El Dorado County Library

In Memory of

Willette N. Strong

Opal

Also by Lauraine Snelling in Large Print:

Ruby
Pearl
Dakota Dawn
Dakota Dream
Dakota Dusk
An Untamed Land
A New Day Rising
A Land to Call Home
The Reapers' Song
Tender Mercies
Blessing in Disguise
The Healing Quilt
Hawaiian Sunrise
Sisters of the Confederacy

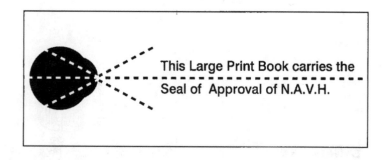

This Large Print Book carries the
Seal of Approval of N.A.V.H.

Opal

Lauraine Snelling

Thorndike Press • Waterville, Maine

Published in 2005 by arrangement with Bethany House Publishers.

Thorndike Press® Large Print Christian Fiction.

The tree indicium is a trademark of Thorndike Press.

The text of this Large Print edition is unabridged.
Other aspects of the book may vary from the original edition.

Set·in 16 pt. Plantin by Liana M. Walker.

Printed in the United States on permanent paper.

Library of Congress Cataloging-in-Publication Data

Snelling, Lauraine.
    Opal / by Lauraine Snelling.
      p. cm. — (Dakotah treasures ; bk. 3)
      (Thorndike Press large print Christian fiction)
    Originally published: Bloomington, Minn. : Bethany
House, c2005. (Dakotah treasures ; 3)
    ISBN 0-7862-7978-8 (lg. print : hc : alk. paper)
    ISBN 1-59415-103-2 (lg. print : sc : alk. paper)
    1. Women pioneers — Fiction. 2. Medora (N.D.) —
Fiction. 3. Sisters — Fiction. 4. Clergy — Fiction.
5. Large type books. I. Title. II. Thorndike Press large
print Christian fiction series.
    PS3569.N39O63 2005b
    813'.54—dc22   2005015636

Dedication

To all those many, many people who
have shared their family stories with me,
I dedicate this book, *Opal.*

As the Founder/CEO of NAVH, the only national health agency solely devoted to those who, although not totally blind, have an eye disease which could lead to serious visual impairment, I am pleased to recognize Thorndike Press* as one of the leading publishers in the large print field.

Founded in 1954 in San Francisco to prepare large print textbooks for partially seeing children, NAVH became the pioneer and standard setting agency in the preparation of large type.

Today, those publishers who meet our standards carry the prestigious "Seal of Approval" indicating high quality large print. We are delighted that Thorndike Press is one of the publishers whose titles meet these standards. We are also pleased to recognize the significant contribution Thorndike Press is making in this important and growing field.

Lorraine H. Marchi, L.H.D.
Founder/CEO
NAVH

* Thorndike Press encompasses the following imprints: Thorndike, Wheeler, Walker and Large Print Press.

Acknowledgments

My many thanks to those who've helped me with this book and others. Doug and Mary Ellison from the Western Edge Bookstore in Medora contributed more than they realize as they steered me in the right direction for books on the era. Diane Rogness of the North Dakota Historical Society provided a wealth of information on early Medora and the historical significance of Marquis de Mores and his family to Dakota Territory.

I can never say enough thanks to my personal team: friend and editor Kathleen Wright; my assistant Cecile Knowles, who is growing in editorial ability all the time; my reunion friends; the Round Robins; and always my best friend and husband,

Wayne. Whenever I need a cheerleader, they are always there. As is Deidre Knight, agent extraordinaire and encouraging friend. I am so blessed with and by the people in my life who love me enough to even say the hard stuff. Hats off to Chelley Kitzmiller, writer and friend, who dared me to write this series.

Without the detailed and fine editing of Sharon Asmus and the rest of the editorial staff at Bethany House Publishers, my books would never see the light of day. How blessed I am.

And without readers who keep asking for more, where would I be? So thanks to all of you who encourage me, share your stories with me, and buy my books so I can keep writing. To God be the glory for all and everything.

Chapter One

Dakotah Territory, May 1886

"Well now, ain't that a purty sight?"

Opal Torvald heard the ribald words through river water in her ears and a haze of dreams in her heart as she floated on the gentle current of the Little Missouri River in her chemise and bloomers. Buoyed by the water, cat-contented by the sun, she was drifting along in a state of bliss. The words and intrusion took a heartbeat or two to register. It was a man's voice, a strange man's voice, and she was next to naked. Or at least in a manner of dishabille that would bring out the caustic side of her sister's tongue. Besides attracting unwanted attention.

Sometimes ignoring danger made it go away.

And sometimes it just got worse. Like now.

Fighting the urge to scream and run, she slitted her eyes open just enough to catch an outline of the man against the sun. She was well enough away from the shore that she could swim, then run to the western bank. However, her clothes were on the eastern bank. As was the man, not to be labeled a gentleman, for a true gentleman would have kept his back turned or would have ridden on by without comment.

Nor could the term gentlewoman be applied to her, nor lady, for no female under those terms would have been swimming in the river without either someone to stand guard or a bevy of other females in attendance.

She had thought of going in without even the benefit of thin cotton between her skin and the river water. But there was one count in her favor. She'd opted for decency — sort of.

Who was he, anyway? She considered various ranch hands she knew from the area, or the men in Medora who were still building for Marquis de Mores. Oh no. What about former visitors to Dove

House, the hotel she and Ruby had inherited years earlier that had burned to a trash heap after a lightning strike?

No one came to mind. The man wore a hat she would have remembered had she seen it before. One side of the flat brim was pinned up to the crown, not a very practical method of protecting one's face and neck from the elements. Protection was the purpose of the wide-brimmed felt hats worn by so many out here in the badlands of Dakotah Territory. The crown was shaped differently too. She noticed all this while trying to decide what to do next.

Why did he have to come and spoil her unexpected break from school? She had truly felt sick when she told Mr. Finch she needed to head on home while she could still make it. Her head had been pounding like stampeding cattle, and she'd felt hot. His droning voice hadn't helped the headache any, nor did the antipathy she'd begun to feel toward the classroom. Ruby might call it spring fever, but after saddling Bay and heading toward home, the river had been singing her name. Headache and heat, two things that might be cured by a dip in the still-cold-from-spring-runoff river.

A dip had turned to a float, and now she

was caught by something worse than a swift eddy.

As unobtrusively as possible, hands fluttering at her sides, she stroked toward the western shore. Any moment she should be able to touch bottom. If the hot weather continued, the river would drop quickly, but right here was a pool that stayed fairly deep year round.

"Hey, missy, you comin' on out and showing off what you tryin' to hide?" His laugh made shivers chase up and down her spine. Suddenly the water felt so cold her teeth started to chatter. "You can't get away, so forget the other bank. I got your horse and clothes right here."

I can give you a mean run for your money, you rattlesnake, you.

He rode his horse closer to the water's edge. "My, my, what a sight for sore eyes."

Going to be a lot sorer before you get what you're thinking on.

The horse put his head down for a drink. The man crossed his arms on the saddle horn.

She could feel his leer clear down to her toes that finally felt bottom. At least he could no longer see anything but her head. Water ran down her face, so she smoothed her hair back out of her eyes. She should have left her hair braided, but after the long winter, all she'd wanted to do was go for a short and simple swim. Free-floating hair was part of the pleasure. What was so bad about that?

She answered her own question. *Some stranger riding up. That's what was wrong with it.*

Mentally she called the man one of the names that Ruby had threatened her with loss of life and liberty for using, but it surely fit here. At the moment Ruby would be right. No lady would let herself be caught in such a compromising situation. Not that Opal had any designs on that title anyway. Much to her older sister's chagrin.

"Well, if'n ya ain't comin' out, I'm comin' in after ya."

"I wouldn't advise that."

"Ya wouldn't? Now, ain't that some terrible shame." He slapped his leg and guffawed loud enough to set the crows to clacking. "And what do you think might stop me?"

Opal glanced beyond him when something moving caught her attention. "Water's too cold for a yellow-livered skunk like you."

"You ain't in no position to be callin' me names like that, missy." He nudged his horse forward, but the animal sat back on his haunches, ears flat against his head.

"Looks to me like your horse has more sense than you do." She kept her shoulders under the surface by bending her knees, not letting him see that she'd moved to shallower water. His horse would have to swim, and it obviously didn't want to do that.

The rider cursed his mount and dug in with his spurs, but all the animal did was spin and try to break for dry ground.

At the same moment, Opal was shocked to see her friend Atticus Grady launch an attack at the rider, pulling him off the horse with a bone-crunching thud to the rocky ground. The horse vamoosed but not before knocking Atticus back on his rear. The man was on him in an instant, and the two fought with fists and feet.

Though Atticus was nearing six feet tall he'd not filled out yet, so he was out-weighed by a stone or two. Out-experienced too, from the looks of it.

Dear Atticus, for sweet pity's sake, why didn't you think before you leaped?

Chapter Two

Western Pennsylvania

Guilt could drive a man to his knees — or to the woodpile.

Jacob Chandler swung the ax, splitting the oak butt in half with one blow. He'd learned that hard physical labor, something that a young preacher never got enough of, was about the best antidote to bad memories and regrets. He set the split half back in place and, with ease born of practice, chopped that one in two. If only he could split the memories down to kindling and burn them the same as wood.

"Forgiving one another, even as God for Christ's sake has forgiven you." His sermon text for Sunday. Along with, "If

thou bring thy gift to the altar, and there rememberest that thy brother hath ought against thee, leave there thy gift before the altar, and go thy way; first be reconciled to thy brother, and then come and offer thy gift."

"Ought against thee." But it wasn't his brother. That would be so easy. The person he'd wronged had disappeared from his life after that one mistake. Not that loving her had been a mistake, but when Satan tempted, he'd not run the other way. Flee from temptation. . . . So the Bible said. But not him, no, instead he'd leaped right in and . . .

He chopped off the memories, the re-criminations, and stood another butt on the chopping block. He'd begged, pleaded, for God's forgiveness. But he'd never seen her again and could not ask for hers. He drove the ax down with such force that he not only split the oak but also embedded the blade in the chopping block. The two halves landed three feet from the block.

He had enough split wood stacked to last for three winters.

"Reverend Chandler?" The voice came from the front of the house.

"Be right there." He snagged his shirt off the tree branch where he'd hung it out of the way and with it wiped the sweat streaming down his face before shoving his arms in the sleeves. He had to get presentable before Miss Honey Witherspoon took it upon herself to come looking for him. He buttoned his shirt and stuffed the tails into his breeches, settling his suspenders back on his shoulders. After slicking his hair back, he set his black flat-brimmed hat in place before striding around the side of the cottage that belonged to the Valley Bible Church, his first parish. *What do I say this time?* But then, with Miss Witherspoon one rarely had the opportunity to speak.

At twenty-six and unmarried, not even betrothed, he was considered one of the better catches in this small town that was spreading up the hillsides of the Dubuque Valley. He knew the designs of the valley mamas, having been warned by one of the well-seasoned men who thought all men should remain free of encumbrances for as long as possible. Not that the man's own state of servitude to the wife of his youth had anything to do with his sentiments.

"Why, Miss Witherspoon, how nice of you to come calling." The young woman fit the name she'd been christened with. Honey. Gold of hair, sweet of smile, and

17

cloying to the ear and palate as she simpered her way through life — most recently with her sights on the single minister. Or perhaps it was her mother's sights.

Her laugh grated on his ears. But perhaps after the discussion he'd just had with the woodpile, even a visit from an archangel would have grated. He kept his smile in place, but under no circumstances was he inviting her inside.

"I brought some chocolate cookies, still warm from the oven. Mama said you would be in need of some refreshment after your grueling hours of chopping wood."

"Why, thank you." He took the proffered basket and, peeking beneath the napkin, inhaled the aroma of fresh chocolate. "And thank your mother for me too." He set the basket down on the stoop and eased her toward the gate. How had they known he was chopping wood? Surely the village grapevine didn't include the daily activities of the local pastor.

"Mama said to invite you for dinner, that surely when you've been working so hard —" she gave an approving stare to his sweat-darkened shirt — "you might like a home-cooked meal."

"Thank you, but I must finish my sermon. I find that chopping wood helps clear my brain and gets the thoughts flowing."

"Oh, well . . ."

"Again, thank your mother for me and extend my most humble apologies."

"Another time, perhaps." After reaching the outside of the gate, she glanced from it to him, perplexity obvious on her brow.

Neither she nor her mama were used to being turned down, he suspected. "I'll see you in church in the morning, then?"

"Yes, of course. I'll be practicing my solo later this afternoon if you . . ."

"Thank you, but I'll be working through until supper, most likely." He touched a finger to the brim of his hat and backed toward the house. "Have a good afternoon." When she twirled her parasol over her shoulder, he picked up the basket and entered the front door. With a sigh of relief, he took out one cookie and made swift work of it in two bites. After two more cookies he set the basket on the kitchen table and crossed to the cookstove to rattle the grate and add a couple of small pieces of kindling to the blinking coals. By the time his pot of soup warmed, he'd be cleaned up and ready to attack the sermon

19

again. Glancing out the back window, he resolved to stack the newly cut wood before dark. After all, neatness was next to godliness, at least according to his father.

As long as he refused to let any thoughts of his own life intrude, he applied the Bible verses, added a few thoughts about the meanings of the verses according to the Greek, and tied it all up in a neat bundle of remonstrance and encouragement, being careful to stay far from any accusations or judgmental phrases. As one of his professors in seminary had said, *"Let God's Word speak for itself. It has far more power than you."*

As he finished his preparation, Jacob remembered he needed to call on Mr. Dumfarthing, one of the founders of the congregation and now bedridden due to a fall on the last ice of the winter. Leaving the spare bedroom that he used for an office, he noticed a slight distaste in his mouth. Not that the distaste was for the task of calling, but the sermon still rankled. If he'd managed to become so convicted himself, he was sure to hear about it from one of the parishioners. Hellfire and brimstone didn't go over well in such a fine Christian community as Dubuque Valley. Not that he'd ever been much of a hellfire man himself.

He stacked the wood before he left, tucked a couple of the cookies into a napkin, and set out down the street to the Dumfarthing residence, one of the larger homes of gray cut granite. Five large houses faced Valley Avenue, protected by cast-iron fences and shaded by ancient oaks that never had the temerity to drop branches on the slate roofs or disfigure the stately matrons in any way. With window-eyes half lidded by shades, the stately dowagers were falling into disarray, as the mining had played out and the land wasn't much good for farming. It was too steep for crops, though sheep did all right.

He turned in at the middle drive and strode on up the walk that was lined with primroses and pansies, the only bright colors, as even the lawns were looking shabby because of the deep shade from the newly leafed-out trees. A squirrel chattered at him, flicking his tail and darting for the tree trunk. A robin sang for his mate somewhere in the tops of the trees.

Jacob leaped the three stone steps and let the lion-headed knocker fall against the plate on the front door. The oval cut-glass pane housed two spiders with opposing webs woven down in the lower curve of the frame. When nothing happened he knocked again, this time clapping the chin of the lion's head on the plate with some force.

The door slowly opened, and the housekeeper stood back, motioning him to enter. "Mr. Dumfarthing will see you, but don't wear him out with a long visit."

"Of course not. Thank you, Mrs. Howard." Jacob removed his hat as he stepped into the foyer, which was in desperate need of some lighting, by candles or gas, he wasn't sure which.

"Have you taken Mr. Dumfarthing out for an airing on the back verandah, as the doctor suggested? Or here on the front porch when the sun is warm?"

"He said he did not feel up to it." She shut the door behind Jacob. "I can do nothing if he is not willing."

"If it is as nice tomorrow as it is today, I will come by after church, and together we will just pick him up and move him outdoors."

Was that a smile he saw hiding again after an oh-so-brief excursion into the light? "I brought some cookies, so would you be so kind as to bring up hot tea?"

"Of course." She hid a snort behind her

ever-present handkerchief. "Who was it this time?"

"Miss Witherspoon." He almost added, "Miss *Honey* Witherspoon," but one should be proper, especially if one was the minister.

"Chocolate?"

"Hmm."

"Nuts?"

"No. I ate several to make sure."

"You are most considerate." She turned before he could be absolutely certain that smile had twinkled out, then led him back to the dining room, which had been turned into a temporary bedroom since Mr. Dumfarthing's fall.

"Reverend Chandler to see you." She might well have been a herald in an old English court. Although she had left off the "sir."

"Well, show him in without all the falderal." The wizened man in the bed pushed himself up higher on his pillows. While his body was failing, his mind and his temper ran neck and neck toward the finish line.

"Good to see you, Mr. Dumfarthing." Jacob stepped to the side of the bed. "I hoped you might be up in a chair enjoying the sunshine on this fine May day."

"I've told you to call me Evan." The withered man pointed to a chair in the corner. "Drag that over here so I don't get a crick in my neck looking up at you. Matilde gone for tea?"

Jacob had a hard time thinking of the dour woman who guarded the house as Matilde, but then, the two of these ancients had known each other for many years and through more secrets than he ever cared to know about. Even though his call on Mr. Dumfarthing had become a weekly event, they had yet to develop any feeling of friendship between them. He sat, they drank tea, discussed Mr. Dumfarthing's view of the medical profession or the weather, and when the old man appeared to be falling asleep, Jacob would excuse himself and leave. His first action on leaving the gloom of the moldering house and its inhabitants would be to take a deep breath of fresh air and resist the urge to dance down the stone steps. His obligation was over for another week.

Today he'd decided to do something different. He'd brought his Bible, and even if the old man huffed and puffed, he planned to read something. Possibly the Scriptures for the week.

Chair in place, he sat himself and crossed one ankle over the opposite knee. "I could help you outside, you know."

"If I wanted to go outside, I'd go outside."

"Really? How would you get there?"

"I'd walk. Same as you."

"Wonderful. I didn't realize you'd been up and around."

"Goes to show you don't know everything. Now, why'd you come?"

Jacob kept his relaxed posture in spite of the zing to his midsection. "Because you belong to my congregation, and I try to visit all those who cannot make it to service."

"What if I said don't come any more?"

Jacob thought for a moment, sending a plea for wisdom upward. The Word promised wisdom in liberal doses to all who asked.

"Ha. Cat got your tongue?"

"Being of the stubborn sort, I would most likely come anyway."

"Hoping to wear me down so I'll leave more of my money to the church, eh?"

Leaning forward, Jacob looked the man straight in the eyes. "Mr. Dumfarthing, Evan, I want you to understand something and understand it well." He spoke softly but enunciated most clearly. "I do not give a fig or a farthing how much you give or leave to the church. That is between you and God. I come to visit you because, when I took on this congregation, every member became part of my family, and I agreed to be the shepherd of that family. Visiting the sick and shut-ins is part of my job as shepherd, and I don't ever want to stand before the Lord God and have to admit to failing my flock. I know I fail in untold ways, but I do what I can and count on God for the blessing." *And the increase of faith for all.* But he kept that part to himself.

Mr. Dumfarthing nodded, then nodded again. "Well said, young man. Guess I was just testing you. And you passed. Now let's have our tea, and since you brought that book along, you might as well read me some. My eyes being not what they used to be, I don't read much anymore."

"Would you like me to read to you more often?"

"That would be fine, long as you don't go pestering me to get out in the sun."

"Agreed." *But you can't stop me from praying for you, and one of those prayers is that you will get out in the sun and let God's warmth flow through and heal you.*

26

They chatted on their usual topics while they finished their tea, and Jacob managed to keep from mentioning that the doctor might have wisdom on his side when prescribing sun and fresh air.

"Thought I'd read the passages for this week and the ones I've based my sermon for tomorrow on, if you don't mind."

"As long as it isn't Revelation, anything is fine by me."

"I'll keep that in mind." Jacob flipped to the passages he'd struggled over. How much easier it would be to read a psalm or two or one of the miracles. Instead he turned to the words of Jesus in Matthew. " 'If thou bring thy gift to the altar, and there rememberest that thy brother hath ought against thee, leave there thy gift before the altar, and go thy way; first be reconciled to thy brother, and then come and offer thy gift.' "

Silence resounded in the room, bouncing off the long windows, riffling the sheers and blowing under and around the bed.

"Did you read that on purpose?"

"What do you mean?"

"Come to preach at me, like?"

Jacob kept his finger in the place and set his foot back on the floor. The thud

27

sounded loud in the stretching silence. "No, sir. As I said, I was reading the lesson and the Gospel for the day."

"You don't know about my brother?"

"No, sir. You've never told me." While he'd heard many things, a few of them less than complimentary, about Mr. Dumfarthing, he'd not heard of a brother. Besides, he'd quickly learned that stories told by others tended toward exaggeration. He'd promised himself to believe only what the person under discussion told him and even then to take it with a grain or three of salt.

"Young man, you don't begin to know about forgiveness."

"I know that Christ died on the cross for our sins, for all the sins of mankind. Yours and mine included."

"God's forgiveness is far easier than man's."

"Christ paid the ultimate price."

"I read the Scriptures. It says to forgive others as Christ has forgiven us. But what about when I didn't forgive and now it's too late?"

"It's never too late." Ah, if only he could believe those words himself.

"He's gone."

"Dead?"

"Yes. And I was too stubborn to forgive him for what he done to me. Even when he asked." Mr. Dumfarthing's hands shook, as with the palsy. He raised them, then let them fall back to the coverlet. "And now I can't forgive myself, either."

"Christ says to lay our burdens on Him, to let Him carry them."

"Do you honestly believe that?"

"Of course I believe it." He could hear the sharp stab of his voice.

"Ah, the believing is easy, the doing sometimes impossible." Mr. Dumfarthing closed his eyes, the signal that Jacob should leave.

Father God, how do I deal with this? What do I say to him? Jacob closed his eyes and swallowed, wishing for the ax and the wood. Instead of rising, he leaned forward and took Mr. Dumfarthing's bony hand in his. "Mr. Dumfarthing, could we pray together?"

The old man reared up from his pillow, eyes wide. "I can't pray like that . . . together out loud. I can't." He fell back. "Not for forgiveness. Not anymore."

"Then God help us, because I can't either." Jacob's throat felt as if it might shatter from the glass lodged within it, that his heart would leap out of his chest. *Fa-*

ther, what have I done? This is not what I was taught in seminary.

Forgive, forgive, forgive.

The old man settled back into his pillows and swallowed himself back to normal. "You mean you want to pray for me? Say all those proper words that don't mean a hill of corn?" He sighed. "I been prayed for by older and wiser men than you, son, and it never did no good."

"No, sir. No proper words and pretty phrases. I'm asking you to pray for my struggle with this, and I'll pray for yours. I've written a sermon that is just so much pap, and I feel that God has me by the scruff of my neck. I'd rather go anywhere than to church in the morning."

If Jacob could have forced his shaking knees to work right, he'd have fled the room and the house and most likely the town. Whatever had possessed him to talk like that? Hands clasped, elbows on his knees, he let his head hang. *Thou, O Lord, art the lifter of my head, my sword, buckler, and shield. I have to trust that this is all of thee.*

The silence no longer hung oppressing but as if waiting, listening, like a beloved mother.

Words stuck in his throat. He, who

should be able to pray in any circumstances, couldn't say a word. His eyes burned, and his nose dripped on his thumb.

"Lord God, help us. Amen." Mr. Dumfarthing's voice crackled and cracked.

Even the curtains sighed in relief.

Jacob dug his handkerchief from his back pocket and blew his nose. "Thank you."

"You'll come again soon?"

"Yes, sir." He clasped Mr. Dumfarthing's hand in both of his and shook it with all the gentleness of a mother's touch. "Tomorrow, after church."

"Good. I want a report on that service."

By the time he got home Jacob felt as though he'd been run over by a fully loaded dray wagon with six up.

Chapter Three

"Sweet mercy, I sure hope we didn't kill him."

"Still could." Atticus nudged the man's shoulder with his boot toe.

Opal bent down to see for certain that the man's chest was still rising and falling. The brushy mustache triggered a memory. Back those years before, on the train west, she'd leaned a bit close, checking to see if a mustached man was indeed breathing, and all sorts of a ruckus broke loose. She hadn't even touched that man on the train, but now her icy hand clenched the branch she'd clouted this drifter with, keeping the weapon close beside her, just in case.

Atticus rubbed the side of his head. "You came mighty close to killin' me too."

"Not funny. Besides, he's not dead. He's

still breathing." She stood and glanced to see if her friend had blood on the side of his head. None. "Anyway, I missed you by a mile." She stopped at the look in his eyes, after his gaze had traveled down and then up again. Red flamed his cheeks.

She glanced down at herself and clenched her eyes and teeth. Heat traveled up her body so fast she thought she could hear the steam from her wet garments whistle.

Atticus turned his back. "Ah, you better get some clothes on." His voice strangled on the simple words.

"Oh, for . . ." Opal huffed a sound of disgust. "You keep an eye on him, then. I'm sure he's not going to be too gracious when he wakes up."

"Opal." The misery in his voice calmed her now-racing heart.

"Don't worry, Atticus. Rand isn't going to come after you with the shotgun and force you to marry me for this compromising situation we are in." While she talked to calm him down, she fought the sleeves of a light blue shirt into place and, after buttoning it, pulled on her divided skirt of navy twill. Her wet drawers immediately soaked through her clothing, something else she ignored as she sat down on a log to pull on her boots. "I'll just explain what happened and —"

"Opal."

"And tell him it's all my fault." She glanced over to see his neck beaming red like he'd been in the sun for hours or scrubbed his skin with raspberry juice. "And you came to my rescue like a gallant knight in shining armor." She finished with a flourish. "You can look now. I'm decent again."

"Opal!"

"Sorry." Sometimes she just couldn't resist teasing him. He fell for anything. She finger-combed her mud-riddled blond hair back and dug a plaid ribbon out of her pocket before braiding the still-soaking mass and tying it off. She flipped the braid over her shoulder, catching a flash of movement out the side of her eye. "Atticus, watch out!"

The man on the ground snagged an arm around Atticus's knees and, with a twist of his shoulders, sent the younger man toppling.

Opal grabbed her holster and gun belt off the tree limb where she'd hung it for safekeeping, jerked out her pistol, and with the ease of long hours of practice, fired a round that splintered a rock by the man's side. Shards of stone sliced both his face and shirt.

"You done kilt me!" His yelp could probably be heard clear to Medora. Clapping a hand on his upper arm, he bellowed, "You shot me. I'm bleedin'."

"If I'd have shot you, you wouldn't be screaming like that. Get up!"

Atticus picked himself up out of the water and slapped his hat on his thigh. "Low-down . . . Why didn't you just shoot him?" He hauled the drifter up by one arm. "Hand me that rope off your saddle."

Opal kept her gun in one hand and retrieved the rope with the other. "If you move, I'll be glad to shoot you in the knee, so make your choice."

"I'm bleedin' bad."

"No you ain't. Little rock cuts never hurt nobody." Atticus dropped the loop over the man's shoulders and cinched it around his upper arms, then flipped a couple more loops and tied it off. "You want to take him into town, or should I?"

"What good will that do?" Opal holstered her gun, grateful that Rand had had his way over her carrying a firearm. Ruby'd had three fits from west over that decision.

"What do you want to do with him?"

"Let him swing from that tree branch over there."

"I din't hurt nobody. You can't hang me!"

"Says who?" Opal arched an eyebrow and turned to gaze at the tree limb. "It's just about the right height." *He thinks I mean to hang him by the neck.* She kept back a chuckle with difficulty.

Atticus gave the roped man a shove. "Get on over there."

"Sure hate to waste a good rope on him. Maybe we better just shoot him and send the body down the river."

Atticus appeared to stop and ponder before shaking his head. "Nah, bullets cost too much. Rope is better. Will leave a lesson for other varmints too."

"I din't do nothing!" Eyes wild as a roped mustang, the man stumbled and was saved from scraping his knees by the jerk Atticus applied to the rope.

"Get on over there."

Opal mounted Bay and took the end of the rope from Atticus. She flipped two twists around her saddle horn, as if roping a calf, and half-dragged the screeching man toward the tree. Once close enough, she unwound the rope and tossed the end over the stout tree limb, catching it as it looped down. She made two turns around the branch, then two around the saddle horn again.

"Anything you want to say for yourself?"

"I got some gold in my pocket. Take that and let me loose." Spit dribbled down the man's chin.

"You want his gold?"

"Nah, let the poor sucker who finds him empty his pockets." Atticus studied the trembling man. "Face it like a man."

"No, please. For God's sake, I . . ."

"You sure weren't thinking of God when you were leering at me." Opal backed Bay up enough to tighten the rope till the man stood on his tiptoes. "You got anything else you want to say?" Disgust made her wish, just for a fleeting instant, that she had shot him. Not to kill, mind you, shooting a deer was hard enough, but to teach him a permanent lesson. Pain was a real good teacher.

She saw a dark stain spreading on his pants. "Let's get it over with." She backed Bay enough that the man dangled in the air, then handed the end of the rope to Atticus to tie around the tree trunk.

"If someone comes along and lets you down, you might want to get out of the area. Men around here don't take kindly to having womenfolk bothered." Atticus cinched the knot down tight. He glanced up to Opal. "You want to tell someone about him, or should I?"

"Neither. He'll probably yell loud enough to wake the dead. Come on, I'll give you a ride." She drew her foot out of the right stirrup so he could swing up behind her. "Where you going?"

The two of them rode off, the man's screams for help assailing their ears.

"I was on my way home. Been out diggin' up the garden plot for Mrs. Black. Jed's so busy building for the marquis, he don't have time."

To Opal it seemed strange to hear Cimarron referred to as Mrs. Black, but then, Atticus hadn't really known them when they all still lived and worked at Dove House. The more new people who moved in, the fewer would remember Cimarron's former life as a soiled dove before Ruby and Opal inherited the saloon-turned-hotel from their dying father.

"I'll take you back near to town, then I gotta get on home." Home to the ranch, the first real home she'd had of her own in her entire life.

"How come you weren't in school?"

She'd been hoping he wouldn't ask that.

"I had a headache and felt sick to my stomach, so I told Mr. Finch I needed to go home."

"But you went swimming instead."

Leave it to Atticus to hit the nail on the head. He had a talent for that. Opal sighed. "The river was calling my name." She thought a moment. "How come you showed up?" The bend in the river where she'd gone swimming was not on his way home, more like a mile out of his way.

"Thought I'd take home some fish for supper."

"And I messed that up for you. I'm sorry." She looked over her shoulder, suddenly realizing how close he was, her back warming from the heat of him.

"Never mind. I'll get Robert, and we'll try the second bend north of town. We always catch plenty there too." Robert was Atticus's younger brother.

When they came around the hill, she stopped the horse. They could still hear the man yelling, although faint by now. "Who you going to tell?"

"Charlie?"

"If you tell him the whole story, he'll go string the snake up himself."

"Maunders?"

"That skunk and Jake Maunders are

probably in cahoots. They smell like two of a kind. Word of this gets back to Ruby . . ." Opal shuddered. All she had wanted was to feel better, and a swim seemed the perfect answer. *Why do I always get in trouble when I don't mean to? I wasn't playing hooky. Mr. Finch gave me permission to leave.* Somewhere in all this the drumbeat at her temples had started up again. Once she got home, Ruby would steep up some willow-bark tea, and that would take care of things.

"You can let me off here." Atticus swung to the ground when she stopped her horse.

"Thanks for saving me." She smiled down at him, then cocked an eyebrow at the serious look on his face. "What is it?"

"Don't you never make fun of us gettin' married again, you hear?"

"Atticus, it was . . ." *Of all the nerve.*

"I mean it."

She watched him stride off across the land now rippling with calf-deep grass. Whatever had come over her friend?

Chapter Four

She should be home from school by now.
You know Opal will be here when she gets here. You promised yourself you would no longer worry about her. After all, what can happen between Medora and the ranch?

Ruby Torvald, now Mrs. Rand Harrison, tried to ignore the argument going on between her ears, but she knew only too well all the things that could happen between town and home. Runaway horse, although it would take something pretty catastrophic to set Bay off; step in a gopher hole; a snake bite, although she'd heard no mention of rattlesnakes being out of hibernation yet. Surely Opal wouldn't have gone fishing without letting her know. But she'd done just that in the past. Or gone hunting. But her rifle stood in the gun cabinet Beans had made, along with the others. Even though guns were not allowed at school, she'd taken her revolver along, thanks to Rand, who thought she was much safer with a gun when she was riding alone. Surely Mrs. Robertson didn't allow her daughters to wear a gun belt and holster. Not that any of them had shown any interest. Unlike Opal.

"Ma?" One-year-old Per had finally learned to say her name.

"Yes, dear, I'm coming." A more tractable child would take a nap without being tied in bed, but not her son. Therefore, when he awoke she needed to be near enough to hear his call, or for sure there would be trouble to pay. She smiled at the sight of his red cheeks and four-tooth grin. "How's mama's big boy?"

"Get up?" He waved his arms, then pulled at the band she'd tied around his middle. She'd learned rather quickly that she must tie it in the back and without a bow. She untied the knot, blowing on his neck to make him laugh.

"Pa?"

"Out with the horses. Are you wet?"

He shook his head. "Wet."

"You are a parrot." She checked his

soakers and laid him on the table to change him. When she bent over to unpin his diaper, he pulled at the front of her waist, making sucking noises at the same time. "You're hungry, eh?" He was always ready to nurse after a nap, even though he could drink from a cup, a slow and painful process that usually got more on him than in him. As soon as she had him dressed again in the loose dress that all small children wore, she sat down in the rocker and unbuttoned her waist. He nursed greedily for the first couple of minutes, then smiled up at her, milk dribbling from the side of his mouth, one fat little fist reaching for her mouth.

"You tend to your business there, you little scamp." She dabbed at his mouth with her apron. "Don't waste the good stuff. The cow hasn't come in yet." Not long after their wedding two springs ago, Rand had come home leading a milk cow.

"Wouldn't it be just as easy to tame one of the seven hundred cows you have?"

"No. Beef cows and milk cows are two different things."

"Look mighty close to the same to me — four legs, four teats, a head, and a tail. Color's different, is all."

Rand had assumed his patient look and

tried to explain the difference. Finally he finished with, "You saw that long-horned mama take after me that day. You think she'd let me milk her? I'd get kicked clear to Dickinson if I tried."

"If you say so."

"Besides, milk cows give a lot more milk than range cows and for longer."

"How do you know? Those calves out there look mighty fat."

That evening he had called, "Ruby, come on out here so I can teach you how to milk."

"Me?"

Ruby could still remember the shock she'd felt when she realized he was serious about her taking over milking Fawn, as they'd named her. Back at the hotel they'd bought milk and cream from their next-door neighbor. Learning to be a ranch wife took more training than running a hotel. She'd learned to milk but had drawn the line at butchering. At least so far. Between Rand and Beans, there was always someone around to dress out whatever game was brought in. The young chickens hadn't grown big enough to eat, and all the hens were laying, so she'd managed to forestall that grisly job.

The first time she'd tried gutting one of

the prairie hens, she turned away to heave up the meager contents of her meal. That was about the time she realized she was in the family way. Talk about joy-filled. That she'd been.

Good thing Opal didn't mind doing the chores of milking, feeding the chickens, and gathering the eggs.

"All right, young man, enough playing." Ruby sat him on her lap, and while she fastened her buttons, he let out a burp worthy of comment. She chuckled. "Take after your father, don't you?" She wiped his face with the skirt of her apron and settled him in the corner of the kitchen in the pen Rand and Beans had fashioned from willow branches. She handed him a teething ring of braided cowhide, a kettle, some pans, and a wooden spoon. Perhaps he'd be a musician someday, much as he liked to bang on things.

Ghost, the mottled cow dog snoozing by the front step, barked her "someone's coming" announcement, and Ruby walked to the door in time to see Opal trot Bay up to the barn.

Right after the sigh of relief that her little, or rather younger, sister — Opal now equaled her five foot seven inches — was home safe, Ruby wanted to go out and

45

shake her. How many times had she reminded her to come straight home from
school?

"Come on, young man, you can help me
get my point across." She hoisted Per to
her hip and headed out, thunder on her
brow and gratitude in her heart. As soon as
she saw Opal, she had an inkling something had happened. "Your hair is wet.
How could you fall in the river from the
road?"

Opal turned from unleashing the cinch.
"I didn't fall in. I went to wade and then
couldn't resist the water, so I went swimming."

"That river's still cold as ice. You're
going to catch your death swimming this
early in the season."

Per leaned toward Opal, arms outstretched, jabbering his plea.

"Not all I almost caught," Opal mumbled under her breath as she took her
nephew in her arms. "You want to ride, big
boy?" She set him in the saddle and held
him there.

"Don't let Bay walk off with him."

"Bay is ground tied. She won't leave."
Opal motioned to the reins that reached
from bit to ground. She grinned up at the
baby now flapping his arms and his jaws at

the horse. "He sure isn't afraid of anything."

"I think boys out here are born wanting to ride." Ruby lifted her face to the sun. "Soon as you get unsaddled, you can help me bring the clothes in off the line and explain this adventure to me."

Opal made a face, which made Per chortle with glee. Of course, just about anything made him laugh. A happier baby would be hard to find anywhere. "Here, you hold him up there a minute." She glanced at Ruby over her shoulder. "I know. I'll help right away, but I can give him a ride around the barn and the corrals." While Ruby held Per in the saddle Opal tightened the cinch instead of releasing it and swung up behind Per, her arms circling him safe in the saddle in front of her.

"You be careful now."

"Ru-by." The drawn out word adequately conveyed Opal's long-term patience with her sister's worriment.

"Drop him off at the clothesline." Ruby smiled at the laughter floating back from the two on the horse. Opal and Rand both had been taking Per on the horses since he could crawl, and now that he could walk around furniture, she'd have to bar the door to keep him safe. Mrs. Robertson had told her to tie him on a long line to the clothesline. That would give him some freedom, yet he wouldn't get away. Knowing Per, he'd go from two steps to a dead run, anything to keep up with his father and Opal.

Thinking on these things, Ruby grabbed a clothes basket off the porch and ambled on back to the clothesline behind the house. Ankle-high grass, grazed once by the riding horses, made her think of the weekly mown grass back at the Brandons'. The backyard had been like a park, with roses, flower beds, a kitchen garden, and both fruit and nut trees. No fruit-bearing trees here yet, but Rand had brought her two apple saplings from his last trip to Dickinson. The two starts could hardly be seen from the rail fence they'd put up to keep cows and deer out. Heard tell, Marquis de Mores had a fruit orchard well started, but she hadn't gone to see it.

She removed the clothespins, dropping them in the bag hanging on the line for just that purpose, and buried her face in the fragrance of sun-and-wind-dried sheets. They had used an abundance of lavender sachets in the linen closet in New York, but nothing smelled better than those dried by prairie sun and wind.

"Here he is." Opal stopped at the west post. "You're acting a bit strange."

"After this last winter I am intoxicated on the smells of spring." Ruby crossed and took Per from Opal's hands. When he looked over his shoulder and chattered at Opal, they both laughed. The frown on his wide forehead meant he'd rather ride.

"Where's Rand?"

"No, Opal, you're not going to find him. I have need of you here."

"All right. But if I headed out with the rifle, I could maybe find a nice buck. We're a bit low on meat."

Ruby shook her head and sat Per in the basket. With a giggle he set it to rocking. Everything moved when around that busy little body. Ghost wandered over and greeted him with a quick tongue swipe, then stood patiently while Per entwined his fingers in her hair. He pulled himself up, wobbling a bit and setting the basket to the same dance. His shout of glee made her laugh too.

"You did it, son. Ghost, you are the best dog any little boy could have." Ever since Per had been crawling, if the dog was in the house, he made a beeline for her. And even when he pulled her ears, she never growled or even moved away.

Ruby had folded the sheets and towels and was beginning on the underthings when Opal returned. "You start with the socks, and put the ones that need mending off to the side. Those men go through more socks than I'd ever dreamed. I need Cimarron and her nimble needle to catch up on the mending."

When Opal failed to respond, Ruby paused. "All right. What is it you need to tell me?"

"Nothing."

"Opal, how many years have I been your older sister?"

"Going on fifteen."

"Right. So what is bothering you?"

"Well, I told Mr. Finch that I felt sick, and I did. My head hurt so bad my eyes were crossing, so I left school early. But when I saw the river, I thought maybe that would make my headache go away, so I was just going to wade, but then it felt so good I went swimming."

"Opal."

"Oh, I had my drawers and camisole on. I wasn't indecent or anything."

"And . . . ?"

"This drifter found me, and . . ." Her words picked up speed like a cow running from the lasso. "And he was coming after me but his horse refused to go into the water and Atticus got in a fight with him and we left him strung up on a tree branch."

"You hung him?" Ruby dropped the pants she was folding.

"No. We wrapped the rope around his arms and left him just high enough his feet didn't touch the ground. He was hollering something awful. Then I gave Atticus a ride back to town and came on home. I wasn't going to tell you, but . . . well, someone most likely should go let him down, and if I tell Rand or the guys the whole story, they'll probably shoot him or really string him up."

Ruby closed her eyes, the scene painted all too clearly on the back of her eyelids. "Opal, you could have been —"

"I know. It was dumb of me. But no one ever comes by that bend in the river unless it's roundup time."

"You don't know who he was?"

"Never saw him before, but he wears his hat some funny. His horse ran off, so I suppose someone should go let him down. He probably stinks pretty raw by now. We scared him pretty bad."

"Leave him there for the crows to pick

on." Ruby pinched the bridge of her nose between thumb and finger to ease the dull throbbing that had started behind her eyes.

"Ruby!" Shock saucered Opal's eyes.

"I know that's not very Christian, but so many men out here are lower than the animals. Whatever happened to common decency?" Ruby picked up her son, who'd just thumped on his rear when Ghost barked and headed for the field. "I don't know what to do, Opal. Why do you get in such scrapes? If you'd just come directly home, this wouldn't be a problem."

"We could leave him there and hope someone finds him in the next day or two." She looked up in time to see Rand leading a saddled but riderless horse. "Uh-oh."

Ruby shook her head. "You got yourself into this one, dear sister, and you are going to have to get yourself out. And I wouldn't suggest playing dumb. Rand knows you far too well for that." Ruby laid the folded clothes in the basket, pulled a stalk of grass from her son's mouth, and with Per on her hip and the bag of clothespins in her other hand, motioned toward the high-piled basket. "You can bring that in after you go talk with Rand."

"You could come with me, you know?"

"Nope, not this time." Ruby ignored the

look of pleading and continued on to the log house that looked as if it had sprouted years earlier right there out of the meadow instead of having been built only two years before.

Standing down by the barn and the strange horse, Opal told Rand her story as simply as possible. When she could see his jaw whitening, she finished with, "But, Rand, I didn't do anything wrong."

"Specifically, no, but without thinking ahead, you put yourself in harm's way, and it's come out wrong all over the place." Rand tipped his broad-brimmed hat back with one finger. He shook his head as he studied Opal's face. "That man blabs around town, and you'll never live it down. He'll be the laughingstock, but it's your reputation that is on the line." He shook his head. "Ruby's right."

"What do you mean by that?"

"Opal, no matter how hard you try, you just can't be one of the men. You're female, and that puts you in a different place."

"I can outshoot most of them, rope and ride as well as any, and put in as long a day as anyone we know." She wasn't boasting, just stating facts. She'd worked harder than anyone could know to learn the ranching skills that were needed. "And I'm better at breaking horses too, thanks to Linc." Linc, short for Lincoln, and his Sioux Indian wife, Little Squirrel, had ridden up one day and asked if Rand had work for them. Hard workers both, everyone was glad they'd come.

"All that is true, but what are we going to do with that drifter?"

"Dig a hole and bury the skunk."

"Opal, this is no joke."

"Hogtie him and throw him in one of the freight cars going west? Tell someone to let him loose on the other end of Montana?" She banged her fist on the top rail of the corral. "He made me so mad I could have shot him right then and sent his body floating down the river."

"Killing a man is far different than killing a deer."

"Yeah, in this case the deer is nicer."

Rand sighed. "Well, I'll take a couple of the guys along, and we'll go let him loose. About all we can do is threaten that we'll come after him if he talks around here. Go on up to the house and get some food we can put in a sack. That will take away one reason for him to go on into town."

"I'd really like my rope back."

Rand gave her a look that made her hang her head. She had a feeling she hadn't heard the last of this yet.

Chapter Five

Western Pennsylvania

Sunday morning arrived, and his stomach hadn't bothered to take a rest.

Jacob looked out over his woodpiles to the maple and beech grove that angled up the hill. He'd heard a coyote singing during the night, along with an owl that kept the rodent population under control in the small meadow off to the west of his plot. Usually Sunday morning wore a mantle of peace, and he looked forward to the service with joy. Jacob Chandler loved and honored his calling — until this last week. How could he preach on this text when he failed to live it? Why hadn't he just chosen an alternate text?

Because God told me not to. That's why. But that didn't make it any easier.

Memories of Melody's eyes seemed to sour the cream in his coffee. He tossed the dregs against one of the unsplit butts and rose to return to the house. It wasn't as if he'd never tried to plead her forgiveness, but when he'd gone to her father's house, the man had met him with clenched fists and threats. Melody had left home, and it was all his fault. And no, he'd never find out where she'd gone, so leave well enough alone and don't show his face around there again.

He'd gone intending to ask for her hand in marriage.

"So, Father, how does this Scripture apply when there is no way to rectify the wrong?" he asked as he lathered up his cheeks. "You know that I tried to ask her forgiveness for taking advantage of her that night." He stroked down one cheek with the razor. "But did I do my very best?" His shoulders slumped. "I thought this was all behind me. I asked your forgiveness, and I know that you forgave me. What else could I have done?" He finished shaving and wiped the leftover dabs of foam from face and neck, then cleaned his razor and hung it from a hook beside the mirror.

You just put it out of your mind and called it good all these years. The accusing voice had a note of authority.

At least I tried to. He remembered the dreams he'd had for a long time and that had reappeared the past two nights.

Father, is this prompting from you, or is the enemy trying a frontal attack? Jacob well understood that Satan knew and used Scripture also. And his favorite ploy was to render Christians ineffective through worry or fear — or reliving past sins.

Still ruminating on the internal debate, he took his hat from the row of pegs by the front door, brushed any lint off the shoulders of his black suit coat, and clenching his Bible with sermon notes close to his chest, started for church. Not since the first time he'd preached had he felt so apprehensive about a sermon.

The organist was warming up her fingers on the keys, children and adults alike gathering for Sunday school, when he entered the white clapboard church by way of the outside door to his office. He had about ten minutes until the brief opening worship, after which those in the pews would scatter for their classes. At least he wouldn't be leading the Bible study for the adults today. He'd finally found someone

58

to take over that duty. However, that left him with more time to think, or rather to stew.

If only he had someone to talk this over with. But while there were several families he'd drawn close to, he didn't know how he could ever admit to such a sin without destroying their trust in him. He knew of no one who could counsel him except the Lord God himself.

The organ notes drew him into the sanctuary as everyone stood to sing the opening hymn, "Onward, Christian Soldiers." The stained-glass window of the Shepherd with His flock threw rich colors on the polished floor. He made his way to the front and smiled at his own flock while they found their seats again, the rustle of clothing, papers, and mothers shushing their broods dear and familiar sounds.

"Good morning."

"Good morning."

The halfhearted return widened his smile. "Surely you can do better than that on this glorious May morning. Good morning."

Bobby Englbrecht in the front row shouted his answer, and the Peabody twins giggled into their Sunday gloves. Mr. Jensen shook his head, while most of the people just raised their voices or at least took part this time.

"That's better. This is the day that the Lord has made."

"Let us rejoice and be glad in it."

"Yes, indeed, let us do that. Now, how many memorized their Bible verses for this week?"

Hands went up all around the room.

"My mama thaid I got them all," Timothy Garrison, still missing his two front teeth, proudly announced from his usual place in the center aisle, right side, second pew. Any moment now his cowlick would stand straight up, no matter how much water his mama had applied.

Jacob noticed such things and loved his flock all the more for their efforts. Before he came, things had been much more serious, or so he'd been told. "On your honor now, all who have done their memory work, please stand." Miss Witherspoon could have been plying a fan, her smile was so coy. Old Mrs. Hackenbacker thumped her cane, then leaned on it. She'd confided to him one day that her mind seemed to work better now that she'd joined the memory brigade.

"Let's say it all together now. Romans 8:28: 'And we know that all things work together for good to them that love God, to them who are called according to his purpose.' Romans 8:28.

"And the Christian's bar of soap?"

A hand shot in the air. "First John 1:9."

"All right, all together. 'If we confess our sins, he is faithful and just to forgive us our sins, and to cleanse us from all unrighteousness.'

"And the Beatitudes in Matthew. 'Blessed are the poor in spirit. . . .'" Several people sat down while the rest stumbled their way through. "We'll keep working on that one." He led the group in applause for those who'd accomplished their memory work, another thing that hadn't been done before he arrived. "Let us pray." He waited out the settling noises while everyone sat down.

"Heavenly Father, we thank thee for this glorious morning and for bringing us all together again to study thy Word and to worship thee. Make us a people with grateful hearts, for thou hast given us so much. We ask thy blessing on our worship today. In Christ's holy name, amen."

As he dismissed the children for Sunday school four-year-old Linnie Springer stopped in front of him. "I thanked God that our mama cat had kittens. I could bring you one when they can see."

He stooped down to her level. "Guess we'll wait and see how they do, all right?" The week before someone had tried to give him a puppy. That had been a real temptation, but so far he'd declined. Often he'd thought of having a pet, especially when the winter wind howled around the eaves of his house. A dog slumbering on the hearth had real appeal, but housebreaking a dog or a cat had never been one of his favorite things.

He watched the children file out the back and down to the basement while the adults came to sit in the front pews. Harland Hammerskold stopped to answer a question, giving Jacob a chance to slip out the side door before the class could begin and before he was asked a theological question, which Harland was famous for doing.

"Good morning, Pastor."

Had Mrs. Witherspoon been waiting for him? He kept a smile in place because of hours of practice. "And how are you this fine day?"

"Fine, fine. I thought I'd catch you quick and invite you over for dinner. I'm making my famous Hog Maw today, or rather, Honey is, and I know how you enjoy that."

"You make the very best Hog Maw, but I'm sorry to say I must decline. I have another engagement." *Thank you, Lord, for Mr. Dumfarthing.* "And now if you'll excuse me, I must finish preparing for my sermon."

Often the brief walk he took during the Sunday school hour was just what he needed for all the pieces to fall into place, no matter how many weekday and Saturday hours had already gone into the preparation. He needed a story for today, and the only one he could think of was his own. His stomach felt like the tangle of knots in a fly-fishing line when miscast. The tangle only tightened as the time for his sermon drew near.

When he stood behind the carved wooden pulpit and looked out over the expectant faces, he threw himself on God's mercy and began with the ancient words, " 'Let the words of my mouth, and the meditation of my heart, be acceptable in thy sight, O Lord, my strength, and my redeemer.' Amen." He withdrew his notes from his Bible as he waited for the congregation to settle.

"I know you've already heard the Scripture passages for the day, but I'd like to read them again. Mark 11:25: 'And when ye stand praying, forgive, if ye have ought against any: that your Father also which is in heaven may forgive you your trespasses.' And Matthew 5:23: 'Therefore if thou bring thy gift to the altar, and there rememberest that thy brother hath ought against thee; leave there thy gift before the altar, and go thy way; first be reconciled to thy brother. . . .' "

When he finished, he paused, trying to gather his thoughts, sending pleas for help heavenward. "Some texts are easier to preach on than others." He glanced at his notes. They might as well have been written in Chinese for all the good they were doing him. He looked out across the congregation, some serious faces, some bored, old Grandpa Peabody nodding off already, others nodding encouragement. "Ought against any," he repeated, then studied his hands. Finding no inspiration there, he sucked in a deep breath, sighed it out, and started again. "We think of Jesus as our loving Savior and friend, just as we sang only a few minutes ago — 'What a Friend We Have in Jesus.' And we do. But Jesus spoke some hard sayings, some confusing sayings, and this is one.

"Perhaps it is more so to me, since I have been reminded so forcefully of a situ-

64

ation in my own life where, after wounding a friend of mine, I sought to ask for forgiveness and that person had disappeared. I never was able to make it right. Yes, I tried, but did I try hard enough? Did God forgive me? Yes, I believe he did, because the Bible says" — he held up his worn leather-bound book — "right here that if we confess our sins, God 'is faithful and just to forgive us our sins and to cleanse us from all unrighteousness.' I believe that.

"So then, what do I do with the words 'ought against any'? Do I leave my gift at the altar as Scripture says and go search for this person? How do I do that? There's another verse, found in our Lord's prayer. 'Forgive us our debts, as we forgive our debtors.' Does that mean that unless I forgive others, God will not forgive me? Yes, it does. Matthew 6:15 says, 'But if ye forgive not men their trespasses, neither will your Father forgive your trespasses.'

"As I said, these Scriptures are heavy and confusing and burdensome. Let me ask of you — is there someone you have not forgiven, someone you've been bearing a grudge against for a short time or a long time because, after all, it was their fault and not yours? 'Ought against any.' "

Another silence stretched. Boots scraped

against the floor as someone shifted in his seat. "We are told to never let a root of bitterness grow, and yet family members or friends might not speak to one another for years.

"We know Scripture says, 'Be reconciled to thy brother.' But we say, 'But, Lord, they do the same thing over and over.'" Jacob nodded. "So then what? We go back to the Bible, which teaches us how to live. Peter asked the same question, and Jesus answered, 'I say not unto thee until seven times, but, until seventy times seven.' That's a whole lot of forgiving." Jacob looked out at his people. Some were no longer looking at him. Some were nodding. A scowl or two creased other faces. "I pray that God will give each and every one of us the grace to be 'doers of the word, and not hearers only.' Amen."

He stepped from behind the pulpit and raised his hands for the benediction. "The Lord bless us and keep us. The Lord look upon us with favor and grant us His peace. Amen."

A moment of silence followed, then he nodded to the organist. "Our closing hymn is number 315. 'Abide With Me'."

That was the shortest sermon he'd ever preached.

Perhaps he'd keep his notes for another time, since they hadn't been used today. During the final stanza he made his way down the aisle to the front doors where he shook hands with everyone who didn't slip out the side doors. Some did. Was that an acknowledgment of guilt or just that they were in a hurry?

All the way to Mr. Dumfarthing's house he castigated himself for being too hard on his people, for using his own life as a poor example, for failing his Lord so miserably for so long. To his surprise, Mr. Dumfarthing was sitting in a rocker on the front porch, a robe spread over his knees and a shawl tucked around his bent shoulders.

"You look mighty down in the mouth, young man," Mr. Dumfarthing said after the exchange of greetings. "Matilde will have dinner ready in a few minutes." He smoothed the robe with fingers knobbed and bent by arthritis. "I hear you gave 'em what for."

"You heard already?" Jacob looked up from studying his clasped hands, elbows resting on bent knees. He'd loosened his tie on the walk over and slung his suit coat over his shoulder so he could roll back his shirt sleeves.

"Oh yes. Things get around right fast here in the valley."

"I just read the Scriptures." *And declared my struggle with it. If I can't get it right, how can I expect anyone else to?*

"That's what's different about you, son."

"What?"

"You admit you're as human as the rest of us."

Jacob snorted. "Was there ever any doubt?"

"Dinner is served." Matilde pushed open the screen door. "I could bring it out here."

"No. We'll eat in the dining room since you have it all set up." Mr. Dumfarthing held out a hand. "Could you give an old man an assist?"

"Speaking of changes, the other day you about bit my head off, and today you are out here enjoying the sunshine." Jacob held on to Mr. Dumfarthing's arm while he got his balance. "I can carry you, you know."

"I might be old, but I'm not an invalid." The snap had returned to his voice.

Taking as much of Mr. Dumfarthing's weight as possible without actually lifting him, Jacob assisted him back into the house and down the hall to the dining room. The drapes had been pulled back off the windows, and the table that had been pushed back against the wall to make room for the bed was now set, and the candles lit.

After a fine dinner and enjoyable conversation, Jacob thanked his host and whistled his way down the walk. On the way home he pondered the change in the old man. All he could come up with was that it must be the grace of God. All those times he'd performed his perfunctory visit, counting the moments until he could politely leave, and today it had been like talking with his grandfather, a man now gone on to his reward.

His being in the ministry was thanks to his grandfather's prayers and the money he'd invested in Jacob's schooling.

What a glorious day it was. Perhaps he'd use some of this lovely weather to set out the tomato and pepper plants he'd started on the windowsills. Surely the danger of frost was past, and if it got cold again he'd cover the tender seedlings.

Later that evening after planting a small garden and eating a supper of the leftovers Matilde sent home with him, he sat reading the weekly newspaper with a refill of tea in the mug beside his chair. But his mind kept returning to his sermon. *If only I could remember all that I said.* That was the advantage of writing out his sermons. He had the notes for later. But not today. He leaned back and let his eyes close. "Ought against any." His mind drifted back those seven, nearly eight, years ago when he was about to be graduated from high school. When he'd been so in love with Melody Fisher that he thought of little else but her. Even when he was milking the cows in the morning before leaving for school or helping his father build the new machine shed in the afternoons, he'd thought of her. They'd been hammering shingles on the roof when he nearly slid off because he wasn't paying close attention. He could feel the heat of the hammer handle in his hand, hear the *tap, bang, bang* it took for his father to drive the nails home.

The tapping continued as he roused himself to reach for his now cooled tea. Was someone at the door? He heaved himself to his feet. "Coming."

He blinked to clear his eyes before opening the door. "Yes?"

"I hate to bother you. . . ." Matilde paused and half shrugged. "Mr.

Dumfarthing would like to see you."

"Is he all right?" Immediate thoughts of deathbed confessions raced through Jacob's mind. *Please, Lord . . .*

"I think he had a bit of a spell this evening. Scared me somewhat, you know."

"Of course. Come in while I get my coat." Jacob stepped back. "Forgive my poor manners."

"No. I think I'll start on back. You can outwalk me by a country mile." She turned to leave. "You'll come right away?"

"Yes. I just need to put out the lamp." Jacob left the door open, and before the smoke from the kerosene lamp dissipated, he was out the door. His prayers accompanied the rhythm of his stride. *Please, Lord, let this not be the end but rather a beginning. Please, Lord, I need your wisdom. Please, Father God.*

He passed Matilde before she reached her gate.

"You go right on in. He's in bed." She paused with a hand to her chest. "Got to get my breath again." `

"No rush. You needn't hurry now." Jacob patted her shoulder, all the while his thoughts on *Please, Lord.* He leaped up the steps to the front door and made his way down the hall to the dining room turned bedroom. Mr. Dumfarthing lay with his eyes closed, the flickering candle by the bedside casting deep shadows in his closed eyes and highlighting the prominent nose, hawklike due to the weight the man had lost with his illness. Jacob had seen pictures of the man when he was younger, a very imposing figure with a large girth due to rich living — a far cry from the wizened creature that awaited him.

"Mr. Dumfarthing?"

"I thought we agreed you would call me Evan."

Jacob breathed a sigh of relief. Appearances could indeed be deceiving. "Yes. You called, Evan?"

"I did. And thank you for coming."

"You're most welcome."

"Don't go looming like that. Take a seat. I'm not dying, at least I don't think yet."

"I'm glad to hear that. And don't you dare make mention of the church, meaning me, looking toward your money."

A slight cackle brought on a coughing bout. "Caught me out, did you? So if I offered you something, you'd turn it down?"

"If you mean for me personally — I'd turn it down. For the church? That I would consider. I need to be a good steward, you know."

"Don't burn your bridges, and all that?"

"Correct."

"The church has many needs."

"Yes." Jacob set a chair close by the bed. "It does. But how can I help you this evening?" He heard Mrs. Howard walking down the hall. She would feel obligated to offer him coffee or tea and be offended if he turned her down. He sat, then leaned forward, elbows on his knees.

"I didn't hold truck with the former pastor, you know."

"I heard mention of that, but I learned long ago to not believe too much in gossip."

"Obsequious, that's what he was."

Jacob leaned against the back of his chair. "I'm sure he did his best."

"Ha. His best to get money out of me."

" 'God loveth a cheerful giver.' " Jacob fought to keep a straight face.

One eye opened halfway. "Don't you go all pious on me."

"I have no intention of it." Two could play this game. "Just doing my job as the pastor of Valley Bible Church."

"Is that your tongue bulging that cheek?"

Jacob shrugged and leaned forward again. "What is it you need?" He wanted to reach out and cover the thin fingers that plucked at the quilt edge.

"I need to know one thing."

Jacob waited, as did the silence.

"If I die tonight, will I go to heaven?" Both eyes opened, and the hand stilled.

"Do you believe Jesus Christ is the son of the living God?"

"I do."

"Do you believe He died for your sins, as well as the sins of the whole world?"

"I do."

"Have you asked Him to forgive your sins?"

"I have."

"Then, yes, if you were to die this instant you would join Him in paradise."

"You say that with certainty."

"Because that is what the Bible says."

The old man nodded, slowly and with care. "Thank you. Just thought I'd better make certain."

"Are you planning on dying tonight?"

"Nope, nor tomorrow night either. But with my ticker, one never knows."

"Seems to me you are healthier than I've ever seen you."

"As I said, just wanted to make certain."

"Would you like me to read you the promises?"

Evan reached over and rang the bell that sat on the nightstand.

Mrs. Howard must have been waiting right outside the door. "Sir?"

"Why didn't you just come in instead of trying to hear through the wood? Can we have some tea?"

"Of course." She glanced at Jacob, caught his slight smile, and left the room with a satisfied nod. "I'll be back in two shakes of a rabbit's tail."

"She was fretting about me."

"She cares for you."

Dumfarthing pointed to a Bible on the long narrow table in front of the drape-covered window. "Read from that one and mark the places."

Jacob did as asked, sipped his tea, ate the cookies, and slipped out when Evan Dumfarthing began to snore.

Mrs. Howard walked him to the door. "Thank you for coming."

"Tell him I prayed for him and will continue to do so. And tell him he can pray for me when he gets bored."

Her chuckle followed him out into the night.

Dancing, leaping, and clicking his heels seemed an appropriate mode of making his way home, but he let his heart do it all for him. This was why he went into the ministry. That others could know, absolutely know, where they stood in eternal life.

Just before going inside his own house, he raised his voice beyond conversation. "Thank you, Father. Thank you!"

Miss Honey Witherspoon might well have been waiting around the corner, her meeting with him the next morning was so fortuitous. He smiled politely, greeting her with perfect manners, rigidly offered.

"Mama said that if I should happen to see you, I was to invite you for coffee." She twirled her parasol over one shoulder.

"I . . . ah . . ." He sighed in resignation. He had no excuses, none that could be dredged up without sounding like exactly that. "Thank your mother for me. I'll put my letters in the box and come right along."

"Oh, I shall walk with you, then, as I must do the same." Her smile and fluttering eyelashes looked to have been well practiced but did nothing to accomplish their intended purpose.

He could hear his heart slam the door as he sighed. Should he offer his arm or would that only encourage her? How could he be polite and not show undue interest?

When he escaped the Witherspoon home half an hour later, the earliest he could manage, he longed for the woodpile. Surely there must be some young man in the neighboring hamlets that would love to be the recipient of this mother and daughter's adoring machinations. At the moment he knew of none. What was a man to do? This situation should have been covered in seminary. Escaping Mamas' Clutches 101. Surely he was not the only young minister to encounter this predicament.

That week two of his congregants stopped him on the street to thank him for his Sunday sermon. If only he could put his own struggles out of his heart and get some sleep, he'd have been more able to rejoice with them.

If only there were some way for him to make amends.

By Saturday he'd given up on finding inspiration for a new sermon and decided to use his notes from the previous week. Unless the Holy Spirit took over again. The stacks of split wood had grown too. Perhaps he should go into the business of providing split wood instead of spiritual counsel for the members of his congregation.

The lower attendance at church the next morning could be attributed to the thunder and pouring rain, but he wondered. Had some folks found his message offensive? Had he probed too deeply? Yet it was amazing how the sermon he'd written for last week was the ideal follow-up for him to preach this week. God surely had planned that well.

Standing at the front door after the service, he shook hands with all who exited the church. "Thank you, Pastor," one of the women said with an extra shake of his hand. "One of these days you and I got to talk about what you said last Sunday." She leaned closer, tears glistening in her eyes. "And it's all good."

"I'll look forward to that." She'd never know how much her tears meant. *Thank you, Father.*

One by one the remaining congregants took his outstretched hand as he thanked them for coming and gave them a "God bless you." Some looked him in the eye and thanked him; others, with downcast eyes, mumbled a greeting and hurried out the door.

The storm had passed, leaving the world washed new, the air so fresh as to be intoxicating as he made his way to visit with

Evan Dumfarthing again. This was indeed the day that the Lord had made.

~ஃ

That night while he sat reading, he heard a knock on the door. When he opened it, a young woman stood on the porch, her hands locked on the shoulders of a young boy.

Jacob blinked once and then again. "Melody?" Surely the wraith before him wasn't her. Surely he was sleepwalking or dreaming or something.

"Yes."

He stepped back. "Please, won't you come in? You won't believe . . ."

"Jacob, I cannot stay." She covered her mouth with her hand to cough, a deep cough that shook her so severely the boy turned to look up at her. Was that a streak of blood on her chin?

"You all right, Mama?"

"Yes, Joel." She pushed him slightly forward. "I'm sorry, Jacob, but I have nowhere else to turn. I want you to meet your son, Joel."

"My son? Surely you . . ." But he took one look into her pain-wracked eyes and knew she wasn't fooling.

"You must have him now. I'm very ill, and I cannot —" She coughed again. She pushed the boy forward. "Good-bye, son. Be good for your papa." With a blood-stained handkerchief covering her mouth, she turned and ran.

Jacob stared at the boy, who in turn stared back at him for a heart-stopping moment before they both jumped to follow her.

"Mama!"

"Melody, wait!" Jacob leaped from the porch. "Stay right there," he ordered the boy and ran down the walk. But he was not in time to stop the buggy from being pulled westward by galloping horses. "Melody!" His cry echoed from the valley sides.

Chapter Six

"Miss Torvald, would it be too much to ask for you to pay attention?"

Opal jerked back to the schoolroom. She blinked a couple of times. "Ah, ah sure."

Snickers from the other pupils in the room told her she'd not made quite the right answer. Even Mr. Finch ducked to hide his smirk. Emily Robertson, who shared her desk, nudged her with her foot.

"Say sorry," she hissed in a whisper.

"Sorry, sir." Opal sat up straighter and plastered a smile on her face, a smile that never made it farther than her skin. No, maybe a smile wasn't the best idea. She sobered up and kept herself from glancing back out the window. Outside where the birds were singing, the sun shone warm and golden, the breeze would cool her neck, and she could ride Bay out across the breaks, searching out the hiding cattle, fishing the pools and rifts of the river. Anything would be better than staying here.

If she had anything to say about it, this would be her last year in school. Especially with this joke of a teacher. Out of his hearing, they often referred to him as Flinch. She knew more than he did about the really important things, like riding, roping, ranching, hunting, fishing, and if she had her way, she'd take on horses to train for others. Rand had recognized early on that she had a way with horses, and with all that Linc had to teach her, she figured she could make a good living as a horse trainer. Someday.

Now if she could only convince Ruby.

She carefully kept at least one ear on what was happening in the classroom. Embarrassment bit like a mosquito, itching for a long time after. If only Mrs. Hegland had continued teaching. Opal had loved school then. But their former teacher, the first in the area, had married a carpenter named Carl Hegland, and they had a little girl and another baby under the apron.

Opal had overheard that phrase and thought it especially appropriate when womenfolk tried to talk without letting on what was really going on. What did they think? Kids were blind or deaf? Of course, she'd overheard it down at the barn when one of the hands made a comment about Ruby, then ducked away when he saw Opal standing there.

Opal felt another nudge on her ankle, enough to bring her back to the warm and airless schoolroom. Her mind would just not stay corralled this day. She'd rope it and drag it squalling back, like a calf being drug in for branding, but before she knew it, it would be gallivanting off and she'd have to start all over again. Lucky Atticus. He was out in the fields. Sure he was working hard, but at least he could move.

She knew if she wiggled again, old Finch would stare at her with what he thought a glare and she thought a joke. Keeping from laughing at times was as hard as sitting still. When she was waiting near the deer trail down to the river, she could sit still as a rabbit froze under a bush when an eagle flies over. The deer never knew she was there. But here?

She stretched her head to the side to pull a crick out of her neck. Surely it must be about recess time. The seat seemed sunk permanently into her rear. A sigh brought another nudge. How could Emily sit so perfectly still? Opal glanced over. Emily had a different book propped behind the history text she was supposed to be reading.

Mr. Finch droned on like a fat bumblebee over a bed of marigolds. Only he wasn't fat. He was skinny like a . . . let's see — she needed a simile or a metaphor. Opal found her chalk and scribbled a sentence on her slate. *Skinny like Cat got when nursing her babies — simile. Rail thin — metaphor but a cliché.*

"Miss Torvald?"

She looked up. "Yes, sir?"

"You are to be listening. You will be tested on this lecture material tomorrow."

"Yes, sir. I was just working on our English lesson. I find metaphor and simile most fascinating, don't you?"

"Oh, well, I see. But we are in history now, and I'd rather you paid attention to this."

"Sorry, sir. Of course I will." *In a pig's eye. And that's a cliché too.* She knew she could look innocent if she made some kind of effort. For that look she received another ankle nudge. This time she nudged back.

⌁

By the time school was dismissed Opal

felt as if she'd been dragged by a runaway cow. "You want to ride with me as far as the turnoff?" she asked Virginia.

"Sure." Virginia glanced at her sisters. "Beats riding dumb Blaze." The Robertson girls had two horses on which they took turns riding double. Blaze was both hammer-headed and hammer-footed. Even his walk was a trial. And since they usually slow-jogged homeward, the two who suffered through riding him were ready for anything else. But horses were expensive, and Mr. Robertson said they were lucky to have horses to ride at all and they should quit complaining. Blaze did fine pulling the sleigh in the winter.

After letting Virginia off at their lane and riding on home, Opal dismounted at the corral and dropped Bay's reins to the ground. She set her saddle over the rack braced on the wall and took off the bridle, freeing her horse to graze. She hung up her bridle and headed for the house and something to eat. Amazing how hungry one could get in a boring classroom and after a strenuous ride home.

They should have stopped to catch some fish for supper.

"How did your day go?" Ruby asked

when Opal came through the door.

"Fine."

"Really?"

"No, not really, but how did you know?"

"Your 'fine' wasn't." Ruby set a flatiron back on the stove. "There are fresh ginger cookies in the jar, and the buttermilk should be cool in the springhouse by now. Help yourself." She attached the handle to a hot iron and returned to the ironing board. "Days like this I sure miss Daisy doing the ironing." Daisy, who had married Charlie, was one of the "girls" from Dove House whom Ruby had agreed to care for when her dying father asked. Charlie had been the bartender.

"Where's Per?"

"Still asleep. He didn't want to take a nap."

"About as much as I wanted to sit in that stifling classroom and listen to a dull teacher. Why they ever hired him is beyond me." Opal chomped into a cookie and, shaking her head, headed out the back door.

The springhouse was snugged up against the hill behind the house. Water trickled into a wooden trough and out a hollow wooden pipe at the other end to wend its way to the creek again. A peeper frog greeted the squeak of the opening door, and Opal paused to let her eyes adjust to the room lit only by the open door. Jugs of milk and cream sat in the cool water, and baskets of eggs lined the shelf above. Haunches of smoked meat hung from the low rafters, while clay crocks of salted sausage and pickles stood against the thick stone-and-mortar walls. No cooler place could be found during the hot summer days unless one floated under a wide-branched tree on the river.

Retrieving the jar of buttermilk from the water, she shook it before pouring herself a cup. After swigging half of it, she refilled the cup before returning the jar to the cold water.

Now that her stomach had calmed some, she nibbled the cookie and sipped her drink on the way back to the house. Perhaps this was not the best time to confront Ruby about not returning to school in the fall. But when was a good time?

At least she'd heard no more of the drifter, so perhaps he'd heeded the warnings and taken his sorry hide on west or north. Maybe he'd freeze to death if he went far enough north. She'd not let on to Ruby she'd had that kind of thought, just like she didn't say she wished she'd shot him. If Christians shouldn't have such thoughts, what did that make her? That wasn't a good thought either.

She leaned against the south wall of the log house, letting the sun sink into her bones to drive out the cold and apathy of the long dark winter, playing the future discussion with Ruby out in her mind. . . .

"If you weren't going to school, what would you be doing?" Ruby would ask.

"Training horses. Whatever Rand needed to have done on the ranch."

"I see. And what if there are no horses to train?"

"Once I build a good enough reputation, people will bring me their horses to break and train."

"What if they can't afford your services?"

"I could take a colt or calf or something in exchange."

"That's true. But . . ."

Opal heaved a sigh. The conversation would just go around in circles. With Ruby there would always be one more "but."

The heat felt good on her closed eyelids, soaking into her body. She listened to the sounds of spring. One of the hens was cackling. Must have laid an egg. A cow bawled somewhere off in the distance. A bee buzzed past her nose. The breeze tickling the cottonwood leaves set them giggling.

That same breeze brought a whiff of the outhouse. Most likely needed to dump lime down the holes again. Per called for his mother. Ghost stuck her nose into Opal's palm and nudged her silent request for an ear scratching.

Opal tried to ignore all the sounds and smells so she could continue dreaming about rounding up wild horses to train.

Ghost whimpered.

"Oh, all right. How come you're with me instead of Per, anyhow?"

She rubbed the dog's ears, headed into the house to set her cup in the dishpan on the stove, and went down the hall to change into work clothes. Chores were calling her name. The discussion with Ruby would have to come at some other time.

~

"Hey, Miss Opal, how about you goin' out and findin' Fawn? We let that fool cow out of the fence to graze with some of the others, and she done left. I got me a feelin' she's hidin' out to have her calf." Linc leaned over the corral fence.

"Sure. Walk or ride?"

"Better take Bay."

Opal whistled, and Bay, who was grazing some distance away, threw up her head. Opal whistled again, and the mare broke into a jog, then a lope.

Linc, his black skin glistening in the sun like he'd been oiled, chuckled and shook his head. "That horse minds better'n most kids."

Opal fetched her bridle.

"You might want to saddle up in case you need to rope that cow. She might be a bit testy when you try to drive her in."

"I will."

Once she was mounted again, Opal rode up to the house and dismounted. "I'm heading out to look for Fawn. Linc said she took off, and he thinks she is calving somewhere. I'm taking the rifle in case I see a deer."

"Get home before dark."

"I will." Opal paused. "Ghost! Hey, dog. Ghost, come on. Cows."

Ghost trotted around the corner of the house, tongue lolling. The word *cows* took precedence even over Per.

Opal nudged Bay into a lope and, with rifle secured in the scabbard, headed north across the meadow in the direction Linc had pointed. Farther up the draw oak trees, Juneberry bushes, and other brush offered good shelter for both calving cows and resting deer. The closer to dusk, the more likely the deer would take the trails down to the river to drink. On the edge of the wooded area she waved Ghost to go searching. Having a cow dog trained to hand signals was sure easier than beating her way through the brush in search of a cow that wanted to stay hidden. As she rode on up the game trail, glued to Bay's neck to keep from being dragged off by low-hanging branches, she heard something crashing off to her left. She stopped Bay, but her own heart picked up speed. When two steers crossed the path in front of her, she breathed a sigh of relief. Rand had warned her that bears were out of hibernation now, and if riled, they didn't go through the brush lightly.

She patted Bay's neck. "You'd have told me if it was something to be afraid of, wouldn't you, girl?" Bay snorted, ears pricked as Ghost took up her place just ahead of them.

"Good dog, Ghost, but wrong cows. Go find."

Ghost headed out again, tongue lolling, eyes bright and eager. Ghost loved to find cows probably even more than Opal loved to train horses. She nudged Bay forward again.

A cow bellering, sounding full of panic, brought the hair up on her neck as she heard growls and yips at the same time.

Ghost barked once, imperatively.

Opal drove Bay through the brush. There's more than one dog there. What else could it be? Coyote? Wild dog? She threw up her arm and ducked her head to keep branches from flaying her face. Bay snorted and plowed to a stop.

The wild-eyed cow stood in front of her still-wet calf. Three snarling coyotes, two in frontal attack position to the cow, one circling behind to get at the calf. Ghost lit into one with a growl.

Opal unsheathed her gun, held it to her shoulder, and fired. The coyote attacking the calf was lifted from the ground with the force of the bullet and crumpled. She pumped another shell into the breech, sighted on a second coyote, and dropped it.

"Ghost!"

The third coyote dodged away with Ghost after it.

"Ghost. Drop!"

With a confused look over her shoulder, the dog bellied to the ground, her whine pitiful in its beseeching.

The cow snorted, turned to nuzzle her calf while Opal dismounted and walked toward her. "Easy, girl. You're all right now." Opal spoke gently, all the while checking the cow for slash marks from the marauding attackers. Fawn spun like a longhorn and, head down, charged toward Opal.

"No, girl, no!"

Opal dodged behind a tree as Ghost lived up to her name, appearing between cow and girl as if by magic. With a nip to the cow's nose, she drove her back to her calf.

"Good dog." Opal leaned against the tree trunk and patted her chest, willing her heart to settle back down and not leap out of her throat.

Ghost returned to sit right in front of her and wriggle from nose to the bit of fluff called a tail. Her whimper pleaded for attention, and Opal gave it wholeheartedly, sinking down to her knees to look the dog in the eyes as she rubbed the dog's ears and down her shoulders.

"What a good dog. Good dog." When she pushed herself to her feet again, her knees felt like sodden river grass. She took in a deep breath and let it out slowly before turning to watch the calf nursing for the first time.

"They've been busy while we caught up over here. Now how can we get cow, calf, and two coyotes home, preferably all in one trip?"

She returned to Bay, slid the rifle in the scabbard, and took her knife out of the sheath hooked on her belt. After bleeding the coyotes, she dragged the carcasses back near the now skittish Bay.

"Don't like the idea of packing coyote, eh? Well, neither do I, but these pelts will look and feel mighty nice come winter." They'd been collecting coyote pelts to make a blanket for her bed. The one she'd seen made up had been beautiful. And warm.

Fawn lowed, a gentle moo that comforted the calf but also let Opal know someone else was near. Bay had already pricked her ears and whinnied just as Opal walked in front of her.

"Ahh." She rubbed her left ear. "You didn't have to make me deaf, you know."

"Opal?" a welcome voice called.

"Over here." So Rand had come looking for her. While she'd not shot twice in the instant succession of the call for help, Linc must have told him where she'd gone.

Fawn licked her calf, all the while keeping a wary eye on Opal and Ghost.

"Looks like you've been busy." Rand came into sight and stopped, crossing his arms on the saddle horn.

"Could have been bad. Three coyotes were after Fawn and her calf. Ghost chewed on the other one, then ran it off."

"I see. And the two shots were for those?" He motioned toward the carcasses on the ground. "You did well, I'd say."

"Thanks. Fawn was aiming to take out her ire on me, but thanks to Ghost and a big tree, I'm fine."

"Mad mama, eh?"

"No gratitude." Opal picked up one of the coyote carcasses. "You want to carry these or the calf?"

"Let's skin them first. Leave the rest out here for the scavengers."

Between the two of them they skinned out the carcasses and, rolling the hides with fur side out, tied them behind Rand's saddle. Buck sidestepped only once, but his ears spoke loudly of his displeasure.

"I'll put a rope around Fawn's horns and tie her to a tree. Then we can catch the calf and put it up in front of you. Okay?"

"Fine with me, but don't go giving her the benefit of the doubt. She'd as soon hook you as look at you."

Rand roped and snubbed the cow up tight to the tree, ignoring the bawling fight the critter put up. "Good grief, Fawn, you aren't a wild longhorn mama. You're a tame milk cow."

"She forgot to read that line on the bill of sale." Opal reached for the calf and caught only air. "Feisty little thing, aren't you?" She grabbed again and got an arm around its neck. Rand took it from her, and when she was mounted, he laid it across Opal's lap.

"You better hang on to him."

"I will."

Together they made their way back to the trail and on homeward, Fawn trotting beside Bay, talking all the way.

"Think we've been cussed out in cow language," Opal said when she and Rand were riding side by side.

"Probably a good thing we can't understand cow talk."

"Oh, I think she's getting her point across."

"Just so she doesn't implant those points into one of us or the horses."

Back at the barn they ran Fawn into a box stall and slid her calf in through the door before slamming it in her face as she charged them.

"She always going to act like this?"

"No. Once she's in the stanchion, she'll calm down. Think she's been too long with the longhorns. They've been giving her lessons."

"I'm going to work with Missy for a while before supper." She'd not had time to work with the filly for three days.

"Probably not. There's the bell."

Opal groaned. She pulled her rifle from the scabbard, knowing she had to clean the gun before she went to bed. That was one of the rules Rand had taught her. You took care of your horse, your rifle, and your rope, and they'd take care of you.

Ruby thought she should take care of more around the house. But how could Opal build a reputation as a horse trainer if she never had time to train horses?

Chapter Seven

"I want my mama."

Jacob stared at the boy. Was this really his son? When he forced himself to think, he knew there could not be much doubt, considering Joel looked enough like Jacob's younger brother to make him homesick. And his younger brother was not only too young to have a seven-year-old son, but he had not been the one to make love to Melody.

All Jacob wanted to do was go kill some more firewood.

"I'm sorry. I don't think she plans to come back." *What a cruel monster you are!* He squatted down to be eye level with the child. *What would my mother do in this situation? First of all, she'd never be caught in such a mess, and secondly, she'd . . . she'd offer food.*

"Are you hungry? Have you eaten?" he asked the boy.

"Not since breakfast."

"I see. I have some cookies and . . . and . . ." His mind searched the larder. "Do you like bread and cheese?"

The boy nodded. "But I don't want to stay here. I want to go with my mother."

"Yes, I'd like your mother to come back too, but in the meantime why don't you come and eat something?"

The boy hesitated. His brow furrowed in a manner that Jacob had seen on his father all his life and been told he did the same. *How can that be? The boy has not been around any of us.* Jacob stood and held out his hand. "Come along, and let's see what we can find."

The boy looked toward the door, then up at Jacob. "Maybe she will come back soon."

Jacob only nodded. He had a very definite feeling Melody would not be back. She had always lived up to her word.

Jacob indicated the chair by the table, and the boy sat on it, his dark eyes tracking every movement Jacob made. He took out a loaf of bread, sliced two pieces, and asked, "Can you eat three?" At the shake of the boy's head, the father brought out a block of cheese, some jam, and butter, freshly churned the day before by one of his flock.

Often members of his congregation who lived out in the country brought him gifts when they came to church. Those in town dropped things by the church or the house. Jacob cut off several slices of cheese, motioned toward the jam, and waited until Joel nodded. "All right, bread and jam, with cheese on the plate. As soon as you finish this, I'll bring out the cookies."

Am I talking just to hear myself make noise? Or because I don't have any idea what to say? I can talk with children easily. I do so all the time. They even appear to like me. But this . . . ? What do you do when you meet your son for the first time and he is seven years old? And his mother leaves him and flees?

He pushed the plate across the table. "There's water or buttermilk to drink. Which would you like?"

"Water." The boy nibbled on a piece of cheese.

After dipping out a cup of water from the bucket, Jacob set it in front of the boy and went to stand at the back door, looking out over his garden and to the woods covering the hillside that grew steeper the farther he looked. *Dear Lord, what do I do here? What would you do? Dumb question. You'd welcome him and surround him with love.* Did Joel bring a suitcase with him? Jacob had been so shocked, he'd not thought to look.

"Pardon me, but did you bring any extra clothes with you? A nightshirt?"

Joel nodded. "By the door." He went back to nibbling on the bread and jam. Mouselike, he ate around the edges, small bites as if being polite.

"Would you rather have something else?"

"No. Yes. I want my mother." His eyes filled with tears, and while Jacob watched, one tear meandered down the boy's cheek.

Jacob could feel his heart crack. He crossed the room and knelt beside the chair. "Ah, Joel, I am so sorry she left. Of course you want your mother. If there was any way to get her back here, I would do so." He put his arm around the now shaking shoulders and leaned his cheek on the boy's soft hair.

"I-I wa-want my m-mother." Sobs so strong it shook them both made Jacob scoop his son up in his arms and carry him to the big chair in front of the fireplace.

Sitting down, he held the shuddering body close and murmured words he hoped were comforting.

The shudders turned to sobs, the sobs to sniffs, and periodically the child's body jerked as he fell asleep, his head on Jacob's chest.

One minute Jacob felt like crying too, the next minute he wanted to rage at the woman who had been so heartless as to leave her son with a total stranger. What was the matter with her? Why had she not let him know of this child? How had she found him now? Questions tumbled through his mind like rocks from a cliff. Would there be a landslide to bury everything?

Where would Joel sleep? There was only one bed in the house, and Jacob had never shared a bed since he left home. Tall as he was, he slept kitty-corner on it already.

Only two choices, he told himself. *A pallet on the floor or he sleeps with me. What if he wakes in the night and is terrified?*

He rose with the child in his arms, carried him to the bedroom, and laid him on the bed. He returned to the front room, where a tattered satchel waited by the door. He snatched it up and headed back to the bedroom, not opening it until he set it on the bed. Joel hadn't moved. He lay on his back, long eyelashes like his mother's feathered on cheeks red from crying. Dark shadows purpled under his eyes, and a narrow line of scar on his right cheek looked like a cat scratch.

Jacob sank down on the foot of the bed. How could his life have changed so in an instant? One moment he'd been alone, and now he had a son and a whole mess of muddle. What a heyday the gossipmongers would have with this.

Forcing himself to tend to the matter at hand rather than succumb to the dither going on in his head, he unbuckled the flap on the satchel and reached inside. He withdrew a sweater, a shirt, trousers, drawers, a nightshirt. Several pairs of socks lay in the bottom, and an envelope. With his name on it.

He put the other things back in the bag, keeping out the nightshirt and the envelope.

While he unlaced Joel's shoes, he fought the anger that attacked again like a waiting cat. A big cat, one that threatened to rip his throat. What kind of mother would dump her son on a stranger and run off? What kind of mother never let the father know he had a son? Where had she gone? How had she found him? Where had she been all these years? Questions snarled at questions, fighting and clawing for supremacy.

But no matter, he couldn't let his feelings loose on this poor scared child. Hadn't he been through enough?

At the thought of how she — he could scarcely think her name or say it — had hurt her child, it was probably a good thing she wasn't around. Once Jacob had him undressed and in his nightshirt, he tucked the covers around him and left the room, leaving a small candle burning on the washstand in case he woke and was afraid in the dark.

Out in the front room he lit the kerosene lamp by his chair and collapsed into it. "Dear God, how could she do such a thing?"

Only the silence answered him, a friendly silence but for the songs of the peeper frogs now that spring had arrived.

He stared at the envelope. Her handwriting was familiar except for the hint of wavering — from weakness or hurry? What did it matter? It was addressed to him. Staring at it would not change that. He leaned back in the chair to dig out his pocketknife, opened the blade, and slit the envelope. After closing the blade again, he leaned back in the chair to return the knife to his pocket. Had the fire been burning, he might have succumbed to the temptation of throwing the letter in the fire, but the warm night had saved him from the action. No fire. No cheery fire, only an envelope that could be the snake or rat in his woodpile, ready to leap out and bite him should he draw too close.

"Jacob Chandler, you are not a coward," he declared.

Right. As if saying the words was sufficient to make it so. His hands shook with reluctance. He pulled the single sheet of paper from the envelope and flipped it open.

Dear Jacob,

How often he'd seen those words on the notes they'd exchanged.

When you read this, I will again be out of your life, this time forever, as I had thought once before. Were the situation not so dire, you would not be reading this now. How life changes, and we are unable to control that. While I have never been strong, I have provided a life for Joel. My husband, Patrick O'Shaunasy, who believed Joel to be his son, died in an accident last year. Shortly after that the consumption, which I have battled forever, it seems, became rampant, and I know I do not have long to live. I wrote to your mother and asked for your address, something I should have done long ago, but I thought I had everything taken care of.

Is God in his heaven laughing at my pitiful attempt to keep our sin from tarnishing our son? Or is this his judgment? I can no longer be depended upon, and I cannot leave Joel to the mercies or lack thereof of fate. So I have brought him to you with the prayer that you will treat him well. He is your son and a good lad. I cannot bear for him to suffer watching me die. May God bless and keep him and you. I have told him you are truly his father.

Do not waste your time trying to find me, for I shall be gone.

Please tell Joel that his mother loved him beyond life itself. If you can find it in your heart to forgive me for keeping him from you, I will rest in peace.

Yours,
Melody

Jacob ignored the tears that made him blow his nose and read the letter again. He checked the envelope. No return address. No forwarding address. Nothing. Nothing but a single sheet of paper that described the havoc one hour of heaven had cost.

Though he lay down beside the boy later, sleep eluded him and memories haunted him.

Their dreams so long ago had been fresh and full of aspirations. They had talked of the life they would have together, a life that would start when he had finished his schooling. She would wait for him. *Wait.* The one thing he had been unable to do.

He got up, lit the lamp, and read the letter again. *Do not try to find me, for I shall be gone.* What did she mean by that? She'd disappear? Die? Surely she wouldn't kill herself. Not one more thing on his conscience now so raw as to be dripping blood.

Blowing out the lamp, he lay down again, only to stare at the ceiling he couldn't see, his arms locked behind his head.

The boy puffed gently in his sleep, a sound so innocent it rent Jacob's heart even more.

He watched the window, waiting for the light. After all, the Bible promised that joy would come with the morning. How often he had promised that to others suffering through a long night. Could his heart, which felt as heavy as an ancient millstone in his chest, not feel it? Or was the Scripture only for others, not applicable to a sinner like he?

When dawn barely lightened the windows, Jacob rose and returned to the chair, where he stared at the ashes left over from previous fires in the fireplace. Gray and black, charred bits — like his life. And it was no one's fault but his own.

Chapter Eight

Reading letters was such a pleasure, and a lazy Saturday morning was the perfect time to partake.

Ruby sighed, one of pure delight rather than of exasperation, which seemed the more usual, at least as far as Opal was concerned. Here she was, on the brink of young womanhood, and she'd become more hoyden than ever. If only Rand would stop encouraging her.

"Stop thinking of Opal and enjoy your visit with a friend."

Per looked up from playing with some blocks of wood at her feet. "Ma?"

"Yes, dear little one, I am your ma." He said few words yet, but Ma and Da could be said many ways.

She returned to her letter.

Dear Ruby,

How good it was to hear from you. I long for a real visit to catch up on these years that have fled so swiftly. The children still speak of you and Opal with delight, and even little Bernie says your name, feeling he remembers you even though he was still a baby, all because the others talk of you so often.

To think you are married and have a son of your own. God grant you wisdom and joy as you watch him grow. It is hard to believe that Alicia is graduating from high school this year and will leave for Philadelphia Women's College in the fall. My first child to leave home, other than you and Opal. I felt at that time much as I am feeling now. That is how dearly I love you both.

Forgive me for sounding so sentimental here, but now that Penelope has her health back, I am more aware of time passing than ever. She was so ill this winter that I was beginning to think we might need to find a warmer climate for her health. I thank God that the others contracted only light cases. Influenza is a vicious beast. I know I should be grateful that we have remained so healthy — except for Jason's broken arm, which happened when he fell out of a tree.

You would not believe how Bernie has grown. He loves school, as do the others, and for that, much of the thanks goes to your years of encouraging them to think and dream. You have a gift for creating a love of learning.

Ruby looked up. Her eyes misted so that she had to blink several times to clear them.

"Per?"

"Da." Thankful again that he always answered when she called, she laid the letter aside and went to the bedroom to fetch him. She would have to remember to put up the small gates Beans had built for her to keep her son corralled where she could see him. He had learned to pull himself up now, and any day she was sure he would break out in a run. Walk would not even enter his mind. She brought him back to sit by her chair and handed him a piece of the bread she had left in the oven until it was solid as the hardtack of early years. While he chewed on that, she returned to her letter.

I do hope that one of these days you

will see your way clear to sending Opal back to visit us. This summer would be especially wonderful because Jason is helping his father in the business, and the rest of us miss him. I know it is good preparation for his future, but that doesn't make me any more cheerful about the whole thing.

I hear the schoolchildren at the door, so I must bid you good-bye for now. Please don't wait so long to write again, although I know you must be far busier than I can imagine.

Love from your New York friends,
Lydia Brandon

If Opal wanted to go east, Ruby would use some of her savings from the hotel to buy the ticket. Perhaps Mrs. Brandon could get her to wear more suitable clothing.

Opal would need an entirely new wardrobe to travel back there. No britches or split skirts, no leather vest or jacket. And no pistol or gun of any kind.

"Mrs. Brandon, dear lady and friend, you have no idea what you are asking." Ruby chuckled.

Early that afternoon a lone rider rode

the trail up to the house. When Ruby went to the door in answer to Ghost's announcement of company, she looked in amazement. Mr. Finch, dressed in a high collar and cravat, gray suit coat and vest, sat the horse with a distinct look of discomfort.

"Mr. Finch, please dismount and come in."

"Ah, good day, Mrs. Harrison. Where might I tie my horse?"

"Oh, I'm sorry. Take him over to the corral and tie him to the wood fence by the barn. I'll heat the coffee."

"Thank you, ma'am." He pulled on the right rein, clucking with his tongue. The horse just stood there, ears flicking back and forth like a semaphore.

Ruby caught her upper lip with her lower teeth. "Ah, horses out here are trained to neck-rein, Mr. Finch."

He swallowed his frown. "Neck-rein?"

"Yes. You hold the reins in your right hand and lay the left rein across the horse's shoulders." *Opal, where are you when I need you?* "Then you nudge him in the ribs with your heels."

She could tell he was trying, but the horse had yet to move. "You need to rein and nudge at the same time."

113

If his red face was any indication, he had not only gotten too much sun, but his patience had about reached its limit too. Should she go down the steps of the porch and show him what she meant? Or would that destroy his pride forever? Men could be so silly that way.

"I-I'll go get the coffee ready." She turned, scooped Per up, and kept the door from banging behind her in case that spooked the horse. Or the man.

That thought almost made her giggle. No wonder Opal had a hard time respecting her teacher. The stories she brought home had given them many a good laugh.

But now he was at her door, and good manners were imperative. Had he come on a social call or what?

It was most likely not a social call since she'd been seeing him regularly in church, which met in the school building ever since its completion.

"Uff da."

"Da?" Per looked toward the door.

"Da will be home later. He's out with the cows."

She set a plate of cookies on the table as she made her way to answer the knock at the door. "Come in. Come in."

Mr. Finch removed his hat and held it with both hands against his chest as he stepped through the door. "Thank you. It sure smells good in here."

"That's the bread I took out of the oven a bit ago. Please sit down. Do you take cream and sugar with your coffee?"

"Just cream, thank you." He sat and rested his hat on the table beside him. "I wish this were just a social call."

Ruby placed the cups in saucers on the table and pushed the cream toward him. *Why am I not surprised?*

"What has Opal been doing now?"

"She has a very good mind, you know."

"Yes, and had the blessing of good schooling, both before we came west and then with Mrs. Hegland."

"But she doesn't really want to use it."

"Really?" Ruby tipped her head slightly, as if she'd not heard right. This was not what she expected.

"She spends much of her time daydreaming and not paying attention in class. The younger children look up to her, and I wish she would set a good example."

"Have you talked to her about this? Is she disruptive in class?"

"No and no. But I have called it to her attention when I observed her woolgathering."

"Does she have plenty to keep her busy and to challenge her? Are her grades suffering?"

He stiffened slightly. "I am doing the best that I am able, Mrs. Harrison."

"I'm sorry. I didn't mean to sound critical. I will speak to her about this."

"I would appreciate that."

"I have a question though. If she finishes her work ahead of the others, what would you like her to do with her spare time?"

"She can help with the younger children. I'm sure you know how good she is with them."

Better than you, I wonder? "Or?"

"She can read a book. As you know, we have quite a collection now."

"Of which she has read most. Unless you've gotten new ones in recently."

"She has?"

The man obviously had no idea how quickly Opal read. "More coffee?"

"Please." He stared at the red-and-white-checked tablecloth, looking up when Ruby filled his cup. "Do you think she will return to school in the fall?"

"I assume so. We have not discussed a different plan."

"I . . . ah . . . I just thought perhaps a finishing school might be a good idea. Not that I presume to tell you what to do, but since she is so obviously disinterested . . ."

Isn't that part of your job? To make learning so interesting that you hold your pupils' attention? I never saw the day-dreamer side of Opal. She's always been a do-it kind of girl. Now, if there had been a snake in your desk, that would not surprise me. Ruby looked up to realize she'd been lost in her thoughts. Would he think sister like sister?

"Thirty students of all ages in one room gives little time for individual attention."

"That is true. Perhaps it is time to petition the school board for another teacher?"

"I wrote to them, but they don't believe the school here will grow to accommodate another teacher."

Ruby shook her head. They surely had not spoken with the Marquis de Mores. Granted, cows outnumbered everything except ants and rabbits out here, but new families were coming in, much to the resentment of the ranchers.

"Well, since I plan on visiting the Robertsons while I am out this far, I had better get back on that horse." The look on his face left no doubt as to his feeling about his mode of transportation.

"Would you like Opal to ride along and

show you the way?" Now, what sort of devilment made her offer that suggestion? Ruby schooled her face in a polite smile.

"N-no thank you. I have a map."

"I see." Ruby stood so he could. "Please greet Mrs. Robertson from me."

"Oh, I will. Thank you for the coffee. You surely do have a beautiful child there."

Per looked up from the rusk he'd been chewing. He'd managed to smear his face from ear to ear. "Da?"

Ruby refrained from pointing out that Per was a boy. It was hard to tell, since all small children wore a shift until age three or when they were potty trained.

"Godspeed, Mr. Finch."

He stopped in the doorway. "And you'll talk with Opal?"

"Yes, of course."

"Thank you again." He tipped his hat and headed down to the corral for his horse.

Ruby watched as he struggled to mount and then, once in the saddle, tried to turn the animal by pulling the left rein. He looked like some kind of puppet, arms straight out, swinging his legs rather than squeezing.

Ruby rolled her eyes. Thank heavens Opal was off with the hands, or she would have burst out laughing. It was all Ruby could do to hold her own laughter in. She knew Rand would enjoy her description once they were in their room, where Opal would not hear.

She lifted Per and propped him on her hip. "It's not her fault, I'm sure, that she's daydreaming. That man could put anyone to sleep."

Chapter Nine

"But, Ruby, I was never rude."

"I should hope not. But you weren't doing what you were supposed to be doing — listening to your teacher."

"I try." Opal sighed and shook her head. "I try so hard, but he has a kind of sing-song voice, and pretty soon my mind just takes off and all of a sudden he is saying, 'Miss Torvald,' like it's a bad word, and then I come back and I don't know what the question was, and . . . and I think he likes to . . . to . . ."

"Embarrass you?"

"Yes." *It makes him feel like a big shot or something, and then I get disgusted. But I can't tell Ruby all this, can I?*

"So to come right down to it, he's boring."

Opal nodded. "And he likes to lecture." *Mostly just to hear himself talk.*

"What do the others do?"

"Virginia keeps a book up like she's reading, and she is, but it's not the history book that he sees."

"Could you do the same?"

"I guess I'm going to have to." Opal chewed on her bottom lip. "I wish Miss Hossfuss, er, Mrs. Hegland was still our teacher. Or you."

"Well, they won't allow women with children to teach, so that leaves Pearl out. Besides, she's too busy."

"Like you."

"I don't know where the time goes."

"Ma?" came from the bedroom, where Per had been napping.

"I'll get him." Opal fled the room. "Hey there, little guy, you ready to get up?"

Per reached out for her, chattering his own little song, one that sounded the same whenever he saw her.

"Wish I could understand you." She untied the belly strap and picked him up. "I think you understand us much better than we do you."

Another run of sounds.

"I know. Pretty soon you'll be running and jabbering up a storm. You wet?"

He shook his head, his latest accomplishment. When she nodded, he imitated that, then giggled, his red cheeks crinkling in a grin.

"You want to go riding?"

He shook his head, the widening smile showing off his two new bottom teeth, chattering at the same time. He pounded on her shoulders with his tiny fists, nearly jumping out of her arms.

"Per wants to go riding."

"Is that what he's saying?" Ruby arched an eyebrow.

"He can sure understand a lot more than he can say."

"You better put a sweater on him." Ruby handed her one off the back of the chair.

"We won't be gone long." Opal swung him up on her shoulders and galloped him out the door. Whistling for Bay, she grabbed Per's fists. He loved to tangle them in her hair and pull. "All right, let go. Ouch." Now he pounded on the top of her head, making both of them laugh.

Once she'd saddled Bay again, she lifted Per to the saddle and swung up behind him almost in the same motion. Per's crow made Bay's ears twitch.

"You sure do love to ride, little guy." She squeezed Bay into a gentle jog, Per giggling all the while, then singing his own song. They rode down to the river, scaring up a flock of ducks and setting the grazing cows to moving a few feet before dropping their heads to pull at the nearly knee-deep grass. Spring sometimes came late to the badlands, but all growing things tried to make up the lost time. When they returned to the house, Ruby came out to the porch.

"You ready for a cookie?" She held up her arms, but Per shook his head and clutched the saddle horn.

"Not even bribery will work." Opal loosened his fingers and handed him to his mother, getting a wail and beseeching look in return.

"Sorry. I've got work to do." She turned Bay away and they loped to the corral, where she unsaddled Bay and let her loose. "Thanks, girl. That was perfect."

Whistling, she took a rope from the fence post and entered the corral. The filly she'd been working with waited at the far side of the enclosure.

"Going to be stubborn today?"

The sorrel's ears flicked, but she continued to hug the far fence. Opal swung the loop gently and settled it over the horse's head, reeling her in hand over hand. Once she had the lead rope snapped on the halter, Opal snubbed the filly to the post sunk in the middle of the corral and went for brushes, saddle blanket, bridle, and saddle, which she set horn down in the dust. Opal kept up a steady stream of conversation as she brushed the horse she'd named Firelight because of the way the sun reflected off her coat and light mane.

"You try to act so tough, when you're just an old softie. Now, try to tell me you don't like this. Think how much fun we'll have out riding the hills instead of working around in this dusty corral."

"Hey, Opal," Chaps called from the barn. "You goin' out with her?"

"Hope so."

"I could ride with you."

"Give me a few minutes, and we'll see." Opal had ridden the filly out of the corral before, but not with another horse. Perhaps that would help calm her down.

Mounting took a couple of tries, but finally the horse stood quietly as Opal mounted and dismounted a few more times before walking around the corral.

"It's like you have to be convinced each day that I am indeed your boss. You know, that kind of slows things down. Wouldn't you rather be free from here?" She glanced up to see Beans and Chaps, crossed arms resting on the top rail, watching the work session.

"She's sure come on quick."

"No. She's a bit stubborn." Opal touched the horse's side with her stirrups to signal a lope. "Not a gallop, mind you." She kept the reins tight enough to get her point across.

When sweat darkened the red hide, she stopped the filly in front of the men.

"You two look mighty good together," Beans said as he stroked the filly's nose. "She's sure a pretty thing."

"Rand ought to be able to sell her for a goodly amount if we can find the right buyer."

"Be interesting to see what kind of cow horse she becomes." Chaps tipped his hat back, the easier to look up at Opal. "Her mama is a good one."

"You been workin' her, what, a couple of weeks?" Beans asked.

"About. Should have started earlier, but school takes up so much time." Opal patted Firelight's shoulder. "You still want to ride with us?"

"Nah, unless you want me to," Chaps said.

"You want me to open the gate?" Beans headed to do just that.

"Thanks," she called as she rode on through to work the horse in the open field.

As dusk blurred the land she rode her among the cows, cutting out first one, then another, all at a walk so as not to spook anyone. One long-horned mama shook her head at them, making sure she was between them and her calf. Others kept on grazing, ignoring both horse and rider. A couple of calves, tails in the air, raced ahead of them.

When Opal brought Firelight back to the corral, she stripped off the tack and let her loose in the corral again.

"About time you hobble her to graze." Rand now joined her at the wooden rails.

"I suppose. I've had them on her."

"You ready to start working that dark gelding?"

"I'd have more time if I didn't have school."

"Don't even begin to think like that. Ruby would skin you alive, and me too."

"I know." She glanced at Rand, relaxed beside her. Should she say what she'd been thinking? Why not? "Don't think I'll go back in the fall."

"To school?"

"Um-hmm."

"Ruby will be right disappointed."

"I know. But I'm going on fifteen now. What can Mr. Finch teach me about the stuff that's really important?" She indicated the horse and ranch with a nod. "Besides, he doesn't teach much of anything. I can read it out of a book myself."

"You're going to have to take that up with your sister."

"Will you stand behind me?"

"I need to think on that." The clang of the triangle echoed through the valley. "Supper's ready."

And I should have been at the house to help. Good thing Little Squirrel is such a good worker. Better not bring up school tonight. Best to wait until after it's out, anyway.

Rand started walking to the house. "You coming?"

"Yep." She pulled herself away from the fence and strolled beside him up to the wash bench along the west side of the house. Tucking her gloves in her belt, she washed her hands and dried them on the towel hanging from a nail driven into the log wall.

At the table Rand waited for everyone to settle down, including Per, who sat in a high chair with a wooden tray, tied in by the usual belly band, before he asked them to bow their heads for grace.

"Heavenly Father, we thank you for the food you have given us, for our home and the work we all do. Thank you for sending us your Son to show us how to live. Bless the work of our hands and this food to our bodies. In Jesus' precious name we pray."

Everyone joined in on the amen.

Linc had protested eating with them at first, saying he and Little Squirrel would be better off by themselves, but Rand had insisted. "No sense cooking two meals, and we have room here," he'd said and repeated it until Linc finally gave in.

Opal still had a hard time understanding why there had been a problem. They worked here, they ate here. Everyone else did. One day after Ruby took her aside and explained how other people acted and felt, even in their own part of the world, Opal had gotten mad.

"Just like with the 'girls,' right?"

"I'm afraid so." Ruby's apron had mounded over the soon-to-be-born Per at the time.

"That stinks worse than polecat — a dead polecat."

"I agree, but that's the way the world is. The way some people are." Ruby flinched.

"Baby's kicking again?" Opal stared at the mound, always fascinated by the thought of a real live baby living and growing inside her sister. "There, I saw it." Delight had made her giggle. "That must hurt."

"A bit."

"Just like that cow Rand and I watched earlier."

"Thanks."

"Well, you know what I mean."

Opal was pulled from her thoughts as everyone at the table laughed heartily at a story Linc was telling. *They all feel like family — including Linc and Little Squirrel.* She was quite certain life didn't get any better than this.

Later, after the hands had left for the bunkhouse and the dishes were finished, Ruby took out her letter from Mrs. Brandon and read it to Rand and Opal.

Opal propped her chin in her cupped hands with her elbows on the table. "Sure would be fun to see them again. You think maybe they'd come out here this summer? They've talked about it before."

"I think I read that they were inviting you to come back there and visit."

"And not be here for summer?" Opal's

129

heart picked up speed like it might jump out of her chest. "I'd miss branding and haying. And who would finish training Firelight and the gelding?"

"I thought you wanted to see your friends again."

"But not there — here. They can afford to come here. We could go camping and fishing and swim in the river. Oh, so many things we could show them and do. Wouldn't that be the most fun?" She leaped from her seat and spun around the room. "Guess I better write them a letter and get it mailed."

"But, Opal . . ." Ruby shook her head when Opal turned to look at her. "You go write your letter. You haven't written them one for a long time."

When she described the afternoon's visit that night to Rand, Ruby got the laugh she'd been expecting.

"Typical easterner. They think you steer a horse rather than neck-rein. Arms straight out?"

Ruby snickered into his shoulder. "And he says Opal spends her time daydreaming instead of listening to his lectures."

"I assume he is a droner?"

"I suspect so. But I agreed I would speak

with her. She has to be respectful."

"That is easier to be with some than others."

Ruby sighed and laid her arm across his chest. "It would help if you did not encourage her in her wild ways."

Rand stroked her hair with one hand. "Ruby, she's not like other girls. She wants to be outside. She loves this ranch as much as I do. She loves all the chores and has the skills to do them. I know that concerns you, but would you have her free and happy outside or miserable indoors?"

"Can't she do both? Medora surely seems to have the best of both worlds."

"I heard on that last hunting trip, she outshot the men every time."

"And yet, she needs to learn the importance of being the perfect lady in dress, speech, and manners. She has to learn all that too."

"Opal can do that."

"I've been thinking about the letter from Mrs. Brandon — inviting Opal to come for a visit this summer."

"You would send her away from the ranch?" His hand left her hair.

"No. She would have to want to go. Please help me encourage her?"

"But she'd miss roundup and fishing and

swimming in the river." He locked his arms behind his head. After a deep sigh he turned to look at her in the moonlight streaming through the window. "That drifter is back in town. There are snickers going round."

"About Opal?"

"I'm afraid so. The conversation stopped when I walked into the room, but I heard enough as I approached."

Now it was Ruby's turn to sigh. "What are we going to do?"

"When the man saw me, he disappeared out the back real quick."

"Where were you?"

"Stopped by Williams' to hear the local goings-on."

"Gossip, you mean?"

His chuckle echoed in his chest under her ear, a comforting sound.

"You didn't drink any of his rotgut, did you?"

"Ruby, do you think I'm stupid, or what?"

"No, not stupid, but how can you bear to go in that disgusting place?"

When he didn't answer, she sighed again. His breathing had changed. A gentle snore confirmed it. He'd fallen asleep just like that. Men!

What was she to do about Opal?

Sunday morning they woke to the patter of rain on the roof.

"The garden will sure appreciate this." Ruby settled Per into his high chair and gave him a spoon to bang. Making noise kept him content for a few minutes, then a rusk would help hold him until breakfast was ready.

Little Squirrel came through the back door, a narrow blanket over her head. "Creek up."

"I'm not surprised. How about you do the sourdough for pancakes? Rand, would you bring in the haunch of venison so we can slice that?"

"You want the milk strained in here or the springhouse?" Opal paused in the door on her way out to milk Fawn.

"We'll use yesterday's, so do it out there. Let's take some in to Charlie and Daisy. Their cow hasn't calved yet, has she?"

"Got plenty cream for butter." Little Squirrel took the haunch from Rand and set it on the table. After giving the knife a couple of licks on the whetstone, she sliced off steaks for frying.

Opal whistled her way out to the barn, bucket swinging in one hand, her hat keeping the rain off her head and shoulders. *If we didn't have to go to church, I'd take Firelight for a long ride upriver and give her a real workout.* Satisfying as the thought was, she played with it more while she brought the cow in and threw a scoop of grain in front of her once she stood in the wooden stanchion. Fawn's calf bellered from the pen. He'd not appreciated being weaned from his mother and let them know about it.

Opal tipped her hat back on its string and, after positioning the three-legged stool and sitting on it, leaned her forehead into Fawn's soft flank. The good smell of cow, barn, and hay, the ping of milk in the bucket, and a cat twining about her ankles were all parts of early morning on the ranch. She could hear the rooster crowing. The calf bellered again, and the ping changed to two-part harmony rising from the bucket along with the rich fragrance of warm milk. She squirted a shot at the cat, one of Cat's many descendants, who caught it openmouthed with minimal splatters.

When she'd stripped the cow dry, she rose, hung the stool on a peg on the wall, and poured enough in the other bucket for the calf to drink, poured some in the dish, and set the bucket for the house on the feed-bin lid.

"Now, take your time. I'm not going to take away the bucket." No matter what she said, the calf guzzled the milk as if starving. "Just think, as soon as we get that fence up, you'll be running in the pasture and grazing like the others." His tail switched from side to side like a metronome.

"Scat, cat! Get out of that bucket." She shooed the cat away before it got a paw down in the froth. The sow they'd raised last year snorted from her pen in the corner. She'd be having babies soon too. That was one of the great things about spring. There were all kinds of babies running all over the ranch.

She gave the calf a last pat, picked up her other bucket, and headed for the house. She'd have to get a move on if they were going to make it to church on time.

The rain had stopped by the time everyone came to breakfast slicked up and ready to ride to Medora. Ruby insisted that Opal wear a proper skirt for church, so much to Opal's dismay she had to ride into town in the wagon.

Opal waved to the Robertson girls as the wagons arrived at the school now turned church. With the ten families that regularly attended their church, the school building bulged at the seams. Since Mrs. de Mores had had the Catholic church built, some people attended there, especially when the Marquis and his family were in residence during the summer. Ruby kept a tight hold on Per's shift as his legs pumped and arms flailed in eagerness to get down.

"Better watch him. He's going to fly." Rand halted the team and wrapped the reins around the brake handle. Beans dismounted, tied his horse to the hitching rail, and removed the bridles from the team, tying them with a rope to their halters instead.

Opal scrambled over the wagon side and used the wheel spokes as a ladder. "Hi, Cimarron."

"Hi, yourself." Cimarron, one of the former doves, who was now happily married to Jed Black, waited for her husband to help her down from the wagon seat.

Being careful not to stare, Opal appraised the growing bulk of her friend. This would be Cimarron's first.

Cimarron tucked her hand around her husband's bent arm and gave him a look from under the broad brim of her hat that made Opal feel a catch in her throat.

Would she ever feel that way? She knew she cared a lot for Atticus. Was there a difference between friendship kind of love and the kind she saw in Cimarron's gaze? The smile Jed gave his wife and the way he covered her hand with his other one made Opal swallow before looking away to answer a call from Ada Mae.

"Coming." She needed to get inside to run through the song the choir — if six people could be called a choir — would be singing. Rand could be heard tuning up his guitar, the signal to get going.

Times like this, when they were about to sing, she always thought of Belle, their former pianist and director, the first one who'd coached her singing.

Where was Belle? Had something happened to her, or did she just not want to keep in touch with her old friends? Perhaps she had never really thought of any of them as her friends.

Daisy joined them after handing her little girl to Ruby, and Charlie laid his Bible on the wooden stand.

"Someday we're goin' to have a man of God leading our services."

Rand looked up from plucking guitar strings. "You saying you aren't a man of God?"

"I mean someone who's got some training." Charlie shook his head. "My ma must be dancin' on the clouds watchin' her hell-bent son lead a church service."

"Now, dear," Daisy chided.

Charlie flinched at the sound of his wife's gentle voice. "Sorry, but that's what she called me."

The choir took their places, ready to sing. "All right, on three." Rand strummed three chords, and the music burst forth.

Opal let her voice soar on the high melody notes while the others sang harmony. Singing was almost as good as riding. Either way she could forget about things like the drifter and Atticus and a meanspirited schoolteacher.

The practice went well, and their singing at the service was even better. They sang full harmony on the "amen" and sat down. Opal knew they'd done well. Ruby was dabbing at her eyes, as were others.

On their way home the rain took up again, and they huddled under the blankets to keep dry. After dinner even Rand took a nap, and Ruby sat reading near the fireplace. But Opal couldn't bear to remain inside.

"I'm going down to the barn," she said to Ruby.

"You want to bring in the eggs on your way back?"

"Sure. I'll feed the chickens too."

"Take the scraps for the pig."

"Chickens like them too." Opal felt a proprietary caring for the chickens, since they were considered hers.

"You're funny."

"Thanks a heap." Opal paused. "How about we make taffy after supper?"

"Good."

Opal left the house, wishing she'd gone riding, rain or no rain. She scattered the potato peelings and eggshells for the chickens and dumped the slops in the pig trough.

"Mabel, you stink."

The sow, getting heavier daily, looked up at her, jowls bulging as she chewed with leftover oatmeal clinging to her long white snout.

"Thanks for the gratitude," Opal replied to the *oof*s of the pig.

When she stood outside under the barn eaves she heard laughter from the bunk-house. She ambled over and knocked on the door.

"Come in."

She stepped into a smoke-hazed room where three hands were gathered around a table, a kerosene lamp lighting their card playing.

"You want to play?" Chaps stopped in midshuffle.

"Sure."

"Pull up a chair."

Opal did so, taking her place with ease. "What are you playing?"

"Five-card draw."

"What's the ante?"

"Nickel."

"I'll stake you." Beans slid five nickels her way.

Opal studied her cards, as did the others. "I'm in."

By the time the triangle rang, she'd collected quite a pile of coins, even after repaying Beans for his stake.

"Better keep that here. If Ruby knew I'd been gambling, she'd have a cow." She shoved her winnings toward Beans.

"Why didn't you tell us that? We coulda done with matchsticks."

The door opened at the same time as struck by knuckles, and Rand stepped in. "You guys seen — Oh, there you are, Opal. Ruby was asking for you." He took in the stacks of nickels, the guilty look on

Opal's face, and grimaced.

Opal pushed her chair back. "We were just having fun. We weren't playing poker. I taught them a new game, vingt et un."

"Twenty-one?"

"I guess. But Ruby only told me I couldn't play poker."

"Looks like you did all right."

"I know."

"She's good as Belle." Chaps slapped the cards down in the middle of the table.

"Cards like her." Joe rose and snagged his hat off the wall pegs.

They trooped out the door, laughing and teasing Opal about her skill.

How do I ask them to stop talking about this?

~~~

"We need to talk." The set of Ruby's lips later that evening made Opal flinch. If only she'd asked the guys not to talk about the afternoon, that look might have been prevented.

"So you were playing poker." It wasn't a question.

"No, I taught them vingt et un."

"Twenty-one is still gambling."

"Just for nickels. You said no poker, and I didn't play that . . . much."

"Opal, what am I going to do with you?"

"But, Ruby, it was just us. That's not gambling."

"But you were betting?"

"Well, yes, but that's just to make it more fun, a challenge. What's wrong with that?"

"A true gentlewoman does not make money off her friends."

"I never wanted to be a gentlewoman or a lady anyway. Besides, I read about people playing whist. They played for money, and they were aristocrats in England. What's the difference?"

Ruby sighed, the kind of sigh that let Opal know she'd better stop the discussion.

Instead she gritted her teeth. "Well?"

"We'll talk about this later."

"What's wrong with now?"

"That's enough." Rand looked up from the newspaper he was reading.

Opal glared at Ruby first, then at Rand, before stalking from the room. How unfair could they be? And after she'd been having such a good time too.

Chapter Ten

"Hey, Jacob, you have company yesterday?" Marshall from the livery hailed him from the side of the house.

Jacob parked his ax blade in the chopping block. "Why?"

"Well, strangest thing. A young woman with a little boy rented a horse and buggy yesterday for an hour, and she never brought it back." He tipped his hat back farther on his balding head. "She asked for directions to your house."

"Yes, my cousin." The lie slipped so easily from his lips. "Said she had to hurry to catch the train."

"You saw her leave?"

Jacob nodded. He'd seen the dust that churned up behind the wheels. "But she headed west. Didn't tell me where she was going. She was in a hurry." *Careful, you are talking too much.*

"Think you could help me look for her? In case something happened, you know."

"I'm sorry, but her son is here. I can't leave him by himself, and he's still sleeping."

"I see." Marshall stroked his chin. "Real strange, wouldn't you say?"

"You sure the horse isn't tied up down at the train station?"

"Be hard to miss. And if he got loose, you'd think he'd come back to the barn." The man turned to go. "You hear anything, you'll let me know? Horse thievin' is a crime, you know."

"She, Melody, Miss Fisher wouldn't steal a horse. She's honest as, well, as anyone I know." *How can you say that? She kept your son from you, lived a lie for the last seven, eight years.* "I'd help you if I could."

"I know you would, Pastor." He nodded toward the door. "Guess your guest woke up."

Jacob turned to see the boy standing in the doorway, dressed again in the clothes he'd worn the day before. "Good morning."

144

Joel nodded. "Did Mama come back?"

"No, sorry. You hungry?" Jacob heard Marshall ride off. "I cooked some oatmeal, and I could toast some bread." The breeze chilled his sweaty skin, so he took his shirt from the hook by the door and slid his arms into it.

Joel stepped back to let him in, all the while keeping his sober gaze on Jacob. "She's not coming back."

"How do you know?"

"She said I was to live with you now. . . ." His voice caught on a sob. "But I want her to get better and come back."

"Me too." But Jacob had the same feeling as the child. Melody was not coming back. *But, God, please don't let her be dead.* There had to be a good reason the horse didn't return. What if there had been an accident?

What if what happened to her was no accident?

Get such broody thoughts out of your head, man, he scolded himself as he dished up the oatmeal that had been keeping warm on the back of the stove.

"You like molasses on your oatmeal?"

Joel half nodded, half shrugged.

"Well, what'll it be?" Jacob dug a spoon down into the crock.

Joel nodded and slid onto a chair. "That's plenty."

Jacob added milk and pushed the dish over to the boy. How could he call this stranger his son? He poured himself some lukewarm coffee and added sugar, something he never did, but right now life called for some sweetness. He'd never tried molasses in his coffee.

Joel ate without speaking, all his concentration on the bowl and spoon and the action of bending his arm to move the spoon.

He was small for his age. Jacob noted that and the pallor of his skin, as if he'd not been out in the sun. "You go to school?"

Another shrug. His son certainly hadn't inherited his father's love of conversation.

"Was that a yes or no?"

"Used to."

"Until?"

"Pa died."

"When was that?"

Shrug.

"Did you go back to your grandma and grandpa Fisher?"

"Who?"

"Guess not. Where did you live?"

These shrugs were getting on his nerves.

"In a town? The country? What state?"

146

A tear dripped off the boy's chin.

Jacob Chandler, where did all your ministerial skills hie off to? He'd never been accused of badgering a child, and he never would be, far as he was concerned, but that might not be the feeling this boy had right now. Jacob softened his voice. "Look, Joel, I need to know something about your life. Perhaps your grandma and grandpa are looking for you."

Joel shrugged again. "They don't like us."

"I see." *What is going on here?*

"You have any uncles, aunts, or cousins?"

Again that funny half shrug and grimace.

"I'll take that as either a no or you don't know."

If a child could cave in on himself, this one did. His spine curved, his shoulders hunched. Only his hands lay open and vulnerable, as if he were waiting for someone to fill them. Or was he letting go of all hope? Another tear tracked down his thin cheek.

Heavens, does he have the consumption also? The thought struck terror like a spear into Jacob's heart. He looked more closely at the closed-in bundle of misery. No bright spots on the cheeks, no coughing, no rattle in the breathing.

He laid a hand on Joel's shoulder to comfort him, but the boy flinched away. So much for that good deed. None of the children in his church acted like this. They ran up to him, chattering away as only happy children could. One even called him Pastor God, since the children were sure he lived in God's house.

Are you sure this is my son? He wanted to scream the words at Melody. But how could he dispute it?

He squatted down beside the boy, keeping his hand on the back of the chair, though he'd rather wrap the child in his arms.

"Can I get you something else to eat?"

Joel shook his head. "I'm going to watch for my mother."

"Where?"

"Out there." He pointed to the front door.

But someone may see you. What did it matter? By now the entire village knew who came, who went, and who stayed. *Lord, why am I so double-minded? You said you despise double-minded people who are blown about by the vagaries of life like a small boat at the mercy of the winds at sea. I've never been at sea, but I can tell you, I hate this feeling.*

The boy shrugged, but his eyes spoke volumes of pain and fear.

Lord, what can I do to help him?

Find his mother.

How?

Go look.

But someone will stop me, and I'll have to lie again, and . . . Jacob sagged under the burden of the lie he'd offered so blithely. But he couldn't tell the truth either.

"Look, Joel, you can watch for her through the window if you like, but I don't want you to sit out there and catch cold in that brisk wind. How will that be?"

Another shrug, but this time accompanied by a slight nod.

"Here, I'll carry the chair for you."

Joel barely shook his head, but another of those looks dug right into Jacob's heart. He clamped both hands on the spindles of the chair back and dragged it to the window, almost daring Jacob to help him.

He's only seven. How can I leave him here to go look? I can't. I don't want to go look. Fear had not been one of Jacob's sins before, but it had him by the throat now.

He washed the breakfast dishes, put more wood in the stove, brought in an armful to fill the half-empty woodbox, paced the kitchen, stood in the arched doorway watching the boy stare out the window, and finally drew out a kitchen chair to hold his body while his elbows, propped on the table, held up his head.

The weight of it all pounded like surf on a rocky shore.

"Someone's here." Joel's voice came as if from far away.

Jacob roused himself and smoothed his hair back with weary hands before heading for the front door even before the knock came. Pulling the door open, he made sure he smiled at the livery man. "Come in, Marshall, come in. Have you learned anything?"

"I think you better step out here, Pastor." He kept his voice low, nodding to the boy he'd seen in the window.

At the somber face and tone, Jacob stepped outside and closed the door behind him. Fear manacled his heart.

"I found the horse and buggy."

"Yes?"

"Up to the bridge. He was tied to a tree there."

"You mean the bridge west of here?" His heart thundered so loud he could scarcely hear. *God, no!*

"No sign of the woman. I'm sorry, Reverend. I think she jumped."

"She could have met someone, and they took her onward."

"True, but there was a bit of this" — he held out a scrap of blue dress material — "caught on the railing. If I remember right, she was wearing blue."

Jacob closed his eyes, the memory of her seared on the backs of his eyelids. Yes, she'd been wearing a blue gown, covered by a dark wool cloak. The river was fierce there at this time of year, the thunder from the waterfall a hundred yards down a constant reminder of spring's fury.

"Will you set out a search party?"

"I thought to inform the sheriff downriver, at Donkenny."

"I see. May God have mercy on her soul."

"I got to feed and water my horse. Strange, why didn't she just let him go back to town on his own?"

Because she was afraid someone would stop her. Jacob kept the thought to himself. *Why, Melody, why?* He kept himself upright by sheer force of will, though his entire being wanted to crumble and scream at the outrage.

My fault. This is all my fault. How do I

tell Joel that his mother threw herself off the bridge and into the river? That he needn't watch and wait any longer?

Do I not tell him at all? And live another lie?

"Thank you." Jacob shook Marshall's hand.

"I guess knowing is better than not. I'm sorry, Pastor. Her bein' your kin and all."

"Oh yes, of course." Close kin. Of the most intimate kind. And my son in there is the fruit of that sin. He backed toward the door. *He's probably wondering why I don't volunteer to help find the body. Jacob Chandler, be a man and say the right words.* "I-I need to take care of the boy." He waved a shaking hand and almost groaned in relief when Marshall took the hint and waved back as he headed for the road.

Joel stared at him, waiting. Jacob shook himself, at the same time ordering some semblance of control.

"The man found his horse and buggy." Joel made it sound more statement than a question.

"Yes." Tears burned the backs of Jacob's eyes.

"Where's my mother?"

"I don't know." That at least wasn't a lie.

152

I don't know where her body is, and if she killed herself, I don't know where her soul is. Lord God, can I tell him she is safe with you?

"I-I'm afraid she had an accident." He crouched beside the chair so that he and Joel were eye to eye. "But we're not sure yet."

"Is she dead?" Joel's eyes narrowed; his chin quivered.

"I don't know. All I know is that Mr. Marshall found his horse and buggy. That's all I know." When he laid a hand on Joel's shoulder, the young boy flinched away.

Joel kept watch from the front steps throughout the long day, ignoring the comings and goings of villagers, some who whispered in consideration of the hunched little figure. Others brought bread and cakes, accompanied by consoling pats and condolences.

By evening Joel lay asleep on the couch, and Jacob didn't bother to light any lamps, hoping that if anyone else came, they would think him not at home.

Later that night he wrote two letters in the glow of the kerosene lamp. He tucked Joel into bed, walked down to the post office, and dropped the letters into the slot.

One was for the deacons at the church that was no longer his, the other for the overseeing pastor of this district. Once back at the house, he gathered his few personal items and packed them in a carpetbag, leaving the house neat and ready for the next occupant.

He woke Joel before the rooster crowed. "Come, we are going now."

"To find my mother?" the boy asked, sleep still befuddling his gaze.

"To find . . ." The breath caught in his throat. *We are going because I cannot live the lie here.*

Chapter Eleven

Lord, what is the best for Opal?

The question had been beating Ruby into the dust ever since she had heard of yesterday's card game. Gambling, a vagrant attack, hostility, a lack of concern for womanly things. Where had her sweet and loving little sister gone? In all their lives they'd never had a shouting match like the one when Opal had returned from school this afternoon. While more than once Rand had calmed altercations in the past, this one had gone beyond what even he would have been able to control, had he been near the house.

All because she asked Opal to help with the spring cleaning. Yes, she knew Opal was training the horses, and yes, that was important. But with Rand gone to

Dickinson for supplies, Ruby had hoped to get the spring cleaning done before he returned. Beating rugs, scrubbing floors, and ironing curtains were part and parcel of womanly duties.

Not according to Opal.

Ruby slammed the bread dough back down on the table. In a few days school would be out for the summer. She rammed the heel of her hand into the spongy dough, flipped an edge over with her other hand, at the same time turning the dough on the floury surface. Three times, then she flopped the entire mass over and repeated the kneading. At the rate she was going, they'd have the lightest bread in the territory. Kneading bread dough was always a good way to work out one's frustrations. But did Opal know how to make good bread? No, not really. *Slam, bang.* Did Opal care if her future family would starve because she had no idea how to manage a household? No. *Thud, slam.*

"You beating bread to death?" Little Squirrel stopped at the table.

"Something like that." Ruby formed the dough into a smooth round and laid it back in the wooden bowl to rise again. After covering it with a clean dish towel, she set the bowl back in the square of sunshine painting a golden window on the counter.

She paused to stare out at the trees still leafing out, the grass so green and supple, tall enough now to bend with the breeze. Woolen long johns danced on the clothesline, mute testimony to the end of winter.

Her arms ached from the pounding she'd given the bread dough. She'd tell Rand of her decision tonight.

Opal was going to visit the Brandons whether she wanted to or not.

✂

Lying in bed beside Rand, she hated to bring up anything unpleasant, but there'd not been time earlier. At least not time when they were alone.

"So are you asking me or telling me?" His voice came gentle through the dark.

"Does it make a difference?"

"I reckon it does."

"Well, I haven't bought the ticket yet."

"So you want my opinion?"

"Yes."

"You know how much I've come to count on Opal's help. She's good as any hand, or almost. She has a good sense with all the animals."

"I know. I just wish she had more sense about herself." Ruby turned on her side and laid her arm across her husband's chest, loving the feel and the sound of him. Seemed the only cross times they had were about Opal.

"She doesn't want to go."

Ruby sighed. "I know that. It's not like I'm sending her away —"

"Isn't it? Seems so to me. She won't fit into the womanly role, so you hope Mrs. Brandon can do more than you."

"She's wiser, and the girls there would be a good influence."

"Isn't it just the trappings you're looking at? No one has a kinder heart than Opal. Her sense of humor brightens all of our days. She loves this ranch like she was bred and born here."

"So you are taking her side?"

Rand slid his arm beneath her neck. "I'm not taking sides, just trying to work this out for everyone's good."

"But she loved New York and the Brandons. There'll be theater and libraries and the park. They'll go to the shore and shopping."

"Sounds to me like you're the one who wants to go to New York."

"Rand, if she were a young lady in New York, she would be attending a finishing school, taking lessons in art and music."

"If she were of the Brandons' class. Where would the two of you be had you not come west?"

"Still working for the Brandons, where they were giving her all the advantages their daughters had." Ruby chewed on the inside of her cheek. "I know what you are getting at."

He stroked her cheek with a gentle finger. "I know she is your little sister, but when I married you, she became my sister-in-law."

Ruby shifted just the slightest but created a bit of space between them. "If she wants to go, then you would allow her to?"

"If that's what she wants."

"And if she doesn't?"

"Maybe we ought to cross that bridge when we come to it. I sure would like her to be here for roundup."

Opal managed to ride out for school the next morning without speaking a word to Ruby.

With a cup of coffee in hand, Ruby took Per out to sit on the back porch, not that Per ever sat still for more than an inch of time. Rand and Beans had fenced the back porch, which stretched the length of the house, with chicken wire and had built a gate so that Per had a safe place to play. Ruby sat down in one of the rockers and leaned her head back. Heartsore. She'd read that word somewhere. That's how she felt about Opal lately. Yet there seemed to be nothing she could do to fix it.

She rubbed her middle and stared into the fragrant dark liquid in her cup. Though nothing had sounded better to her, for some reason, the coffee didn't set well on this lovely morning.

"Ma?"

"Yes."

Per's unintelligible babbling made her smile. He pulled himself up on the fencing and used it to make his way over to her. When he drew up even, a good two feet separated them.

Per looked over at her, waved his free arm, and jiggled in place. His gyrations shook his balance, so he grabbed the wire with both hands again, still grinning at her over his shoulder.

Ruby held out her hands, elbows resting on her knees. "Come on, big boy, you can walk to Ma." She wiggled her fingers. "Come on."

Cat, enjoying the sun in the other chair, meowed, arched her back, and stretched all the way from whisker to tail the way only cats can do. Then she leaped to the floor and crossed to rub against Ruby's skirt.

Per chattered again, flapping his free arm, bending and straightening his knees so his shift brushed the floor.

"Come on, you can walk this far. See, Cat is waiting for you."

"Ma, ma, mmm." Drool glistened on his chin. He reached as far as he could, but she deliberately kept her hands a few inches from his.

He stamped one foot, then again, leaning as far as his arm attached to the fence allowed.

"Per, you are so funny. Come on, let loose and walk here." She wiggled her fingers. Cat arched her back, then sat to wash her face, licking a white paw and rubbing it over ear and cheek.

Per mumbled and stared, his fist clenching and unclenching. He took one step, let go of the fence, took two more steps, wavered, and collapsed into her hands.

"Per, you did it. You walked all by yourself." She held him up for kisses and hugs, loving his chortles, kissing his cheeks. She put him on her lap, but before she could kiss him again, he was sliding to the floor to tackle Cat.

Cat tolerated his fingers for a bit, then rose and stalked back to the other chair. She leaped up into the seat and turned around three times before settling in.

Per, eyes focused only on Cat, rolled to his knees and crawled over there to pull himself up on the chair. He thumped the patient animal with one hand and crowed his delight. Cat shook her head, glared at the intrusion, and leaped to the floor in one sinuous movement, stalking off, tail stick straight.

"She got you there."

Per turned to look over his shoulder.

"You're more fun than a pile of kittens. Wait till we tell your pa that you walked all by yourself."

Per kept one hand on the chair, walked around it, and took two steps to the wire, then followed it over and walked right into his mother's waiting hands.

Ruby cuddled him for the moment he allowed and let him go when he began to squirm. She tossed the dregs of her coffee into the bridal wreath bush and glanced over to the garden where Little Squirrel was planting corn. The peas were already climbing up the willow branch trellis Rand had tied together. Potatoes showed green hills, and carrots feathered in lines straight as the string used to mark them.

Opal had caught enough fish that Little Squirrel was able to plant part of one under every hill of corn. Hoe a hole, drop in the fish, cover, drop five corn kernels — one for the crow, one for the worm, and three to grow — cover, and tamp. Take a full step and repeat. Thanks to the plow Rand had bought, they had a huge garden this spring compared to other years.

Ruby rose and walked to the west end of the porch, where she could see him with two of the horses hitched to the plow, rows of sod rolling over at the bite of the shear. He planned to plant oats for cattle feed. Beans and Chaps were digging holes for fence posts.

Ruby absently rubbed her middle and leaned against a post. Her husband was taking a ribbing for turning sodbuster, but it didn't seem to bother him any. He and Robertson were talking about buying a mower together so they could put up more hay.

She looked down to find Per had followed her, using his friend, the fence, for support. She picked him up and pointed off across the field. "There's Pa out there."

"Pa?" Per nearly jumped out of her

163

arms, running the *p*'s off into funny little sounds.

Of course he did not show off for all the men when they came up for dinner, laughing and washing at the bench outside the house. He crawled to meet them at the door and rode to his high chair on Beans' shoulders. The older man had taken a strong liking to the little guy, and the way Per grinned and beat on the bald dome let everyone know he felt the same.

Beans grabbed the baby's hands and swung him down into his chair. "So you can walk, eh? Well, you just get yerself on down to the barn and slop them hogs, you hear?"

Per waved his arms and banged his spoon on the tray.

"He got to be the happiest baby I ever seen." Beans took his place at the table.

"Not that you seen too many, old man." Joe sat down beside him, giving Beans a cuff on the shoulder.

"No, that's one of the sadnesses of my life. Been with lotsa cows and roughnecks like you but not with much of the softer and sweeter side of life."

Ruby patted his shoulder as she leaned over to set the meat platter in the center of the table. "You can be grandpa to our children all you want, Beans. That's the only way they'll get one."

"Thank you."

From the look in his eyes she knew he'd meant what he'd said. "You are most welcome."

~ʌ

"Only two more days to go." Opal blew in, setting her lunch pail on the counter. "I can't wait."

"Shh, Per is sleeping."

"Sorry. I'm starving."

"There's bread and cheese."

"Any sour cream?"

Ruby shrugged. "Not sure, but bring in the buttermilk too. You can make biscuits for supper."

"Ruby, I have to work with Firelight before I start the regular chores."

"It's time you help with the cooking more." Ruby knew her tone had a bite to it, but the obstinate set of Opal's chin got her dander up.

Opal muttered under her breath as she stomped out the back door, the screen door making a healthy slam behind her.

"Ma?"

Ruby was hoping for a bit more time before he awoke, but thanks to Opal, that wouldn't be.

"I'll get him." Opal slammed back in the door.

"If you'd been more careful, he might have slept longer."

Opal spun in place. "Why are you so crabby all the time? I can't ever do anything right anymore." She clomped down the hall, her boot heels taking the punishment for her ire.

She brought Per back into the kitchen a few minutes later, set him in his chair with a rusk, made her bread with sour cream and jelly, and left without saying another word.

Guess I won't be telling her the good news about Per's first steps in the near future.

When the time came the biscuits should be in the oven, Opal had not yet returned.

Little Squirrel set the ingredients out and cut the lard into the flour. "I do."

"That girl . . ." Ruby felt her stomach roil. She started out the back door to the outhouse. Something sure hadn't agreed with her. The smell of frying sage hen made her want to gag.

Opal met her at the door. "Sorry I'm late, I — Ruby, are you all right?"

"No." Ruby pushed on by but never made it to the building out back before she

166

had to stop and heave. Coffee tasted even more bitter coming up than it had going down.

Opal handed her a wet cloth when she finished. "I'm sorry you are sick."

"Ja, me too. Thanks for the cloth."

"Can I get you some water?"

"No. I'll sit down a minute, and then I'll be fine." Ruby sank down on the edge of the porch.

"Put your head between your knees. That's what you tell me."

"No. I'm better. Little Squirrel already started the biscuits. You go help her."

Opal sighed but did as ordered.

All the mess with Opal, and now I feel so sick. Lord, what is going on? Ruby rubbed her forehead. *Am I really crabby?*

Chapter Twelve

"Look at that. Per is walking." Opal turned to Ruby in surprise.

Ruby looked up from her mending. "He has been for several days."

"Thought it was yesterday." Rand held out his hands. "Come on, little man. Come to Pa."

"And you didn't tell me?"

"Sorry. Guess I was so busy throwing up in the bushes I forgot."

How come everything I do lately makes her crabby at me? Opal picked Per up and blew on his neck to make him laugh. "Can you say Opal?"

"Da, da. Mmm da."

"Opal." She spoke her name slowly.

"Ma?"

"No, O-pal."

He blew a raspberry.

"Now, don't go getting him all wound up. It's about bedtime."

"I won't." Opal rolled her eyes. *Can't even play with the baby right.*

"So are there games and races and such at school tomorrow?" Rand laid his copy of the Medora newspaper, *The Badlands Cowboy,* in his lap.

"Yes, and prizes. I had perfect attendance this year." She set Per back down at his father's knee, then knelt on the floor a couple feet away. "Come on, little guy. Walk to me."

Per grinned at her, banged his fists on his father's knees, did his deep knee bends, and then, arms in the air, took the four steps to Opal's arms.

"Does he always do the sort of bobbing up and down first?"

"Has to get wound up to go." Rand folded his paper and, setting it aside, leaned forward. "Come to Pa. Come on, Per."

Per did his little dance and struck out, his steps growing more sure with each foray.

Opal glanced up in time to catch Ruby in a yawn. *She doesn't look good. She's got huge circles under her eyes. Please,*

God, don't let Ruby be sick. Maybe that's why she's so crabby.

Ruby closed her Bible and laid it on the table beside her chair. "I'm never this tired." She rubbed her eyes. "I can't even read my Bible without falling asleep."

"You go on to bed. I'll put Per down." Opal clapped her hands, and Per copied her, but the effort plunked him down on his diapered rear, which made him giggle as he rolled to his hands and knees and crawled back to Opal.

"Drool face." She clapped her hands again while he pulled himself upright on her knee.

"Thank you. I'll feel better in the morning." Ruby stood, trying to cover her yawn and failing, which made Opal yawn, and then Rand caught it too.

"Good night, everyone."

" 'Night." Opal turned and watched her sister walk down the hall to her bedroom. Ruby was usually the last one to go to bed.

Ghost crossed the room to lie beside Opal. She patted her head, watching Per walk around her knee, jabbering and drooling, and throw himself on the dog.

Ghost looked up at her. Opal chuckled. "You don't have to put up with that, you know. You could move."

"I never dreamed she'd be so good with a baby. But they say cow dogs will take care of any little critter. They've even been known to nurse kittens." Rand wiggled his fingers, beckoning Per, who gave him a toothy grin and laid his head on Ghost's side.

"No." Opal couldn't believe what Rand said.

"True. Happened back home. Cow dogs, sheep dogs, they have such a mothering instinct."

"Bet those old cows don't think so when Ghost rounds them up. They'd just as soon hook her with the tip of a horn."

"She's too smart to let that happen."

"Easy." Opal removed Per's clench on Ghost's ear. "Pet her nice." At his babbling, she covered his hand with her own and gently stroked the dog's head. "See?" She picked him up and sat him in her cross-legged lap. "Just think, after tomorrow, no more school."

"Until fall."

"I think I've had enough schooling." There, she'd said it again. Perhaps the more it was said, the more it could become real.

"Ruby wants you to go on longer."

"I know, but what for? I don't want to be

a schoolteacher, and half the time that's what I do, help with the little kids."

"You could go to high school in Bismarck."

"And leave the ranch?" Horror struck like a ravaging wolf.

Rand leaned forward, resting his elbows on his knees. "You know Ruby wants the best for you."

"Ruby wants what *she* thinks is the best for me."

"Many kids your age would be jealous that you can go to school."

"That's not my concern." She leaned her head against Per's head as he rested against her shoulder. He was so little and sweet. "I better put you to bed, little guy." She looked up at Rand. "There's plenty of work for me here on the ranch, and I could start training horses for some of the other ranchers around here."

"You're right, we have plenty to do, and you could do worse than apprenticing to Linc." He rubbed the bridge of his nose with one finger. "It's just that you should take every advantage to better yourself."

"You want I should apply to be a maid over at the big house or in town?"

"No. That's not going to help you out."

"I could get married, I suppose." But she

shuddered inside. While that might be what would happen down the road, least if Atticus had his way, she knew she wasn't ready for that yet. Being cooped up in a house sounded worse than Indian torture. She rose without uncrossing her legs, Per in one arm.

"Say good-night to your pa, little guy." She held him out for a kiss and took him back to change his diaper and pull his nightshirt over his head. Sitting down in the rocker, she set it to singing and hummed a little tune while she patted his back. Moonlight painted squares on the pine flooring. A nighthawk called. Coyotes yipped far enough away to be faint as a whisper.

"Oh no." She laid the drowsy baby down in his bed, tucked the covers around him, and headed back to the living room and the door.

"Where you going?"

"I forgot to lock the chickens in."

"Check on the sow then too, would you? She's going to farrow any night now."

"Sure."

Opal stopped on the porch and looked up at the sky, easily finding the Big Dipper and smiling at the density of the Milky Way that arched directly overhead. An owl hooted, and she heard the rush of its flapping wings as it hunted for careless rodents. Tonight would have been perfect for lying out to watch the stars.

Moonlight drew the shadows dense black, the barn, house, even the blades of grass etched around by silver light.

She inhaled and held the breath, savoring the fragrance of pine, a hint of woodsmoke, green growing grass, and a slight tinge of horse and cow. The slightest breeze floated from the west, carrying the moo of a cow and the whisper of cottonwood leaves sharing secrets. The sounds of her feet swishing through the grass and of her own breathing glided in the air as she made her way to her charges. To ride across the plains, to run and throw herself into the river, to fly like the owl, to stride the Milky Way bridged across the heavens — anything seemed possible on this most perfect night.

Instead, she closed the door to the chicken house, hearing the flock inside rustle and peep, aware of her intrusion into their rest. The sow lay on her side, back against the fence.

"You all right, girl?"

The pig grunted in answer. One flapping ear caught an edge of moonlight. The smell of the pigpen melded with the others, all inherent elements of ranch living.

Opal headed back to the house. The rooster would crow far sooner than her eyes would want to open.

"Some night, isn't it?" Rand was leaning against a porch post.

"Wish I could go riding."

"Me too."

"Maybe tomorrow night?"

He dropped an arm across her shoulders. "We'll see."

"Sow's outside, sleeping against the fence."

"She's not started a nest yet?"

"I threw some of the old hay in for her this evening."

"Good girl."

Later Opal stared out her bedroom window. *Ruby thinks I'd want to trade this for a visit to New York? You could hardly see the stars there. Not like here. The sky is so huge, like a bowl with pinprick holes in it for the stars to shine through.* Even when she crawled under her covers, she turned to see the sky. A shooting star bisected her window.

Ah. Make a wish. She closed her eyes. *I wish . . . I wish I was the best horse trainer in Dakotah Territory. No, in the whole West.*

～⋇

She returned from milking in the morning to find Ruby puking into the bushes again. Opal set the milk pail down so fast it sloshed and went to wrap her arms around her sister's midsection.

"Ruby."

"I-I'm fine." She slumped against Opal, eyes closed, wiping her mouth with the hem of her apron.

"Sit down. I'll get you some water." Opal eased her over to the porch and kept a hand on her shoulder as she sank to sitting and leaned against the post.

"I thought I was better this morning, but now at least I'm sure what is wrong."

"What?" Opal laid a hand against her sister's sweaty forehead. "You don't have a fever."

"No, but I think I have a little brother or sister for Per."

Opal paused, her smile widening by the moment. "Another baby?"

Ruby nodded. "All the signs are here."

"When do you think it will be born?"

"Might be a Christmas baby."

"Ohh." Opal sat down beside her sister, glanced out to where she'd left the milk bucket, and leaped to her feet. "Get out of there, Cat." She ran over, scooped up the bucket, and took it into the springhouse so she could run it through the strainer, a clean cloth clamped to a square frame that fit over a jug that Little Squirrel had set up.

She poured the milk slowly so as not to run it over, all the while thinking, *Baby, a new baby in our house.* She remembered when Ruby had been with child before. She'd been tired then too, and yes, she'd been crabby. Not as bad as she'd been lately, but that must be what was causing it. As soon as the milk had run through, she dipped water out of the cooling tank to scrub the bucket, rinsed out the cloth, and dumped the used water into the slop bucket. Like the whey from cheese making and milk that turned sour, all was fed to the pig and the chickens.

Whistling, she headed for the house, grateful Ruby was no longer sitting on the step. She must be feeling better.

After chores and breakfast Opal met the Robertson girls at the road, if one could call the track a real road, and they whooped and hollered their delight as they loped the horses into town.

Most everyone got to school early and

were lined up to go in before the ringing of the first bell.

"My goodness, you must all be excited to study today." Even Mr. Finch wore a smile.

Once they were seated, he announced, "We will start with the spelling bee. There will be a prize for the two finalists. Line up on both sides of the room, please, young ones closest to the front. I will give you words according to your reading level." He waved his hand, and the room whooshed into two lines like the parting of the Red Sea.

"There will be no prompting." He stared at them until they all agreed.

Opal and Virginia Robertson were the last two standing.

Mr. Finch nodded to them both and read the next word. "Fugacious."

Opal listened hard. "Would you use that in a sentence, please?"

The teacher did so. "The fugacious boy disappeared in the woods."

Opal scrunched her eyes half shut. She locked her bottom lip between her teeth. "F-u-g-a . . ." *Which one* — c *or* sh? "F-u-g-a-c-i-o-u-s. Fugacious."

"Correct."

They could most likely hear her sigh of relief clear to the ranch.

He gave the next word to Virginia, who spelled *granivorous* promptly.

"Miss Harrison, leucoderma."

Opal smiled. She knew that one and spelled it.

"Miss Robertson, nihilistic."

This time it was Virginia's turn to fidget. She rolled her eyes, chewed her lip, started, stopped, started again. "N-e-h-i-l-i-s-t-i-c."

"I'm sorry, that was incorrect. Miss Torvald."

Opal spelled the word correctly.

Mr. Finch's smile didn't look anywhere near as warm as it had to the others, but Opal collected her prize, a book of Shakespeare's sonnets.

"Thank you."

"You must thank Mrs. de Mores. She donated all the prizes for today."

"Congratulations. You did well," Virginia whispered as they returned to their seats.

"We will now have an arithmetic spelldown. Take sides again."

This time Robert Grady won the prize. The smile on his face made Opal wish Atticus had been there to see him.

The red team won the geography contest, and everyone received a tablet and a pencil.

"Now for our attendance awards." He called out the names according to age, with the Robertson girls and Opal all getting perfect attendance awards. Each received another book and a certificate.

"How many years does that make it for you?" Mr. Finch asked Opal.

"Two. I had the measles the first year." Opal took her seat again.

"We will now adjourn to the outside for the races."

By the end of the day Opal had two blue ribbons to add to her stack of books. She put all her treasures in her saddlebags and mounted Bay.

"Am I glad that's over," she muttered when they were out of earshot.

"Why, I thought you had fun. I did," Virginia said from behind her.

"I did. Today. I meant I'm glad school is over."

"Oh, me too."

Opal stared up the street. A man riding into town looked familiar. No, it couldn't be. She reined Bay off between two buildings.

"What are you doing?"

"Did you see that man up the street?"

"No. I didn't pay any attention."

"He's the one Atticus and I strung up."

"Oh no."

"Oh yes. What am I going to tell Rand?"

"Well, it's not your fault."

"Maybe I won't say anything."

Emily and Ada Mae met them as they came out the alley.

"What happened to you?"

Opal told them and finished with "Let's get on home."

Do I tell him? Do I not tell him? The words kept beat with Bay's easy lope. A covey of prairie chickens thundered up from their right. "Wish I had the shotgun along."

"I don't ever want to shoot anything." Virginia raised her voice to be heard above the thudding hooves.

"You help butcher chickens. What's the difference? We need to eat."

"I know. But wild things like the grouse and the antelope are so beautiful out where they belong."

Opal heard her, but her inner voice was louder. *That man is back, and he was riding with another guy. It's a free country. He can go wherever he wants. He's either pretty brave or stupid dumb to come back after the men warned him away. What will Rand do?*

I hate to have to tell him. She clamped her teeth on the argument. *I am not afraid. I am not afraid. I'm not. I'm not.*

Chapter Thirteen

How could his life go to the dogs so quickly? Jacob wondered as the train clacked westward. He stared at the small body sleeping huddled under a quilt in the seat opposite him. *My son. Part of me. And his mother committed suicide. All my fault.*

He'd not allowed his mind to even speak the word up until now. There was always the hope Melody did not throw herself off the bridge, but that bit of fabric snagged on the railing was pretty conclusive evidence.

I should have stayed in the valley and helped search the river for her body. He turned his attention to the land passing outside the window. Small farms, woods, small towns. Newly planted fields. New life everywhere but here on the train heading west and taking him from all he'd known.

He'd seen no alternative. He couldn't face the lie. All his careful planning gone.

Coward! Coward! Coward!

Lord, what am I going to do? I cannot be a pastor again. I thought I was following your plan for me. My church will wash their hands of me. I should have gone to see the bishop. I wish I'd gone to Mr. Dumfarthing. All my life I've been so circumspect. All but that one time, and it has come back to haunt me, nay, not just haunt me but to tear my life limb from limb. Drawn and quartered and all but my head stuck on a spike in the town square.

And look who is suffering for my sin. Joel's dark eyes haunted him. *My son.* The words still felt foreign to Jacob.

How will I care for him? Where will we go? Surely he could get a job somewhere.

The train's *clackety-clack* lulled him to a half sleep.

"Sir."

The small voice snapped him alert. "Yes, Joel."

"I gotta go."

"You know where it is. Do you need me to open the door for you?"

"Yes, please."

Jacob stood, picked up the quilt, and

folded it in half and then half again to lay it on the seat. "Come on."

He opened the door to the necessary and waited until he heard his son call again from the other side. *He's so little. Is he small for his age?* He'd counted the months. *He just turned seven.* Jacob led the way back to their seats.

"Are you hungry?"

Joel nodded.

Jacob dug down in their satchel and handed him a sandwich, their last. They'd have to eat in the dining car or buy food at one of the stops, both outrageously expensive.

He could see his small hoard of cash disappearing like mist in the sun. His own stomach grumbled from lack of food. They'd already been on the train twenty-four hours. Should they get off in Chicago and he go look for work there?

The thought brought on a shudder of revulsion. Country was what he needed. Country where he could find work on a farm or a ranch until he could get enough of a stake to homestead. Dakotah Territory had opened more land for homesteading. The Sanders family had left Pennsylvania and gone west to homestead. He'd had one letter from them saying they'd found a good place, that God had led them to a place where someone else had already broken the sod and then left.

Jacob stared at his hands, calloused from chopping wood but not tough enough to guide a hand plow behind a horse. And where would he get enough money to buy a horse?

It all came back to money. While he'd never had extra, at least up until now he'd known where his next meal was coming from.

I should have gone home. That thought brought on another wince. To bring Joel there would have been an admittance of his former lack of character.

"I'm thirsty."

"Oh, sorry. You know where the water is. Do you need help?"

Joel shook his head.

"Go on."

He watched the boy sway back down the aisle, a small hand seeking safety by hanging on to the seat armrests.

"Hiram, did you read about Medora in that paper?" The voice came from the seat behind him.

"Hmm."

"That marquis sure dreams big dreams, don't he?"

"You mean with shipping all that beef and such on refrigerated cars?"

"Yes, I find it fascinating."

"He'll never make it. Mark my words, the big packing houses will never give him a chance."

"I heard he shipped salmon clear from the West Coast."

"Hmm."

"We might have eaten some of it at the Stanleys'." The woman's voice carried well.

Jacob knew better than to eavesdrop, but perhaps this was a gift from God. Medora. He liked the sound of the name. A woman's name for a town. How had that come about?

Joel returned and rolled up the quilt so he could sit on it to see out the window.

Where was this Medora? Dared he ask?

"He has no chance, a Frenchie like that taking on the establishment."

"From what I've read, he has plenty of backing." The woman seemed insistent on keeping the conversation going.

How can I find out more about this place?

"There was that scandal about him killing a man, gunned him down without a qualm."

"I don't believe that what we read was the whole story." She rattled the paper she was reading. "You know those reporters, always going for the sensational."

"Now, don't you go making disparaging remarks about reporters. Remember, I was one for a time."

"I know, but owning the paper is so much more satisfying."

What paper? Who were these people? Jacob took a huge bite of courage, put his most charming smile in place, and stood. He motioned for Joel to stay where he was and took the three steps that brought him even with the seat behind him.

"Sorry to bother you folks, but I couldn't help overhearing your talk of Medora. I was wondering if you could tell me more of this place."

"And you would be?"

"Jacob Chandler, ma'am." Had he a hat on, he would have doffed it. His name sounded naked without the title in front of it.

They both laid down their newspapers, the man folding his just so, leaving the headlines showing. "What is it you want to know?"

"First of all, where is it located?"

"Western edge of Dakotah Territory,

right on the Northern Pacific Railroad. Little Missouri River flows through there."

"I see. This Frenchman, what was his name?"

"The Marquis de Mores. He married Medora von Hoffman, the daughter of a New York banker." The woman smiled up at him. "Are you thinking of going there?"

"Possibly."

"What is it you do for a living?"

Ah, you would ask that. "I'm thinking of teaching school. But I wouldn't mind working for a man like that. He sounds like a real forethinker."

"Ach, dreamer is more like it. You'd do well to stick to teaching."

"So the region is good for raising cattle?" He figured that, since they'd mentioned shipping beeves.

"They drive them up from Texas to fatten there. Quite the frontier — cowboys and Indians and all. Pretty rough life if you ask me." The man gave him a nod. "But you're young and strong. Takes that to make it out there, or so they say."

"You and your little boy . . ." The woman hesitated.

Please don't ask about his mother. "They say there is land in Dakotah for homesteading. Is that around Medora?"

"I doubt it. Those ranchers don't like sodbusters coming in. Free range is what makes it possible for them to raise cattle the way they do."

"Where are you from?" the woman asked.

"Pennsylvania." Jacob smiled at her but turned back to the man. "How could I learn more about this place, short of going there?"

"I grew up in Pennsylvania, near Philadelphia. Lovely city." She leaned forward. "What part did you come from?"

"Now, Mrs. Thornwald, don't badger the young man so," her husband admonished.

Jacob nearly sighed with relief. How difficult this was, trying to get information without sharing much about himself. He'd gone to school in Philadelphia. Perhaps they knew much of the same area. Conversations were built that way. As a pastor he'd enjoyed just such chances to meet people as this. The lie. It always came back to the lie. Was it going to color the rest of his life?

"I thank you for the information. Please forgive my bothering you like this."

"Not at all. If you have more questions, we have hours yet before Chicago," Mrs.

Thornwald assured him. "Mr. Thornwald likes nothing better than talking about the West. Why, I think he'd go be a cowboy himself like Mr. Roosevelt did, if he were younger."

"Mr. Roosevelt?"

"Yes, Theodore Roosevelt. He's from New York. Ailing son of a wealthy family, who went west for his health after the tragic death of his wife and fell in love with the country and the people. He has a ranch there now and runs cattle somewhere near Medora."

"Oh really." Jacob glanced over his shoulder to see Joel staring at him again. Those dark eyes so sad. What could he do?

"My thanks again for your time." He backed away and turned to sit down in his own seat.

Surely this was providence.

~

The next day he waved good-bye to the Thornwalds as they departed and then, taking up their possessions, he nodded to Joel. "Stay right with me now. We have to change trains, and I have to buy new tickets. We'll get something to eat here too."

Joel nodded.

How could this child sit so still and

never say a word unless asked a direct question? This extra burden weighed far heavier than the satchel carrying the few books he brought along with his clothes.

Once they had their tickets in hand, Jacob took Joel up to the counter to eat. "What would you like?" He pointed up to the reader board.

Joel shrugged.

"Can you read what it says?"

This time he gave the barest shake of his head.

"Can you read at all?"

A nod small as a blink.

"So you've been to school."

Another blink.

"Good. You can have a ham sandwich or beef or cheese, unless you'd like a bowl of soup. And there is milk for you to drink. Which would you like?"

Joel stared at him, eyes rounder than normal.

"Joel, you can make a choice." Jacob kept his voice gentle, for whenever he raised it at all, the boy closed the shutters to his soul as though a big storm lurked just over the hill.

"Ham, beef, or cheese? I'm having ham."

A slight nod.

I do hope that means he wants the

same. Is it always going to be like this, me trying to understand sign language? Ah, Melody, how do I reach him? I know he can talk, and he isn't slow. But he certainly has shut me out.

"That'll be two ham sandwiches — if you could put cheese on them, that would be better — one glass of milk, and a cup of coffee. Oh, and two of those cookies you have there." He indicated the cake plate with a glass cover.

They took their meal to a table and chairs out on the black-and-white squares of marble set in a diagonal pattern.

Jacob set out the food and bowed his head. "Lord, we ask you to bless this food we have, and we thank you for caring for our every need. Amen."

Joel sat with one bite in his mouth, as if chewing might be cause for trouble.

"We say grace before we eat, and from now on I will ask that you pray some of the times too."

Joel's eyes flinched. No other part of him moved, but his lashes came halfway to his cheeks, giving him a pinched look. Just the tiniest motion indicated a no, but had Jacob not been watching so carefully, he would not have seen it.

"Eat your sandwich. I'm not going to

bite you." *Are you just shy? Frightened with all this change? I know I would be. How, Lord, do I decipher this puzzle?*

By the time they'd slept another night, changed trains again in St. Paul, and chugged west, Jacob felt they might fall off the end of the world. At last the conductor stopped at their seats and announced, "Medora, next stop." Joel had not uttered enough words to fill his hand should each word be the size of a dried bean.

No matter how often he looked up, he'd felt the boy's gaze on him. Unless the child slept. How much of the time he'd been lying under the quilt had he really been sleeping? Or was he merely hiding?

When the train screeched to a stop, Jacob lifted his valise out of the overhead rack, folded Joel's quilt up as small as possible, and stuffed it into the top of an already overloaded satchel.

God, I certainly hope I've made the right decision. "Thank you." He nodded to the man who'd answered many of his questions since St. Paul. Now to find out if the man had been spinning yarns or telling the truth.

Chapter Fourteen

"Opal, what's the matter?" Ruby asked.

Guess I didn't do too good a job hiding my feelings. Opal gritted her teeth and clenched her fists at her sides. *I am not scared.*

"I thought you'd have such a good time this last day of school." Ruby wiped her hands on her apron and came to Opal, who dropped her saddlebags and reached out for her sister. "What is it, dear heart? Opal, are you crying?"

"N-no." Opal sniffed back the tears that burned so bad her eyes felt on fire.

"Are you sick? Hurt? What is it?" Ruby clasped Opal's shoulders and leaned back so she could look into her face.

"We were riding through town to come home, and th-that drifter was riding toward us, along with another guy who looked about as bad." There, she'd said it.

"Oh, dear Lord." Ruby hugged her again. "Did he see you?"

"I don't know. I ducked between the buildings. How come he was so stupid as to come back?"

"I don't know."

"I should have just shot him when I had the chance." Opal glanced over to the gun rack. "I should have."

"Opal, don't talk that way! There's a big difference between killing an animal and killing a man."

"He's worse than any animal I ever saw."

"Yes, some men can be like that."

Opal stared out the window, then spun around, her face alight. "We could invite him out here to talk and go dump him in one of those quicksand places on the river."

"Opal Marie Torvald, I don't ever want to hear such words again. You know what the Bible says about killing." Ruby set the stove lid aside with a clatter and picked two chunks of wood from the woodbox.

"Ah, Ruby, I was just teasing. Besides, that way the river would get him, not us." Opal gave her sister a sideways glance along with an appeasing grin.

"Opal." She stuffed the wood into the firebox and carefully set the lid in place.

"A joke, Ruby, a joke." Opal raised her hands halfway and let them fall to her sides. *I never should have told her he's back. Now she'll be more after me than ever.* "Where's Per?"

"Sleeping." Ruby stared at the stove. "If I didn't wake him."

"Here." Opal hefted her saddlebags. "Come see what I got. I could have brought home prairie chickens if I'd had my gun. A whole covey blew up along the road home. Fried prairie chicken would taste real good for supper." She set her saddlebags on the table. "Where's Little Squirrel?"

"She and Linc went fishing. Beans came back and took Rand and Chaps out to help rescue a couple of steers that got caught in a bog."

"Here's all my prizes." Opal set her books, tablets, pencils, and blue ribbons on the table. "Pretty good, huh? I won the spelling bee. Virginia failed on *nihilistic*."

"Good for you."

Opal could tell her sister was still distracted. "You should have seen Robert win the arithmetic bee. Atticus must be busting his buttons, he's so proud." Opal studied her sister. "It's started to rain."

Ruby nodded.

She's not listening at all. The sun was glorious outside. Opal gathered her things together to carry to her room. No sense wasting time with Ruby. She should never have mentioned anything about the drifter. Here she felt better, and now Ruby was all worried.

Dumb bunny, why don't you just keep some things to yourself or wait and tell Rand? He'd know what to do. Opal scolded herself as she changed into chores clothes — britches and her old boots. She buckled her belt back around her waist and rolled up the sleeves on her shirt. The filly was ready to take out to work the cows, although most cowboys refused to use a filly or mare, since they caused trouble when they were in heat. Firelight had good enough bloodlines to make a good broodmare, but if she was cattle trained, she might sell easier and for a larger profit.

Opal peeked into Rand and Ruby's room and saw Per still sound asleep. She tiptoed back out and stopped at the table to cut herself two thick slices of bread to spread with butter and jam. Today she'd not even take time for buttermilk. Even though she was home earlier than usual, there was so much to do.

Ruby was sitting on the back porch, her Bible in her lap, eyes closed.

Opal started on by but stopped at Ruby's pronouncement.

"Stay within sight of the house."

"But, Ruby."

"No argument. Stay close to home."

"But I was going to work Firelight with cattle today."

Ruby opened her eyes. "I said, no argument."

Opal stomped off the porch and down to the corral. *Wish I had never told her. Dumb, just plain sheep dumb. That's what you are.* At the moment she couldn't think of anything dumber than sheep. Unless it was her.

She took her rope off the hook in the barn and headed for the horse pasture. While Bay always came when she whistled, the filly hadn't learned that yet. She walked on down to where the horses grazed, dropped a loop over Firelight's head, and led her back to the corral. "You're next," she warned the dark gelding. He really needed a name, but so far she'd not come up with a good one. He was low on personality, not nearly as smart as the filly.

"All right, with no cattle nearby, I guess we rope the post." She'd been working her on backing and standing. The first time the rope flew by her head, the horse leaped to the side. "Easy, girl. That's no way to behave." By the time Opal lassoed the snubbing post a dozen times her mount knew enough to ignore the whirl of the flying rope.

After about an hour Opal had forgotten all about the drifter, Ruby's concern, and school being over, concentrating instead on freeing the filly and catching the gelding, only to start all over again on reining, leg work, and sliding stops. Soon sweat spots dotted the animal's neck, and Opal took him out of the corral to cool him out. She patted his neck. "You did good, son. Maybe we should call you Will, short for willing. How'd you like to be called Will?" His ears swiveled back and forth, listening to her and keeping track of all else around them.

The sun was angling toward Chimney Butte by the time she let him go back into the fenced pasture with the broodmares, two of which should be foaling any time.

After putting away her gear, Opal checked on the sow, picked the eggs, and headed for the springhouse with the basket.

Ghost's barking stopped her short. The drifter. She'd forgotten all about him. Could it be . . . ? But she turned to see Ghost dashing toward the river where the men and horses were swimming across the last stretch, Rand in the lead. At this time of year the Little Missouri was treacherous with shifting sandbars, holes, and quicksand. Not too many places were safe to cross, but the stretch that bordered the homeplace was blessed to be one.

Even the memory made her jaw tighten. That man had the ability to ruin an otherwise perfect day. Better to get this over with before Ruby talked with Rand.

"You guys look like you been rolling in the mud."

"You should see those steers. You'd think if one got caught, the others would stay out of the mud, wouldn't you?" Chaps stepped from his horse and glared down at his leather chaps. "Shoulda swam across the river."

Rand dismounted and gave a jerk on the leather strap holding the girth of his saddle tight.

Opal gnawed on her bottom lip. If she didn't talk quick, she'd be late milking

Fawn and even later for supper.

Catching a movement out of the side of her eye, she looked toward the river where Linc and Little Squirrel were carrying their catch back to the house.

"Looks like fish for breakfast."

Rand glanced over the rump of his horse. "Looks like we'll be smoking some too. They really did well."

I'd rather have been fishing too. Opal sighed.

While the others were teasing Joe, who had ridden down from the buttes on the eastern side of the river and hadn't had a mud bath, Rand glanced down at her, at the same time working on the rear cinch. "So what's happened now?"

"The last day of school was great until we were riding out of town and I saw that drifter again. He had another man with him." She watched Rand's face but caught only a slight tightening of his jaw. "We ducked between two buildings. I don't think he saw us."

"I'd heard he was in town. He knows where you live by now."

"Why'd he have to come back?"

"Plenty going on in Medora."

"Not for his kind."

"No, but Little Missouri still has an

abundance of booze and gambling." Rand swung the saddle off his horse. "Sure wish I'd been riding Buck today. This knothead doesn't have the sense God gave a goose."

"So what do we do?"

"Nothing tonight. Give me some time to think on it." He handed the reins to Chaps. "You take them out to the pasture, please."

"Sure, Boss."

"You told Ruby yet?"

Opal nodded. "She's some upset."

"No doubt. You done milking yet?"

"No, sir. I was just getting to it."

"Keep this under your hat for now, all right? I don't want anyone going off half-cocked."

"Yes, sir."

Rand gave a tug on her thick braid. "It'll be all right, Opal."

"I sure hope so."

"Hope's not good enough. We need to do some serious praying. God promised to be our protector, remember?"

Opal didn't answer but whistled for Ghost to bring Fawn in. Not that the dog was really needed, since the milk cow was standing by the gate waiting for them. Somehow she just felt safer with Ghost around.

She studied the buttes around the rim of

their valley. Everything looked as usual. The blackbirds sang from the thickets; two crows flew overhead scolding each other or the dog below them. Fawn mooed gently; a horse snorted and then, knees buckling, dropped to the ground and rolled, legs kicking, his grunts of pleasure carrying on the cooling air. When he finally rolled completely over, he surged to his feet and shook, dust flying in a cloud around him.

Opal let down the bars on the fence, Fawn walked through, and she slid the bars back into their slots. She and Ghost followed the cow to the barn, where she dropped the block to hold the stanchion closed, then went for a scoop of grain. Fawn's calf came into his stall from outside, announcing his impatience at the wait for his feeding.

The cats wound around her ankles, mewing for their share. Just a normal evening in the barn. A separate world of peace and dust motes. Would that all her life had the quiet comfort of a barn.

My first day of freedom. Opal stretched her arms above her head and turned to look out the window. The sun had yet to come up over the buttes, but the world shimmered in that crystal moment, transparent, filled with birdsong. She slipped from the bed and knelt at the windowsill to peer through the window that could now be opened to the life outside after being sealed shut all winter. While each season had its own particular fragrance, Opal always said she loved the fresh, invigorating sip of spring the best. She caught a movement in the woods, and a doe with two spotted fawns stepped from the tree line into the clearing.

Ghost barked, and they disappeared as if they'd never been. Opal breathed in deeply again before rising to dress. Today she could go barefoot. It was time to toughen up her winter feet.

Rand was giving the day's orders after breakfast when they heard a horse galloping toward the house.

Ghost flew off the front porch, barking her "it's a stranger" announcement.

"Stay here." Rand's order stopped Opal in midrise. "I'll see who it is."

"Mr. Harrison!"

They heard the call before the horse stopped. "Mr. Harrison. Opal!"

"That's Robert." Opal was right behind Rand as they tore out the door.

"What is it, son?"

Robert, eyes running, gulped out, "It's

Atticus. Someone beat him so bad he might be dying."

"Where? When?"

"We found him this morning. He crawled as close to home as he could. Mr. Rand, they beat him near to death."

"Who?"

"Don't know. He can't talk, other than to say 'Opal.' Opal, you got to come. Atticus, he needs you."

Rand strode past Robert and headed toward the corral. "Go in and eat while we get the horses."

"No, I ain't hungry."

"I'll get my boots." Opal ran down the hall. What a morning not to have put on her boots. *Oh, Atticus, hang on. We're coming.*

Chapter Fifteen

Not Atticus. Why would anyone hurt Atticus?

"Opal, stay with the rest of us." Rand shouted to be heard over the pounding hooves.

Opal tightened her reins, bringing Bay back to a steady lope, the kind that a fit horse could keep at for miles. Bay pulled against the bit, always wanting to be the front-runner.

Oblivious to the beauty around her, Opal could think only of Atticus. The only one she could think of who would want to hurt Atticus was the drifter. And that made the beating all her fault.

All because she'd gone swimming. Why did such a simple and innocent thing cause such troubles? That foul and rotten man.

Why didn't I just shoot him. I know God says do not kill, but had I known what could come of that, his death would have been a gift to mankind. It wasn't Atticus's fault. Please, God above, Atticus was just trying to save me. My fault. My fault. The words kept an even beat with the thud of hooves along the road.

The drifter — she didn't even know his name. Why did he come back?

To get even. The words still didn't make sense. She knew Rand had threatened him with his life if he came back.

And he was back. She'd seen him.

They slowed to a jog through town, giving the horses a bit of a breather, and picked up a lope once past the cattle corrals now empty until the steers fattened again from the winter losses.

When they reached the Gradys' log cabin, Opal let Bay out and skidded to a stop right at the door.

Mrs. Grady threw the door open. "Right this way."

Opal blinked in the dim interior, then followed Mrs. Grady into the lean-to on the back. She fell to her knees beside the wooden bed. If she hadn't known this was Atticus, she would not have recognized him. His head looked like a misshapen ball with eyes swollen closed, a slash across one cheek, and bruises already turning colors. His right arm was bound to a board and that across his chest. While the rest of his body lay hidden under a sheet, one foot was propped on a pillow.

"Atticus?" She took his free hand in hers, fear at the heat of it making her stutter. "A-Atticus, can you hear me?"

A slight pressure on her hand was her only answer.

"Do you know who did this to you?"

Another squeeze. His breath rattled in his chest.

Opal glanced up when she felt a hand on her shoulder. Rand stood right beside her.

"He can't talk none," Mrs. Grady whispered, tying her apron in knots.

"He can hear, though." Opal held his hand against her cheek. "Oh, Atticus, we have to know who did this to you."

"Don't make no difference. We just got to get him healed. Been praying ever since we found him." Mr. Grady spoke from the corner of the room.

Rand squeezed Opal's shoulder, the spot feeling cold when he withdrew his hand. "Let's go outside, Grady." He led the father from the lean-to.

Opal knew Rand would try to get as

much out of the man as he could. How much did his family know of that day at the river? How could she ask Atticus questions without making things worse?

Opal fought back the tears that welled at the sight of his mangled body. She leaned closer. "Give me one squeeze for yes, two for no."

One squeeze. She breathed a sigh of relief. They could communicate.

"I'm goin' to fix coffee. You need anything, you just holler." Mrs. Grady patted her shoulder. "Robert, you see if you can do anything for Miss Torvald here."

Miss Torvald? When did she cease being Opal? It wasn't like they were strangers.

"Ah, Robert, could you bring a basin of cool water and a cloth? Let's see if we can make Atticus more comfortable."

"Sure can."

As the boy left, she leaned closer to Atticus's head. "Now, I must know. Was it the drifter?"

One squeeze. A wait then another.

"Was he alone?"

Two faint squeezes.

"I saw him with another skunk who didn't look any better than him."

One squeeze.

"I'll kill them." Rage bit the words off,

and she almost missed his two rapid squeezes.

"What do you mean, no? They tried to kill you. An eye for an eye."

His face worked, and a faint moan came from his closed mouth. His hand fluttered in hers, then tightened.

"Easy, easy. I'm right here." She forced her hand to gentleness and turned to thank Robert when he set the basin down beside her.

"We found him about a mile from home. No idea how far he had crawled."

"Where had he been?"

"Went to town to help out at the Blacks. Pa was out plowing. June and I went fishing. All came home but Atticus. We figured he stayed over to work late or start work early in the morning." He sniffed. "I shoulda gone lookin' for him."

Opal dipped the cloth in the water, wrung it out some, and laid it across the broad forehead that looked like it had been scraped across gravel.

She took his hand again and felt a gentle squeeze.

After a time she changed the cloth. Bit by bit she saw him relax and realized he was sleeping. "You rest, my friend. That's what you need to do to get better."

She could hear the others in the kitchen, the low murmur of their conversation indecipherable.

June, her gaze stuck to the cup she carried so carefully in both hands, made her way in the dimness, the candle by the bed the only light but what seeped between the chinks in the logs.

"Here. There's sugar in it." She handed Opal the cup.

"Thank you."

Just as she took the cup, Atticus groaned, then jerked as if struck by lightning. His back arched, arms thrashed, knocking the cup out of her hands, catching her on the shoulder, and nearly throwing her off the chair.

"Rand, someone, help!" Opal leaped to get out of the way as her friend bucked and heaved on the bed.

"Oh, my God." Mr. Grady reached for Atticus and then backed off. "If I hold him down, I might hurt him more."

Opal knelt at the bedside again, crooning the same gentle song she used on the horses, no specific words but calming. She didn't know where the song came from, but she knew the name of Jesus was laced through it.

Atticus, breath heaving like he'd run a

mile, lay flaccid, sweat running, blood seeping from the side of his swollen mouth.

"H-has he done that before?" Opal could scarcely speak, tears leaking down her face.

"No. No one in our family has fits."

"Probably from the beating on his head. I've seen it happen before." Rand dipped the cloth back in the pan and gently wiped Atticus's face. "You poor man. God, please bring healing here. Restore Atticus to his former self. Bring him back strong and able to breathe freely. Give him rest and peace. Amen."

Opal repeated the amen, as did the others. She had kept her gaze on Atticus during the prayer, had watched color come back into his face, but now she turned to stare at Rand and felt her jaw dropping in awe. Never had she heard him pray with such authority, as though God were standing right on the other side of the bed and they were having a discussion.

Please, God, make all that happen. Please, let me find the sorry animals who did this to him. Her insides heated up, as if preparing for branding. Branding would be too good for those two. *God, why do you let people act like that? You could stop them. I know you could, but you didn't.*

Why? Atticus is good, and he loves you. Seems to me that if you love someone, you take care of them. You protect them.

She took Atticus's hand again, but this time there was no answering squeeze.

He was indeed asleep.

Rand placed his hand on Atticus's forehead. "He will most likely sleep for some time. If he starts to run a fever again, lay wet sheets over him. A fever can sometimes cause attacks like he had, especially if there is a head injury."

"Thank you, Mr. Harrison." Mrs. Grady shook his hand. "I'll stay right by him. Please God that our son will live."

Opal followed the men out of the room. If they were going after the drifters, she was the only one who would recognize them. No, Rand saw him before. She stopped but didn't return to the lean-to.

"I can send Linc and Little Squirrel over to help you," Rand said.

"Why, that would be most kind of you." Mr. Grady pushed his hat back on his head. "Rand Harrison, you sure do live by the Good Book. Not like some we know. Don't know why anyone would beat on my boy like that. He never hurts no one."

Rand nodded. "Some things just can't be explained. Little Squirrel is real good with caring for someone wounded." He gathered his reins and mounted his horse, indicating for Opal to do the same.

They waved and rode away from the house.

"Now, don't you go getting any wild ideas."

"Shooting those varmints is not a wild idea. I asked Atticus, using hand squeezes for yes and no, and he said it was that drifter, and I saw the other man with him. I'll bet we could find them over at Williams' or Maunders'. They don't take to those kind in Medora." *Why did they go after Atticus? They should be coming for me. I'm the one so stupid as to go swimming. None of this would have happened if I'd gone straight home like I'd told Mr. Finch.*

"We should get ahold of the army," Rand said.

"Right, and they'll take care of it like they did for those guys who attacked Cimarron. No one ever caught them. Besides, the army is too far away." Opal felt like screaming. Here he was so calm and Atticus lay back there suffering. Why, those sidewinders could be watching them right now, ready to shoot them from behind a rock or up on a butte.

Bay jigged and tossed her head.

"Sorry." Opal loosened her hand on the reins.

"We're goin' straight home. No stopping to look for them, do you understand?"

"I know. We got to get the rifles."

"No, we will not get the rifles. A young woman does not go on a manhunt."

"But, Rand, I'm a good shot, and I . . . I . . . it's my fight." She zinged him a look that should have singed his hat brim.

"I won't discuss this, Opal, and if you are wise, you won't bring it up when we get home."

"But, Rand, I —"

"Sometimes you have to leave things to others."

As soon as they cleared Medora, Opal let Bay have her head and left Rand far behind. If only she could leave her rage to blow in the wind also.

Soon as I get home, I'll get my gun and be out of there before you get to the house. Just because I'm a girl, you think I should stay home and let the men take care of things. Or wait for the marshal. Like he'd come for a guy getting beat up. He doesn't care. Her thoughts slammed around her head like Bay's hooves slammed against the ground.

When she finally let Bay slow down, she realized tears were flowing. And it wasn't just the wind making her eyes water. *Ah, Atticus, this is all my fault. If you die, it's all because of me.* "God!" She screamed at the air. "What are you doing about all this?" She shook so hard, she could have fallen out of the saddle. Leaning forward, she wrapped her arms around Bay's neck and sobbed into her mane.

By the time she reached home she had herself under control. Rand wasn't far behind her, but she didn't wait for him. Let him deal with this. She headed for the barn and stripped the saddle off her horse, turning her loose in the corral so she wouldn't go drink while she was so hot.

Taking her rope off the pegs, she shook it out and headed for the pasture. She'd start with the gelding today, then the filly.

~✄

Thoughts of ways to get the drifters woke her during the night. Nothing seemed better than cougar bait. Only shooting was faster. Once her breathing calmed she could hear the low murmur of Rand and Ruby talking. She got up and padded to their room.

"Is Per all right?"

"Yes. Why?" Ruby asked from the darkness.

"I heard noise and thought maybe he was sick or something."

"Thank you, dear one, but all is well. You go on back to bed."

"All right." Opal stopped, then turned the other way. "I'm going to get a drink." Out in the kitchen, she filled the dipper and drank from the edge. The cool water dripped from her chin but calmed the raw feeling in her throat. Had she been crying? That's the way her throat felt. She made her way back to bed and snuggled under the sheet and light blanket. Compared to the heavy quilts of winter, her bed felt free, not smashing.

The rooster crowing was the next thing she heard. No school. *Ah, freedom. But Atticus*. The thought made her leap from the bed. If she hurried with her chores, she could ride over there before she started work.

"I'll milk. You help Ruby." Rand met her in the hall.

"What's wrong?"

"Just the morning sickness, and Little Squirrel isn't here to help. I'll send Beans up too."

"Sure." Opal tiptoed into the bedroom.

"What do you want me to fix?" She whispered so as not to wake Per.

Ruby moved ever so slightly under the bedcovers. "Bacon and eggs, pancakes."

"Can I bring you anything?"

"No. I'll be better in a little bit."

"Coffee?"

"Oh, no."

A groan sent Opal scurrying. *If that's what happens, I sure don't ever want to have a baby. Ugh.* She headed to the springhouse to get the eggs, slab bacon, buttermilk, and milk.

She'd never been left alone to do this, not that Beans wouldn't take over as soon as he got to the house.

They made it through breakfast without a hitch, Joe taking care of Per, who greeted them all with a happy crow.

When they finished, Opal dumped all the dishes in the dishpan and started to wash. Per banged his spoon on the table.

"I'm coming." *How does Ruby keep up with all this? At least she has Little Squirrel to help.*

"You want me to stay and help?" Beans came in with an armful of split wood.

"No, I'm better now." Ruby entered the kitchen, looking pale but with a smile, tying her apron as she came. "Thank you all for the extra rest."

"Are you sure you're all right?"

"Yes, Opal dear. Think I'll just have a slice of bread, then we can get busy."

"Busy?"

"Rand and I made a decision last night."

Opal took a step back. "Why do I get the feeling I'm not going to like this?"

"We need to hurry so you won't miss the train."

"The train?"

"You are going back to New York to visit the Brandons."

"But, Ruby!"

"There will be no argument. This is the only way we can be sure to keep you safe until they catch that man."

"No-o-o."

Per wailed right along with her.

Chapter Sixteen

"Will we find my mother here?"

Jacob looked down at the boy by his side. He would have to tell him. But how? *Your mother took the coward's way out and flung herself over the bridge?* He didn't know that for sure. And yet he couldn't be more certain than if he'd seen her fall. *The coward's way. What a self-righteous, judgmental excuse for a man you are. You who've never been really sick a day in your life, who are you to know the torment one suffers with consumption? Dying bit by bit, and after losing her husband too.*

If Jacob could have fallen to his knees without making a fool of himself, he would have. But in his mind he was on his knees, pleading for forgiveness.

Who could he ask where there might be work? And what would he do with the boy — he still had a hard time referring to him as his son — while he worked?

Had he stayed in the valley, any one of the church ladies would have helped him out. *But I'd be living a lie, a bigger lie than ever.*

At this bend in his life there were no easy answers.

"Come." He made his way to the ticket window in the station house. "Excuse me."

The man in the green eyeshade turned from the counter and smiled. "How can I help you?"

"We are new in town, just got off the train, and I need both a job and a place to stay for both of us." He indicated the child by his side.

"I see." The man nodded, appearing to be thinking. "What kind of work do you do?"

"I-I've been a farmer and a teacher." He had taught, that was for sure, just not in the local school for children. "I'm good with my hands too. My pa made sure I learned how to do most anything that needed doing on the homeplace."

"I see." A nod accompanied the words. "Well, we don't have much farming here, all ranching. Can you ride a horse?"

"Yes."

"Rope cattle?"

"I could learn."

The man rolled his eyes. "Roping is not something you learn overnight. Can you handle a hammer and saw?"

"Yes."

"Perhaps you better go on over to see Adams at the general store. He'd have a better idea than I do about available work. As for a place to stay, you'd best buy yourself a tent and pitch it with the others out there." He motioned toward the other side of the railroad tracks where various kinds of shelters had been put up. "Medora's booming, that's what she is, thanks to the marquis."

"De Mores?"

"Yeah. All this you see around here is due to one man's dream — Marquis de Mores. He should be arriving any day with his family from New York. They live there during the school year and here during the summers. Named the town after his wife, he did."

"I'd heard there was a lot of building going on here."

"Biggest slaughterhouse — they call it an abattoir — west of the Mississippi. He ships the beeves in ice-cooled railroad cars. You wouldn't believe all the cattle coming in here."

"I see." Jacob glanced behind when he heard someone clear his throat. "Sorry." He turned back to the stationmaster. "Thank you. You've been most helpful. Come, Joel."

The man had motioned toward the northern section of town. The two-story building must be the store. Off to the west he could see a tall brick smokestack with several large buildings surrounding it and a plethora of corrals and chutes. As they walked he studied the buildings. Several very nice houses, a brick Catholic church, log buildings, and off to the south on a hill sat a huge two-story house, perhaps where the elite family lived. Dust rose from the dirt streets as horse carts and oxen-drawn drays, many filled with building materials, passed by. Horses jogged down the street, being ridden by what must be cowboys, with their leather-covered legs and wide-brimmed hats. A sign on one building said Boardinghouse, so he motioned Joel to follow him through the gate and up to the porch. He knocked at the door and, while waiting for an answer, continued studying the surroundings. From the looks of things, there weren't a lot of women living here.

Joel sat down on the porch floor, propping his elbows on his knees, his back to his father. If dejection needed a picture, he was it.

Jacob turned when the door opened and touched the brim of his hat. "Good morning, ma'am. My son and I, we're looking for a place to stay."

"Sorry, I'm all full up, same as all the other places here."

"I see. Well, thank you."

"If I was you, I'd check on over at the store. Adams might know of something."

"Thank you. We were on our way there." Jacob nodded and touched his hat again. "Come, Joel."

"Your boy is lookin' a mite peaked. You eaten today?"

"Well, yes, early."

"Wait here." She returned in a couple of minutes and handed a bag out the door. "Something to tide him over."

"Thank you. You've been most kind." Jacob took the package and turned to go. "Come on, Joel."

Without a word, the boy rose and followed him out the gate.

"Are you hungry?"

Joel only shrugged.

"Thirsty?"

A brief nod.

Jacob exhaled a breath of frustration. "Joel, I cannot read your mind. If you need something, you must ask me."

"Yes, sir."

Lord, give me patience, and I need it right now. "I wonder if there is a public well here. Have you seen a pump or anything?"

"No, sir."

"We'll ask at the store."

Paint had not touched the general store, the wooden siding bleached into a silver sheen. Two rocking chairs took up a goodly part of the front stoop, topped by a slanted shake roof.

"You want to wait out here? You can help yourself to whatever that kind lady gave you."

Joel took the package and settled into one of the rocking chairs, paying no more attention to Jacob than if he'd been a total stranger.

Jacob watched him carefully fold back the paper, then, sure that the boy would be fed, he pushed open the door, setting a bell to tinkling.

The ripe and varied smells of a store that

carried everything from pickles to pots, beeswax to beans, waxed familiar. There had been a similar store in his hometown when he was young. He looked up to see tools hung high on the walls, bridles draped under the shovels, saddles on sawhorses, men's pants and shirts, hats and boots. A wheel of cheese sat under a glass dome. Spices and tobacco tins lined the wall behind the tired wooden counter. A roll of brown paper on a frame and a cone of string on a pole held places of honor, along with a scissors connected by twine to the underside of the bar.

A man dwarfed the sorry apron tied with a many-knotted string around a nonexistent waist above equally lacking hips. The brush on his cheeks more than made up for the thin stubble on top of a knobby head. His nose, a big hooked knob, perched between deep-set eyes above a small mouth and a chin that forgot to show up.

"What can I get you, son?"

"Mostly information, I think. I'm Jacob Chandler. My son and I arrived on the train, and I had no idea there would be no place to stay. Besides that, I need a job. The stationmaster said you might know where I could get both."

"I see. What can you do?"

"Whatever I need to. Grew up on a farm, went to school, got a good education."

"Can you keep books?"

"If I need to. I heard there is already a schoolteacher here."

"Was. He left for the summer. We're hoping he comes back." He glanced out the front window. "What about your boy?"

"Be good if I could work somewhere that he can be near. We don't know anyone here."

"Hmm. Let me think on this. If you got tent, bedrolls, you can make camp anywhere you find a bare spot."

"No, we have none of that. Just our clothes, personal things." *All because we left in such a hurry I didn't take time to think. How could I have been so careless?*

"You plannin' on stayin' round here?"

"Looks that way. I have to get work, and soon."

"Tell you what. I generally only run a tab with fellers I know, but you seem an honest sort. You want to buy some bedding and a tent, some supplies, you can pay me when you get work. Fact is, if you'd like to catch up on my bookwork for me, that could be a first payment."

"How much would those supplies run?"

228

He choked at the amount the man quoted. "Let me think on this. There any other places needing a good hand?"

"Well, roundup is about to start. Sometimes some of the spreads put on an extra man or two."

"Spreads?"

"The ranches. Lot of cattle being run, got to be rounded up, calves branded, cut. Stock treated. Roundup's a big operation." He turned to a man who had just walked in. "What can I do for you, Robertson?"

Jacob stepped back and let the proprietor take care of his customer. He wandered around the store, looking at the tools for both building and ranching. What would he need to keep a home not only for himself but for his son? *Lord, why did I run off so half-cocked? Plain, stupid old pride is why. I was ashamed, so I ran. And now I can run no farther because I have no money, or very little.* He thought to his comfortable little parsonage house with the huge pile of split wood. How must his congregation be feeling about his just disappearing like that?

I cannot go back, and I will not repeat the mistake of letting too many people depend on me. I will make a life for us here. I close the door on the past and live in the day of today. No one needs to know what has gone before. I am not the man I was then.

He stared at the wall without seeing, without hearing anything but the slamming of the door and shooting home the bolt on his past.

It is finished.

"Young man."

The sound finally penetrated. Jacob turned, tapping his chest with his finger and raising an eyebrow.

"Yes, come here." The store's proprietor waved him back to the counter. "I want you to meet Mr. Ward Robertson. Oh, guess I don't rightly know your name."

"I am Jacob Chandler." He held out his hand. "Good to meet you, Mr. Robertson." Glancing at the man behind the counter, he waited.

"I could use another hand." Robertson looked Jacob over. "Sorry, but I can't offer much more than room and board. Adams says you have a boy?"

Jacob stepped to the window. "Joel. He's sitting out front in that chair. He's seven."

But the chair was empty. As was the one beside it. Jacob sprinted for the door. "Joel!"

Chapter Seventeen

"Joel! Joel!" Jacob ran from one side of the storefront to the other, searching up and down the street and along the sides of the building.

"We'll find him." The storekeeper stopped him with a hand on his arm.

"I told him to sit in that chair, and now he is gone."

"He can't have gone far. Besides, everyone knows everyone in this town. Don't worry."

Robertson, the man who'd come into the store, joined the two men. "I'll help. You go that way, and I'll go this."

"Good." Jacob nodded his thanks and headed to the left. Ahead of him he could see the scree at the bottom of the cliff striped with layers of rock in gray and brick and tan. He turned to the right and strode between the buildings, calling his son's name. Where could he have gone?

Worry and fear met up with anger, and the three formed a partnership. They rode Jacob's shoulders like harpies of ancient Greek tragedies, lashing him with scorn. *You left him. He's too little to be left alone. What kind of a father are you? You don't care about him anyway. He's nothing but a burden.*

"Joel?" Jacob called again and then followed the answer that came from beside the pump. "Joel, I told you to stay put in that chair."

"But I was thirsty." Joel gave another pull down on the pump handle. "I can't get any water."

"But you have to do what I tell you. Why didn't you come ask me?" Was that a glare he saw before the boy ducked his head and stared at the ground? Jacob took the handle and pumped with quick jerks until water gushed from the spout. "Help yourself."

"I don't have a cup."

"Use your hands, like this." Jacob cupped his hands, but by the time he got them under the flow, the water slowed to a trickle. "Put your hands like that, and I'll pump water into them."

Joel did as told and slurped from the water fast draining out. He cupped his hands under the flow again, a lesser volume now that Jacob pumped more slowly. He drank four times before stepping back.

"You finished?"

"Yes, sir."

"Good, then we need to go back. Other men are looking for you. You must never just take off like that. You understand me?"

"Yes, sir."

"Did your mother allow you to just go wherever you wanted?"

Joel kicked at a chip of wood, his hands rammed deep in his pockets.

"I asked you a question." Jacob flinched at the sideways look he caught from the boy walking beside him. Sullen, no. Angry, yes. Was the boy harboring anger at him?

"Mr. Robertson." Jacob waved as he called the man's name. "I found him over at the pump. Thank you for your help." He laid a hand on the boy's shoulder, only to have him flinch away.

Was finding a place to work and a roof over their heads not enough to handle without an obstreperous child?

"You want to ride out with me? I got the wagon right around the side of the store." Mr. Robertson stopped on his way back into the store. "You can help me load up."

"Of course." Jacob sat Joel back down in the chair. "Now, listen to me. You stay right there, you hear?"

Joel nodded and clamped his arms across his chest. Wet marks darkened his shirt and down his pants, proof that he'd drunk.

"There's more inside." Mr. Robertson came out with a sack of flour over one shoulder.

Jacob reentered the dimness of the building. "What can I carry out?"

"That sack of beans. There'll be more."

Jacob hefted the hundred-pound sack and threw it over one shoulder, grunting under the weight. He staggered slightly and regained his footing. While he was used to swinging an ax to split wood, he'd not often hoisted heavy sacks over his shoulder. Once outside, he rounded the corner and dumped the sack in the back of the wagon Mr. Robertson pointed to.

Five sacks and many more bundles, some in tow sacks, some wrapped in paper, joined the flour and beans.

"Okay, that's it." Mr. Robertson climbed

up on the wagon seat. "What's your boy's name again?"

"Joel . . ." He almost slipped and said Melody's maiden name. If he used his name, he could add one more lie to the load he already carried, but if he didn't use his name, he left himself open to questioning. No wonder the Bible had such strong injunctions on telling the truth.

"Joel, come now. Bring your satchel." He leaned around the building to make sure the boy was still in the chair. He was. The thudding he'd been hearing was the sound of a boot toe slamming against the post holding up the slanted roof. If the arms and the kicking foot were any indication, Joel had picked up sullenness and brought it along for the ride.

Jacob felt like snatching the boy up by his collar, but instead he stopped in front of him, one foot up on the porch floor.

"Joel, Mr. Robertson has offered me a job and us a place to live. We are going home with him now, so pick up your satchel and come along."

"I want to find my ma."

O Lord, be merciful to us. How do I help this child? "Joel, we'll talk of this later. Right now we are keeping a busy man waiting."

"She's dead, ain't she? You just don't want to tell me."

"I-I'm afraid —"

"No, she isn't. You're lying." Joel leaped off the stoop, ran around the corner, and climbed into the back of the wagon. The brief glimpse Jacob had of his face was mute evidence that Joel was fighting tears and didn't want anyone to know.

Well, so much for all his ministering skills of helping people with grief. Jacob castigated himself repeatedly as he stepped on the wagon wheel spoke and climbed up to the seat. Perhaps if he sat beside the boy . . . But he remained where he was, and Mr. Robertson hupped the team toward home, wherever that might be. At least they would have a place to lay their heads tonight and a roof over their heads, along with full bellies if the rear load was any indication.

"Is his mother really dead?" Robertson kept his voice low, so as not to be heard above the squeaking wheels and trotting horses.

Jacob wanted to say that it was none of his business, but since the man was good enough to take them in, he deserved more than a surly response.

"I don't know. She had severe consumption, and she . . . ah . . . disappeared." He tried to keep his voice dispassionate, but the lump in his throat caused a stumble. Like a cat gone off to die was the way it sounded. *Ah, Melody . . .*

"I'm sorry for your loss. Long time ago or recent?"

"Last week."

Robertson nodded slowly. "I see."

"So we came west." Not an excuse but a statement of fact.

"Land here has a way of easing a burden. Plenty of hard work to hide in."

Jacob glanced over at the driver. Eyes that gazed far beyond the distance, hands gentle on the reins, Ward Robertson looked over his shoulder and nodded. He gave a slight dip of his head, as if they'd formed a pact and needed no more for a signature. If the man thought anything peculiar about his new hand and son, he'd most likely keep it to himself. Jacob figured that if he ever needed to go to battle, he'd want Ward Robertson on his side.

~

Not having seen a single dwelling along the road for a long while, Jacob was pleased when they finally topped a rise and saw a ranch house snugged against the hill's south slope. Walls that looked to have

237

grass growing like fur on the sides and a roof of split cedar shakes used the hill for its backside. Two young girls came running to meet them.

"What'd you bring, Pa?" The slightly taller one ran alongside the turning wheel.

"Stay back now, or there won't be any treats for nosy sisters." Mr. Robertson sounded gruff, but the smile that fell in easy creases said otherwise. "The smaller one is Ada Mae, then Emily. I've got a wife and five daughters."

Both girls ran behind and scrambled up over the wagon tail.

"Who are you?" Ada Mae plunked down beside their young guest.

Jacob turned to watch.

Joel looked away without answering.

"Pa, where did you find the boy?"

"In town at the store. This here is Mr. Chandler, our new hand, and his son, Joel."

"Howdy, sir," they both chimed and without hesitation swung their full attention back to the boy glowering between them.

Ah, Joel, how disappointed your mother would be in your manners today.

"How old are you?"

No answer.

"Cat got your tongue?" No trace of sarcasm colored Emily's question, only curiosity.

"With my girls, your boy might get right spoiled."

He could do with some spoiling, Jacob thought, *but he needn't be rude.* "Joel." One word could speak for many at the right time. Jacob glanced over his shoulder and gave a parental nod to put emphasis on the command.

Joel glowered, shoulders hunched. "Seven."

"I'm Ada Mae, and I'm eight. Do you like school?"

"Some."

Jacob turned to study the house. Two posts off to the side held up twin ropes of drying wash. Cattle grazed down the slope toward the flat field before the creek that leaped and bounded over and around the rocky draw. Grazing cattle dotted the pasture; calves raced through the grass, tails high in mock terror.

"You have a good-looking place."

"Thank you. It's home and keeps food on the table. You and your son can bunk in that soddy off to the right. You'll eat at the house with the rest of us. Mrs. Robertson is a right good cook."

"Thank you."

"We'll unload the wagon later." He raised his voice. "You had dinner yet?"

"No, Pa, we was waiting on you." Emily grabbed one of the tow sacks.

"Good." Turning to Jacob, he said, "I'll introduce you to everyone when we get inside."

The girls leaped off the wagon before it stopped completely at the hitching post in front of the porch.

"Leave your things here, and let's go eat."

Jacob beckoned to Joel, and the two followed Mr. Robertson, who was slightly favoring his right side, into the house.

"Well, I'm most pleased to meet you," Mrs. Robertson said after her husband had introduced her. "We've been needing some extra help this season. Sit down, sit down. I see you've met Ada Mae and Emily." She laid a hand on a girl with long braids. "This is Virginia. Edith is next, and Mary, our eldest, is married and moved away."

"Pleased to meet you all." Jacob smiled at each of them. *What a fine family.* "This is my son, Joel." He nearly tripped over the words, but each time he said them, it became easier.

Mr. Robertson said grace as soon as all had taken their places. It was like a flock of birds settling down at once, first one fluttering up, then another. The fragrance of stewed meat and fresh bread nearly undid Jacob. His stomach responded with such a growl, the littlest girl, on his right, giggled behind her hand.

"Ada Mae, mind your manners." Mrs. Robertson set another bowl, this one of baked beans, on the table. "Help yourselves, now. We don't expect anyone to leave the table hungry, thank the Lord."

When she'd finally dished up her own plate, Mr. Robertson was already raising his coffee cup for a refill.

"Now, Edith, you pour the coffee, and Virginia, since you are finished, you serve the cake." Mrs. Robertson glanced over to Joel. "Son, you better have another slice of bread. It's a long time until supper."

By the time they left the table, Jacob knew he'd eaten twice what he needed.

"Let's get that wagon unloaded, and then I'll want you to run through some things for me."

"Fine." *What kind of things?*

Some time later one of the girls brought a horse in from the field. "Pa wants to see how you ride."

"Ah, fine." Jacob looked at the saddle.

"We never had a saddle, however, we just rode bareback."

Virginia looked toward her father. "Should I give him a lesson, then?"

"No, you can do that later. Right now, young man, I'd like to see you ride."

"You mount by putting your left foot into the stirrup, left hand on the horn, right on the cantle." Virginia identified each piece by a touch of her hand. "Then pull yourself up, swinging your right leg over the horse's rump."

Jacob knew his thank-you was not heartfelt, but since when had he needed a young girl to explain something so simple? He turned the stirrup with one hand, raised his left foot to shove it into the stirrup, and the horse moved off just a couple of feet, swishing his tail at Jacob's clumsiness. Three times and he finally swung his right leg over as advised and settled into the saddle. "Very good, Mr. Chandler." She flipped each rein up around the horse's neck so that they crossed on the withers.

Jacob picked up the reins, one in each hand, and clucked the horse forward.

"You might want to walk him around the corral, get the feel of his mouth."

Jacob did as told, but when he pulled on the right rein, the horse stopped.

"That horse is trained to neck-rein, son."
Mr. Robertson sat watching, arms crossed
on the horn. "Let me show you." He exag-
gerated putting the reins together evenly in
one hand with the ends of the reins coming
up past thumb and forefinger. Nudging his
horse forward, he laid the reins to the right
to go right and left to go left. "Very easy. It
gives you a free hand for your rope or a
quirt or sometimes to hang on with. Some
of our gullies are mighty steep."

Jacob followed the instructions, feeling
like a failure at first but gaining confidence
quickly. He settled back in the saddle as
his boss did and followed him out the
corral gate down along the creek. Watching
Robertson work his cattle gave Jacob a hint
of how much he had to learn.

As they rode past the house, Robertson
whoaed his horse. "Wait here." He strode
into the house and returned with two rifles
and two kids on his heels.

"Can we go along, Pa? We promise to
stay out of the way."

"I guess." The man mounted his horse
and pulled his daughter up behind him. He
pointed to Joel. "Go on. Get up behind
your pa."

Jacob reached down and, grasping Joel's
hand, pulled him up. Not as smoothly as

Virginia and her father but he managed. The feel of Joel's arms about his waist made his heart do a two-step flutter dance. *My son.*

"Come on along."

His horse automatically followed the other.

"We'll go on up the creek where I set up a target range for the girls to learn on. Everyone needs to be able to shoot out here, if for nothing else but to keep meat on the table. Snared rabbit gets awful tiresome after a while."

Jacob swung Joel down, dismounted, and took the rifle offered.

"You know how to load and fire?"

"Yes, sir."

"Good." Robertson handed Jacob a couple of shells. "See if you can hit that tin can nailed to the tree." He pointed at a distant tree.

Jacob loaded, sighted, fired, and missed. Second shot missed.

"How about that can set on the stump?"

Jacob sighted, and the can pinged off the wood. *Thank you, God.* He sighted on a stick poking up from behind a rock. "I think your sights need some adjusting."

"Good. You'll do."

Jacob let out a breath he just realized

he'd been holding. If he'd been as bad a shot as he was a horseman, he and his son might have been hoofing it back to town with no job in sight.

"My pa could shoot better'n that."

Jacob spun around to catch a gleam in Joel's eyes. Was that malice? Or just ordinary spite?

Chapter Eighteen

I won't have summer on the ranch. Ruby, how could you do this to me?

Opal stared out the dirty train window. She was being sent east to the Brandons for her protection like a little kid being sent to her room. How could they be so cruel? All this mess because she'd had a headache and asked to go home from school early and had listened to the siren song of the river and had gone for a swim. Surely you ought to be able to go for a swim without the whole world crashing down around your ears. But it had. And it was all her fault. Atticus had been beaten to within an inch of his life, and those drifters were still loose. *Atticus. Oh, Atticus, you've got to get well, or I'll never forgive myself.*

Ruby had already packed Opal's bag, and they were in the wagon on the road to town before she could do much more than catch her breath.

"Is this seat taken?"

The voice jarred her out of the scene raging in her head. She looked up to see a man dressed in a black wool suit coat, his eyes dark as the coat, cigar smoke wreathing his dark hair.

Opal glanced around. There were plenty of seats available. "No, but I can't abide cigar smoke." She sat up straighter and studied him through slitted eyes.

"And if I put it out?" His voice had a nice ring to it. He could be interesting.

Sure, just like that drifter, only dressed better. "No, thanks." She turned back to face the window. She didn't even have her gun along. Rand made her leave it at home.

He took the seat right across the aisle. Out of the corner of her eye she saw him grind out the cigar on the windowsill and stick the remaining portion in his breast pocket.

He reminded her of the hustlers that used to come into Dove House. They'd spend their days doing who knew what and the evenings in the cardroom.

"I know we haven't been properly introduced, but we could perhaps carry on a
conversation, or I could go get the conductor to conduct an introduction. Makes
the time pass."

Opal turned slightly so she could see
him better. He *had* put the cigar out.
There were some manners taught him
sometime. And Ruby hadn't said she
couldn't talk to anybody. Why, all those
times she'd carried her tray of food to sell
out to the train, she'd talked to most anybody.

True, they'd never been introduced. She
turned a bit more and smiled slightly.
What could they talk about?

"Nice weather we're having."

"Yes, miss, it most surely is. You from
around these parts?"

"Yes, and you?"

"You know where Seattle is?"

Opal shook her head. "No."

"It's about as far west as you can go,
right on the shores of Puget Sound in
Washington Territory. I work for a packing
company out there."

"So where are you going now?"

"Chicago. What about you?"

"New York. I used to live there."

"Never been there, but I hear it is some

place. Where do you live now?"

"On a ranch outside of Medora." *Don't you go saying too much. You can get in trouble here too.*

"Not much to see out here."

"Not since we left the badlands. There you can never see enough."

"You like the ranch?"

"Oh yes. I have a horse named Bay and a nephew named Per. He's the cutest thing."

"So why are you going to New York?"

Opal stared at him a moment. *Because I'm being banished.* "You ever play cards?"

"Sure. Why?"

"Just thought it might pass the time. It's a shame we don't have more people. We could play a round of poker."

"That's not exactly a lady's game."

"Depends on where the lady is from." *Not that I'm a lady, and if I were, I sure as shooting wouldn't be stuck on a train heading east.* The thought of Bay and the filly that would most likely be sold before she got home again made her clamp her lower lip between her teeth. All because of the drifter. *Just one man, if you could call him that.* She glanced back at the man across the aisle. Perhaps it wasn't fair to tar him with the same brush, but what did she know about him? Other than being well

249

dressed, having decent manners, and almost handsome. She'd never bothered to be much of a judge of people's looks.

"I could perhaps find some more players."

"Anyone you know?"

He shook his head. "There are tables in the second car back. Several card games are already going on. But that's not a good place for a young lady like you. I'll go see who I can find."

After he left, she thought back those few short years to the trip she and Ruby made west. She'd been scolded soundly for spying in the men's car. Besides, it would be full of smoke, and she didn't care for smoke at all.

But card games were more fun with more players.

Mr. Waters — he introduced himself as Hank Waters — returned with two other men and pointed to them as he said their names. "Bud Jamison. Miss Torvald. Tack Sanders."

Opal nodded. "I'm pleased to meet you." She motioned to the flat case that would be their table. "Shall we play?"

"We're playing poker with a girl?"

She ignored the muttered remark and remembered Belle's admonition. *"You'll get a lot further with a sweet smile. Remember, bees and honey."*

"Five-card draw, or do you have another preference?" She looked at all three, one by one.

"That'll be just fine."

The look in Tack Sanders' eyes, nearly hidden by brushy eyebrows and whiskers, sent a shiver up her spine. A vision of a man against the sun flashed through her mind. She glanced around the car. Two ladies were chatting a few seats away. A little boy and girl were listening to a story being read to them. A silver-haired gentleman was snoozing with his head back. Surely nothing bad could happen to her here.

"You sure you know how to play? Five-card draw is a man's game." Bud Jamison's gold tooth caught the light.

Hank Waters drew a deck of cards from his breast pocket. "Shall I deal or would someone rather?"

"Let her." Brushface, as Opal renamed Sanders, nodded toward her. His tone made Opal smile inside. He so obviously thought she was a chicken ready for plucking.

Opal shuffled the deck, then, thumbs on top, she riffled the cards together. She wanted to look at the heckler to see his reaction but instead repeated the process. After dealing the hand, she waited for them to check their cards and dealt out the number they asked for.

"Beginner's luck," Brushface muttered after she won the hand.

Hank Waters raised one eyebrow, reached in his pocket to draw out his cigar, caught her look, and put it back. Either the other two men didn't smoke or he'd warned them.

"Winner deals?" She kept her smile inside.

"A'course." Goldtooth — Bud Jamison — twisted his mouth slightly to one side. His eyes narrowed.

Opal shuffled again and set the cards to the right to be cut.

"Who taught you how to play?" Brushface asked when she scooped in the next pile of coins.

"A friend. Would you care for a different game?"

"Nah. You can't take three in a row . . . less you're cheatin'."

"Mr. Sanders, I don't need to cheat." *Cheating is against my principles.*

What about obeying your sister? The small voice slid over her right shoulder.

If it weren't for her, I wouldn't be on this

stupid train going to New York. I would be home where I belong.

She shuffled and dealt with a snap to the cards.

This time she tried to lose, but the two men played so stupidly she gave up. When the bet was down to between her and Waters, she folded.

"You two in cahoots or something?" Goldtooth stared at the cards. Waters had bluffed. She didn't bother to show her cards.

When Waters dealt, and she won the hand again, Brushface roared and slapped both hands on the leather case. The coins jumped, as did Opal.

"You're cheatin'!"

Opal sucked in a deep breath to still her rampaging heart.

"You chit of a girl, you gotta be cheatin'!" He leaned across the playing surface, blowing stale beer and bad-breath fumes in her face.

"She won fair and square." Hank Waters spoke clearly, his voice soothing. His steely eyes said more.

"You set us up." Brushface slammed Waters with an elbow.

The case tipped up, coins flying in all directions, many sliding right into Opal's lap, as the two men surged to their feet.

"Now, now!" Goldtooth waved his hands. "No need to fight about this."

Hank blocked a thrown punch but tripped over the arm of the seat across the aisle. Brushface went after him with a snarl.

"Stop it!" Opal pushed away the leather case. Oh, for her gun. Oh, for an escape. She was caught in the corner unless she scrambled over the back of the seat.

Keeping one eye on the two combatants, Goldtooth knelt down to scoop up some of the scattered coins.

"Oh no you don't." Opal took a step forward and brought her boot down on the back of his hand.

He yelped and clutched his hand with the other. "You little . . ."

A woman screamed. Men hollered.

The conductor slammed a knotted stick on Brushface's head. "Enough!" His roar stopped all action. He hefted the baton again, but Brushface shook his head and raised a hand in surrender.

"If you can't play a fair game, get on out of here. Any more of this, and you'll be off at the next stop."

The conductor hustled the two men on to the next car, then returned to glare at

Hank Waters. "There wasn't anything underhanded here, was there?" He glanced over to include Opal. "Did you know this man before?"

"No, sir. Just thought to pass the time."

"I'd suggest you take up knitting or some such. A lot safer."

"St. Paul coming up." He nodded toward Hank Waters.

Opal sat back in her seat, trying not to laugh out loud, ignoring the voice trying to remind her she'd brought on trouble again. She should write Belle and let her know what had happened. Belle had taught her well.

After changing trains in St. Paul, Opal splurged with a good meal in the dining car, then snuggled under her quilt for some much needed sleep. For safety's sake she tucked all her paper money down into her chemise, another lesson learned from the mistress of gambling. Good thing Ruby couldn't see her now.

Opal woke shivering in the night. Brushface, Goldtooth, and the drifter had melded into one man in her dream and had pursued her across the country. No matter how hard she pushed her horse, her pursuer stayed right on her heels. Each time she looked back, he'd grown larger, till the arms reaching out to grab her seemed to brush her skin.

She sat up, struggling to catch her breath. She'd done it again. She'd caused someone else harm because she didn't think things through. Mr. Waters had worn a cut lip and a blackened eye when he left the train, and although he'd told her more than once it wasn't her fault, she knew it was. *When am I going to learn? No wonder Ruby worries I'll never be a gentlewoman. She'd never play cards like that.* She blew out a breath. *But Belle would.*

She dozed off again sometime later but woke at each noise. When dawn lightened the windows, she finally felt free from the night demons. *From now on, you play only whist.* And this time she meant it.

"I heard you had yourself quite a time, young lady." The conductor stopped by her seat when she woke up. "You didn't really cheat, did you?"

"Of course not." Opal stared at him as if he'd sprouted scales. "I don't need to cheat. They just underestimated me because I'm a girl. Serves them right. Where are we?" She stretched her neck from side to side to banish the crick that had settled in due to the way she'd slept.

"Coming up on Chicago. Where'd you learn to play cards like that?"

"From a friend. Are they still serving in the dining car?"

"You can get something to eat there most all day long. Good part of the night too."

"Thank you. Could you please watch out for my things here?"

"Tuck them under the seat. I'll put up a Taken sign."

"Thank you." Opal stopped by the necessary and smoothed her hair back with dampened hands. She should brush the snarls out and rebraid it, but her growling stomach sounded about like two dogs going at each other.

Once resettled after Chicago, she read a book, got bored with the scenery, ate her meals in the dining car, read some more, chatted with an older woman who took the seat across from her, and was thoroughly bored by the time the train finally went underground to pull into New York.

She gathered her things, grateful that she'd taken time to wash up and do her hair, and followed the passengers down the steps.

"Opal. Opal, over here."

She stood on her tiptoes to see who was

calling her name. A waving hand caught her attention. That slender, fashionable young woman coming toward her couldn't be Alicia, could it? Of course it was. She looked enough like her mother for them to be sisters. Same sealskin brown hair, the same welcoming smile, gracious to a fault. It was Alicia, all right.

"Opal." Even the younger fashion plate strolling beside the elder had her hair up. No long thick braid hanging down her back. It must be Penelope, but it couldn't be. Penelope was the same age as Opal. "Opal, is it really you?"

"Last time I looked." Opal could feel her cheeks burning. The last time she'd looked, she was dressed in a well-used dark skirt, and while it was clean, it had never even made an acquaintance with style. Her waist too had seen better days. If only she'd been allowed to wear her divided leather skirt and the soft fringed jacket she'd grown into, the one that had belonged to Belle. Opal sucked in a deep breath. It was all Ruby's fault for hustling her off like that. Plastering a smile on a face that would rather frown, she squared her shoulders.

"Yep, it's me. But whatever happened to all of you?"

"What do you mean?"

"Why, you're all grown up."

Alicia and Penelope laughed and hugged her. Jason gave her a wide smile, touching his hat brim in a one-fingered salute. "Wait until you see Bernie. He's in school now too. Mother says she has the first peace she's had in seventeen years."

"They'd be here too, but Bernie fell out of the oak tree this morning and cracked his head a good one, so Mother had to stay home with him. She said to tell you she can't wait to see you." Alicia took her arm on one side and Penelope the other, leaving Jason to deal with the baggage.

"Not fair." But his grumble was accompanied by a wink.

"We need to locate your trunk." Alicia stopped her with a hand on her arm.

"I didn't bring one." Not that she'd had enough clothes to even fill the bag she brought, since britches were impossible to bring along. That would have really shocked her friends.

Only the slightest pause betrayed their astonishment. "Good. Then we shall have to do lots of shopping."

"Come along. The carriage is waiting. And Mrs. Fleish can't wait to see you either."

Feeling she was caught in a hurricane, Opal let herself be guided through the crowd, one or the other of her captors pointing out people and places, a dress, a hat, until she wanted to stand still and scream.

But screaming had never been her way of dealing with things. Instead, she finally planted her feet and let their hands slide off her.

"What's the matter?" Alicia turned a baffled gaze on her.

"Too much. This is too much. I'm used to air and sun and a wind that blows where it will. Give me a moment to catch my breath." *As if I want to breathe in these obnoxious odors.* She felt her nose pinch in protest.

Jason stopped beside her and plunked her valise down on the floor. "So what's the difficulty here?" Even though his voice cracked, he already sounded like his father.

I'm the difficulty, and I cannot go on any longer. Opal swallowed the tears that burned behind her eyes. *I want to go home. Please, Lord, I want to go home.*

"It'll be all right, Opal. Truly it will." Jason spoke softly while both the girls studied Opal as if she were some strange kind of creature. "You don't have to hurry if you don't want to. I hate to shop too."

"Thank you."

"I'm sorry, Opal. I'm just so excited to have you back with us." Penelope stepped closer to Opal. "I want to show you everything. Life is terribly exciting here, and I thought you'd want to see it all." Her grin had remained in spite of the fancy clothes. "Besides, I haven't had half as much fun since you left."

But you don't understand. I don't want to be here. I want to be home on the ranch, back to the time before the drifter. I want to be working with the horses, playing with Per, riding the ridges, and seeing the fantastical forms and shapes of the badlands.

"I was hoping you would come to visit us out West."

"You don't want to be here?" Alicia's eyes grew round.

Wonderful, Opal, now you've hurt their feelings. "Oh no, it's not that at all." *And now you're a liar too.* "I just need some time to adjust. Even a little bit of time." She stepped forward and hooked arms with the two again. "Lead on. I'll be all right." *Please God, I'll be all right. As soon as I no longer look like a poor relation, I'll be better.*

Chapter Nineteen

"Why did you say that about your pa?"

Joel stared down at his loosely clasped fingers. Sullenness rode his eyebrows and molded his chin.

"Joel, I'm speaking to you. I know your ma taught you good manners." Jacob waited, but the boy refused to answer. What was he to do with him? Mr. Robertson had given him a strange look at the boy's comments.

"My name is Joel O'Shaunasy." The mutter could scarcely be heard.

Jacob blinked. His name. Of course that was his name. Did he need to go explain their sad tale? How could he do that without giving away more than he desired? He thought longingly of the comfort of his little house and the foibles of his parishioners back home. There, he'd finally been making headway with Mr. Dumfarthing, and now a new pastor would need to start all over again — if he'd have the patience to try, or even the desire.

He glanced around the ten-by-ten room with dirt walls that gave off a dank odor. Maybe it smelled good to gophers and moles, but the aroma did nothing for his sensitive nose.

Tell him.

The voice came so clear he almost turned around to see who had spoken. *I can't.*

Tell him.

Jacob rammed his fingers through his hair. How do you tell a boy his mother is not only dead but might have hastened her own death?

A sigh escaped before he could swallow it. "Joel, I need to tell you something." *Look at me, show me you are listening.* The boy sat on the lower bunk only two feet away, but the walls he'd raised between them were so strong as to be nearly visible.

Jacob swallowed the next sigh. "Something about your mother."

Not even a muscle twitched. Had the boy. . . ? He had to quit thinking of him as *the boy.* Joel was his son. "We won't be looking for her anymore. I am fairly certain she died before we left the valley."

Joel's slitted gaze nailed him to the wall. "Why?"

"Remember the man from the livery coming?"

He gave a nod so brief as to be almost nonexistent.

"He said he thought Melody, er, your ma, fell into the river. The horse and buggy were tied up at the bridge."

"You said we were going looking for her."

"I know. I didn't want to tell you, but . . ." Jacob knelt in front of his son. "I'm sorry."

"You told a lie." Only the tightly clamped jaw kept the tears at bay. He swiped his sleeved arm under his nose.

"I know." *I've told many lies lately, and like this one, they all want to return to haunt me.* "I was trying to make it easier for you." Jacob reached out to smooth Joel's hair back, but the boy scooted against the wall.

Jacob sighed again. So much for trying to make things right. He rose and leaned against the bunk-bed frame. Mrs. Robertson had brought out quilts for them to use for mattresses and sheets to cover them. She'd promised to sew tickings to fill with hay as soon as the grass was tall enough to cut.

"Joel, son, I'm sorry." The words hung in the dimness, broken only by the twilight coming in through the open door. "I'm going to the outhouse. You go ahead and get ready for bed. The top bunk is yours." He waited a long moment, but when there was no response, he left, sucking in a deep breath of clean air as soon as he cleared the doorway.

The evening star hung in the west as he strolled out the path. A cow bellowed in the distance. Birds twittered in the branches of the cottonwood trees, settling for the night. He'd not fared at all well with the riding, let alone the roping and working with the cattle. Why would Mr. Robertson even keep him around?

When he returned he heard Joel breathing in the top bunk, an errant sob causing a hitch in the rhythm. He should have asked for a candle, but knowing the early time work would start, he needn't spend time reading anyway. He hung his clothes on the bed frame and slid under the covers. What a day they'd had.

~

"Don't you have any work clothes?" Mr.

Robertson stared at Jacob's pants and shirt in the dim morning light.

Jacob shook his head. "These are my work clothes." At least, he'd cut and split wood in them and dug up his garden.

"You're going to need something tougher than that."

"These will have to do for now."

"Can you milk a cow?"

"Yes, sir."

"Buckets are up to the springhouse. We have two milk cows. Ada Mae is bringing them up now. You take the Guernsey. Gotta watch her. She kicks some."

"You have any kickers?" Jacob asked.

"Kickers?"

"Guess not. I can make some if you want. The ones on our farm were a piece of chain to hook around each hock. A short chain connects the two."

"Maybe later. Tried hobbling her. You just need to grab that bucket as soon as you've finished. She puts her foot in real quicklike."

Jacob nodded.

"We eat after chores."

Jacob nodded again and headed for the rock building indicated. He brought both buckets and joined Ada Mae in the barn. She'd already poured a small mound of grain in front of each of the stanchioned cows.

"You sure you know how to milk?" She peered around her cow's haunches.

"Haven't for a long time, but I'm sure it will come back real quick." He took a three-legged stool from the peg on the wall and stopped behind the tan and white cow that stood with her udder bulging.

"Easy, boss." He patted her on the rump and set his stool in place. Ada Mae already had milk singing into the other bucket. As soon as he sat down, the cow shifted her back feet, her tail catching him on the ear. He set the pail between his knees and clasped the two far teats, squeezing and pulling in the age-old motion of cow milkers. Milk streamed into the bucket, playing counterpoint to the slosh of the other milker.

He nestled his forehead into her flank and inhaled the rich fragrance of fresh warm milk, cowhide, and barn.

"Remember to watch her. She twitches her tail just before trying to kick the bucket." The voice came from behind him.

"Thanks." He switched to the near teats, his hands remembering the drill without conscious thought. Surely there would have been a better way to tell Joel about his mother. He'd heard the boy crying during the night.

The cow's tail caught him across the back of his head at the same moment her near back foot caught the bucket and, in spite of his quick grab, sent it toppling. The barn cats leaped to get what they could. Jacob stifled the words he'd like to have used. They'd warned him. He heard a snicker from the other milker.

"She's quicker than a snake striking."

Jacob picked up the stool and hung it again on the peg. About a pint of milk, perhaps a quart, remained in the pail.

"Pour it in here, and I'll take them up." Ada Mae gave him a commiserating shrug. "She's done it to all of us."

Why would anyone keep a sly, sneaky cow like that? They should have turned her into stew meat. She'd be too tough for roasts. "She won't catch me again."

"Hope not."

Jacob went by the bunkhouse and rousted Joel up for breakfast. The boy's swollen eyes told their own tale, but when Jacob laid a hand on his shoulder, the boy flinched away. He walked behind Jacob up to the house.

"Joel, you can sit here." Virginia patted the chair between her and Ada Mae.

"Hear she got you," Mr. Robertson commented as he pulled his chair out.

"I'm sorry, I —"

"You'll be ready next time." That sounded like he'd be on the milking detail permanently in spite of the fiasco in the barn.

After grace not much was said, as everyone ate swiftly, passing the platters of ham and eggs and pancakes when asked.

One good thing, Jacob thought as he forked in sustenance, *we'll eat well here.* He hoped time would ease Joel's grief, and in the meantime he had the younger girls for company. All in all, perhaps coming west wasn't a bad move after all.

Or so he thought until he tumbled off the horse two hours later. He dusted himself off and watched the creature run back to the herd, stirrups banging his sides, spooking him further. What on earth had startled him, anyway? Or did horses in the West jump straight up in the air and buck on the way down just for pure ornery spite? Jacob glanced around to see who had witnessed his fall and caught Virginia turning away to hide what he knew was laughter.

"Go ahead. Laugh!" He dusted off his rear.

"You want me to go rope him again?"

I would rather bash him about the ears with a sturdy pole, but until I have my hands on those reins again, I have no alternative but to humiliate myself further. But he answered, "Yes, please." Robertson had given strict instructions that he was to learn to ride and rope and Virginia was to help him. The rope too was banging against the sides of the disappearing horse.

The young lady sighed. "I'll saddle up, then." She put two fingers in her mouth, and a piercing whistle floated across the meadow. A black-and-white horse raised its head and came trotting toward them. She whistled again, and the horse broke into a run.

"Opal taught me how to do that."

"Opal?"

"Opal Torvald. My best friend. The Harrisons are our nearest neighbors. She went to New York for a while, but she'll be back. She can train a horse better than anyone around here."

The pinto trotted up to them and nosed Virginia's pockets until the girl pulled out a cookie and rewarded her mount. She grabbed the horse's mane and led it over to the corral.

Jacob watched as she bridled and saddled her horse with a minimum of fuss, took a rope off the barn wall, mounted, and loped off toward the herd.

While he waited he wandered over to the well and pumped full the bucket that hung on the spout, then dipped out a drink, using the tin cup hanging on a hook attached to the pump side.

Since Mr. Robertson had included splitting wood on Jacob's list of duties, he headed for the chopping block and set to. At least he knew how to do this well.

He glanced over to see Joel and the two younger girls kneeling in the garden pulling weeds. A burst of laughter floated on the warming air. At least someone was having a good time.

Virginia led his horse up, and Jacob exchanged baleful looks with it.

"You got to show him who's boss."

I think he already knows. Jacob nodded. "Thanks." He mounted, gathered his reins, and with a little extra force, reined the brute around and headed back to the corral.

By the time the dinner bell rang, both he and the horse had worked up a fine sweat. But the horse now knew who was boss. At least for today.

While they ate, Mr. Robertson gave instructions for the afternoon work. "After we finish eating, we'll take the wagon and go on up the draw to bring back those corral poles we cut last winter. You know how to dig postholes?"

"Yes, of course."

"Good. I thought you could get started on the new corral. Got to sink the posts first. You'll find an extra pair of leather gloves in that box on the front porch."

Jacob glanced up to see Edith by his side.

"You want a refill on that coffee?"

"No thanks. I've had enough." Was that a blush or were her cheeks always that bright? Turning back, Jacob caught a calculating look on Mr. Robertson's face. *Don't worry, sir, I am not in the habit of falling for innocent young women. I can run faster than any of them.*

He needed to start running sometime later when, due to the sweat pouring from his body, he'd removed his shirt and hung it on a pole. Digging postholes was hot work, in spite of the breeze.

"Ah, Mr. Chandler."

Edith's hesitant voice made him grab for his shirt. *Idiot, you're not behind your little house where no one would come without an invitation.* He rammed his arms into the sleeves, which stuck to his wet skin and refused to budge. He heard the sound of fabric ripping and realized his face was now hotter than before, and it wasn't due to the sun. With his shirt finally in place, he turned to see her studying the ground, her cheeks shaded by the broad brim of her straw hat.

"Sorry. It was hot and, ah . . . I . . ."

"I thought you might be in need of refreshment, some liquid, a d-drink." She handed him the glass. He reached for it and bumped it instead, and the glass not only fell to the ground but shattered. She stared at him, down to the pieces, and back up.

"I'm sorry. So sorry." He knelt, she knelt, and their hands brushed in their haste to pick up the glass. "Please, let me do this."

She stood. "I'll go get more."

"No, please. I'll get a drink from the pump later. Where should I dump this?"

"Down the privy." She spun on her heel so fast her skirt swirled.

Jacob watched her go. How to embarrass a lovely young woman without even trying. *Jacob Chandler, this certainly is not one of your better days.*

He watched as a stranger on horseback

approached the house. He appeared to be no stranger to the family as he visited with Mrs. Robertson and rode out the way she pointed.

Jacob returned to his digging.

"You need some help setting those posts?" Ada Mae, his fellow milker, appeared at his side.

"I got one more to dig; then you can hold them straight while I fill in the holes."

"You dug 'em plenty deep. This ground sets up like rock once we water 'em in and the dirt dries."

Jacob slammed the posthole digger down, spread the two long handles, and pulled out the dirt to stack off to the side. It was about time to sharpen the digging end, but he wanted to finish first. Good thing the ground was still some wet, or he'd not have gotten near as far.

Robertson had shown him where the gate was to be and said they'd do six rails. That would make it too tall for a horse or a cow to be tempted to jump over.

He caught the sound of galloping horses and turned to see what was happening. The stranger and Mr. Robertson galloped across the meadow and slowed down as they neared the buildings.

"Uh-oh," Ada Mae said, looking at the riders.

"What?"

"Pa don't look too happy. Mr. Harrison neither."

While his curiosity itched, Jacob ignored it and walked over to the pile of posts. He grabbed one end of the peeled post, raised it, and plunked the other end down in the nearest hole. A resounding thud rewarded his efforts.

"Hold on to this, and —" He turned around to see his helper dashing up to the house. "So much for that." He dumped a shovelful of dirt in the hole and, using a heavy metal rod, tamped it in. He repeated dumping and tamping, working his way around the post, eyeballing it straight as he worked. When he got within six inches of the surface, he brought a bucket of water from the pump and filled the hole. After repeating his actions on the next post, he returned to the first, filled in the remaining dirt, and tamped it down. When he leaned against the post, it never moved.

Ada Mae skidded to a stop beside him. "Pa and Mr. Harrison are going looking for those drifters that beat up Atticus."

"I see." *Actually, I don't see, but no sense asking too many questions.*

She leaned a rifle down against the first upright post. "Pa said to keep an eye out for any strangers skulking around here." She nodded toward the rifle. "Just in case."

Jacob tamped the last shovelful in hard. Perhaps it was indeed important that he could shoot straight.

"He said to tell you the nails are in the barn for the rails. I know where." She waited until the next post thudded into a hole, then wrapped an arm around it to keep it straight. "Atticus near to died."

"Shouldn't the law take care of something like that?"

"The law?"

"You know, the sheriff, deputy, police."

She looked at him like he'd mumbled something in Latin. "There's no law but the good men out here. Unless you go clear to Bismarck. But there's no time for that."

"I see." So the stories he'd heard of the Wild West might be true? A posse did ride out after the bad guys? Who was Atticus, and what all had gone on before he arrived? "When will they come back?"

"When they catch them or lose them."

"I see. Lean that a bit to the right." He might not be much good in a posse, but he could build a solid corral. And keep an eye out. The thought of someone with violent tendencies watching the place raised the hair on the back of his neck. And he'd brought his son out here?

Chapter Twenty

"Opal, are you all right?"

Opal brought her mind back from dreams of the sun setting over Dakotah Territory, the shadows thrown in bizarre shapes, the river musing with the willows. "What?"

Alicia sat down beside her friend. "I asked if you are all right."

Opal attempted a nonchalant shrug, but her lower lip trembled, much against her will. She shut off thoughts of home and turned to smile at Alicia.

"You are looking lovely, as usual."

"Opal."

"You sound much like your mother."

"We care about you. You know that."

"I know. And you have all done so much for me, the lovely clothes, seeing the sights.

Taking me to the theater, the museums, our stay at the shore. I'll never forget our week there, but here we are in July."

"And you're homesick?"

"Yes." Opal wrapped her arms around her raised knees, sharing the bench beneath the weeping willow.

"Tell me more of your ranch in the badlands. It's such a strange name for a place that you see as beautiful." Alicia brushed a leaf from her skirt.

"The rocks are worn by wind and water into strange shapes, some like round houses with a capped roof, some like fingers pointing to the heavens. There are fires burning along underground coal deposits, and the rocks turn red like bricks where they've been heated. There's a prairie dog town, with acres of holes and burrows. One sits up as sentinel while the others find grasses and grains to eat. When he sees danger he whistles, and they all dive down in their holes. They're like fat chipmunks with skinny little tails that point straight up when they run."

"You love it there, don't you?"

"It's home. I never had a real home before, and there I do. Linc, one of our ranch hands, has taught me to train the horses, and I've never loved anything so much as that. It's like I can read their minds, and they can read mine. Horses are willing creatures, when you understand them, and loyal too. About as much as a dog."

"You have a dog too?"

"Her name is Ghost. She's a cow dog. Mostly she likes to watch out for Per. Ruby depends on Ghost to help keep Per out of trouble." Opal tipped back her head and stared up at the sun outlining the slender leaves in gold. "It's a harsh land, but when you look across the grass flowing before the breeze, you're sure it's a green ocean topped by a huge bowl of blue sky, a blue so bright you are sure there can be no other blue just like it. When a meadowlark trills, no song on earth could be more beautiful or more fitting."

"Is it hard for you to be here?"

Opal started to answer but caught herself, her eyes popping open. "Oh, no. I mean, how can I ever thank you for being so generous to me?"

Alicia, her eyes as gentle as the hand she used to pat Opal's, smiled. "We had hoped you would stay and go to school with us in the fall."

Opal dropped her gaze to her hands that had unconsciously clamped together. "I . . . I thank you for the invitation, but . . ." She swallowed hard, trying to get the words out. *I want to go home. Oh, dear Lord, I want to go home.*

"But you'd rather be home?"

"Please don't think me ungrateful."

"Opal?" The call came from the veranda at the back of the house.

"Back here, Jason, under the willow." Alicia leaned forward and gave Opal a hug. "Thank you."

"For what?"

"For giving me a glimpse of the land you love."

"Opal, you got a letter." Jason ducked through the trailing branches that hid them from the outside world. "Mother thought you would want it right away."

Alicia stood. "Come, Jason, let's let Opal read her letter in peace."

"It's from Ruby. I'll read aloud if you like. You'll learn more about my home that way."

Jason sank down on the leaf-and-twig-strewn ground, legs crossed, and Alicia resumed her place on the bench.

Opal slit the wax seal on the envelope and pulled out a sheet of paper. So many times she'd watched Ruby write letters while at Dove House. She'd even written some herself to the Brandons.

"Dear Opal,

I never realized how much I would miss you. No matter how busy Per is, I seem to be waiting always for you to call me from the porch and come bursting through the door. I hope and pray you are having a wonderful time. I'm sure you will have all kinds of stories to tell when you return."

Opal looked up with a grin. "Shall I tell her about Mr. Furstenburg?"

Alicia turned pink, and Jason trapped his chortles behind his spread hands. "His ears . . ." Jason rolled his eyes, then cupped his thumbs behind his own ears and spread his fingers.

"Jason, you are being rude. He can't help . . ." Alicia dissolved into giggles along with Opal. Charles Furstenburg had called on Alicia to ask her to walk with him in the park. He'd called only once.

When the three of them got over making sport of Mr. Furstenburg, Opal continued reading her letter.

"Per has grown inches in the weeks since you left. He tries to run, but his belly gets going faster than his feet, and he sprawls, usually over Ghost. That poor dog is so patient. She never growls at him, even when he pulls himself up by her ears."

"Ghost, what a funny name." Jason propped his elbows on his knees.

"She got that name because she is such a mottled gray and black and brown that she disappears into the long grass or into a shady place, and you won't even see her until she moves again." Opal sighed. "She's better than two cowboys at working the cattle."

"You weren't fooling when you described branding and roundup?" Jason dreamed of becoming a cowboy like his hero Teddy Roosevelt.

"Not at all. You should have seen Joe hustle when that old mama cow came after him. He let her calf go and ran for the fence. Took him three tries to get a brand on that baby." Opal chuckled at the memory.

"You ever been chased by one?"

"No, they won't let me work the ground, but I'd rather be on a horse any day." Opal returned to her letter.

"In answer to your question, Atticus is recovering very slowly. He still has fits at times and scares his family half out of their wits, but he doesn't have them so often now. We pray for his full recovery."

Opal cleared her throat. *Oh, Atticus, you have to pay for my foolishness.* She started to read again, stopped, cleared her throat, and sniffed.

"Roundup went really well. Rand is pleased at the calf crop — we lost so few to the winter. I am feeling much better. Thank you for your concern. Just part of life."

"Was Ruby sick?" Jason leaned forward.
"Ah, morning sickness. That's all." Opal stopped. That wasn't something young boys needed to know anything about. Having babies was not discussed in polite company. She glanced at Alicia for support.
"No, she's fine, like she says."
Opal turned the page over.

"The Robertsons have a new hand. A man from the East with a seven-year-old son. Virginia plans on writing to you. Her tales of teaching Mr. Chandler to ride and rope rival your own for humor. I must get back to work. I hear Per stirring from his afternoon nap. Haying will start in a week or so, and the Juneberries are now canned and made into jam. The peas are ready, and tonight we will have your favorite, creamed new potatoes and peas with ham. Greet the Brandons from me and tell them how much we would love to share our western world with them.

With all my love,
Your sister, Ruby."

Opal looked up from the letter. "She means it too. Maybe next summer you can come stay on the ranch, Jason, and become a real cowboy."

Jason propped his elbows on his knees. "Tell me more about the badlands. I read that there are rattlesnakes there."

Alicia shuddered. "Ugh, snakes."

Opal shared a smile with Jason. "True, we have rattlesnakes, but we also have bull snakes that eat a lot of gophers, and a funny one called a hognose snake. When you startle him, he rears up hissing and puffs out like an adder. I was scared near to death the first time I saw one." Opal shook her head at the memory. "But if you don't run away, this snake falls to the ground, belly up, mouth open, tongue hanging out, playing dead. You push on him, and he flops back again. I heard that someone tied one in a knot when it was playing possum and never even got bit."

"You're making that up."

"Nope. Cross my heart." She crossed and raised her hand. "You'd like the fawns, Alicia. They run on matchstick legs and leap so daintily."

Penelope's piano practicing floated out an open window. Opal thought back to Dove House and the piano she'd been learning on. One day she'd love to learn more. So many things had been lost in the fire catastrophe.

~

True, the new gown and short jacket were nowhere near as comfortable as her divided skirt and deerskin jacket, but since first Opal had no proper clothing, and then they'd gone to the shore, this Sunday morning all the family readied for church. Opal took an extra moment in front of the mirror to smile at the image she saw. The two tones of blue in the gored but full skirt reminded her of the bluebells that nodded in an early summer breeze across the prairie. The fitted jacket with leg of mutton sleeves and twin points on the lower front edge, all in a deeper hue, gave her a hint of womanhood. Her eyes seemed to sparkle more, and wearing her hair caught up on the sides with the wavy mass streaming down her back set off a tiny hat with a bit of a feather.

Was this really her?

"Must be." At the sound of her own voice, she knew for sure. *How I wish Ruby could see me now. She'd be pleased as punch.*

"Oh, Opal." Alicia and Penelope stopped in the doorway, then laughed at each other for saying the words at the same time.

"We need to be leaving to get to church on time," Mrs. Brandon called from the bottom of the stairway.

"Do you have a hanky in your bag?" Alicia asked.

"Now you really sound like Mother." Penelope swooped up the blue reticule that matched the jacket and slipped it over Opal's hand so that the drawstrings hid under the hem point that extended to the back of her hand. "You look just perfect."

"Thank you."

The three girls made their way down the stairs to where Mr. Brandon stood watching them, his smile of pride lighting his entire face.

"Delphinium, lemon lily, and pink peony — you three are a sight to behold."

"Thank you, Father." Alicia laid her hand on the arm he offered, leaving Opal and Penelope to giggle in her wake.

"Have any of you seen Bernie?" Mrs. Brandon stopped in the doorway. "Now, don't you all look lovely? Mrs. Davis surely did herself proud with those gowns."

"No. Haven't seen Jason either." Mr. Brandon raised his voice. "Now, boys, I don't care what you are doing, but we are leaving now."

"Coming." Jason thundered down the stairs.

"Where's Bernie?"

"This always happens when it is time to leave for church," Penelope whispered to Opal. "Bernie hates sitting still for ten minutes, let alone an hour."

Opal only nodded. *Me too.* But she didn't voice the thought. Since she was dressed like a young lady, she would have to act like one. Bernie thundered down the stairs just as his father started up to get him.

"Sorry." He ducked under his father's arm and flew out the door to scramble up on the seat next to the driver.

"You look lovely, miss," Mr. Klaus murmured as he assisted her into the coach.

"Thank you. No running races dressed like this, eh?"

"No, miss, but you better watch out for the young men."

She felt a blush heat up her neck and cheeks and finished settling herself in the seat. Young men, indeed.

"Opal, Miss Torvald, is that you?" Rupert stuttered in his greeting in front of the gray granite church.

She smiled, practicing a ladylike demeanor. "Hello, Rupert. Do you still have a pony?" Well she remembered his lack of generosity in sharing pony rides.

"No." His look said "Of course not" — easily done when looking down one's nose. "Now I have a jumper. I compete in shows and do some fox hunting in the fall."

"Really?" She'd hardly recognized him, but he'd grown into a rather striking young man. "That must be exciting. Most of our horses are trained for working cattle."

"You did get a horse, then?"

"Yes, and I train young horses for some of the ranchers near us."

"You must come to the stable and go riding with me."

Penelope took her arm. "We must go in now. Sorry, Rupert."

"You still don't like him much?" Opal whispered when they entered through the ten-foot-tall carved wooden doors. The organ swelled as they filed into the sanctuary, taking Opal's gaze clear up to the peak where the rose window broke the sunlight into iridescent jewels of every hue. So much time had passed since she'd been in a real church with an organ, a choir, and wooden pews.

The Shepherd's window backing the altar, with Jesus holding a lamb and other sheep surrounding His feet, made her think of home again.

She settled into the pew between Alicia and Penelope, blinking back tears. Had they come on because of the beauty of this house of God or because of homesickness for the school building that substituted for a church on Sunday back home? Ruby and Rand would be there, trying to keep Per quiet. Cimarron and Jed, Daisy and Charlie, the Robertsons, Linc and Little Squirrel with the other hands. Would Atticus be there? And his family? *Atticus, my dear friend. Father God, please make him well again.* The memories returned of his body arching on the bed, those guttural sounds he'd made, the thrashing of legs and arms. As they stood for the first hymn she clutched the back of the pew in front of her. *God, please. It's my fault, and I can't do anything about it.*

She held her half of the hymnal and tried to see the words through a veil of tears. If only she could go home, surely there was something she could do to make things easier for him.

She stumbled over the clog in her throat at the first words but then threw herself into the music as "Holy, Holy, Holy" lifted voices and hearts. ". . . Lord God almighty. Early in the morning our song shall rise to thee." Her voice soared on the high notes as she forgot herself and the mess she'd made for Atticus. She glanced to see why Penelope had stopped singing, only to catch openmouthed awe staring at her.

"What?"

"Your voice. Opal, your voice." They both turned back to the hymnal. "Holy, holy, holy, all the saints adore thee . . ." A hush fell after the final amen.

Opal remained standing for the opening prayer but dug in the reticule dangling from her wrist for the handkerchief she'd stuffed there. Her eyes needed mopping now.

Alicia handed her a hanky, passed over from her mother. Mrs. Brandon leaned around her daughter and, taking Opal's hand, drew her to her side and put an arm around her waist.

The tender touch, the beauty of the music, and the prayer all combined to make Opal weep even more.

I need to go home. Father God, please, I need to go home. She mopped her eyes and clamped her teeth against further tears, but in spite of her best efforts, the tears only slowed.

"It's all right," Mrs. Brandon whispered. "I often cry in church. Don't feel bad or embarrassed. It's all right."

Opal finally won the battle and gave Mrs. Brandon a watery smile. "Thank you." Her whisper was more a mouthing than a murmur, but the smile in return confirmed the hearing.

Did God hear as well as Mrs. Brandon? Or had He quit listening to her since she'd been so bad? Neither question did she dare ask. But she was sure God used to hear her. After all, Rand had brought her Bay, and now she had the filly too. Unless, of course, Rand sold her, which had been the original plan.

How strange it seemed to have a real minister stand up in front and preach instead of Charlie or Rand reading from the Bible. Every time she thought of home, the tears tried to get loose again, and her mind refused to pay attention. Something like in school. But that brought up another thought. Would Mr. Finch be back again? If only Pearl could or would go back to teaching, she, Opal, would want to stay in school, but not with Mr. Flinch, as the students dubbed him. Or she'd be in trouble all the time.

"Seventy times seven? You want me to forgive that many times? I can't even count that high."

As the minister's words broke through her musing, Opal's attention clicked back to the sermon.

"Aren't we a lot like Peter? And are we required to forgive someone who wrongs us seventy times seven? Now, I don't believe that God wants us to keep count, but as He forgives us over and over, so must we forgive others."

Not that drifter, God. You can't mean that. Why, he nearly killed Atticus, and Atticus is good through and through. Now, if he'd attacked me, that would make sense. But I don't see how I can forgive him for what he did to Atticus.

Opal joined in the final hymn. Singing always made her feel better.

~⁊

"What happened?" Alicia asked later after they'd eaten dinner and retired to their rooms to change into play clothes.

"I guess I got to thinking of home, and then I couldn't stop crying. I never had that happen before." Opal carefully hung her bluebell gown in the chifforobe. "That surely is a lovely gown." Her hand trailed down the fabric.

"And you looked lovely in it." Alicia propped herself against the bed pillows, her book on her lap. "Tell me about Atticus."

So Opal told her the entire story as she sat on the end of the bed, her arms hooked around her raised knees. "So you see, it is all my fault."

"No, it isn't. It's the drifter's fault. He chose to attack you. Men can't be allowed to act like that. That's what we have laws for."

"Not where we live."

"No wonder Ruby thought you would be safer here."

"There you are." Penelope and Jason

stood in the doorway. "You want to play croquet? Father is setting up the wickets."

"Sure." Opal scooted to the edge to stand up. "Thank you."

"Do you mind if I talk to Mother about this?"

"No. I'll tell her if she wants."

"Good. I guess things really are different out West."

"Well, one thing sure, we don't have any grass flat and smooth enough for croquet."

"What would you like to do today?" Alicia paused in the doorway to Opal's room.

Opal looked up from the letter she was writing. "I'd like to take the trolley all over."

"A trolley rather than the carriage?"

"Yes. All the way down to the Battery. And I'd like to see as much of the Statue of Liberty as possible."

"Let me ask Mother." Alicia turned, then paused and said over her shoulder, "It's going to be hot today and sometimes the smells . . ." She shuddered delicately.

"Thanks." Opal dipped her pen in the ink and continued describing the electric lights and the huge buildings ten and twelve stories tall here in New York City.

Higher than the bluffs behind the house, I think. But, Ruby, there are people everywhere here. They remind me of our herds of cattle at roundup time. They pour off the ferries and the trains. We walked across the Brooklyn Bridge yesterday. There's a special layer for pedestrians; the traffic flows along eighteen feet below. It is one of the marvels of modern construction with huge towers and steel cables. Jason gets all sparkly eyed when he talks about it. He has studied the building of it extensively. I think that's what he would like to do someday, after he becomes a cowboy, that is. Working at his father's firm is not what he wants to do forever.

She stopped and gazed out the window. A tall elm tree sent shadows dancing on her floor. At home she could look out her window and see the waving grasses and sometimes a deer at the edge of the brush. A sigh escaped before she could catch it. Lovely as this room was with its light green embossed wallpaper and matching curtains and bedspread, she'd take the cold floor with the bearskin rug by her bed any day. She'd just signed the letter with an admonishment to Ruby to hug Per for her and not let him forget who she was when Penelope rushed into the room.

"We're all going on the trolley like you want, and Mrs. Klaus is packing a picnic basket. You have the best ideas." She stopped by the tall carved post of the bed. "Maybe tomorrow we could go play lawn tennis again."

Opal groaned. She'd rather lasso cattle any day. If she'd been able to wear her divided leather skirt, the game might have been fun, but in the skirt and petticoats and drapes they all wore, why, it was lucky someone didn't fall and break something.

They took the elevated train down to the Battery District and stared out across the river to Fort Wood on Bedloe Island, where the Statue of Liberty's granite pedestal could be seen with an iron framework rising above it. While she'd seen pictures of the various pieces of the gift from the people of France, the size of it made her shake her head.

"It's going to be taller than the buildings."

"I know." Mrs. Brandon stood beside her, Alicia on the other. "When I read the poem that Emma Lazarus wrote to help raise money for this project, I weep for joy. It is so fitting a picture of our country.

'Give me your tired, your poor, your huddled masses yearning to breathe free.' "

Alicia added, " 'The wretched refuse of your teeming shore. Send these, the homeless, tempest-tossed to me. I lift my lamp beside the golden door.' "

"That sounds mighty fine, but there's a lot more room for those immigrants out West than there is here, let me tell you."

Mrs. Brandon laughed and, shaking her head, put an arm around Opal's shoulders. "Leave it to you, my young realist, but here is where most of the jobs are."

"True, but we have free land for those willing to work hard enough to homestead it." Opal stared upriver, where ships lined the docks like piglets at a sow. People and cargo came off those ships every day, then other wares were loaded on, and the ships left again. She stared down at the water, the sheen of oil on top, floating boxes, barrels, and bottles, the water a sluggish gray. *Uff da,* as Ruby so often said. One surely would never swim in this water. She'd take the muddy Little Missouri any day.

On the trolley ride home the emaciated face of a little girl digging in the trash haunted Opal. There was a lot of money in New York to be sure, but people were starving just the same. Wasn't there something that could be done about that? She wished she could have given the child the food left in the picnic basket. One thing she knew for certain. She preferred the vast open spaces of Dakotah Territory over this teeming city of New York.

At supper that evening the discussion came around to Theodore Roosevelt.

"I know him," Opal said. "He's a fine gentleman, a good cowboy too."

"You know Mr. Roosevelt?" Jason stared at Opal, his eyes taking up his whole face.

"Yes. He has been to our house for supper several times. He showed me the pictures he'd drawn of our prairie hens and grouse. He really likes our part of the country and said that toughening up to become a cowboy and hunter saved his life. He likes to write and draw, and he loaned me one of his books."

Jason looked from Opal to his father. "Can you believe that?"

"Well, his ranch, the Maltese Cross, borders ours. Not that we own the grazing land, just that around the ranch house."

"Do you realize who he is?" Mr. Brandon looked over his glasses.

"Well, I know he is from New York and he comes back here a lot. I think he'd rather stay in Dakotah Territory, though."

"I've heard there are some who want him to run for mayor of this city." Mr. Brandon tapped his coffee cup to signal a refill by the maid.

"I like the way he writes of the West." Jason propped his elbows on the table but jerked them back at the sound of his father clearing his throat. "He goes hunting all the time. And does roundup, like you do." He smiled at Opal. "I would give my right arm to ride in a roundup."

"You wouldn't be much good without a right arm." Opal kept a straight face. "But I can teach you to rope if you want." *If I'd only brought my rope.* "And riding out there is as different from riding in the park as walking is from riding the train."

Jason shook his head. "I don't care. I want to try."

"We'll see" was the only answer his father gave, no matter how imploring the looks.

That night Opal woke in the darkness, her pillow wet from her tears. "I'm turning into a crybaby," she muttered as she turned the pillow over and slammed it into shape. "I've got to get back home soon."

Chapter Twenty-One

"Rand, did I do the right thing?"

Rand rolled over and tugged his wife up next to his heart. "I thought you agreed not to worry about this anymore. What's done is done, and after we prayed about it, *we*" — he emphasized the *we* — "decided that a trip to New York would be good for her in lots of ways."

"But she is so homesick."

"When I'm gone from here, I am too. I count the minutes until I can be home again." He brushed wisps of honeyed hair back from her brow and then smoothed away the furrows digging into her creamy skin.

She closed her eyes, and the slightest of smiles lifted the corners of her mouth. Rand leaned down and kissed her, the kind of kiss that promises love forever.

Hesitant to let his lips go, Ruby threaded her fingers through his hair and tugged to bring him close again.

"Oh, Mr. Harrison, you do know how to chase away my worries."

"At least for the moment." He kissed the spot where the furrows had been. "We'll bring her home soon. I was more worried about her wanting to stay there. The Brandons have a lot to offer that we don't."

"Perhaps if you shipped her horse back there . . ." Ruby nipped his chin. "But if you think of doing that, I might have to resort to firmer measures."

~�æ

Rand listened to the rooster creak out his first announcement of the approaching dawn. The second cleared his rusty pipes, and the third reached troubadour quality.

"Time to get up."

"I know, and I can never tell you how grateful I am to be over the morning sickness. Even bacon tastes good again."

"I'm glad. I was missing it." Rand stepped into his pants and went to stand at the window.

Ruby watched him welcome the dawning of a new day. Seldom did he take time to pause, instead charging ahead from one chore to the next. The brightening light outlined his strong shoulders and trim waist. He stretched his arms, hands locked high above his head, then wiggled his shoulders.

Thank you, Father, for such a man as Rand. She heard Little Squirrel in the kitchen and knew she should rise. A robin's song echoed another raise-the-dawn order from the rooster. *Lord, please protect this bit of your heaven.* She pushed away the thought of the drifter and went to wrap her arms around her husband's middle, laying her cheek against his naked back. He crossed his hands over hers and squeezed her arms into his ribs with his.

"All will be well."

"Please God."

"No. We have to believe that or the enemy will have won. He likes nothing better than to get God's children on the run."

Ruby inhaled the scent that was Rand. "How did you get so wise?"

"I read His book. He says to stand against the evil one, and that is just what we are doing. Taking a stand against evil."

"Ma?"

"What's he doing awake?"

"Greeting the dawn like the rest of us." Rand turned and dropped a kiss on her nose. "Unhand me, woman, so I can go forth."

"To the outhouse?"

"Show some respect." He pulled on his boots, snagged a shirt off a peg, and stuffing his pocket watch into his pocket, headed out the door.

Ruby dressed and tied a clean apron about her thickening waist. At the rate she was growing, she might have twins inside. The thought brought a smile on one hand and stark terror on the other. How would she ever keep up with two like Per?

She swooped into his room and untied the belly harness that kept him in bed. Without it he'd be out and into things in the middle of the night. Or out the door. Ever since he could walk, he lived life at a run.

"Ma." Multiple sounds. "Da." More gibberish.

Ruby needed someone to translate. Obviously Per thought she should understand.

He repeated "ma" and what sounded like the same lingo he'd spouted before.

"Sorry, little man, but you'll have to speak more clearly if you want me to understand. And saying it louder won't help either." She kissed his chipmunk cheeks and pulled up the wool soaker over a clean diaper. It would be nice for him to be trained before the new baby came.

She set him on her hip and headed for the kitchen.

Rand walked in with Joe behind him.

"Where did you see him?" A frown furrowed Rand's brow.

"At Williams' last night."

"And no one in Little Missouri had the common courtesy to send him on his way? Or lock him up?"

"Didn't appear so. Them squatters don't get much sympathy when something goes wrong for *them*."

"They aren't squatters. They have as much right to the land as the ranchers."

"You know that's not what others believe."

"I know. Grab something to eat, and go get Robertson. I'll send Linc over to get Charlie and Hegland. Perhaps by the time we get to town, they'll be sleeping off a drunk."

"Here." Little Squirrel handed Joe two pieces of bread hiding a thick slice of ham. She had another for Linc when he came through the door. By the time the two men

305

rode out, Chaps had brought in the pail of fresh milk, and Beans had announced that the rest of the horses were saddled and ready.

Breakfast was a hurried affair with no conversation other than "please pass" and "thank you."

"What do you plan to do with them when you catch them?" Ruby finally asked the question that had been ricocheting around her mind.

"Take them to Bismarck to the law."

"Riding?"

"No. On the train." Rand wiped his mouth, then stood and strode to the gun cabinet where he kept the rifles and ammunition. He handed one to each of the men, along with a supply of shells.

"Make sure you fill your canteens. I hope we get them in town, but who knows."

Please, Lord, bring them all home in one piece. Ruby couldn't force food past the lump in her throat. And here she'd been rejoicing to be over the morning heaves.

"Don't waste your time worrying, but you might send up a prayer or two." Rand kissed her and headed out after the others.

"Pa?" Per banged his spoon on the table.

"Call Ghost," Rand told Ruby.

Ruby went to the door and called the dog away from the horses. "Good girl. You take care of Per today."

Ghost looked over her shoulder one last time, then followed Ruby into the house.

"I go hoe the garden." Little Squirrel headed out the back door, leaving Ruby to finish the dishes and strain the milk. She took that out to the springhouse and returned with the older cream to churn into butter. She filled the wooden churn half full and set it in front of a chair out on the back porch. Fastening the gate in place, she brought a sack of wood scraps out for Per to play with and started the churning. The paddle beat and swished. A breeze blew tendrils of hair on her neck and two sparrows scrabbled in the crab apple tree at the corner.

A perfect day, other than the fact that the men were out seeking destruction.

"Please, Lord, bring them all home safe. 'I will lift up mine eyes unto the hills, from whence cometh my help. My help cometh from the Lord, which made heaven and earth.' Lord God, be thou our deliverance, our strong right hand. Fight the battle for them."

"Ma?" More gibberish followed, then

"Opa?" Per leaned against her knee.

"I know. I miss Opal too." She slammed the paddle a little harder as the forming butter made it heavier. She leaned over and kissed the top of Per's head.

He rubbed his eyes with his fists, a sign that he was tired.

"Ready for a nap already?" She felt his forehead with the back of her hand. Sure enough, it was warm to the touch. What else could be going wrong?

Chapter Twenty-Two

Rand looked at the men assembled and ready to go. Everyone was accounted for.

"You all be careful now." Daisy stood on the porch while Charlie mounted up.

"Don't you go worrying." Charlie tipped his hat back. "All we're goin' to do is rope those two worthless hides and haul 'em in to the law."

Ward Robertson shook his head. "My wife said the same thing. I'd have brought my new hand, but we'd have to wait for him to catch up. He's got a ways to go yet on his ranching skills."

"All right," Rand said. "We'll wait this side of the river and let Chaps wander in and see if those two are still in Little Misery. Hopefully we can surround the town and take them down." He looked around the circle to see if all agreed. With their nods, he reined Buck around and headed out.

Once in Medora they mingled with the traffic on the streets while Chaps headed across the ford to Little Missouri, or what was left of it since Dove House burned down. The livery had moved across the river into Medora, and Mr. Nelson had closed his store so he could go work in the abattoir.

Rand waited in the shade of the general store, arms crossed on the saddle horn. While Chaps was the one most likely to not cause a stir, Rand hated waiting. Too many things could go wrong. Perhaps they should have just gone in together. There was a good chance the two had moved on again.

After what seemed like hours, Chaps came jogging back as if he had not a care in the world.

"The snakes went out the back way. They're heading downriver."

Rand raised a gloved hand to signal the others and jogged back to the main street, heading out of town. "Do they know we're on to them?"

"I think so. You know Williams. He'll do anything to cause trouble."

"Shame we didn't put someone out in the back field." Rand called himself a name for not thinking of it. "Did you hear them leave?"

"No, they snuck out real quietlike."

"They probably think they're safe. Charlie, why don't you take Linc and Robertson, go on out past that big snag and see if we can scare them into one of the box canyons. Joe, you climb on up the butte and see if you can see them. We'll go real slow, so as not to spook them."

With the plans in action, the men rode without talking, keeping down the dust that could give them away.

Joe slipped back into the group. "They're about a mile ahead. Seem to be taking their time."

Rand pulled his pocket watch out and checked the time. "The others can't be in position yet." They slowed to a walk for the next fifteen minutes, then Rand nodded. "Now remember, no shooting unless they shoot first."

They picked up the pace.

A single rifle shot announced the others were in position.

"Here we go." *Please, Lord God, make this work.*

Coming around a rock face, he saw the

two ahead by less than half a mile now. They looked back and kicked their mounts into a gallop, suddenly veering to the right, away from the river.

"They saw Charlie. We got 'em."

"Don't they know that draw don't go nowhere?"

"Guess not. Unless their horses are half mountain goat."

The two groups formed up and followed the drifters into the box canyon, stopping to dismount as soon as they saw the riderless horses.

With all of them taking cover, Rand waited, then hollered to the drifters. "You might as well come on out. You got nowhere to go."

A rifle shot was the only answer.

"We can wait as long as you want."

A bullet pinged off a rock.

"Keep your heads down," Rand told his men. He turned to Chaps. "Make sure you watch those buttes so they don't try climbing out."

They waited, each finding a spot of shade and hunkering down.

"You got a better chance with the law," he called. "I'll take you there myself."

One of the drifters yelled a couple of obscenities and wasted another shell.

"Such talk. What would your mama say?" Rand leaned against a boulder, cleaning his fingernails with the tip of his knife. "What say you throw out your guns and come out nice and easy. We don't want any bloodshed."

A volley of shots answered him.

"Sounds like you're gettin' to 'em," Charlie called from his hiding place.

"They don't have the brains God gave a goat. Worthless, that's all," Joe answered loud enough for the men on the run to hear.

The sun beat down. The canyon heated up.

"I din't do nothing. I'm comin' out," one of the drifters called.

"Throw your rifle out first."

Metal clattered against rock.

Rand glanced above his cover to see one man with his hands in the air rising from behind a rock. "Come on down, nice and easy."

"Don't shoot."

"Don't aim to."

Rand started to step out but thought the better of it. Two shots came in quick succession. A grunt came from the right. The man dropped behind some rocks.

"Bullet ricocheted. Robertson's been hit."

Rand closed his eyes and groaned. A freak accident. He ducked around the rock and darted to where Ward Robertson lay slumped over, blood pumping from the side of his neck.

Rand clapped his hand over the wound. "Hang on, man. God, help us."

"T-tell Cora I-I'm sorry." Ward crumpled in his arms.

"Godspeed, my friend." Rand laid his neighbor on the ground, fighting a rage that burned red before his eyes. Random shots were returned as the two penned-in miscreants fired back. *Not Robertson, Lord.*

Get them, his insides shrieked.

He fought to keep reason. *Let the law deal with them.* "We —" Rand had to clear his throat to make his voice heard. "We aren't a vigilante posse here, boys."

"They killed a good man. What do you mean, take 'em in? Hanging's too good for them."

"You know the law." *How will I tell his wife? And the girls? God, a stupid accident.*

A scream came from up the canyon.

"One down."

"Stop your fire."

"There he goes." One shot brought the

314

man down from his escape attempt up what must have been a game trail.

Silence fell on the draw.

"Should we go get them?"

"Be careful. One might still be alive. If so, we'll take him in."

Guns at the ready, the men made their way from rock to rock.

"This one's still alive."

"This one's gone."

They brought in the one body, and two men half dragged the other.

"Tie them on their horses." Rand gave orders, but all the while his heart lay in the dust with Ward Robertson.

"Sorry, Boss." Chaps shook his head. "Bullet hit the rock and did a ninety degrees to hit him. Can't believe it."

"Yeah, well, help me get him up on Buck, and I'll ride behind him." The temptation to leave the wounded man to his fate in the rocks ate at him like a starving badger.

How was he to live with himself anyway? Would this make any difference?

"Charlie, take him into town."

"Going to treat that bullet hole?"

"Someone wrap a kerchief around it." Two men held Robertson upright, and Rand swung up behind him. "Let's go."

"I'll take him on to Bismarck." Carl Hegland rode beside Rand.

"Go ahead if you want."

The road to the Robertson ranch was the longest ride of Rand's life.

"Oh, dear God, no." Mrs. Robertson flew off the porch as soon as she saw them. "Is he . . . ?"

"Yes, near to instant. A ricocheted bullet hit him. I'm so sorry."

"And the drifters?"

"One dead and one wounded."

Chaps dismounted to help lower Ward to the ground.

"Bring him in here." Dry-eyed and stone-faced, Mrs. Robertson led the way.

The girls clustered together, weeping and holding one another.

Jacob came in through the door right behind them. "Is there anything — ?" He stopped when Rand shook his head.

"Lay him on the table."

The men did as Cora said.

"I'll bring a box by in the morning," Rand said. "My boys will dig the grave. You tell us where."

"I don't know. Let me be for a while, then I can make some decisions."

"You want the girls to come home with me?"

"No, Ma, we'll stay here." Virginia stepped forward, tears streaming down her cheeks.

Ada Mae flew across the room to her mother. "Don't let them put Pa in the ground."

"Hush now. We'll talk in a bit." Rand motioned to the men to follow him.

"I'll dig the grave as soon as she tells me where." Jacob stopped by the horses. "I'll help her all I can."

"Good. I'll bring the box soon as we can get it nailed together."

"I cannot do it." Jacob stamped the shovel in the ground again, certain that any moment he would hit rock and have to begin again, for the third time. "I should volunteer to conduct this funeral, but if I do, they'll know." He tossed the shovel of dirt on the growing pile. *Lord, I told you I can never be a pastor again.* Right, a shepherd who can't find his own way, let alone lead a flock.

But my flock needs a shepherd. Did you think I did not bring you here for a reason?

You didn't bring me here. I ran. I ran from you, from my calling, from my people.

He tossed a shovelful on the growing pile. *All because I could not control my baser instincts. Say the truth, man. It was carnal desire. And a woman died because of me.*

Amazing how anger and fury dug even a gravesite with dispatch. He stomped the shovel in deeper. If only he could clear the debris from his heart and soul as well as he did the dirt for the grave.

And then bury the detritus of his life as they would the fine man who should not have died yesterday.

Lord, you make no sense. And here I am yelling at you again when I swore I would not. I would not yell. I would not pray. He leaned on the shovel handle. *And so, I cannot rejoice. I have no right.*

A meadowlark took wing, spilling drops of joy as he flew.

"Come unto me, all ye that labor and are heavy laden, and I will give you rest."

Jacob stared at the hole that surrounded him. Nearly hip high. He'd paced out six feet. Ward Robertson had been just under six feet, all muscle and sturdy rectitude. But with a heart big enough to welcome a man on the run and ask no questions other than *"Can you ride? Rope? No, then what can you do?"*

I can build. Jacob looked to the finished

corral. *And I can bury. No, I can dig the hole, but I cannot say the words.*

You can.

But then they'll know.

Is that so bad? I am the Good Shepherd, and I have appointed you.

All right. Just this once.

A crow flew over, his caw sounding more like a chuckle. The breeze giggled with the oak leaves.

Jacob scraped the floor of the grave flat, then using his shovel as a post, climbed out. He stuck the shovel in the top of the mound and headed back down toward the house.

Mrs. Robertson had been baking and cooking since dawn or long before. Had she slept at all?

Jacob entered the kitchen. "I finished."

"Thank you." She wiped her eyes with the back of her hand, leaving a streak of flour on her cheek for the tears to track through.

"Ah . . ." He sighed.

She glanced up from rolling pie dough. "Yes?"

"I'll conduct the service for you if you like."

"You've done that before?"

"Yes, a few."

"Thank you. Could you mention that no one bears the guilt of him dying the way he did? The Lord just figured it was his time. There's a verse to that effect, isn't there? I couldn't find it, but I know I've heard it."

"Yes, Psalm 139 assures us that God knows the length of our days. He knows our going out and our coming in."

"Good. If you'd read that, I'd be most grateful."

"What will you do? About the ranch, I mean."

"Keep on. Neighbors will help. The girls and I will learn to do more. Are you in a hurry to go somewhere else?"

"No."

"Good. Then you'll learn too, and we'll make do."

"I'll get on with the milking, then."

"The girls have already gone out. We know how to do the home things. When Opal comes back she'll be over here to help too. Now, there's someone we need to be praying for. She's going to take on all the fault for this. If God thought we needed to live under fault and guilt all the time, He wouldn't have bothered to send us His Son, leastways that's the way I understand it."

Jacob watched her lay the pie dough in

the pan, rolled just the right size so as to lap over the sides only a little. All the while she uttered the most profound faith he'd heard in a long time. Was that what he was doing? Laboring under guilt and blame instead of . . . He turned and left the house. Sounded like he and Opal had a lot in common.

~✂

Friends and neighbors gathered the next afternoon to bury Ward Robertson on a slight knoll north of the house. An oak tree shaded the plot.

After reading Psalm 139, Jacob continued. "Lord God, we commend our brother to your most merciful care, trusting that you have set the length of our days before we were even born. Believing in your divine goodness and your grace, which gives us the courage to go on living in a world gone awry with sin. Your grace sent your Son to die that we might live. Ward Robertson now walks with you in your kingdom of light. May we rejoice for him as we lay his earthly remains into the ground from which we came. Ashes to ashes, dust to dust, until we meet again in paradise. Please pray with me. 'Our Father which art in heaven . . .' "

The age-old words drifted upward as incense on the breeze, a sacrifice of faith through the veil of tears.

After the amen Jacob lifted his arms. " 'The Lord bless thee, and keep thee. The Lord make his face shine upon thee, and be gracious unto thee. The Lord lift up his countenance upon thee, and give thee peace.' In the name of the Father, and of the Son, and of the Holy Spirit. Amen."

Silence reigned for a time as eyes were wiped. Finally Mrs. Robertson spoke. "Please come to the house for coffee and the food we have all prepared. Mr. Robertson was a quiet man, but he loved all of us and loved sharing what we had." Cora Robertson wrapped her arms around her daughters and led the way down the gentle slope.

Jacob took one shovel and, with a toss, dirt thudded down on the box. Rand took another, and the pile diminished swiftly.

"I got a feeling there is more to you than an ordinary ranch hand." Rand dumped another shovelful on the mound.

Jacob leveled the dirt by standing on the edge now, the grave nearly filled. Was the hole within him being filled at the same time?

Chapter Twenty-Three

Opal's fingers shook as she opened the letter.

"Why are you afraid?" Penelope sat cross-legged on the grass, one of the baby bunnies nibbling a clover stem in her lap.

Opal closed her eyes. *I'm not afraid. Yes, I am. I am terrified Ruby will say I cannot come home, that I have to stay here.*

Guilt from her lack of gratitude weighted her shoulders. The Brandons had been nothing but good to her, and still all she could think of was home — and Atticus. He had not answered her letters.

She pulled the paper from the envelope and unfolded it. All her tension released on a sigh.

"You're going home."

"How do you know?"

"Your face. I haven't seen you smile like that since you got here."

Opal closed her eyes again, and with top teeth clamping her bottom lip, she shook her head. "I'm sorry I've not been a better guest."

"You've been a fine guest. It's just that I remember you laughing all the time and making me think anything could be all right if Opal thought so."

"Thank you, dear sister."

"You're the same age as me, you know. But since you came back, you seem older than Alicia."

Opal glanced back at her letter. Now that she knew she was about to receive a reprieve, she could well afford to wait.

"Go ahead and read it. We all want to know what is happening in Dakotah Territory."

Opal did, skimming the letter. "Oh no."

"What?"

"Mr. Robertson was shot and killed in a . . . a . . ." Her voice refused to work. *The drifters. All my fault. Atticus beaten up, now Mr. Robertson killed. All my fault.* She forced herself to finish reading. One of the drifters was dead, the other badly wounded but now in the Bismarck jail. And no news of Atticus. She let the letter fall in her lap, her initial joy overwhelmed by the tragic news.

"Opal, what is it? Opal?" Penelope shook Opal's hand.

Opal heard her call as if from across the river or a butte. "I-I'm fine. Really I am."

"Here." Penelope handed her the pink-nosed bunny and leaped to her feet. "I'll be right back."

Opal cuddled the softest creature imaginable under her chin. The whiskers tickled, but she ignored that, concentrating on the little heart beating beneath her fingers. The baby sniffed her fingers and up the tender skin of her throat and chin.

How will the Robertsons manage without their pa? They don't have hired hands like Rand does. Haying must be starting now.

"Opal, dear, what is it?" Mrs. Brandon knelt on the grass beside her.

Opal slowly turned her head, blinking to make sure she recognized the woman backlit by the sun.

"Mr. Robertson, our neighbor, was shot and killed when they cornered the two drifters."

"The two drifters?" She laid a tender hand on Opal's shoulder.

"The ones who beat Atticus near to

death." *The one who tried to attack me.*

"Oh, dear God." Mrs. Brandon sank down and gathered Opal into her arms. "You poor darling."

The comforting arms, the sweet-smelling headrest, and the stroking hands all combined, and Opal disintegrated in tears.

"It's all my fault. All of it is all my fault. Just because I went swimming." She rambled on, half the time incoherent, other times the sobs drowning any words she tried to utter.

Mrs. Brandon rocked her, murmuring mother things, bits of love and snatches of comfort that came from a well of mother love, ready always to bind up the broken-hearted.

"Go get us something cool to drink," she instructed Penelope.

Penelope dashed away tears of compassion as she jumped up. "And a cold cloth?"

"Yes, dear." Mrs. Brandon settled herself more comfortably and smoothed back the strands of hair that tears glued to Opal's cheeks.

The sobs lessened, tending more to sniffs and cries that caught in the throat.

"Here." Penelope handed her mother the cold cloth.

Mrs. Brandon laid it across Opal's eyes.

"Just rest now, and then we'll talk."

Opal nodded and caught her breath on a leftover sob. The cushioning grass felt cool beneath her. "The bunny. Where's the bunny?" She pushed upright, horror sending panic clear to her fingertips.

"There, in your skirt. Penelope, take it."

"Oh, I might have killed the bunny too."

"Here, drink this." Mrs. Brandon put the glass in her hands. "Drink."

Opal gulped the tart lemonade. She set the glass down in the grass and used the cloth to mop her face. When a hankie appeared near her hand, she used that too.

"Now are you ready to talk?"

"I-I guess."

"I gather from what you've said and from what little Ruby wrote to me that you feel responsible for all the rough and cruel things that men have been doing in Medora."

"Well, not everything, but . . . well . . . what has happened since I went swimming that day. If I'd —"

"Opal, dear, we can say 'if I' did this or didn't do that, things would be different, but what you did was an innocent thing, a —"

Opal interrupted her. "Would your girls

have gone swimming in a river all by themselves?"

"Would that they could have. How I
envy the freedom you've had out there."

"Really?"

"Really. When I was young, I would have
gone to Africa or China had God called
me there. I dreamed of adventuring in Cal-
ifornia or sailing the open sea."

"You did?" Opal sniffed and stared at
the same time.

"I did, but life doesn't always give us
what we dream of, and we learn to enjoy
what we have and are. That's part of being
the kind of Christian Paul talks about.
Being content with what we have."

"But I thought, I mean you . . ."

"Oh, I like nice things. I try to be the
best mother and wife I can be. I like order
and beauty around me. But life here can be
very circumscribed, as you well know.
Now, let's get back to you."

"But if I had stayed in school that day —"

"Opal, dear. That was an innocent action. True, you might have been more
careful, but that man chose to sin against
you. That is where the fault lies."

"I could have handled it differently. I
goaded him."

"Yes, you might have done differently, but

328

we can never go back and undo what we did. We learn from our errors and go on. God does not want you to haul this burden of guilt around for the rest of your life."

"But —"

"Did you tell those men to go out and beat Atticus within an inch of his life?"

"No."

"Of course not. And the men went out to keep those two criminals from committing more violence. That too was beyond your control."

"I still wish I had shot him at the time."

"That, my dear Opal, is what is within your control."

"But it is too late."

"I know. And I will thank God for the rest of my life that you don't have to carry the burden of killing a man."

"So what do I do?"

"You go home, and you help the Robertsons deal with their grief. You comfort Atticus, if he will let you, and you strive to listen for God's direction in everything you do."

Opal sat up and turned to face Mrs. Brandon. "You think He'd tell me?"

"Oh yes. In His Word and in your heart. God our Father loves you, Opal dear. He always has, and He always will.

On that I will stake my life."

Mrs. Brandon leaned forward and cupped her hand around Opal's cheek and jawline. "I will miss you, my dear. I was hoping you could learn to be happy here again and go to school with my children, but I know God has something special for you to do back home. I do see how much you love it there."

"You'll come to visit?"

"I would love to. Perhaps next summer."

Mrs. Klaus came out and set a tray on the table between the two loungers. "I brought some more lemonade and cookies."

Mrs. Brandon stood and helped Opal to her feet. "Come, let's enjoy our treat, and then we will help you pack."

~✴

The next morning the Brandons waved her off at the train. They were sending her home with an entire trunk of new clothes and gifts for the family.

"Thank you." Opal hugged Mrs. Brandon one last time. "I can never tell —"

"Just let it all go, my dear. It is over." She leaned back and cupped Opal's face in her gloved hands. "There is always a place for you here, though I doubt Ruby will let you leave again."

"No, with two little ones, she will really have her hands full. And besides, I need to teach Per to ride."

"He just learned to walk."

"Oh, he runs already, and you should see him on horseback. You'd think he could fly the way his arms get to going so fast." Opal hugged Jason, or at least as much as he could stand. "Remember, you are spending part of next summer on the ranch. You might even get to meet your hero."

"And you'll send me a rope so I can practice up?"

"Yes. Wish I'd brought mine so you'd have a head start. If you see Mr. Roosevelt, greet him for me."

Lastly she hugged Alicia and then Penelope, who burst into tears. "I so wanted you to stay and go to school with us," she said, wiping her eyes. "But I know how you love the ranch and need to go home. You'll write to us?"

Her own eyes wet, Opal gave Penelope an extra squeeze. "Yes. And you write to me too."

She looked over her shoulder and waved one last time before entering the railcar and finding a seat by the window so she could wave even more. Now that she was truly on her way home, she could feel sad that she was leaving. And appreciate more what the Brandons had done for her.

But the train could not go fast enough to suit her.

~✗

Several days later, on July 31, 1886, she stood in the doorway as the train pulled into Medora, brakes screeching and steam billowing. If she hadn't had all those skirts in the way, she'd have leaped down before it fully stopped. Instead, she waited for the conductor to put the step in place and assist her down. Her teal blue traveling gown had a slight bustle with the front skirt in a straight panel falling just to the tops of her fine leather boots. She'd just put the jacket back on, since even moving, the train felt like an oven. The tiny boat-shaped hat nestled in the waves of her hair, and a feather swooped backward.

"Opal, is that really you?" Rand held Per in one arm.

"Per?" Opal stopped at the sight of Per hiding his head on his pa's shoulder. "He's forgotten me."

"No. He just doesn't recognize you dressed so lovely." Ruby gave her little sister a long hug, then stepped back to look at her again. "We sent them a girl, and they returned a young lady to us. Opal, you look like you stepped right out of the pages of *Godey's Lady's Book.*"

"Wait until you see the rest of the things. I don't know where I'll ever wear them out here." She dug in her reticule and pulled out a packet of peppermint drops. "Think this will bribe him?" She handed it to Per. "Candy. Put it in your mouth."

He did so, then pulled it out again and waved it in the air, a grin buckling his cheeks. One swipe caught his father on the cheek.

"Get that in my mustache, young fellow, and we will have a serious discussion."

"That's my trunk over there."

Rand handed Per to Ruby. "You take him. I'll get the trunk."

Per on her hip, Ruby linked arms with Opal. "I'll never be able to tell you how much I missed you."

"They want me to come back. I think at least Jason will come here next summer. I have to send him a rope with instructions. I can see him roping Mr. Klaus."

"No, Per." Ruby kept him from grabbing Opal's hat.

"You should have seen the look on Alicia's face when I told her I usually wear britches." Opal held her skirt with one hand while Rand handed her up to the wagon seat. Ruby and Per climbed over the wheel and into the back. Rand stepped up on his side and unwrapped the reins from around the brake handle.

"I should just let you drive them home. Get you back in the swing of things."

Opal turned her gloved hands palms up. "I think I lost all my calluses. I'm going to have to start toughening them up again." She paused and turned to look at Rand. "Did you sell the filly?"

"Yes. Mrs. de Mores bought her."

"Medora bought the filly?"

"For four hundred dollars. All because you had trained her so well. She said you should come by and visit her if you like. She also said she would like you to go along on the next hunting trip."

Opal leaned against the seat back. "I can't believe you got that much."

"I was some surprised. She asked how much, and off the top of my head, I said five hundred. She said three. I said four and she said sold."

"Firelight's a flashy mount and rides nice and easy." Opal sighed. "You sold the gelding also?"

"Yep."

"So I don't have anything to work with."

"Oh, I wouldn't say that."

"Why?"

Rand turned and looked over his shoulder and winked at Ruby. "Should we tell her or make her wait?"

"Tell her."

"No. I think she should wait."

"Rand." Opal stopped for a moment and inhaled fresh, sweet Dakotah air. "All right, I'll wait, but two can play at that game."

Ruby laughed, and that set Per to laughing, which made Opal giggle. She reached up and unpinned her hat, then un-buttoned the pearl buttons going up the points from the sleeve hems and those up the front of the jacket.

"Getting warm?" Rand glanced over at her. "You do truly look lovely, young lady. Welcome home."

"Thank you." Opal nibbled her lip. "How are the Robertsons?"

"The girls are waiting for you to teach them ranch stuff. Their pa never did want them helping at roundup or such. Other than the cooking and serving," he added after a poke from Ruby.

"I promised them you would go over as soon as you got home and settled." Ruby reached up to take Opal's hand.

"You mean change my clothes?"

"Well, I didn't exactly expect you to come home looking like a fashion plate, but then, I wasn't surprised either."

"There are some things for you in my trunk too. Although what you and I think of as serviceable and what they think don't exactly match."

"I'm sure." Ruby unwound Per's fingers from her hair. He'd used her as a standing post and grabbed whatever he could when the wagon hit a rut. "We have some more good news at home too."

"What?"

"We'll be having another baby."

"Twins?" Opal turned, shock turning eyes and mouth to Os.

"No. Little Squirrel is in the family way too. She's so happy. Linc is popping his buttons."

"How wonderful." *And Atticus? How is he?* "Thought I'd go see Atticus soon as I can."

When neither of them commented, Opal turned to look at her sister. Rand had donned his poker face.

"All right. What is it you don't want me to know?"

"The Gradys are leaving the badlands."

Rand's words struck like tiny arrow

points, each drawing blood.

"Atticus too?"

"Yes. He's still too weak to manage on his own, and though the fits seem to have tapered off, he has to use a crutch to get around."

"His foot was broken too?"

Rand nodded. "We don't see much of him."

"Have you gone over there?"

"They were at the burial. That's when we learned they were leaving."

"Atticus never answered my letters."

"His right side is more affected."

He could have had Robert write for him. Dear, gentle Atticus, what has all this done to you? Please, Rand, pick up the pace.

The rattles and squeaks of the wagon, the clip-clopping of the team's hooves, Per's jabbering to whatever he saw while standing at the side of the wagon bed with Ruby holding securely to the back of his shift, were all part and parcel of an ordinary trip from town. Other than no one had much more to say.

Opal leaned down and began unbuttoning the sides of her shoes so she could undress more quickly. She thought back over the conversation. "You said there was a surprise."

"That's right. I did, didn't I?" Rand glanced out the side of his eye. "Took you a while."

Seems I got some heavy stuff on my mind. "I sure hope it has to do with horses. They're much simpler to deal with than life in general."

"Got to say an amen to that." Rand tipped his hat up with one finger. "We were rejoicing over a good roundup, healthy cattle, and then trouble blindsides us. Keeps us from getting cocky, that's for sure." He put his feet up on the kickboard and rested his elbows on his legs. "One good thing though, that new hand over at Robertsons', he handled the burial like a preacher. Makes me curious about his background. We sure could use a real preacher around here."

"He's not said anything?"

"No, but then you never know what drives people to head west. I heard he was from Pennsylvania. Not much of a cattleman but good on farming. He cleaned and oiled that used mower we bought, sharpened the blades, got it running better than new."

"Edith blushes every time she looks at him. He gets the biggest piece of cake whenever she is serving." Ruby's chuckle brought a "ma" and a giggle from Per.

"Is he always this happy?" Opal turned sideways in the seat so she could watch him.

"Seems so. Hope the next one is the same." Ruby grabbed him and gave him a big smacker on the cheek.

"Ma." He wiggled and giggled and chattered at her.

"Lord help us when he can talk." Rand eased the team back to a walk when they crested the final hill.

Opal stared out at the ranch, painted in the greens and golds of pure peace. What she wouldn't give to never leave again. But what if Atticus and his family had already left? What about all her dreams to take good care of him? To help make him whole again?

Chapter Twenty-Four

The sound of someone crying in the night woke Ruby. She slid out of bed without disturbing Rand and tiptoed down the hall to Opal's room. Once seated on the bed, she stroked Opal's shoulder.

This had to be about Atticus. Opal had come home from the Gradys' and gone about her chores without saying a word. Her eyes were deep pools of hurt.

"He h-hates me." Opal's weeping shook the bed.

"No, I don't believe that for a moment. I'm sure he hates what has happened to him."

"I said he should stay here. I'd take care of him."

Oh, Lord, and him so proud and wounded. "I see."

"I could make him better. I know I could." Opal rolled onto her back, using the sheet to wipe her face. "Sometimes healing takes a while."

"That it does." *And you have no idea how bad hurt he was. It's a miracle he's still alive. His poor ma said he wants to die rather than live crippled.*

"He told me once not to tease about us marrying." She rubbed her eyes like a tired child. "Now he wouldn't even look at me." She sat up and folded into Ruby's loving arms. "Told me to go away. He didn't want me around, getting underfoot and all."

Oh, Atticus, how you've wounded my dear sister.

"He blames me. I know he does."

"No. He blames those men. His ma told me that. Said he smiled when he heard they got shot. But then he cried when he learned of Robertson's death. Sometimes people get better from head wounds like his. We have to pray for that."

"I'm glad he's dead."

"The drifter."

"Um-hmm. Why do men do such terrible things?"

"No one taught them about Jesus and God's love. When we don't have that, people can do the cruelest, most vicious, most despicable things imaginable." Ruby shuddered. "Some even beyond imagining." She stroked Opal's hair. "But we live in the light of the cross, in God's love. And you can't be bitter. Somehow God is going to work all this out for His glory."

"How?"

"I don't know. But I've seen Him do so in the past. Why would this time be any different? He's the same yesterday, today, and forever. Remember how we thought it was so awful when our father died the night we got to Dove House? Remember how we came all that way and looked at the mess we walked into?"

Opal drew in a shuddery breath.

"And now those girls, all but Belle, know Jesus as their savior. And they are happy and married and have all the good things they thought they would never have."

"Mrs. Brandon said I can't think this is all my fault, but it sure seems like I started it all."

"Life seems that way at times. But she's right."

"Mrs. Brandon is pretty wise."

"Yes, she is. And a wonderful friend."

"She wanted me to stay back there."

"I know."

"But I live here."

"Thank you, God. I've missed you so." Ruby squeezed her close. "Putting you on that train was one of the hardest things I've ever done. But I had to get you out of harm's way."

"I know that now. Or at least I think I do." Opal reached over and took a handkerchief out of the drawer of the stand beside her bed. After blowing her nose she flopped back on the pillow. "I told Atticus I'd pray for him and that he has to send me his address so I can write to him. But I don't think he will. Robert might, though."

Ruby sighed. "It's hard to let go of people we care about."

"Uh-huh. Thank you, Ruby. I love you."

Ruby sniffed back the burning behind her own eyes and in her nose. "And I love you. Good night."

She made her way back to her own bed and slid carefully under the sheet.

"Things all right now?"

"I hope so. I think our Opal has done some growing up."

Rand laid out his arm so she could put her head on his shoulder. "Life kind of forces that at times."

"She's had to face some pretty hard things. Life seems so much easier back in

343

New York, and I was afraid she would stay."

"Our Opal doesn't go for easy." Rand kissed the side of her forehead.

⟿

Opal was out milking by the time Ruby entered the kitchen in the morning. She'd heard the screen door slam while she was dressing. Little Squirrel already had the coffee made, so Ruby poured herself a cup and took it out on the back porch where the sun was drinking dew, lending sparkles to the droplets on the spider web between the yellow rosebush and the cream hollyhock. A big brown spider waited in the center of the fine web.

Ruby watched it groom one leg and then the other. "Catch as many flies as you can. They're especially abundant this year."

A pair of house finches brought in their first offerings of the day for the noisy brood that had hatched in their nest in the upper corner joining porch roof and house.

She could hear the clatter as Little Squirrel put more wood in the firebox and set the lids back in place, all morning sounds, kitchen music.

Cat paraded up the path, tail straight in the air, a field mouse dangling from her jaws.

"So you're bringing in breakfast too."

Cat chirped and padded over to the box where her current batch of kittens were old enough to begin eating solid food. Cat called them out and laid the mouse in front of them.

Two dashed to her side, ready to nurse. One sniffed the mouse, and the largest one yawned, his pink tongue and white teeth bright against his gray face.

Ruby leaned against the porch post and watched.

Cat pushed the mouse with one paw. The watching kitten leaped backward as if attacked. The yawner hunkered down and hissed. The chorus of two pleaded for her to lay down or stand up, whatever, but let them eat.

Cat settled down on her paws and ripped the mouse open. One kitten came over and licked the open spot, then growling, sank his teeth in.

"Well, good for you, Cat, you got one going." Ruby tossed the dregs of her coffee into the rosebush and reentered the house. It was time she helped with the breakfast for her family.

"I see Cat has kittens again." Opal set the frothing pail of milk on the table. "Is the strainer in the springhouse?"

"She's trying to convince them a mouse is good for eating." Ruby turned from the stove where she'd been stirring the oatmeal.

"They're all lying in the sun, nursing now. How long do cats live?"

"All depends on whether a coyote gets them or not," Rand answered from the doorway. "Sure smells good in here."

"Rand." Opal didn't like the thought of coyotes going after the kittens.

"Well, coyotes like cats and dogs and any critters smaller than they are that they can catch."

"I heard them howling last night. They sounded wild and free and so much like home. Coyotes don't sing in New York."

"No. There's all that caterwauling of trains and trolleys and drays and carts and horses and people yelling." He shuddered. "Give me wide open skies and trees any day."

"Me too." Opal headed out to the springhouse.

"What do you know about New York?"

"Same as any big city, all noise and commotion. Not fit for man nor beast."

After breakfast, where Opal regaled them all with stories of her trip, she saddled Bay and headed on over to the Robertsons'.

"Opal!" Virginia leaped from the porch and ran out to meet her. "I'm so glad you're home."

"Me too." Opal took her foot out of the stirrup. "Come on up."

Virginia reached for her hand, stuck her left foot in the stirrup, and swung up behind her. "Thanks."

"Sure sorry to hear about your pa."

"Yeah. Been bad. Edith couldn't quit crying yesterday. Good thing we got Mr. Chandler here, or I don't know what we'd do."

Opal fought her own tears as she heard Virginia sniff. "All the neighbors will help." *Especially me, since this is all my fault. If only I'd . . .* But she knew there was no going back. Like Mrs. Brandon had said, there's no going back. We can only pray we don't make the same stupid mistake again. Easier to say than to do.

"Yes, the neighbors have been helping. I told Ma you would teach us girls how to work the cattle. Mr. Chandler isn't too good on roping and such." She sucked in a deep breath. "Maybe you could teach him too."

"Rand said Mr. Chandler started mowing?"

"Yep. Leastways we should have hay."

They rode on down to the barn, where two horses dozed in the corral.

Opal looked out across the meadow to see a team pulling the mower and laying swaths of green grass, straight as you please. "Got any cattle nearby?"

"Like for roping?"

"No, for driving." She stopped Bay at the corral where the two horses came over to visit the newcomer. "Who else wants to learn?"

"Joel. He's seven, almost eight." At the question on Opal's face, she added, "He is Mr. Chandler's boy."

"Oh. And Emily?"

"She'd rather stay in the house, but Ada Mae is all set to learn."

"Let's saddle up those horses, then, and one of you can ride Bay. I'll bring another horse tomorrow."

"Hey, Opal. Ma says to tell you you're staying for dinner." Ada Mae came running from the house, her braids flopping in the breeze. Behind her trudged a boy, his overalls held up with one suspender, wearing a flat hat.

Opal looked at the two girls. "You got any boots? And hats?"

"Sunbonnets."

"Better than nothing. Go get them, Ada Mae. And bring boots too, or shoes." She turned back to Virginia. "How many saddles?"

"One. Pa's."

"I see. Well, we got our work cut out for us." She turned to the boy leaning against the corral. "You're Joel?"

He nodded.

"I'm Opal Torvald from the next ranch downriver. I hear you want to learn to rope."

Another nod.

"Guess you don't waste too much energy on words, eh?"

He shrugged.

"Do you know how to bridle a horse?"

He shook his head.

"You ever been on a horse?"

A nod this time. He held up one finger.

"Then we will start with the basics as soon as Ada Mae gets back. How about letting down the bars to the corral?"

He nodded and went over to pull out the bottom one, letting it hit the ground without sliding it farther back.

"Let me show you something." Opal slid the lowest rail back far enough for Bay to walk through easily. "You do that with all the bars so you or your horse don't trip.

Strange things make a horse panic, so you do your best to keep them calm. Once your horse trusts you and you trust him, your life will be a whole lot easier on the range." She waited while he finished the rails, then walked Bay through.

"Close it up?"

"Yes, thank you." He could talk. Maybe he was just shy.

"Ada Mae, you want to catch those horses?" Opal asked, now that boots and hats were in place.

"I can't."

"They need to be roped?"

"Uh-huh. They're broke but not real trained."

Opal untied her rope from her saddle and, shaking out a loop, walked toward the two horses hugging the far side of the corral. She waited until one was clear and settled the loop over the animal's head.

"You made that look mighty easy."

"Takes practice, is all." She led the horse back and then, taking a short rope, knotted it around his neck and did a tie knot over the railing. "You see the way I did that?"

"What?"

"The knot. You want to make it so you can pull it loose by jerking on the tail, but if the horse pulls, it tightens down. Virginia, show them how while I catch that other knothead."

She loosened another loop and headed back across the corral. The rope whirled through the air, and she led that horse back to tie it up.

"All right, here's the way we'll do this. I'll show you how to bridle Bay and then each of you take a turn while I see how well these two behave."

I should have brought over some of our horses, she thought as she explained the bridle and how to put it on. Bay stood patiently, only her tail swishing as she fended off flies.

By the time they'd each bridled Bay a couple of times, she'd worked the kinks out of the first horse. Then she showed her students how to put on a saddle.

"There's no way Joel can reach that high, so someone will have to help him."

When she approached the second horse, he flattened his ears and pulled back against the tie rope. "Oh, forget it. I'm not going to let you get away with that, so just behave yourself." But he resisted the bridle, sidled away from the saddle, and spoke his piece with flat ears, mean eyes, and a twitching tail.

Once she had him saddled, she glared

back at him. "You just stay right there and get used to that. I'll see you later."

She turned back to the others and had them each bridle and saddle Bay in turn. "That's good. All of you. Joel, you had the most to learn, and you did well."

For the first time a smile twitched his mouth before he ducked his head so she couldn't see it.

"I guess you'll have to take turns on the two horses. Joel, you ride Bay. I'll show you how to mount. We can shorten the stirrups on my saddle easier."

While Ada Mae, who was tall for her age, mounted easily, Joel couldn't even get his foot near the stirrup.

"You'll have to use the fence. Lead Bay over there. She'll stand for you."

With both of them mounted, she explained reining, stopping and starting, and watching for what their horse was saying.

Joel looked at her kind of funny, but she grinned and shrugged. "You think a horse can't talk? Watch." She turned and walked toward the tied horse. He immediately laid back his ears and shifted his rear feet. "What do you think he is saying?" Opal paused for a moment. "Joel?"

"Go away?"

"Or?"

"I don't like you."

"Good. Now pay attention to Bay. She likes riders, but she doesn't like to have someone jerking on the reins. She has a tender mouth."

By the time the triangle rang for dinner, all those in the corral were sweating except for the tethered horse, which had gone to sleep.

"This afternoon we'll do some rope work." She lifted her flat felt hat and wiped the sweat from her forehead. When she walked into the house, Opal stopped by Mrs. Robertson. "I am so sorry to hear your sad news. Mr. Robertson was a fine man."

"Thank you, dear. Sometimes it is hard to remember that the Lord knows best." She gave Opal a hug.

"I'll do all I can to help you."

"I know. You have no idea how much that means to all of us." She mopped her eyes with the hem of her apron.

Opal glanced up in time to see a shocked look on the face of the man coming in through the back door. He covered it quickly, turning it into a polite smile.

"Oh, Opal, I want you to meet our hand, Jacob Chandler. Mr. Chandler, Miss Torvald."

Opal stretched out her hand. "Glad to meet you." Interesting. He'd almost not shaken her hand. Was he offended by her unladylike attire? Did he think she'd bite?

"Y-yes."

"Welcome to Medora." *Silly. Women don't shake hands like that. Whatever possessed you?*

"Thank you."

"Ma, I need britches like Opal wears. Riding a horse in a skirt is real uncomfortable." Ada Mae took Opal's hand. "You sit here by me."

Opal glanced up to catch Edith's slight arching of the eyebrows. *Ah, so that's the way it is. Don't worry, my friend, I have no interest in your man — if you really think he's yours — or in any man.*

Chapter Twenty-Five

Finished. Jacob stopped the team to look out across the mowed field. He stretched his arms, picked up his hat, wiped sweat from both his brow and the hatband, and set it back in place. There should be several tons in what he'd cut, enough to get the Robertsons' stock through the winter. On the morrow he'd start cutting at the Harrisons'.

He clucked the team forward again, and this time the cycle bar clamped upright. He'd need to spend the afternoon sharpening the triangular blades, greasing the gears, and checking for loose parts.

He stopped the team in the shade of the barn, and as soon as silence fell, he could hear Miss Torvald drilling her not-quite-so-willing students.

To her "No, you can do better," he unhitched the team and stripped off the harnesses to hang on the barn wall pegs. Those needed cleaning too. Perhaps Joel would do it. He had yet to order his son to do anything other than to stay close to the farm, or rather the ranch, buildings. He still struggled to remember ranch, not farm. Farmers, or as the ranchers dubbed them, squatters or sodbusters, were not popular out here on the range.

Joel dropped the loop over the post in the center of the corral just as Jacob arrived at the gate.

The girls all clapped. Joel's face lit up like the sun came from within until he saw his father. The smile didn't fade. It stopped. Without another glance in Jacob's direction, Joel retrieved his rope and turned his back.

Opal seemed to notice the brief exchange, gave Jacob an assessing look, and went on with her charges.

"All right, everyone pick out a corral post and practice until you can rope it three times in a row. Then we'll start with moving targets."

Jacob watched a moment more. *Wish I had time for that.* He'd tried to throw a rope the night before, but the fool thing had a tendency to twist. Tendency, ha! It lived to twist. Even his seven-year-old son was better than he.

He turned away. Too much to do to stand gawking. He shook his head. Girls in britches. It still didn't seem proper, but he could sure see the reason behind it. And Joel, wasn't it about time he — *He what? What do you expect from him?*

"No, come on, Ada Mae. Remember the wrist. And keep your eye on the rope. You'll make it."

What was the sadness he saw in Opal's eyes when she thought no one was looking? What brought it on? He bent over the mower. The first day's cutting was ready to turn. Mr. Harrison said he'd do the raking. Jacob had asked Opal to let Rand know. Had she forgotten?

Heading for the pump, he glanced over at the corral again. Now she had them roping one another. No wonder the laughter had escalated.

On his way back from the drink he stopped at the corral.

"Miss Torvald."

She spun around from showing Ada Mae how to lift the loop again. "Yes?"

"Did you tell Rand we'd be ready to rake this afternoon?"

"Sure did. He said he'd be over after dinner."

"Good. Thanks. I'll start cutting there tomorrow." He waved and returned to his mower. Picking up another stack of blades, he set them on the shelf by the grindstone. He sat on the wooden seat and pushed down on the foot pedal attached to the turning gear of the grindstone, setting the wheel to spinning. After dropping water on the rim, he held the blade against the stone. Sparks flew, and the metal screamed in distress.

He had worked a third of his way through the stack of mower blades when he sensed someone approaching.

"Thought you might like a cold drink about now." Edith Robertson wore a clean apron over her faded calico dress and a wide smile.

"Why, thank you, but I came back from the pump not long ago." He indicated the dark streaks on his shirt. "Sure helps one cool off too."

He'd seen that kind of smile before. Too many times. And usually from marriageable-aged young women. *Lord, please, can't I just do my work here and not have to hurt her feelings?* Innocent as a baby bird, her smile would catch some man's fancy, just not his.

However, if he were looking for a wife, which he wasn't, she would have been a good candidate. Tall and slender, graceful, and already an excellent cook. Mrs. Robertson was training her daughters well. With a dimple in her right cheek that joined readily with laughter, Edith would make a fine and engaging wife.

Why not for me? He had no answer to that question. That's just the way it was.

"Oh, well, then I'll leave this jug in the shade by the barn wall for later."

"Thank you." He bent to the next blade, but when he looked up again, she was still there in the shadows watching him. "Is there something else?"

"No. I'm just enjoying being out of that hot kitchen for a bit. We're canning beans today."

"I see." He picked up another blade and eyed it against the light. Sure enough, there was a nick big enough to see through. He'd walked the field to look for rocks but had missed at least one.

The next time he glanced up, Rand was driving a team with a rake into the yard. "That field looks mighty good," he said after the greeting.

"Thanks. I started mowing at the south-west corner. First third is ready for turning."

"So far no rain. A good thing for hay, but bad for gardens." Rand climbed down from the seat. "Where's your grease pot?"

"Right inside the barn door on the left."

After Rand greased the rake axles and left to begin raking, Jacob heard Opal again.

"All right, everyone mount up. We're going to drive cattle, maybe even cut a few."

Cut a few. Had he heard right? Jacob watched as Opal rode out, her three students in a line behind her like goslings following a goose. Joel now sat as comfortably as the girls, swinging his coiled rope with one hand, reins in the other.

Perhaps he could take time tonight to work with that stubborn rope and ride some. Otherwise how would he ever be ready for fall roundup? And from what Mrs. Robertson said, getting those beeves to Medora for sale would get them money for the entire next year.

Supper was a silent affair, as everyone was too tired to talk. Lines of jars on the counter told the story of the kitchen work, along with the good food served, enough to feed twice as many people. The first section of hay was turned, and they might bring in the first load tomorrow afternoon, the next day for sure.

"You want to take the mower home with you?" he asked Rand, who sat across the table.

"I'd rather you did the mowing. You're better at it than I am. If it's dry enough, my men will come to haul and stack what's here. We'll just go from place to place like we talked about."

"And up on the buttes?"

"We'll split it up even. One load here, one to my place." He turned to Opal. "How'd your chicks do with the cattle?"

Before Opal could answer, Ada Mae jumped in. "Some of those old cows got no thought to minding." She thumped her fork on the table. "Pa said some were meaner'n sin, and he was right."

"But you got them going?"

"Finally. They like hiding in the brush better than being driven."

"But you made them come out." Opal nodded her approbation to each of them.

"I almost got knocked off by a branch." Joel reached for another slice of bread. "I was watching that cow, and my horse went after her, and I grabbed that saddle horn

361

like to pulled it right out."

Jacob stared at his son. He'd not said that many words at once since his mother dumped him on the parsonage stoop.

"You did real good. Tomorrow we'll bring in a couple of calves to practice roping." Opal smiled at each of her charges.

"You better warn their mamas. Might make them a bit peevish." Rand nodded at Opal, his smile bringing a return one from her.

"Would you care for more beans, Mr. Chandler?" Edith picked up the bowl to hand it to him.

"No, thank you, Miss Robertson. I've had about all I can eat." Jacob glanced over the table to catch Opal in a knowing look. She arched her right eyebrow at him and returned to finishing the meat on her plate. Now, what was that all about?

After supper Jacob found Joel in the corral swinging his rope, but it missed the horse's head twice. He'd pull it back, loop it carefully in his left hand, loosen the loop with his right, dog the horse, throw, and start again.

"You were close that time."

Joel threw him an over-the-shoulder look

that clearly stated the importance of close. He readied his rope again and dropped it over the snubbing post nice as you please.

"If you could teach me to do that, I'd be much obliged."

Joel shrugged. "There's a rope in the barn on the right wall. Make sure you coil it right before you put it back."

Jacob fetched the rope and joined his son in the corral. The two horses hugged the far side.

"You got to learn to hold it first." Joel demonstrated holding the loop and the remainder of the coiled rope.

Jacob shook out his rope like his son, and immediately the loop twisted into a figure eight. "See, this happens all the time."

A slight smile touched his boy's face. "Opal says it's all in the wrist."

"Miss Torvald."

"She said to call her Opal." Joel's shoulders stiffened, and he turned away, whipped the loop around his head, and settled it over the snubbing post. He walked over, flipped it off, and looped it back in the coil.

"So what am I doing wrong?"

Joel shrugged. "You better ask Miss Torvald." He trailed after the horse, whirled the rope, and it fell cleanly over the horse's head. The animal turned to face him, and Joel walked up to the critter. He stroked its neck and rubbed the ears. He slipped a hand through the loop to keep it from tightening and, with a slight tug, led the horse away from the other.

What a difference in such a short time. Only three days Miss Torvald been working with the children, and look at Joel.

Jacob shook the loop out on his rope again, and this time it stayed open.

"What did I do different?" He looked from the rope to his son, the twilight softening the edges of both sight and sound. He played the loop in and out, the light-colored rope a thing alive in the gloaming.

Joel let the horse go and came to stand beside his father. "Now you drop it over that post like this." His arm formed a graceful curve as the rope left his fingers and settled over the post.

"When we go to town we need to buy you a proper hat."

Joel glanced up at his father's fedora. "You too."

Later that evening Jacob worked by lantern light, adding a hay rack to the wagon bed. He extended the sides by mounting braces on the wagon frame, then nailed together the two frames for the ends and bolted them to the wagon and wing frame. Now they'd be able to haul a decent amount of hay per wagon. He should have suggested the same to Rand.

When he stumbled into the bunkhouse to bed he knew it was past midnight, but getting the wagon done was of utmost importance. Good thing he'd started it earlier. He shucked his clothes and lay down under the sheet. Life in the badlands was as different from life in his parish in Pennsylvania as red was from black. He'd not had time to read his Bible in days, let alone write a letter to tell his family where he'd ended up. They must be thinking he fell off the face of the earth. *Lord, please understand that I'm not deliberately trying to ignore you. I thank you for . . .* He fell into a well of sleep so deep he didn't hear the rooster crow.

"Pa!"

Jacob could hear the voice but for a moment thought he was dreaming.

"Pa, we overslept." Joel touched his shoulder.

Jacob rolled over, his feet hitting the floor in one motion. "Thanks for waking me."

Joel buttoned his shirt. "Someone banged on the wall and called your name. You didn't hear it?"

"No, guess not." Shrugging his galluses up over his shoulders, Jacob sat back down to pull on his boots. How could he have slept so hard? He blinked to get the sleep out of his eyes. A quick dunk under the pump spout would have to do for washing this morning. Right after breakfast he was supposed to be on his way to the Harrison ranch, and he'd not brought the horses up to be grained or harnessed. As they headed for the house, it dawned on him. Joel had called him Pa. A fine name — Pa.

Everyone else was already seated and grace said when he and Joel walked into the ranch house.

"Sorry."

"Young man, you can't work all night and all day too." Mrs. Robertson set a platter of meat in front of him.

"I had to get that hay rack done. They'll need it this afternoon."

"Hay rack?" She stopped on her way around the table and laid her hands on Ada Mae's shoulders.

"I added a frame to the wagon bed so we can haul a larger load. We used them all the time on my father's farm."

"Oh, I see. Well, thank you. You're heading on over to Harrisons' right after breakfast, then?"

"That's the other reason why I had to get it done." He bowed his head for a quick grace and glanced up to see Edith smiling at him.

"Anyone here ever stacked hay before?"

"Last year."

"You know to pack it down good? The tighter the pack, the better the topping of a stack will keep the weather out."

Mrs. Robertson exchanged questioning looks with her girls. "The men took care of all that."

"When I was young, it was the children's job to tramp the hay on the loads and then on the stack. Pa would spread it with the pitchfork, but we would drive the wagon and pack the loads. Any of you ever driven a team before?"

"Just on the wagon into town." Mrs. Robertson took her seat. "I guess that's something else you girls better get to know how to do. Harnessing the team too." She cleared her throat. "Thank you, Mr. Chandler. Life is some different lately."

Jacob buttered his bread and sopped up the yolks of his fried eggs. He couldn't help much with the cattle yet, but he could help a heap with the home chores. Thank God, Mrs. Robertson had good neighbors.

Chapter Twenty-Six

"So how are your pupils doing?"

Opal looked up from buttering her bread. She shook her head, shrugged, and half smiled all at the same time. "Takes a good while to learn to spin a rope. Joel catches on real quick, but I think he spends all evening practicing. That pa of his, Mr. Chandler, he's mighty good with the haying, but he and a rope, why, it's like they're enemies."

"He'll get it." Rand exchanged a smile with Ruby. "He has a good teacher."

"Thank you." Opal covered a yawn with her hand. "You want us all on the wagons or . . . ?"

"We'll run both wagons again. Mr. Chandler is still mowing. You drive one, and Emily the other."

"That's what I thought. That will leave Joel, Virginia, and Ada Mae for packing." Opal thought longingly of the filly Rand had brought home for her to train. But that would have to wait. She also needed to go talk to the foreman over on the Triple Seven about the two horses he'd mentioned after roundup. He wanted more than the normal rough-and-ready training most cow ponies received.

Thoughts of Jacob Chandler trying to spin a rope circled through her mind. One thing you had to give the man credit for, he didn't give up easy. And he was a hard worker. That was two things. Like Rand said, he'd get it eventually.

"Maybe tonight after we're done haying, we could all go down to the river. We should be done over there, right?" Opal looked to Rand for confirmation, then grinned at his nod.

"I'll pack a dinner basket. Tell Mrs. Robertson that everyone is invited." Ruby glanced over at Little Squirrel, who nodded.

"We start fire early. Cook rabbit over coals."

"Maybe we could even go fishing." It seemed like months to Opal since she'd sat on a log or on the bank and flipped her hook out in the slow-flowing water. Linc and Little Squirrel had done most of the fishing lately. Thinking of fishing took her mind on a ride back in time — to Atticus. Where was he? She couldn't even write to him without an address. Was he getting better? *Please, Lord, he has to get better.* Her thoughts took off at a gallop. Why did a good, innocent man like Atticus have to suffer? What good did that do the world? But the hardest question was why did God allow such a thing to happen? She understood that men caused the grief, but as far as she understood, God could have put a stop to that drifter before all the mayhem broke loose.

But then, if she hadn't stopped for a swim . . . The fault always came back to her. Guilt was a terribly tiring burden.

Even though Mrs. Brandon had convinced her she wasn't responsible, that had been before she'd seen Atticus. The same Atticus who'd made sideways comments about marrying her someday and had now disappeared from her life. She pushed back her chair. "I'll bring up the team."

"Opa!" Per's calling after her did nothing to slow down her headlong flight. If only she could outrun or outwork the voices in her head.

The dew had dried off the raked hay by the time they arrived at the Robertsons', all the men riding on the hay wagon with Rand and Opal.

By dinnertime they'd hauled in four loads, finishing off the second stack by the barn and starting a third. When the men all doused their heads under the pump and shook the hay seeds out of their shirts, the children did the same, the girls going behind the house to shake out their clothing.

"Ugh. I itch all over." Opal turned so Virginia could brush off her back, then returned the favor. Water dripped from her soaking braid, sticking her shirt to her now seed-free back. "A dip in the river would have saved us all."

"We can play in the water tonight. Sure wish our place was on the river." Emily twisted her braids together and wrung more water from them.

As Opal drove the first load back out, she turned at the sound of Ada Mae's scream. "Snake! Snake!"

The rattler was slithering toward the edge of the load by the time Opal reached back and grabbed it by the tail. With the flip of her wrist, she snapped it as Rand had taught her and tossed the limp carcass over the side. She glanced up to see Ada

Mae staring at her, her mouth hanging open in shock.

"Missy, you be faster than dat old snake hisself." Linc leaned on his carved wooden hay fork. "I was gonna pitch him over and let Chaps down there get a thrill."

"Don't need no thrill." Chaps tossed up another forkful of hay. "Just tryin' to keep you all on your toes. Move that wagon on up, young lady, or we'll be here all day. Thought you wanted to go fishin'."

Opal clucked the team forward. While her action had been automatic, her heart pounded as if she'd faced off the snake nose to nose. They'd been lucky so far. This was the first snake to get tossed up with the hay. He must have been dozing in the shade. "I wonder if snakes ever go deaf."

"I'd rather they just went dead." Ada Mae tramped by her, packing down the load. She shuddered, making a face at the same time. "I hate snakes worse than anything."

"Me too." But Opal was thinking more along the variety of two-legged vipers.

"You was quick as a wink," Chaps said later when they were unloading the wagon. "Sorry I didn't see that thing before I flung it."

"No harm done, other than Ada Mae near to had a conniption."

But Opal had to endure the story several times over as Ada Mae made her sound more a heroine with each telling whenever there were new ears to hear.

Linc clapped her on the shoulder when she shook her head in denial. "Let her be. Everyone needs a hero sometimes."

"I wasn't brave like she says. If I'd have taken the time to think, I'd most likely not done what I did." Opal kept her voice low.

Linc lifted the harness from the back of one horse while she did the other. "Real courage is when you are scared to the bone and do it anyway."

"I acted too fast to be scared, but afterward I nearly fell off the wagon I had the shakes so bad."

They hung the harness on the pegs in the barn wall.

"Shame we wasted all dat good meat."

"Linc." Her shuddery face made him laugh, a deep hearty sound that usually brought delight to her face. This time she just shook her head.

Down at the river sometime later, with the fragrance of roasting rabbit drifting out over the water, Opal sat on a log, her cork floating on the surface of the sunset-burnished river, the brassy sheen broken only by the plop of another cork setting hers to bobbing in the ever-widening concentric circles. When hers dipped under the surface, she used the same wrist action as earlier, this time to flip a hooked fish from the water to the bank, where Ghost barked to announce the catch.

"How many now?" Joel glanced back at the flopping fish.

"Six. And you?"

"Four. I missed one."

"You have to set the hook, or some of the old swimmers take your bait and slide right off." Opal bent down and grabbed the flopping fish, disentangled the hook, and slid the stake up through the gill, settling the fish down in the water with the others.

"You got enough to start scaling?" Rand called from near the campfire.

"Is six enough? Joel's got four more."

"Have him bring them over."

She turned to the boy at the other end of the log. "You heard the man."

Joel jerked back on his pole. "Five."

Opal threaded another grasshopper on her hook and tossed it back in the lazy river. She settled on her log and swatted a persistent mosquito. If only there was something invented to keep the bugs off, this would be absolutely perfect. She listened to the laughter and banter from those gathered around the fire. Rand was teasing Ruby, and Mrs. Robertson was scolding him for the teasing. Per toddled too close to the water and wailed when Ghost edged him back. Wood chips flew from the wood-chopping contest between Joe and Mr. Chandler.

"You got one on." Joel's comment snatched her attention back from the wood choppers.

Opal jerked her pole, but all that flew back was the cork and empty hook.

"You got to pay attention."

"Smart-mouthed kid." Opal could feel her cheeks warming. Not that Joel knew where she'd been looking but that she had to eat her own words. She rebaited her hook and tossed the line up toward a log that protruded into the current.

The fish hit it before the hook sank under the surface.

"Like that?" The flopping fish slapped the ground right behind her.

"Some fast. How come they don't just catch their own grasshoppers?"

"Most hoppers are too smart to fall in the water."

"You think grasshoppers can think?"

"God must have given them a brain too. Everything has a brain."

"You sure? Even trees?"

Opal thought a moment. This sounded like one of the discussions she'd had years earlier with Ruby. "No, not trees, but all things that breathe."

"Trees don't breathe?"

"They don't have lungs."

"But my pa said . . ." He paused. "My other pa said trees are good for the air. How can they do that if they don't breathe?"

"I don't know. Maybe by . . ." She paused and squinted her eyes, trying to remember what she'd read, at the same time wondering what he meant by his "other" pa. Should she ask? Or was that being too nosy? Since when had she cared about being nosy?

But Joel seemed kind of private-like. As did his father. She inhaled, sucking the smell of wood fire, sizzling rabbit, and frying fish down deep into her soul. How would she describe an evening like this to the Brandons in New York? The cottonwood leaves tattled secrets in the evening breeze, mosquitoes whined loud enough to deafen one, and supper always tasted better outside. No idea why, but it seemed to.

"Food's ready. Come and eat," Mrs. Robertson called.

She and Joel pulled their lines out of the water, wrapping the strings around the willow poles and grabbing their stakes of fish, then waded back across the shallow river. The Little Missouri lazed on by, deeper in some places but shallow here at the ford.

"Opa!" Per charged toward her, stubbed his fat little foot on a rock, and looked to hit the dirt except for his faithful guard dog who stepped in front of him so he could save himself by clutching her fur.

Opal stopped to pat the dog. "Good girl. He sure keeps you on the move, doesn't he?"

"Opa!" The little prince demanded her attention.

She handed Joel her fish and pole and, crossing her two hands to grab Per's, swung her nephew's little body up on her shoulders. She let him grab her hair, retrieved her hat from where he'd knocked it, and glanced up to see Mr. Chandler's gaze locked on her.

"You do that well." His voice lay like honey on toast.

"Thank you. Lots of practice." Her words snagged in her throat, then tumbled out in a rush. "Huh, Per?"

"Opa!" He drummed his fists on the top of her head, his giggle making those around him smile back.

Opal ponied him up to his father and ducked so Rand could lift him off her shoulders. "Ouch. Per, let go." Between her and Rand, they untangled his fingers from her hair, and Rand held his son while everyone quieted for grace.

"Jacob, would you lead us?" Rand looked to the man across the fire.

Why did he do that? Opal glanced from her brother-in-law to the visitor. Rand always led the grace. She caught a look that passed between the two men, as if they had a secret that she might decipher if she thought on it long enough.

Who was this Jacob Chandler? Joel had referred to his other pa. And yet he'd been introduced as Mr. Chandler's son. Did Mrs. Robertson know more than she was telling? And Edith? She was smitten, that was for sure.

Opal lassoed her thoughts in time to join the amen, not having heard a word of the prayer. Guilt snipped at her ears as she watched Edith make sure she was near Mr.

Chandler. Opal shook her head inwardly when the man deliberately, at least it seemed so, eased Chaps in between them. Edith smiled at something Chaps said, but her eyes didn't agree with her mouth.

"Help yourselves." Ruby pointed to the table they'd created with boards set up on two sawhorses and covered with a blue-and-white-checked oilcloth.

After supper Rand brought his guitar from the wagon, and while the women gathered up food and children, he practiced a few chords, then picked out the tune to "O Susannah!" One by one the voices joined in the song, accompanied by the *basso profundo* of a bullfrog and the tenor voices of a cricket chorus.

"She'll be Comin' 'Round the Mountain" segued into "Shoo Fly, Don't Bother Me," which flowed through ballads and into "Bury Me Not on the Lone Prairie."

"How about 'My Old Kentucky Home'?" Mrs. Robertson requested, drawing Ada Mae closer to her side. After they finished she sighed. "I do miss the sing-alongs we used to have on evenings on the porch."

"How about 'Shenandoah'?" Chaps looked up from whittling, his fingers caressing the smooth wood being shaped by his knife.

When the last strains faded away, Rand set his guitar to the side. "Thank you for coming, neighbors. Wish we could do this more often."

"Morning's going to come earlier than usual." Mrs. Robertson picked up a towel-covered bowl and headed for the wagon. "Come along, girls. Oh, Joel and Mr. Chandler too. Sorry."

"Thank you." Jacob stopped beside Rand. "That was truly lovely."

"I play sometimes for church. We hold it at the schoolhouse in town. You have a good voice. Maybe you would like to join our little choir."

Opal caught herself waiting for his answer. Come Sunday, she and the girls would join Rand and Charlie singing for church, as they had before.

"We usually practice just before the service."

"Thanks, but I . . . we don't hold much with churchgoing."

Joel gave his father a puzzled look that Opal would have missed had she not been waiting for his answer herself. What kind of man didn't go to church, especially after giving Mr. Robertson such a good burial? Ruby had gone on and on about it the day Opal returned from New York.

380

"Sorry to hear that. You are always welcome any time you decide to come. Someday God's going to bring us a real pastor, though right now we take turns with the preaching, mostly just reading Scripture and singing and praying together."

Later that night, on her way to the outhouse, Opal passed Rand and Ruby's room, then paused, caught by their conversation. They were talking about Mr. Chandler.

"He's hiding something," Rand said.

"Everyone's hiding something." Ruby sounded about asleep.

"There's a lot more to that man than meets the eye; you mark my words."

Opal waited, but when nothing more was said, she continued on out the back door. Just who Jacob Chandler was seemed to be a question on more minds than hers.

Chapter Twenty-Seven

Ruby stood at the post on the back porch watching the sunrise gild the leaves of the oak and cottonwood trees and turn spider webs into masterpieces of diamond-spar-kled strands. The rooster crowed, a robin greeted the dawn with song, a meadowlark strewed song pearls on the breeze.

She started to move but paused, her hand finding its way to her belly to cup the new life she'd just felt flutter. Life in her womb, such an inexpressible joy. Mornings like this she knew how Mary had felt and why she said, "My soul doth magnify the Lord, and my spirit hath rejoiced in God my Savior." *Lord, how can I thank you enough?* She had so much to be thankful for. House and home, Rand, her family, friends, the produce of the garden, land

and river, this place, where they dwelled far from the city and with a beauty that caught one's breath and made songs of praise not be a sacrifice but a joy. "My soul indeed magnifies the Lord."

"Talking to yourself again?" Rand stopped behind her and, like the touch of a butterfly, kissed that certain spot on the back of her neck. A spot that sent shivers clear to her toes and fingertips.

"How about running away with me, you lithesome lady, you?" He wrapped both arms around her, crossing his hands over her mounding front.

"Fie, sweet sir, lithesome will not be the case for long." She leaned her head back against his shoulder. "I felt the baby move."

"Ah, my love. So much to be thankful for."

"That's just what I was saying. Look, Rand, just look at all we have. And are."

"I know. Sometimes I feel almost guilty for all the blessings we've been given. We work our hearts out for it, but still, I can't ask for more."

"Nor I."

"Ma?"

She turned and kissed Rand right under his mustache. "Your son calls."

"We could leave Opal in charge and ride up the river a way. Just the two of us. It won't be long before you're too big to ride."

"You think I should?"

"Do you mean able or according to the mores of the day?"

"I don't give a fig about what's proper anymore. The question is, would it hurt the baby?"

"Indian women ride when they are big as a bass drum. That is, if they can find a horse the men aren't using."

"How do you know?"

"I have eyes."

"M-a-a?"

"Coming, Per. Hang on."

"Think about it."

"A day away. Just us? What's to think about? Of course I want to go." *Even though riding is not my favorite thing, as it is Opal's, being alone with my husband would be the perfect gift on a perfect day.*

"Don't you go changing your mind."

"I'll pack our meal." She ducked under his arm and headed for the hall to the bedrooms. Peeking into Opal's room, she was not surprised to find the bed made and clothes hung on their pegs. Opal was most likely down milking.

She swooped Per out of his bed and blew against his neck to make him laugh. "What a good boy you are."

"Ma good?"

"Yes, Ma is good. Are you hungry?"

"Hungry." He nodded and stuck his finger in her mouth as she leaned over him to change his diaper.

"One of these days we are going to have to train you to no more diapers. You can go in the pot like a big boy."

"Pot."

"August is almost over, and school will soon be starting. With Opal gone all day at school, what are you going to do?"

"Do."

"One of these days, and sooner than I think, you'll be talking up a storm. We better be getting some clothes sewn for Opal. She can't go to school in britches. That's for sure." *And the gowns she brought back from New York aren't suitable for school out here.*

She picked up the baby and settled him on her hip, one arm around him and the other hand carrying the diaper out to the pail on the porch. Time to wash again. How could she take the day off and go with Rand? What dreamers they were.

"In every thing give thanks." The Bible

verse floated through her mind as she sliced the smoked venison haunch to fry for breakfast. Today was so easy to give thanks, but what about the days that weren't so easy? And for certain there would be more. Life was just like that, with the ups and downs. Like being so big again she couldn't see her feet, let alone button her shoes. Like the days and nights she had struggled with a new baby, never getting enough rest, even though Little Squirrel helped so much. *Lord, I know Paul wrote of praise when he was in prison and had been beaten. Prison to me is the winter when the blizzard comes or when the children get sick. Please remind me when I grumble that I should praise you instead.*

"Ma-a?" A spoon banging on the table accompanied his request.

How much easier it will be when he can talk and tell me what he wants. She handed Per a crust of bread she'd baked hard just for him.

"Ruby, I strained the milk," Opal said, entering the kitchen. "Are you churning butter today? There's a lot of cream."

"Opa!" Per tried pushing away from the table and banged against his chair back when he couldn't move. His mother had tied the belt tight enough. "Opa-a." He raised his arms, reaching for her, pleading for his freedom.

"I'll be right back. Just a minute."

His wail followed her out the door.

Ruby placed the last of the slices in the frying pan and crossed to her whimpering son. His lower lip protruded, and he squeezed his eyes to force a tear, much against its will.

She dropped a kiss on his thistledown hair. "Big boy, Per. Eat your toast."

He sniffed and dug in his lap for the treat, then waved it at her when he found it.

Ruby returned to the stove to turn the sizzling meat, grateful the meat fragrance didn't force her to make a run to the outside, as she'd done so many mornings a few weeks ago. *Thanks for reminding me, Lord, of one more thing to be grateful for.*

Rand and the hands came in through the back door and took their places at the table.

"Start with the oatmeal."

Little Squirrel nodded and gave the kettle an extra stir before ladling the cereal into the bowls stacked to warm on the reservoir.

"Let's say grace." Rand paused while Opal slid into her chair. "Father in heaven, let us ever be thankful for all you have given us, for home and health and the work we love. Thank you, and bless this food and the hands that so lovingly prepared it. Grant us this day an opportunity to grow in grace. Amen."

What did he mean by that? Ruby pondered her husband's words as she beat the eggs after cracking them in the bowl. An opportunity to grow in grace today? Had the others heard what she did? She'd have to ask him later.

"Opal said she'd help in the house, so we can leave shortly." Rand dropped the information like a pebble into a pool of water.

"But I —" Ruby glanced up in time to catch a raising of his eyebrows and a slight tilt of his head, a sign that he was prepared to fight for what he'd said.

Lord, how do I get it all done today? Opal hates housework, and I can't say as I blame her. I'd rather be outside today too.

So you have the opportunity. Take it. The gentle voice contained a hint of scolding and a heap of reminder. Rand had plenty of work to do today too, and yet he'd rather take her for an outing.

She swallowed her denial and, after a deep breath, nodded. "I'd love to go.

Thank you, Opal." *And you,* her eyes shouted down the table to her husband.

The look he sent back made her insides mush up. Reminders of his love did that to her.

When they finished eating, Rand gave out the orders for the day to the men, and they all pushed back from the table.

"You need firewood?" Linc asked.

"Both here and at the washtub, thank you."

"I put diapers on to boil." Little Squirrel looked to Opal.

"I'll start with the dishes. Per can help me churn on the back porch," Opal said.

"The beans need picking too. Let's dry this last batch for britches and then the rest can go for shelled beans." Ruby set the dishes in the pan.

"You want to hang them on the strings on the porch?" Opal fetched a wet cloth and wiped Per's hands and face, something he liked about as much as getting his diaper changed. "Hold still, you squirmer, you."

"Ma-a."

"I'm not helping you. Be good for Opal." Ruby stopped to hug Opal as she went by. "Yes, just dry them on the strings, and thank you."

"You're welcome. Have fun." She lowered

her voice to a whisper. "Even though I know you'd rather take the wagon than ride."

Ruby winked at Opal, now as tall as she was. "Won't be much longer that I can do this, and it makes Rand happy."

"You could go fishing."

"You could can beans too."

"Just thought I'd suggest it." Opal raised her eyebrows and half shrugged.

Ruby laughed to herself as she headed to her bedroom to change into the leather divided skirt she'd gotten from Belle. So what if she couldn't button the waist. It would still stay up.

Rand had the horses ready at the hitching post in front of the house when she stepped outside.

"I have our dinner." He held up the saddlebags before he slung them over Buck's back and tied them in place.

"I need to say good-bye to Per."

"He's busy out with Opal. Why not leave him be?"

Ruby thought a moment. "I can't do that." *What if something happened to me, to us, and* — She cut off that line of thinking and hurried through the house. The dishes steamed in the dishpan on the stove, evidence that Opal had left to do something else.

Can I depend on her? Of course I can. When Opal gives her word, she lives up to it. A thought stopped her in midstep. *I've never left Per before. I could take him with us. He would love to go. He loves to ride.* She half turned to go ask Rand, then changed her mind. Would this be harder on Per or her?

What if something happens to me? This thought returned on the attack, sharper than the first time. After all, danger lurked everywhere out here in Dakotah Territory. As if it didn't in New York.

She had asked for a break one day, and now, when it came, she was dithering like a sheet on the clothesline set to dancing and flapping in the wind.

"Come on, Ruby, the horses are getting restless." Rand's call made her smile again. Of course, the horses were getting restless because he was.

Taking herself firmly in hand, she stepped through the back door to see Opal coming from the springhouse, a bucket of cream to dump in the churn in one hand and Per's little fist in her other. She was telling him something, and he smiled up at her like the sun rose on his Opa. Little Squirrel had the fire going under the washtub and was carrying another bucket of water from the well.

Bees buzzed in the rosebush by the step. Ghost looked up from her nest in the shade of the rose, checked her charge, and lay back down with a sigh. Of contentment? All was well.

Ruby nodded and stepped off the porch to meet Opal and Per. "Bye. We'll be back before supper." She stooped over and kissed Per on top of the head. "You be good."

He nodded. "Good."

"Thank you, I think." She shrugged as she looked at Opal.

"We'll be fine. Go play." Opal nodded toward the churn. "Open that for me, would you please, and then get out of here before Rand comes after you."

Within minutes Ruby found herself settling into a gentle jog as her horse carried her toward the trail up the east bank of the Little Missouri River. Rand reached for her hand and grinned at her, the broad brim of his hat shading his eyes but unable to dim the love shining there.

"Thanks for coming."

"Thanks for making me."

"You're welcome."

She'd forgotten how much she could

enjoy a ride with Rand. He pointed out the cattle gathered under the shade of an ancient oak tree, placidly chewing their cuds while keeping a watchful eye on the riders. He showed her a ledge where an eagle had her nest, the young already fledged and flying free. They both laughed when a covey of grouse burst from the brush with a whir of wings, startling them. He showed her the entry to a fox den that was nearly hidden by a thicket of bushes.

When they stopped for an early dinner, the sun had yet to reach its zenith, but she was more than ready to dismount.

"I don't know how you men ride all day and are still able to walk without staggering." She clutched his arm after trying one step.

"Take it easy. You'll be fine in no time." He left her to stand while he pulled off the saddles and bridles and hobbled the two horses. Then he guided her to the shade of an ancient cottonwood with bark ridges so deep on the trunk that one could bury a finger in them. "Sit here." He spread the saddle blankets while he spoke.

"I'll stand, thank you."

"Suit yourself." He crossed his ankles and sat with such easy grace she laughed.

"I don't know how you do that."

"Do what?"

"Sit down cross-legged like that."

He shrugged. "Easy." Patting the blanket beside him, he smiled up at her. "Come, be comfortable."

"May I lean against you?" She eyed the tree trunk he leaned against. "That looks too rough for comfort."

"You may lean on me anytime and for all time."

Her gaze caught on his and refused to let go. The flutter in her middle had nothing to do with the baby, but came along with a warmth she'd come to recognize as her loving response to this man. Sometimes she wondered at the strength of it. After all, they'd been married three years now. But all such thoughts flew up to join the birds as she nestled into the curve of his arm.

"Are you hungry?" She glanced over at the saddlebags.

"Not for food."

"Rand, someone might come by."

"Not here. See how secluded we are."

"You planned for this?" Her voice squeaked on the last word. No others were needed.

Some time later he lay with his head in

her lap, staring up at the canopy of sun-speckled leaves. "You know what?"

"No, what?"

"We've never done this before."

"I know." She could feel her cheeks flaming all over again.

"Picnics with just the two of us should happen more often."

"I couldn't agree more." She reached for the saddlebags. "But now I am hungry." She batted his shoulder, laughter dancing in the sun motes. "Aren't you?"

"Ravenous."

"Ah, Rand, how I love you."

"Good." He swung himself to a sitting position. "Let's keep it that way."

They ate their sandwiches, tossing a bit of bread to a curious sparrow. Conversation roamed like the cattle on the plains, grazing here, trailing there.

She'd put things back in the saddlebag when she glanced over to see him watching her. "What?"

"I think there is something else we need to talk about."

"Oh-oh. Why do I get the feeling I'm not going to like this?"

Rand rubbed his upper lip under his mustache. "Opal came to me the other day."

"Why to you?"

"She was asking for help in how to bring up something with you. She hates to upset you. You know that."

"I knew I wasn't going to like it."

"She heard that Mr. Finch has returned to teach school again this fall."

"Oh, rot." Ruby sighed and studied the black beetle strolling the horse blanket, catching a foot in the coarse weave, shaking free, and continuing. Why did her sister so often make her feel like that beetle? "She has to go to school."

"No, she doesn't. She's completed the requirements through eighth grade, and Mr. Finch makes her help with the younger children instead of teaching her and the older girls."

"Then we need to talk with him, explain that they aren't there to teach but to learn."

"I don't think it's that easy."

"Rand, are you taking her side?" She bit back the "again." While she tried to keep the steel from her voice, she knew she'd failed when his eyes narrowed.

"I'm not taking sides. I told her she has to talk with you, but I do see her point."

"See, I told you." Ruby huffed and wrapped her arms around her knees. "Do you realize that the only times you and I get upset with each other are when we talk about my little sister?"

"She's not so little."

"That has nothing to do with it."

"It has everything to do with it. As far as I can see, she's old enough and smart enough to be making more of her own decisions."

"I wonder if you would be so understanding if she were your younger sister. School is important."

"Not if you're not learning anything." His voice had gone softer, a sure indication he was fighting to keep his temper.

"I think we better head on back."

"If you insist. But I don't know why we can't have a discussion without you getting all hot under the collar."

"Me!" Ruby surged to her feet and planted her hands on her hips. "I'll have you know, Mr. Harrison, that I'm not hot under the collar. My collar is just fine. You're the one who is not listening to reason."

Rand saddled the horses while she stamped around the small clearing, murdering ants and any other small critters caught in the grass.

She started to mount when he put a hand on hers on the saddle horn. "Okay, I have no idea how else I could have handled this, so can we agree on one thing?"

Ruby chewed her bottom lip. *I hate being angry at you.* She rested her forehead against his arm. "What?"

"That I love you, and you love me, and no matter what, we can figure out solutions to problems."

"Oh, Rand, this has nothing to do with loving you. I just want what's best for Opal."

"And you think I don't?"

His question stopped her in midbreath. "No, of course not. I mean, of course you do. Oh, Rand, I always wanted her to graduate from secondary school."

"Why? Because you didn't?"

"I had to go to work to give us a home. I wanted her to go to finishing school, to become the young lady I never could be. Mrs. Brandon would have done that for her."

"I know. But Opal loves this ranch as much as I do. She has a heart as big as our Dakotah sky. Perhaps if we really think on it, we can come up with something far better for her than spending hours each day cooped up with a teacher who isn't half as smart as she is."

"Rand Harrison."

"Well, it's true. He has more book learning, but —" he kissed his wife on the tip of her nose — "he lacks a certain amount of common sense, don't you think?"

"I don't know. I hardly know the man."

"Would you like to be friends with him?"

She closed her eyes for a moment, thinking of the teacher who'd followed Pearl. "No."

"Why not?"

"He's insipid, boring, and looks down on us ranchers."

"Oh, really?"

"I think we need to ask the state for a new teacher, or else someone ought to wise him up." She gave him a sideways glance.

"Me?"

"Why not?"

"Get on your horse. We have a few miles to cover." He gave her a boost and mounted Buck. "You're not going to worry about this, are you?"

"No, but I do like to have a plan."

"I know. Worrying doesn't accomplish anything."

"Rand."

He grinned at her and nudged Buck into a slow jog.

"Everybody can't just not do what is

hard. Hard times build character."

"You don't think Opal is enough of a character?"

"There's a difference." But she'd noticed the tightening of his jaw. He'd go talk with the man all right. Perhaps instill in him a little more respect for the rancher breed. *Opal, sometimes you make me so perturbed.* If only Pearl had been able to keep teaching.

Chapter Twenty-Eight

"Opal, I guess you and I have something to talk over." Ruby stood with Per on her hip. His head leaned against her shoulder as if she'd been gone for weeks instead of a few hours. The instant he heard her voice, he'd run shrieking to the door. His "Ma-a" could probably be heard clear to town.

"Now?" While Opal had willingly worked at the house all day, she thought that as soon as Ruby returned, she could head for the horse pasture.

"Can you think of a better time?"

"Well, yes." Opal took a broomstraw from the can on the warming shelf and leaned over to open the oven door, sticking the straw into the cake to test for doneness. When some batter showed on the straw, she closed the oven door very carefully so the cake would not fall. "How about after supper?"

"I suppose. How long until the cake is done?"

"Perhaps five minutes."

"Can you wait that long, or do you need to get out to the horses immediately?" A bite to the words made Opal decide staying would be best.

"I'll wait. Did you have a good time?"

"Yes, we did. How was Per?"

"Busy. He thought he should be able to churn the butter, wash the butter, and salt it too. Ghost played with him for a while."

"Don't know what I'd do without that dog at times." Ruby tickled Per's tummy and kissed his cheek. "You were a good boy?"

"Go boy." He stuck his first finger into his mouth, a favorite trick since he was weaned.

"We got the beans picked and strung. I'd rather do that than can them anytime." Opal checked under the towel spread over a pan of rolls rising. They would be ready for the oven when the cake was done. She'd used the leftover sourdough batter from the breakfast pancakes, kneaded in more flour, and set the rolls rising for supper.

"Did the men get back yet?"

"No. There's a roast in the back of the oven."

"Thank you, Opal, for my day off. I cannot tell you how much I appreciated it."

"Good." *But I thought it might make you more agreeable to what I want, if Rand mentioned it to you, which he obviously did.* She set the wood-slatted rack on the table and pulled the coffeepot to the hotter part of the stove. "Coffee should be hot about the time the cake is done. I thought whipped cream would be good on it." It seemed she'd been cooking and baking all day while the men were over at Robertsons' bringing in the last of the hay loads.

"Don't forget to check the cake and put the rolls in," she said to Ruby as she headed to her room.

Even school might be better than all this housework. The thought made her hustle to change clothes. Working in the heat had been cooler in a dress, something she was rarely willing to admit, but out with the horses she'd never wear skirts or a dress. Although riding sidesaddle in the park in New York, wearing a riding dress of Alicia's, had been a different story. Several young men had come to ride with them. Penelope had teased her about them afterward.

"They never showed up before you came," she'd said.

Opal had made a derogatory sound.

"Opal, you have no idea how fetching you look. That blue makes your eyes sparkle, and you're as graceful on that horse as any woman I've ever seen ride."

"You come west, and I'll show you how to really ride." She nudged the horse forward. "Come on, let's take that trail over there by the lake."

Penelope rode beside her, Alicia trailing. "Do you really ride astride — in britches?"

"Yes. You can't work cattle with all this stuff on." She gestured to her skirts and petticoats. "Why, it would shred in minutes riding through the trees and brush. We all wear chaps to protect our legs."

"Chaps?"

"Leather leggings that cover the fronts of your legs, kind of like an apron that attaches to a leather belt. You tie them behind your legs with leather strings."

"I saw a picture of a cowboy who had furry coverings on his legs."

"Most likely some tenderfoot who wanted to look like a cowboy. Look over there." Opal pointed to two black swans being followed by their half-grown young. They'd looked up the name in the dictionary. Cygnets. French.

"Aren't they lovely?" Alicia said with a sigh. "So graceful. I'm sure they never had to take lessons from Miss Claudette."

"Are they that bad?" Opal could barely repress a shudder.

"Walk with a book on your head, and if you drop it —"

"You can never let your spine touch the back of a chair. What are chairbacks for if not to lean against?" Penelope rode on the other side. For a change the three were alone, the brothers off on a different outing.

Even though she knew the answer, Opal asked the next question. "Why go if you hate it so?"

Penelope rolled her eyes, another of the many things she was not supposed to do. "Mother acts so gentle and patient, but you don't want to cross her on certain things. 'Now that you are young ladies, you must put off the things of childhood and learn to deport yourselves in the manner of your station.' "

"That's a direct quote." Alicia smiled, a serene smile that looked more like her mother's than Opal could believe. "But it's really not so bad once you decide that Miss Claudette is doing her best to help you. I'd be mortified if I made a faux pas in public."

Opal had glanced over to see Penelope make a face.

She shuddered now as she stamped her foot securely into her boot. To live like that, corseted until you could barely breathe, restricted from all things enjoyable, buildings all around until you felt you were in a canyon closing in from the top. Not like here with sky that went on forever, painted canyons that glowed in the sun — even the shadows teemed with life. How could Ruby have even dreamed she would rather stay in New York to go to school?

She grabbed her hat off the hall tree and headed out the door, smiling to herself at the sound of Per laughing out on the back porch. Being with him all day had not been a bad thing. He was fun and funny and learned so fast. And almost as cute as a half-grown colt.

She glanced up at the screech of a hawk overhead. Good thing they had put wire over the chicken run, or he'd have dined at their expense. "Go get those gophers that are tearing up the pasture," she told him.

The bird ignored her. The horses ignored her whistle too, peacefully grazing at the far side of the fenced pasture. The filly had not learned to respond to a whistle yet, but Buck lifted his head and whinnied.

"Bring them all on up here," she called to him. Even now she missed Firelight, the filly she'd trained and Rand had sold. Even though that was the way of ranching and she'd known it would happen, inside she had dreamed that maybe Rand would surprise her and let the filly be hers.

Too many things had changed in the last couple of months. She whistled again, and Bay broke into a trot. While the old mare was rarely used for roping cattle any longer, she still loved attention.

"Good girl." She let Bay snuffle her hair and leaned into the warm, firm shoulder. Bay might be up there in years, but she'd make a good horse to teach Per to ride. Opal swung aboard, her rope looped over her shoulder. Bareback, no bridle, one with her horse. Now, this was the way to ride, not like a dolled-up stick on the trails of a city park. "But I need to get a letter off to them. Wouldn't we have fun if they would come here to visit?"

Bay broke into a lope at the slight squeeze of Opal's legs, the wind lifting her

407

mane and tugging at her rider's hat. Leaning slightly in the direction she wanted the horse to go, Opal singled out the young filly and lassoed her with one try.

"It's about time you learn to come when you're called." She looped the rope over the horse's nose and led her back to the gate. Dismounting, she let Bay go and took the filly up to the barn. "You need a name, little girl, but I've not come up with a good one yet."

After brushing the sorrel's coat and mane and picking up her feet, checking for thrush or a stone in the frog, she saddled the horse and mounted easily in spite of a bit of sidestepping. By the time she'd dismounted and mounted again three times, the horse stood quietly.

Training a horse never seemed like work to Opal. Neither did training her young charges. Perhaps she'd ride . . . *Cinnamon — that's the name.*

"Perfect. Cinnamon." She stroked the filly's neck. "Cinnamon. That's you." She roped the snubbing post from the horse's back, practiced keeping the rope taut, backed her, moved forward again to release the tension, and ran sliding stops and side-to-side spins.

"She's looking mighty good." Rand leaned on the corral fence.

"Thanks. She learns fast. How about we call her Cinnamon?" Opal rode the horse over to the fence. "Thought I'd try her with the cows tomorrow."

"If she's got as much sense as she has flash, she'll be an easy sale."

"She will."

"You've been working her what, two weeks now?"

"About that."

"We've got two geldings coming from the Triple Seven."

"When?"

"In a week or two. They want them ready for fall roundup."

"Nothing like waiting until the last minute."

"You're right about that. As a matter of fact, I talked with Ramsey at the abattoir, and he asked if we couldn't bring some beeves in early. Think we'll round up the fattest and take them in."

"When?"

"Starting Monday."

"Be good training for the kids."

"True. Thanks for the time off for Ruby today."

Opal dismounted and hooked her stirrup

over the saddle horn to unwrap the cinch straps. "You're welcome. Ruby's not real happy with the school idea, is she?"

"Nope. You better have a good plan to present."

"I wanted to talk with Pearl first."

"You hatching something?"

"I hope so. Guess I'll just tell Ruby that it would be better to talk about it tomorrow, and I'll go see Pearl first."

"Good idea." He pulled her saddle off and carried it to the barn.

"Thanks, Rand."

"You're most welcome. That's what family is for."

The next morning Opal took her charges out to rope and bring in a couple of steers to practice on; then she headed on over to Pearl's house, closer to town.

Even after all this time, she still glanced up at times, expecting to see Atticus come whistling over the rise after working for the Robertsons or perhaps for Daisy or Pearl. Even the thought brought the heat of incipient tears.

"Oh, Atticus, I miss you." The thought that he'd never written chased the tears as her teeth clamped on the words she often wished she could tell him. Something about being a coward and not living up to his word. So what if he had a problem? Running away wasn't the answer.

At least that's what he'd told her more than once when she was ready to flee the frustrations of the schoolteacher, who was now back to bedevil her.

She kept her horse at a lope and stopped in front of the white house set on a neat acre or so on the flat just south of the train tracks in Medora.

"Why, Opal, how wonderful to see you. Glad you are home again." Pearl, with one child clutching her skirts and another in her arms, met her on the porch. "Would you like something to drink?"

"That would be right fine." Opal flipped her reins over the hitching rail on the outside of a white picket fence. "Your place looks so pretty."

"Carl is a good builder. He'll be adding on another wing, hopefully before winter. We're hoping to take in a couple more boarders."

Opal leaned over to smell one of the roses blooming up the porch post and across the front of the roof. "Ah."

"Have a seat. I'll bring out a tray."

"I can help. You look to have your hands full."

"Come on, Carly. You know Opal."

The little girl hung back, her tiny hands twisting the front of her shift. She peeped out from lowered eyelids, as if too much of a good thing might send her into hiding.

Opal scooped her up and followed Pearl into the cool dimness of the front room that extended the length of the building. "Do you have a doll to show me?"

With a small nod the little one slid down to the floor and darted out of the room, returning in an instant with a rag doll, yarn hair in braids and a permanent smile embroidered on the flat face.

"This is some doll. What is her name?"

"Libby." Now a finger took up a place between the rosebud lips.

"Libby is a good name." Opal hunkered down on her haunches. Carly was a few months older than Per, the first small child in her life since she'd left the Brandons when Bernie was a baby.

"Come, Carly," Pearl said. She handed the baby to Opal and took a tray with two glasses out to the porch. "Bring your basket."

"Her basket?" Opal glanced around the room. Carl not only built houses but created furniture for his family. The desk he'd made for Pearl to replace the one burned in the fire when they were still at Dove House occupied a place of pride in one corner with a six-foot-tall bookshelf behind it, the shelves full of books read by both him and Pearl. Their mutual love of books had started their friendship back at Dove House.

"Did Carl make the sofa too?"

"Yes. Isn't he an amazing craftsman? I helped upholster it. He's working on a dressing table now. He found a dead oak tree down the river and dragged it home. He doesn't waste an inch of wood."

She set the tray on a small table and took the baby from Opal. Indicating a seat on the porch, she handed Opal a glass of red liquid.

Carly sat on the floor, removing a bonnet for her doll from a small willow basket.

"Raspberry swizzle. Our berries went overboard this year." A sigh of relief accompanied her sitting down, then she handed the now-seated Carly a small glass. "You be careful now."

"I sure wish you were teaching school this fall," Opal said.

"Mr. Finch is back. I saw him getting the schoolroom ready."

"I know." Opal shook her head. "That man."

"I know you don't like him, but he seems to do well with the younger children."

"They don't know any better."

"He's been fortunate to have you and Virginia to help him."

Opal took another sip of her drink. "I'm not going back." She might as well lay it right out there.

"I thought Ruby wanted you to finish your education."

"She does. But I'm not going away again, and Mr. Finch doesn't know enough." *Or care enough.* "I don't think he likes me any more than I like him."

"Not that you caused any problems in the classroom or any such thing, I'm sure." Pearl smiled at Opal as she helped Carly put the bonnet on her doll.

Opal lifted an eyebrow. "Do frogs, mice, or snakes in a desk drawer count as problems?"

Pearl shuddered. "I'm certainly glad I never had such surprising visitors."

"You made learning exciting. I loved school when you were teaching."

"I miss it too, but I have more than enough here to keep two women busy. I'm hoping some young woman will come west looking for a job."

"I've been thinking. I could help you for

a couple hours a day in exchange for tutoring."

"I'd teach you for free."

"But this way Ruby might be more inclined to think I mean to live up to getting more schooling." She started to say more, then paused to give Pearl time to think.

Pearl chewed the inside of her lip while rocking the baby.

"More, Ma?" Carly held up her glass.

"That's enough for now." Pearl looked back to Opal. "Even if I get someone to help, I will gladly teach you in exchange for things like cleaning the boarders' rooms or whatever else I need."

"That would be wonderful." Opal grinned. "You sure you don't have a horse that needs training? That's what I do best."

"Sorry. I hear you're teaching the Robertson girls to handle cattle."

"Yes. Them and Joel. He's the quickest of them all."

"I don't know how Cora is going to manage through the winter."

"Mr. Chandler is a good worker. Not much on a horse yet, but he's learning." Opal set her glass down on the tray. "I better get back to my charges. I left them roping steers. Or rather one steer. I brought a yearling in for them to practice on. The milk cows got tired of being roped."

"Tell Ruby I'm having everyone here after church on Sunday."

"I will, and, Pearl, thank you more than I can say."

"You'll earn your schooling." Pearl patted her shoulder. "This fall I'm hoping to get a quilting group going. The women out here need to get together more often. And my house is pretty central."

"I'll tell her." Opal jumped down the steps. "Bye, Carly."

The little girl clutched her doll by one arm. "Bye," she said and waggled the fingers on her other hand.

~⁊

The wranglers in training were sitting on the corral railing when Opal trotted Bay back to the Robertson homeplace. The steer lay on the opposite side of the dirt enclosure, chewing his cud and keeping a wary eye on the three ropers.

"How'd you all do?"

"He's the only one who got more than one rope on him." Ada Mae nodded toward Joel.

"Mean old thing. He shakes us off. Those horns . . ." Virginia shuddered.

"His horns aren't too bad yet," Opal said.

"Bad enough."

416

"Make your loop bigger." Opal rested her crossed arms on the saddle horn. "Were you roping from horseback or the ground?"

"Both." Joel shook out his loop, then recoiled the rope.

"He got dragged around the corral before we could get that stupid animal snubbed to the post." Virginia looked like she'd been dragged through the dirt too.

"Well, since you've had a rest, why don't you get your horses out again? We'll go find us some calves to cut out, and then maybe we should head on over to the river and cool off."

"You mean it?" Ada Mae perked right up.

"Sure. Bring your corks too." They each had a cork with a hook or two stuck in it, along with enough line to fish with.

"I'll go ask Ma." Ada Mae bailed off the rail and ran for the house while the others headed for the small pasture where the horses had been let loose.

Some time later, with their clothes nearly dry again and strings of fish for both families, they all rode home. The Robertsons and Joel loped on past the Harrison ranch house while Opal stopped to hand Little

Squirrel her string of fish.

"I'm going to milk."

Little Squirrel nodded.

"Opa!" Per waved his arms from the back porch.

Opal let Bay loose in the pasture and waved Ghost on out to bring in the milk cow. If only every day could be like this one. Now if only Ruby would go along with her plan.

Chapter Twenty-Nine

Was it a sin to be jealous of his son?

Jacob watched Joel from the shadows of the barn. The boy worked his rope like it had become a permanent extension of his arm. He flipped loops sideways, spun others over his head, the loop settling over the snubbing post, the milk cow, the small herd of weaned calves being kept in the fence for just this practice, his horse, a tree stump from the back of the horse. While he hadn't as much success over the long horns of cows and near-to-market steers, he'd gained the skill quickly. For a youngster he did better than most young men. Perhaps all the hours spent practicing had something to do with that.

Jacob took his rope from the wall and tried to duplicate the finesse of his son. He could now rope the post three times in a row, the minimum required by Miss Torvald.

He had yet to lasso a live animal, either on foot or from the back of a horse, although he had roped the post from a horse — a horse standing still.

He glanced over at the haystacks to remind himself that he had accomplished something of importance for all his hard work. That and the new corral they'd be using to contain the rest of the weaned calves.

He took his lariat out to the fenced pasture and ambled out toward the milk cow. She seemed the most amenable to getting a rope thrown over her withers or rump or to a bumping of her nose, as his did instead of falling neatly over her head and tightening around her neck.

I should just quit. I could get a job in town.

But you're not a quitter. The voice brought a mantle of comfort.

On the third try he roped the cow over her head. "Finally." He walked toward her, recoiling his rope as he came. "Good girl. Thank you." He slipped the noose off her head and stroked her under the jawline and along her neck, a favorite place. She stretched out her head, a visible reminder of her appreciation, making it easier for him to pet her. "Hope you don't mind if I try again."

After two more successful throws, he left her and ambled toward the horses.

The dark bay he usually rode tolerated his throws, twice shaking off the loop before one settled cleanly.

A sound of clapping from behind him made Jacob turn. There at the gate waited Joel, Miss Edith Robertson, and two of her younger sisters, both of whom were far more adept than he.

"Very good, Mr. Chandler." Edith clapped again.

Jacob felt like ignoring them, desiring to fail in private, but instead he smiled and waved. He glanced to his son, who applauded with the rest. Was that a smile he saw on the boy's face?

"I'm finally getting it."

"You'll make a cowboy yet." Ada Mae slipped between the rails and crossed the field, now followed by the others.

Automatically his gaze went to his son's face to catch a half smile and slight nod, all of which would have been missed, as he said nothing.

That meant more than all the effusiveness of the Robertson girls combined. *You've got it backward,* a voice sneered from his left shoulder, sounding so real he almost turned to see who was talking. *Doesn't matter what that child thinks. You're the father, the man. You know the Bible says, "Honor thy father."*

Jacob straightened his shoulders, almost said something, then stopped. *I'm the father all right, through an incident of passion, but someday I'd like to be Pa.*

"Show me how to lasso a moving animal, please."

Joel shrugged. "Sure, why not?"

"Thanks."

Joel loosened his loop and trotted out toward the horses, swinging the loop above his head, and when the horses broke into a trot, the loop floated out and settled over the head of the lead animal. "Horses are lots easier to rope than cattle with those long horns. They just shake their heads and get loose." He planted his feet and leaned back against the rope to tighten it, and the horse stopped and turned to face him. "You need to throw a bit ahead of a moving target."

Jacob could hardly believe his son had so many words available.

Joel coiled his rope again as he approached the horse, patted his neck, and slipped the rope off his head. "You might find it easier to rope one of us first."

"I see." *I'll never get this. Why is it so difficult for me and easy for you, a young boy?*

"I'll run, then we'll take turns." His son took off running.

"You have to figure a bit ahead of the animal's head." Ada Mae sounded just like Opal.

Jacob nodded again and shook out his rope. He made it on the third try. The grin from his son as he lifted the rope off over his head made every bit of effort worthwhile.

"You did it." Virginia clapped. "I'll run next." Virginia dodged through the gate rails and took off.

Edith made a one-woman cheering section as the others roped and ran and swapped places to run and rope again.

By the time the shadows lengthened toward evening chores time, Jacob had managed to rope a moving horse, the milk cow, the girls, and his dodging son. He laughed along with the others at the mistakes and the near successes, yelling "atta boy" or "atta girl," as the case may be.

"Sounded like you all had a right good

time out in the pasture," Mrs. Robertson said as she set the supper on the table.

"Joel's pa finally got it." Ada Mae plunked into her chair. "Roping's harder than anything else, I figure."

"Harder than arithmetic?" Edith raised an eyebrow.

"Don't remind me. School starts on Monday." They all groaned in unison.

"And we have church this Sunday. Mrs. Hegland has invited us all to dinner at her house afterward." Mrs. Robertson nodded toward Jacob. "I hope you'll accompany us this Sunday, Mr. Chandler. That's the best way for you to get to know your neighbors."

"Thank you for the invitation, but —" He glanced at Joel to catch a look of hope and real interest instead of the shuttered blank look of the summer.

"We'll be glad to go along." He nodded toward Joel. "Won't we, son?" *Now why did I say such a thing? I don't want to go. How can I not leave clues about my other life if I'm back in church?*

"Yes, sir."

Jacob fell asleep that night with real gratitude in his heart and on his lips. *I don't know why you keep on caring for me, Lord, when I ignore you like I have been. I know better. But thank you for your faith-fulness in spite of my actions. Although I don't at all understand it.*

❦

Saturday morning Opal arrived right after breakfast to work with her students.

"May I be a part of your class?" Jacob joined them at the corral.

"If you want. We're going out to work the cattle — roping, cutting, and trailing. You sure you're ready for that?"

"I have to learn sometime."

"How's your roping?"

"I roped a trotting horse yesterday." *And three running children.*

"And your riding?"

"I haven't fallen off."

"A cow pony?"

"One of the horses out in the pasture."

"All right. But you haven't been out with the cattle at all yet?"

"No." *I was too busy haying and fixing the corral.* He kept a pleasant look on his face in spite of the bite of her questions. After all, he wasn't one of the children.

Once the horses were caught and sad-dled, Edith brought out the saddlebags filled with dinner and handed one pair to Jacob and one to Opal.

"You all be careful now." While her

words were for everyone, her gaze never left Jacob.

"You want to come along?" Opal asked.

"No. Ma needs me and Emily in the house." Edith glanced at Opal. "We can't all be ranch hands."

"As if you ever wanted to." Virginia reined her horse around. "You can't look pretty and work cattle."

"That's not . . ." But her words were swallowed up by creaking gear and pounding hooves.

Ada Mae and Joel followed Virginia up the lane toward the buttes and draws. Opal hung back, then caught up with Jacob, who was following the others.

I'm going to have to say something to Miss Edith, Jacob thought as he settled into the jog of the other horses. *I don't want to cause a rift, that's for sure. But it's different when you live on the same place. Back in Pennsylvania if I didn't want to encourage someone, I could just not be available. I didn't eat at the same table every day.*

He glanced over at the young woman riding beside him. Now, why was it he found her far more interesting than Miss Robertson? He was even getting used to the idea of a young woman in britches.

Work like this in a skirt would be even more dangerous than it already was.

When they reached the top of the rise, Opal shouted for the others to stop. After they gathered around her, she gave the orders. "Drive all the steers you find up on the butte. Let the cows and calves go. You can work in pairs. Virginia, you work with Mr. Chandler. One of you hold the herd, the other drive out the steers, then take turns. Joel, you and Ada Mae do the same. Any questions?"

She turned to the man beside her. "I'll show you what I mean."

Now, that's a good thing. I don't even know what to ask. Jacob nodded. *I'd rather cut hay any day.*

"Gather them over there by the spring."

Jacob looked to see where she pointed. He didn't see any water. Where did she mean? Joel and Ada Mae took off up the trail.

"Come on." Opal headed off to a brush-and-tree-filled cut that led toward the buttes in a fairly steep grade. "Cattle like to lie in the shade after morning grazing and to hide there when they hear us coming. You have to look really hard for them, as they disappear in dappled shade. Fan out."

They drove their horses into brush that tore at their chaps. Jacob ducked under a tree branch, one hand clamped around the saddle horn. He leaned forward, hoping and praying his horse knew more about what to do than he did. When he found two cows or steers — how could he tell in all the brush? — lying down, they leaped to their feet and tried to run past him back toward the river. His horse spun to cut them off, and it was all he could do to stay on.

Virginia darted out of the brush and, using her coiled rope in one hand, harried one of the critters back the way they'd come. In spite of him, Jacob's horse shouldered the other, and the two animals headed up the draw.

"That's the way." Virginia grinned at him and pointed ahead. "You keep them on the right track, and I'll find more."

By the time they'd reached the top of the draw and broke out onto the prairie, they had six head.

Opal joined them with two more. "Now we cut out the cows and let them go where they will but keep the steers moving northward."

She nudged her horse into the herd and eased a cow and half-grown calf out to the edge. "Okay, hold the others."

One of the steers broke for freedom, and Jacob's horse drove after it, nearly jerking the man out of the saddle.

"Just hang on," Opal shouted loud enough to be heard above pounding hooves and bawling cattle.

Jacob did as she said, one hand, including the reins, clamped on the pommel, the other bonded to the saddle horn. Each time the steer shifted direction, the horse beat him to it and turned him back to the herd.

"Keep them moving, but no hurry. We can let them graze along."

Jacob wanted nothing more than to get off and walk, but instead he ordered his fingers to let loose of the saddle horn and slumped in relief.

"You did fine."

Sweeter words could not have been spoken.

"I nearly fell off." Admitting such a failure made his stomach clench.

"But you didn't, and that ornery steer is back where he belongs. You hold them now."

"Right."

Before long his heart stopped trying to leap out of his chest through his throat and he could breathe normally again. The steers lowered their heads to graze, tails switching at the flies — not that the wispy stubs looked to be very effective.

Three steers bawled as they broke over the rise, Virginia and her swinging rope hot on their heels. The three newcomers barged into the middle of the grazing herd, sending them all scattering.

Jacob's horse took off like he'd been shot from a forty-pounder, and again he hung on for the ride. They settled down just in time for further additions by Opal.

"Think you can cut out that cow?"

Jacob stared over the moving backs and rattling horns. Which one was the cow? They all looked the same to him.

"The one with the broken horn."

"I see." He sucked in a breath and nudged his horse to a jog.

"Take it easy. There's no need to rush."

He nodded, concentrating on the right animal. He eased into the herd, came up beside the cow and slightly ahead, his horse already aware which animal he was to work. Within seconds the cow was out of the group, and when she whirled to get back into safety, his horse spun and headed her off. This time Jacob was ready and stayed right with his horse, balancing himself on the balls of his feet with only one hand on the saddle horn.

The cow gave up and, shaking her head, ambled back to the brush, her bellow echoing across the valley.

"She's calling her calf."

"Or announcing we beat her half to death."

Opal chuckled. "You did much better that time."

"I was ready for it." He patted his horse's shoulder. "Do these boys do this naturally, or is it all training?"

"Both, but some horses never get it. You might as well put those into harness, because the cows outsmart them all the time."

"I never realized . . ."

"Most people don't. Rand says that back east they keep the cattle in close pastures and feed them corn to fatten them. Ranging cattle is a far different proposition. You take the next draw. Go on back down the one I just came up. During the real roundup, we'll have Ghost along too."

"Ghost?"

"Our cow dog. She chases those critters out of the brush, saves both us and the horses a heap of trouble."

Jacob reined his horse around and returned to the draw, letting his horse have his head on the way down. He leaned back against the cantle, his feet pushing the stirrups forward to the shoulders. Going up or down, neither was easy.

Once down to the fairly level trail — level as compared to the draws — he scouted for cattle in the brush pockets, pushing the two he'd found up into the next draw. He harried them along with his coiled lasso as the others did. But when two broke from under some trees, his horse saw them before he did and spun to stop their retreat. Jacob had no time to duck, and a branch caught him in the chest, sweeping him off the back of the horse. He hit the ground rear first, his head connecting with the dirt second.

The other two riders brought eight head to join the herd as they grazed along.

"You've done well," Opal called as the two groups merged and settled into grazing after a bit of horn rattling.

"Where's the others?" Joel studied the herd.

"Your pa is behind us. Virginia's ahead." Opal checked the sun. "About time for dinner. We'll eat after the others get here."

"We found a bunch of cows and calves,

not as many steers," Ada Mae said, then rode off to the right of the spotted herd, hazing one wanderer back into the group before joining Opal and Joel.

"They're looking good. Some are about ready for market. Has your mother said anything about taking some in early?" Opal gazed out over the herd.

"No, but I know we're short on cash." Virginia rode up beside her. "She wasn't able to pay Mr. Chandler like she wanted to."

"Let's work these on back to your ranch then and see what she says." Opal glanced over her shoulder at the sound of hooves behind them. "We've got trouble!" Opal shouted to the others when Jacob's horse, empty stirrups clapping its sides, broke over the rise. "Ada Mae, you hold the herd. Joel, rope his horse. Virginia, let's go find him."

They headed back the way the horse had come, dropping down over the lip of the butte and into the brush.

God, please don't let him be hurt. Visions of Atticus flashed through her mind. Was there another injury to be laid at her doorstep? After all, she'd given the orders.

Chapter Thirty

"Mr. Chandler!"

Opal could hear Virginia calling when she paused herself. They'd fanned out as they descended the cut, and with only about ten to fifteen feet between them, she expected to find him soon — hopefully walking up to greet them.

"Please, God, don't let him be hurt. Not another man hurt." Opal muttered the phrases over with each step her horse took. "Mr. Chandler!"

With all the noise of the horses, the brush scraping, and their calling, she might have missed him, but his hat snagged on a tree limb caught her attention.

"Over here," he called.

Her feet hit the ground before her horse

stopped. At least he was not flat on the ground. Jacob was upright and leaning against the trunk of the tree, head in his hands, blinking against the light.

"What happened?" She dropped to her knees beside him, her fingers gently probing the bleeding gash on the back of his head.

Her heart pounded so loud in her ears, she could barely hear his stumbling words.

"T-tree caught me. I hit the ground." He rubbed the back of his head and brought a bloody hand to spread in front of slightly glazed eyes. "Must have hit my head." He spoke slowly, carefully, as if searching for words.

Not again. Not again! The words screamed through her mind.

"Here." She whipped off her bandana and folded it to press against the wound. "Head wounds always bleed a lot."

"What happened?" Virginia crashed through the brush to stop dead still, her face blanching white when she saw the blood.

"Not bad. I'll be fine." Jacob's words were still slow.

"Virginia, give me your bandana so I can tie this in place. We need to get him home. You hurt anywhere else, Mr. Chandler?"

He winced when he shook his head. "I don't think so. Arms and legs are working."

"Can you stand?"

"In a minute."

"Virginia, go get his horse. Tell the others to bring the steers down to the corral."

"You want one of them to help here?"

"I think we'll be all right." Although Jacob still looked gray around his mouth, the color had begun to return to his face. Virginia ran back to her horse and galloped up the draw.

"Sorry. Such a stupid thing."

"Hey, we've all been brushed off one time or another. That's just part of cattle ranching." She checked the makeshift bandage, relieved to see that the gash had quit bleeding. "You're going to need some stitching back here."

His groan told her his opinion of that.

"But I don't think anything is broken." She'd read somewhere that the bones of the head felt mushy if broken. His didn't. She sat back on her heels. How was she to get him on a horse?

"Do you think you'll be able to ride?"

"Yes, I think so, but not very fast."

"Are you dizzy?"

"Some."

436

"I could go back to the ranch and get a wagon."

"No. I'll make it." His voice held a hint of his usual firmness now.

But staring into his eyes, she wasn't sure he would. The pupils didn't look exactly right. But he could answer questions all right and seemed able to think for himself.

Silence settled for a bit, just the sound of her horse stamping and the bit jingling.

"Would you like a drink of water?"

"Please." His eyes drifted closed.

She retrieved her canteen and led her horse closer, leaving it ground tied as all well-trained horses learned. She knelt beside him. "Here."

His hands shook when he took the canteen, but he held it to his mouth and drank by himself. "Thanks."

She could hear the horses and Virginia coming down the draw. The others would take the steers back south to a wider, easier way down so they didn't scatter.

When Virginia stopped a few feet away, she dismounted and led his horse over. "You sure you can get up?"

"Yes." Chandler pushed with his legs and used the tree trunk as an aid. Opal stood close, ready to catch him if need be.

He closed his eyes and took a deep breath.

"More dizzy?"

"Yes."

"We're not in a hurry." Opal studied the man, the horse, and the obstacles to getting him mounted. She refused to let herself think about the ride back to the house.

"I could go for the wagon." Virginia glanced from Opal to the man holding up the tree.

"No."

Opal shrugged. "We'll try it his way. Bring the horse right in front of him, then we'll take either side to keep him from falling."

"I won't fall."

"Let's try this." Opal moved to the man's left and waited for the horse to stop a foot from Chandler's chest.

"You ready?"

"As I'll ever be." He took one step forward and leaned against the horse for a moment before gripping the saddle horn with his left. A grunt as he raised his right hand to the cantle said something else hurt, or perhaps just moving his head caused it.

"When you put your foot in the stirrup and start to mount, I'm going to be right behind you."

Jacob's nod was so brief as to be easily missed, but Opal was watching him more carefully than she would a coiled rattler.

"On three?"

"Yes."

"Virginia, be ready. One, two, three." *Is this the best way to help him? No, go get the wagon, a well-padded wagon. Do it, Mr. Chandler, you can do it.* The thoughts buzzed around her head like a swarm of angry hornets.

He pushed his boot toe in the stirrup and with a mighty groan heaved himself upward and hung rigid for a moment — the longest moment Opal could remember. *Come on, swing your leg over,* she urged silently. Slowly Jacob eased his right leg over the horse's rump and, with as little motion as possible, settled into the saddle.

"Oh, good." Virginia let out a long-held breath.

"It's going to be worse when we move out," Opal warned him.

"I know."

I could ride behind him. Hold him upright. Opal chewed her lip. Would he allow that? "I'll lead your horse."

"Right."

"We'll go as easy as possible." If a human face could indeed flash from white to green, his did. Eyes clenched against the pain, he clung to the horn with both hands.

Opal rounded the horse to make sure both of his feet were firm in the stirrups, and then taking the horse's reins, she paused to ask, "You ready?"

"Um-hum."

"It will be easier on you if you can let yourself be loose in the saddle."

"Much looser, and I'll fall off."

"Let's pray that doesn't happen." She mounted her horse and, motioning Virginia to ride on the other side, started out.

They made it to the mouth of the draw and stopped for a break. "The rest should be easier."

"Just get it over."

"Drink of water?"

"No."

"Virginia, head home and tell your mother what's happened."

The girl nodded and nudged her horse to a jog, then a gallop.

"Easy." Opal stopped her horse from taking off too. At least Jacob's horse hadn't started. *Thank you, God, for that.* She chose the smoothest track, keeping watch both ahead and on the man.

"Stop."

She did, only to watch him slump forward on the horse's neck to retch and heave. *If only I knew some other way to help you.*

With a groan he lay still, a shudder rocking his shoulders.

"Water now?"

"Please."

She dismounted and helped him straighten so he could take a sip from the canteen. He swished it around his mouth before spitting. "You could use it to wash your face too if that would help. We're near enough to water."

"I can't."

"You want me to?"

"No, let's just get there."

When they topped the rise so they could see the ranch house, Opal felt like hollering her joy. They'd almost made it.

Jacob groaned and slumped to the side.

Opal was off her horse and at his side before he could ask for help. "Hang on. We're almost there."

"Just . . . rest . . . a . . . moment." Each word came separately as if being drug up from a deep well.

"Take as long as you need."

She released her hold on his arm, stepping back, almost checking her hand at the warmth she felt. That was crazy. She'd not felt something like that before.

She shook out her hand and mounted her horse in a fluid motion. "Ready?"

"Yes."

When they neared the house Mrs. Robertson called from the porch, "Bring him here."

Opal rode up to the house and dropped the reins. How she wished for Rand or some of the hands to help get him down. *If only Mr. Robertson were here. And that's all my fault.* She snuffed the thought like blowing out a lamp. *Concentrate on Chandler. You can still make a difference here.* She dismounted and stopped at his left knee. "Getting down won't be easy."

"I could just fall off."

Opal couldn't help but smile. She had to admit the man had a sense of humor, even in the midst of his pain. "Please don't. But we're here to break your fall if you do."

Jacob leaned over the horse's neck again, resting against the mane. Slowly he kicked free of the opposite stirrup and eased his leg over the horse's rump, lying as flat out as the saddle would allow.

Opal and Mrs. Robertson both braced his waist as he kicked his left foot free of the stirrup and slid down the side of the horse.

"Lean on me." Opal locked her arm around his waist from one side and grabbed his arm to drape over her shoulders.

"The bed is ready, Ma." Edith held open the screen door.

"Okay, son, one foot at a time." When he turned, Mrs. Robertson slid under his other arm so the two divided his weight. Although they made a six-legged creature, two legs stumbled, the weight they held causing the ungainly trio to sway and bounce off the doorways.

"Bunkhouse." The effort it took for Jacob to utter that single word was obvious.

"Don't be silly. I can't be running back and forth to the bunkhouse to take care of you. You'll be fine right here. All right, let him down easy." They sat him on the edge of the bed, then lowered him onto the pillow. Opal knelt to unlace his boots and pull them off before they lifted his legs to lay him flat on the bed.

"Thank you."

"See you stay that way." Opal closed her eyes at the memory of another injured man lying in bed. There too due to a head injury — because of her.

"You two girls get on out of here now. I'll get him cleaned up."

"You want help with that gash on the back of his head?" Virginia asked her mother.

"No. I'll do fine. It isn't the worst thing I've stitched up."

Edith wiped her eyes as she hovered near the doorway. "You think he's going to live, Opal?"

"Live? Of course he's going to live. People don't die from a wound like that — he's just going to have a headache big as Dakotah for a while." Opal paused. "Tell your ma I've gone back to help bring in the steers. We got twenty head or so we could trail in to the abattoir. I think Rand has some to take in too."

"I will." Edith glanced back to the bedroom. "He looks so bad."

"Better than he did out on the trail." Opal headed for the door. "We can be grateful it wasn't any worse."

"What happened?"

"Got swiped off by a tree branch. Happens to all of us one time or another."

"You should have —"

Opal whirled and glared at her friend. "I should have what?"

"You know he's not a good rider, and —"

"You get to be a good rider by riding. He wants to learn, and if he's going to stay in this part of the country, he has to learn. Give him credit for trying."

"I just meant . . ."

Opal straight-armed the screen door. "He's a man, Edith. You can't tell a man what to do." Opal mounted and would have ridden out at a dead run had she not had more sense. She could hear Rand's voice like he rode right behind her. *"Never take your feelings out on a horse."*

What is the matter with that girl? So she thinks the sun rises and sets on Mr. Jacob Chandler. Wringing her hands isn't going to help any. And I never saw her volunteer to get out and make sure this ranch keeps running. Always says her ma needs her in the house. Right, but no cattle, no house. Or at least no food and everything else it takes to keep a family.

By the time Opal met the herd coming in, she'd calmed down enough to answer the children's questions about Mr. Chandler.

"He'll be fine in a while. Virginia is

doing chores, so let's just run these brutes in that new corral for the night."

"How about we run them to the pasture, so they can graze?" Ada Mae pointed to the fenced acres.

"They might decide to go right through that fence, but good thinking. We can take them out to graze tomorrow."

"Tomorrow's church," Ada Mae reminded them.

"Ah, you're right. Let's take a chance on the pasture, then."

Opal loped on ahead and pulled back the poles so they could drive the herd through. When the last one cleared the gate, following the leaders like any good herd animal, she shoved the poles back in place and rested her arms on the top one. "You all did a fine job today, handling an emergency and everything. I am really proud of you."

"Is my father really going to be okay?" Joel asked.

"He'll do."

"Thanks to you."

"We do what we must out here. It's just a good reminder that we always need to be on guard. Accidents happen so quick. At least this one has a happy ending."

"Not yet."

Opal patted his shoulder. "Your pa is going to be just fine. Just give him a few days." *Not like Atticus*. The thought tore at her heart. She could help one man but not the other. What was fair about that?

Chapter Thirty-One

Big help I am. Flat on my back and needy. You'd think my posterior would be the part that's wounded instead of my head. He gently fingered the bandage Mrs. Robertson had just changed. How could such a simple thing as sitting up to be bandaged make his eyes cross and his stomach heave?

Be grateful.

The voice floated through the Sunday morning silence. Everyone had already left for church, including Joel, who had half-heartedly volunteered to stay and care for his father.

Jacob had told him to go on, that he'd be fine.

The Harrisons had stopped by, leaving him Ghost for company. Mrs. Robertson assured him that he'd be all right in a few days. After all, the brain didn't take kindly to being shaken up. And the more he persisted in trying to move around, the longer it would take.

It was not the kind of news Jacob wanted to hear. Keeping his eyes closed made life easier, so he did just that.

Right on the verge of sleep, he heard the voice again. *Be thankful.*

Thankful for a beating drum in his head in spite of the bitter willow bark tea that Mrs. Robertson made him drink? Thankful that he wasn't hurt worse. Yes, he could do that one. Thankful for clean sheets, the sun shining in the window, birds singing, a gentle breeze fluttering the curtains, a place to live for him and Joel, delicious food . . .

For my Son, your Savior? My Word? Me?

That stopped him up short. "God, forgive me." His groan brought Ghost to the bed to put her paws up on the edge so she could peer into his face.

Even the dog was concerned for him.

"Good girl." He stroked her head and down her shoulders and chest, then clasped his hands across his chest.

"So you had to knock me out to get my

attention?" Inside he nodded, favoring the idea of not moving his head any more than necessary. Ghost whined at the edge of the bed. "That's all right, girl. I'm not going crazy. You needn't worry."

The silence within the room felt like a gauzy covering of peace, so transparent he could see through it but so pervasive he breathed it in, a rich scent that made him desire more.

Come unto me all ye that labour and are heavy laden, and I will give you rest.

"Lord, I am coming. I am here, and I am resting. I know your Word says that you forgive, but how do I forgive myself? I've made such a mess of my life . . . my son . . . his mother. Lord God, the lies, the deceit . . . even here I have hidden away like a criminal."

He flinched when he gritted his teeth, clamping shut his eyes.

Do you understand that I love you? I have called you by name. You are Jacob, and as I blessed the man you are named for, I will bless you, and there will be no more deceit. Through you, I will bless others.

"I am not worthy." Burning tears scalded Jacob's skin.

I love you. You are my child. I love you.

Jacob's fingers itched to write. How long it had been since he'd written anything — letters, sermon notes, his journal — yet now he could hardly keep his eyes open to read.

He snorted, gently. Now that he wanted to, he couldn't even read his Bible, that dear book he'd tucked away at the bottom of his bag and not opened once since he stepped on the train. He'd left the Reverend Jacob Chandler behind. He'd buried him, as it were.

Ah, but someone would read to him. He felt sure that all he had to do was ask. Ask for help.

The agony of it, the weight that sat on his chest. Surely if he opened his eyes he would see an ugly creature sitting on his chest, licking its chops and grinning through slitted eyes and sharp teeth.

"Because of Jesus I am forgiven. God, my Father, said so. I am forgiven," he declared firmly.

Forgive yourself, even as I have forgiven you.

That word *forgive*. To give for. Forgive, to let it go. *As far as the east is from the west, that's how far God puts my sin from His mind.* Thinking made his head ache, but he struggled on, putting one thought

451

after the other, feeling the urgent need to do this now.

He would not refuse the laudanum the next time it was offered. But had he taken it before the others left for church, he would have been asleep now . . . instead of being set free.

What if — how could he not think of what he'd done? Joel was a visible reminder. How could he make it up to him?

Just love him. Be his father, as I am your Father.

"But, Lord, that sounds so easy."

Too easy?

"I already love him."

So do I.

"I know." Jacob lay still and let his mind drift. *But he doesn't love me.*

Ah, the crux of the matter. Why should he?

Pictures floated through his mind, pictures of Joel ignoring him, going his own way, glaring, always walking a distance apart.

"Ah, I have been just like that with you, Lord, haven't I? Ignoring you . . . going my own way. . . . But you have forgiven me."

A chuckle billowed the white curtains.

Jacob drifted off to sleep with that heavenly chuckle pouring comfort in his ears and heart.

He woke to the sound of horses and wagon wheels, of laughter and footsteps on the porch that ran the length of the house. Ghost yipped her delight at the family's return.

"Shh, he might be sleeping." Ada Mae could be heard clear to the springhouse when she tried to be quiet.

Mrs. Robertson stuck her head in the door. "You're awake?"

"I heard the horses come back." Jacob turned his head slightly.

"Can I get you anything?"

"Thank you, but no. Is Rand still here?"

"Out on the porch with the others."

"I'd really like to talk with him."

"I'll get him."

What am I going to tell him? The thought made him blink. Why had he said that? Not that he disliked visiting with Rand, but . . . *What do I tell him? Do I need to tell him everything?*

Somewhere he'd read that confession was good for the soul. It most likely went along with "Confess your faults one to another, and pray one for another, that ye may be healed."

"Opal tells me you got caught on the wrong side of a branch." Rand pulled the cushion-padded chair up to the bed after the greetings.

"Makes me feel right stupid."

"It has nothing to do with how good a rider you are or anything else. It happens often when the cattle are in the brush and trees. That's why a good dog is so important. Did Ghost take good care of you?"

"She got a bit concerned when I was talking to myself." *Or rather to God, but that is another story.*

A silence fell while Jacob fought a need to pick at the sheet covering, to stare out the window, to do anything rather than face the man beside him.

Coward. The name echoed in the hallways of his mind. He cleared his throat. "I have something I want to tell you, mainly because God has impressed upon me that I should, not because I have any great yearning to do so." He glanced at Rand from the corner of his eye, half expecting a look of either disdain or confusion but met neither.

"Do you believe God still talks to us today?" Jacob's words burst forth in a rush.

"Of course. He uses His Word too. I

often wish He would speak more distinctly, but when I force myself to take time to listen and the need is great, I hear Him."

"Ah, good." Once he'd asked a professor that question and had been granted a long diatribe on his audacity to expect such a thing. If it wasn't in the Bible, it came not from God.

He started to turn his head, but at the immediate return of the room to fuzziness, he lay still. "I'm not sure where to start."

"I've always found that the beginning is a good place."

Again another stretch of silence.

Jacob heaved a sigh that caused a drum roll in his head, and cleared his throat. "This started the summer I was to graduate from secondary school. I thought I had met the woman of my dreams and truly loved her. One night our passions ran away with us, and we spent the night together." He glanced out the side of his eye again to see Rand's reaction.

A gentle nod and a look of understanding greeted him. Had there been condemnation, he wasn't sure he could have continued. Without justifying himself in any way, he told the remainder of his story, bringing Rand up to date. "So here I am, still living a lie, and I think it must end now."

"Do you believe that you are forgiven?"

"By God, yes. By Melody, yes. By myself, well, that's why we are talking. I have sinned greatly."

"And been forgiven greatly. I'm no pastor, but I can say to you, in the name of Jesus the Christ, your sins are forgiven. A helpful verse I've learned is 'There is therefore now no condemnation to them which are in Christ Jesus.' If Christ and God himself do not condemn you, then where is it coming from?" Rand leaned forward. "I believe Satan himself condemns us so that we cannot trust God to do what He said He would. If Satan can get us to hate ourselves, we can't walk in the freedom that Jesus promises."

"Like me."

"Exactly. Surely God can use you here. He promised to turn evil into good."

"What do you suggest I do?"

"Well, you might not make the best cowhand, but I got me a feeling you'll make a mighty fine pastor. And our little flock is in mighty need of one. You'll have to have some form of support, like working right where you are, but we need the Word of God preached, the sacraments administered, and someone to marry our young and bury our dead without calling a pastor clear from Dickinson. You already took care of burying one of us. That made me certain there was more to you than you were willing to let on."

"You are very perceptive."

"Just observant. I like to see what folks are good at. Like, Opal is a natural at training horses."

"And people."

"Yes. As long as it has something to do with horses or cattle. She does love the ranch and everything that goes along with it."

"She was riding from the time she was little?" Jacob hid a yawn behind his hand.

"Oh no. For just a couple of years. You haven't heard her and Ruby's story?"

"No." He yawned again. "Sorry, I keep falling asleep."

"I'll go on now. We can talk again." Rand placed both hands on his knees. "I expect you're going to be laid up awhile yet. That will give you plenty of time to think. But not on the sins of your past any longer. They're over and done with. The present — it's a gift."

"Wish I could read, but I tried and my eyes . . ."

"I'm sure there are enough young ladies in this family that one or more will find time to read to you." Rand stood and extended his hand. When Jacob met it with his, Rand wrapped his other over the two. "Welcome to the family, son. You made it home."

Home. I made it home. "Thank you, sir."

"You are most welcome."

Jacob watched as Rand left the room, the silence falling again, the sounds of laughter and chattering voices diminishing as Jacob floated away on the cloud of peace that surrounded and upheld him.

~*~

The next days moved by most quickly when he slept a good part of them away. Since the younger girls were out working with Opal, Edith offered to read to him. There was no way he could turn her down without sounding churlish.

"Please don't be offended if I fall asleep while you are reading," he said, trying to cover a yawn. "I can't seem to stay awake for very long."

"I don't mind. When you sleep, I'll go help Ma again."

"I don't want to take you away from your duties."

"Reading to you is a privilege, not a duty." The warmth radiating from her gaze and her smile reminded him of nothing but the amorous glances of Miss Witherspoon from his church in Pennsylvania. But here he was trapped in bed, captive to gentle caring and serving.

I must have a serious talk with Mrs. Robertson. No matter how lovely her daughter, how good a cook, or skillful in wifely duties, I'm not interested. Why?

The other side of his mind snickered. *Because you've got your eye on Opal, that's why.*

If he could have leaped off the bed without paying a heavy price, he would have.

"Are you all right?" Edith stopped in the middle of the sentence. "Can I get you anything?"

"Ah no. I'm fine. But I think I . . . ah . . . I'm just too sleepy to listen anymore. Thank you so much."

"But you look really wide awake. Like something just frightened you."

If you only knew. Frightening is right.

She rose and gave him the smile he'd come to realize she saved just for him. "Can I get you something to drink before I leave?"

"No. No, thank you. I'm sure I'll be lots better when I wake up again."

Jacob sighed a breath of relief when the sound of her footsteps receded down the hall. Taking himself in hand, he began to list the reasons why he should not be interested in Opal Torvald. *She's too young. She wears britches. She would rather be with horses than anyone else. She knows more about ranching than I do. She can outride, outrope, out-anything me when it comes to ranching. She'd never make a pastor's wife. Who said she had to be a pastor's wife? Are you going to volunteer to pastor here? Besides all that, Joel is not ready for a new mother. And Opal is too young.*

Now his head ached as though a herd of steers had run through, a herd of stampeding steers at that.

Chapter Thirty-Two

"How's it working out with Pearl?" Rand took off his hat and wiped his forehead with a shirt sleeve.

"All right. At least I don't have to go for lessons every day." Opal loosed the gelding she was training back into the pasture, then joined Rand leaning on the top rail of the gate.

"He's coming along well?"

"He's willing, at least, not like that knothead." She motioned to a Roman-nosed heavy-boned gelding the Triple Seven had sent over. "I'm going to tell them he'd do better trained to harness. At least that's what I'd do if he were mine. He's not quick on his feet." She shook her head. "I don't want to waste my time on him any longer."

"So tell them."

"I plan to take him back tomorrow. I hate to even charge them. They could probably sell him to one of the sodbusters."

"Sure, as if they'd make it easier for one of them. They're the worst of the free-range advocates."

"I know." She stared across the river to where the sun was setting Chimney Butte on fire. "You really think they've brought in too many head this summer?"

He nodded. "If we'd had more rain, we might have been all right, but the land is grazed too close. Leaves nothing for winter feed. It used to be there was standing grass, all dried and waiting, under the snow for the stock to dig for. If we get a bad winter, there's going to be a lot of dead cattle. Those pesky sheep graze the plains right down to the roots. You ridden down the river lately?"

"I've not had time."

"The marquis brought in thousands of sheep. People think there's plenty of range. I just wish we'd put up three times as much hay."

"How come you didn't buy any steers coming up from Texas like the others?"

"The cattle born and raised here do better, that's why. These last winters have been real easy. But old Beans said his bones were telling him we are in for a bad one this year."

Opal glanced at him out the side of her eye and scrunched a face. "That's pretty superstitious. You don't really believe it. . . ." She paused and turned to face him. "Do you?"

"He's been right too many times to not believe."

The triangle clanged, announcing supper.

"Oh no. I haven't milked yet."

"Guess you'll do that after we eat. You know how Ruby hates holding supper."

"Ghost, go get Fawn," Opal commanded.

The dog left their sides with a leap and tore across the pasture, circled Fawn, and then walked slightly behind her as she made her way to the gate.

"Leastways I'll have her in the barn."

With Linc, Joe, and Chaps helping out over at the Maltese Cross Ranch, the meal would have been pretty silent but for Per.

"Son, you need to eat and not talk all the time." Rand laid a hand on his child's shoulder. "It would certainly help if I could understand you at least somewhat."

"He's like a clock. You wind him up, and

he never quits until the spring is loose. Then he just stops. No medium ground for that one."

"Ma, mo bed. Mo bed." Per pointed to the bread platter.

"What do you say?"

"Pease. Mo bed."

"That's pretty clear."

"He was telling you earlier about Ghost and the snake she brought in." Opal buttered a slice of bread for her little nephew.

"How do you know that?"

"He said Ghost and snake and dog and bad, mixed in with all the other. You just have to listen real carefully."

"It also helps to have known what went on this afternoon." Ruby passed Rand the bowl of rabbit stew.

"What snake?"

"A big bull snake Ghost caught. How she knows to stay away from rattlers is beyond me. She dragged it up on the back porch, so proud of herself she wriggled all over."

"She's brought gophers and rabbits before but not a snake." Rand handed the bowl to Beans. "You ever saw such shenanigans before?"

"Nope. Maybe she thinks we ain't got enough to eat." Beans sopped up the stew gravy with his slice of bread.

"Or she's not got enough to do. I should have sent her with the men."

Opal finished her supper and looked toward Ruby. "May I be excused? I need to go milk."

"Of course. Do you have studies to do tonight?"

"Some."

"Pearl said she thinks your arrangement is working out well."

"I'm keeping up." Opal picked up her plate and utensils and set them in the steaming dishpan on the stove. "I'll do these after I get back."

"Little Squirrel will do them."

"Thanks, Little Squirrel. I've got some geometry to do. I don't know why I have to learn higher mathematics." She put a sneer on the word higher. "I can do multiplying and division, even fractions. What's wrong with all that?"

"Nothing. But higher math teaches you to reason and figure things out. It makes you smarter."

Opal shook her head, muttering as she went out the back door. "Waste of time. What horse cares about the hypotenuse or the radius or diameter? Neither do I."

Milking was always a calming occupation. The sweet smell of hay and grain, the song the milk made in the bucket, starting with a ping and ending in a purr. The cat winding about her ankle was waiting for her to pour some milk in the flat pan for the barn cats, all descendants of Cat, who must have been taken by a coyote or an owl, since she disappeared one night. A ranch needed a lot of cats. The mortality rate was pretty high.

Opal released the stanchion and let Fawn amble out the door, then gave in to the cats' pleas and poured milk in the pan. "You won't be getting this much longer. Fawn is cutting back on her milk."

The three cats lined up around the dish, hunkered down, tails wrapped around their bodies, pink tongues making short order of the meal.

"There was a mouse in the oat bin. You better get on the ball and earn your keep."

They ignored her now that she'd fulfilled their demands.

Opal whistled a tune on her way to the springhouse, then realized it was one of the songs the girls used to sing. That made her wonder about Belle. She had taught Opal to sing and play the piano, to dance too, but Ruby hadn't been too happy about that. At least not the way the girls danced.

I wonder if I wrote to Belle if she'd get the letter. Or if she'd write back. The thoughts entertained her while she poured the milk through the two layers of cloth to strain out any dirt or grass seeds that might have fallen into it. Though she had brushed off Fawn's udder first, some chaff still made it into the bucket.

"You sound happy." Rand spoke from the rocker on the back porch, the evening dusk deepening the shadows so Opal hadn't noticed him.

"I guess I am." She ambled over and took the other chair. "Is Ruby putting Per to bed?"

"Um-hmm. He about fell asleep in his supper, but he still didn't want to go to bed."

"He might miss out on something."

"Mr. Chandler was asking after you today."

"He was?"

"Said he misses those roping lessons."

"How's he doing?"

"Up and around. He's still not ready to get on a horse, but he's working on something out in the barn. The man's real good with a saw and hammer."

"Like Mr. Hegland?"

"Pretty much."

"He'll do all right on horseback, given more time. When's roundup going to start?"

"In a couple of weeks. Think we'll bring in another fifty head or so if we can find them this week."

"I better get on the homework. I still don't think I need higher math." Opal left him chuckling on the porch and went to her room to retrieve her books. At least she didn't have Mr. Finch staring down his nose at her if she asked a question. Why was it he liked to make her feel stupid? Thinking about what fun she'd have if he came out to help at the ranch carried her through lighting a lamp and setting her books on the kitchen table. Little Squirrel had already finished the dishes and set a pot of beans on to soak. Sourdough for pancakes in the morning was rising on the warming shelf, floating a yeasty fragrance through the room.

Opal sighed. Might as well get the hard part over first. Greek or Latin were as easy as loping across the prairies compared to this.

By the time she'd done and redone her ten problems, yawns were chasing each other out her mouth. She moved over to Ruby's rocking chair and set her lamp on the whatnot table beside it. Studying the history of France had caught her attention far better when she started reading *A Tale of Two Cities*. Studying American history the year before had bored her to distraction. It was all dates, memorizing dates. However, the collection of letters written by some of the signers of the Declaration of Independence had made her keep reading.

"Isn't it about time you blew out the lamp?" Ruby stretched her hands over her head, then covered a yawn.

"How come you're up?"

"This baby hasn't figured out the difference between night and day yet." She patted the mound pushing out her nightdress.

"Little Squirrel says you are having a girl baby."

"She does, does she? Has she said what she thinks she is having?"

"Didn't ask. Did you know that human babies and calves take about the same time to grow big enough to be born?"

"And horses take another month. Rand informed me of that. I make enough trips to the outhouse now that I'm wearing a rut in the path."

"Is that usual?"

"Yes. It was the same with Per." Ruby made her way out the back door, carefully shutting it so the slam wouldn't wake anyone.

Opal read to the end of her chapter and replaced the bit of paper she used as a bookmark. She slid her books into her saddlebags so she would be ready to go in the morning and hung them up out of Per's reach. He loved taking anything out of anywhere, but he failed in the putting things back department.

The next morning after chores Opal finished her breakfast quickly and set her bowl and spoon in the dishpan on the stove. "I'm heading to Pearl's now." She turned to Ruby as she wiped her hands on the towel hanging on the hook for just that purpose.

"Will you go by the store before you come home?" Ruby handed her a short list. "You should be able to fit these in your saddlebags or that tow sack there."

"I guess. I'm stopping at the Robertsons' too. I can't let those young wranglers get too out of practice."

"Tell Cora hello for me and that I'm thinking on the quilting bee Pearl suggested. We need to make that a regular

470

meeting this winter. Sometimes I miss how easy we all had it at Dove House, the way we could sit and visit in the evenings on the back porch."

"I never thought it was easy. We worked all the time."

"Think of the taffy pulls and popcorn parties, the singing around the piano, taking turns reading. I was so proud of you, the way you taught the girls to read and write. Opal, dear, you are an excellent teacher. You know that?"

"I'd rather teach horses than people." Opal slung her bags over her shoulder. She stooped down to give Per a hug, then tickled his tummy. "Don't you go sticking out that lip. A bird will come and sit on it."

"Bird. Opa, up." He raised his arms, eyes pleading.

She hugged him quick and beat it out the door before he started to cry. Ignoring his tears, like Ruby said she should do, tore at her heart.

~

The morning passed like two blinks. Pearl even made geometry interesting.

"Now, say you were going to build a barn. You need to know how many square feet you will need, how tall the walls, the pitch of the roof, the angles on the rafters, how to square all the corners."

Opal shook her head. "I never thought of that."

When her lessons were finished, she helped Pearl scrub the floors and bake cookies, wrote down her assignments, and then rode on into town.

Waiting for Mr. Adams to add up her purchases took even more time because he was busy with another customer. So by the time she left town, school had already let out and the pupils gone on home. A glance over at the river reminded her of Atticus. If only they could go fishing again. Some days it seemed like that had all happened in a different lifetime. Other times, especially at night, it came back in a rush. *Oh, Atticus, have you forgiven me? Do you think of me and remember the good times?*

The ride on south smelled like fall. Dry grass, dry earth, sunflowers, and blue asters. She puzzled on Atticus as her horse jogged up the hill. Would he ever write to her? Would he return?

Off to the west, the grand house the marquis built crowned the hill, the orchard and garden closer down to the river. Mrs. de Mores had already left with the children, since they would attend school in New York.

That thought brought on another. She could have been going to school in New York this year. She shuddered and inadvertently twitched the reins, causing her horse to pick up the pace. "Sorry." She tightened the reins just a smidgen and settled back into a slow lope that ate up the miles. Some horses never got the hang of that easy gait, either pounding the rider to death on a hard jog or fighting the bit all the time to gallop. But riding Bay's lope was as easy as sitting in Ruby's rocking chair.

She eased back when they crested the hill that led down to the Robertson place. No one was working in the corral or out in the pasture. Two saddled horses stood at the corral gate dozing in the sun.

She rode up to the house and dismounted, flipping the reins over the hitching rail. "Anybody home?" She could hear a hammer pounding from the barn.

"Opal, come on in," Mrs. Robertson called. "I just poured the buttermilk, and the cookies are hot from the oven."

"Smells good in here."

"Emily, go on down to the barn and tell Mr. Chandler to join us."

"I will." Edith brushed past Opal in her

rush to get out the door.

Opal stared after her. *And hello to you too.*

"Don't mind her. She thinks Mr. Chandler is her own —"

"Ada Mae."

"Well, she's all goggle-eyed over him." Ada Mae shook her head in total disgust.

"Someday you're going to do the same thing." Mrs. Robertson pointed to a chair. "Sit there, Opal. My goodness, girl, but it seems ages since you've been here."

"Where's Joel?"

"Out changing his clothes. He's been practicing like you said to. Every day." Virginia passed the cookie plate. "Me and Ada Mae too."

"Ada Mae and I." Her mother made the correction without a glance.

"Ah, Ma."

Opal rolled her lips together to keep from laughing. "Ruby corrected me all the time too."

Ada Mae leaned closer. "It don't matter, I don't think."

"You don't want to sound uneducated, do you?"

Ada Mae shrugged and took a large bite of cookie.

"The way you talk and your manners say

a lot about the upbringing you've had. Your grandmother would choke if she heard you talking that way."

Ada Mae sighed again. "Yes, ma'am."

Opal heard Edith and Mr. Chandler talking before their steps echoed on the porch. At least Edith was talking.

"Howdy, Miss Torvald." Mr. Chandler removed his hat when he came in the door. "Good to see you."

"You're looking some better than the last time I saw you."

"I imagine."

"Ma's finally allowed him up on the promise that if he gets dizzy he'll take it easy again." Emily reached for a cookie.

Opal caught a look sent by the eldest sister that would fry an egg.

He certainly is a fine-looking man. No wonder Edith is all goggle-eyed. The thought caught her by surprise. What difference did it make how he looked? What counted was what kind of cowboy he'd make come fall roundup. She studied the man as he sat down. He seemed a bit stiff yet, and he held his head as if he didn't want it moving too much. He turned and caught her gaze, a slow smile warming his face. "I thought perhaps we could do some calf roping or something. I could use some more practice."

Opal swallowed and took another bite of her cookie. One sip of buttermilk wasn't enough to loosen up her throat, so she took another, this time choking on the cookie crumbs.

"You all right?" Emily thumped her on the back.

"I will be. Let's get out there before I have to head on home." She coughed again and patted her chest. "Just swallowed wrong."

"Buttermilk too strong for you?"

Opal glanced up at the sting in Edith's voice. Now, what brought that on?

Chapter Thirty-Three

"The way things are looking, I'm thinking we ought to start our roundup sooner than the rest." Rand stared out the window at the frost-painted ground. Just what they needed — an early frost. Not even mid-September, and what little green had been left from all the grazing was quickly succumbing to frost brown. "I'm thinking to keep the cows closer to home if we can. Sometimes fences are not a bad thing."

"If we did it on a Saturday and Sunday, all my young ropers would be available to help." Opal joined him at the window.

"Good point. Let them, and you, see what a real roundup is like."

"Let's see, how many steers have we already helped bring in and ship out for both spreads?" The innocent look she gave him made him smile. Her students, all but for Mr. Chandler, who still got dizzy when he tried to sit a horse, had proven themselves adept at flushing the steers out of the brush, molding them into a herd, and not only bringing them home but driving them to the stock corrals in Medora.

"You can be right proud of them."

"I am." *Of that and of the horses I've trained, even though women aren't supposed to be good at such things.* The teasing she'd gotten at first still rankled at times. But the men had had to eat their words, dust and all, when the horses she'd trained outperformed the half-wild ponies they usually rode. Gentling a horse was proving a lot better than breaking one any day. Not that most of the men would admit such a thing.

"Wish we had a few more horses to be worked this fall."

"We?"

"Well, me."

"Let's get roundup over with and see what happens. I'm hearing rumblings that local beeves aren't in good enough shape to earn top dollar. Sure glad most of ours are already gone." Rand reached for his hat and shrugged into a wool vest. "If we'd get a good rain and a long Indian summer, there'd be something out there for them to eat this winter."

~⌇

The next morning they were on their horses by the barn as the sky paled from indigo to pale cream. Visible clouds of breath from both horses and humans hung on the still air.

"We'll work in pairs like we did before. Each of you men take a youngster under your wing. Mr. Chandler will drive the cook wagon. We'll start west of the river. Most of the cattle are ranging on that side, heading south. Bring in anything, and we'll drive the odds over to the Triple Seven." He whistled for Ghost, and they all headed for the river.

Opal held back, since she'd been assigned the job of horse wrangler for the day. They would all take turns wrangling or searching except for Mr. Chandler, who was filling in for Beans. When the horse herd reached the other side of the river, she whistled and swung her rope to keep them moving. The riders would ride a horse one day, then give it a rest the next, even though they planned to be home by dark on Sunday. She already wished she'd started with Bay but knew the horse she rode needed more experience to become a top cow pony.

They rode five miles or so before Rand signaled the cook wagon to stop. "We'll camp here tonight, so have supper ready just before dark. Opal, you come on with me. Virginia, you keep track of the horses. Don't let them graze too far out. Keep in sight of the wagon." He pointed them all in different directions and the hunt began.

"Wish we had another Ghost." Rand glanced over his shoulder. "The way that wind is picking up, we might be in for a downpour."

"Good and bad either way." Opal pulled her hat down more snugly and slid the bead up the strings that often held the hat on her back rather than her head.

Hours later, after dodging branches and the horns of angry cattle, soaked from the rain squalls that blew through, and feeling as though she'd been in the saddle for days rather than hours, Opal trailed the twenty head they'd found while Rand and Ghost searched the last coulee. A cow and her half-grown calf broke out in front of them, and her bawling made the others restless. Horns clattered as those in the herd shook their heads and bawled back. Opal eased up alongside the outer rim, ready to leap ahead and turn the leaders if necessary.

Her heart thumped, pumping warmth into her arms and hands and down to her feet, feet that seemed without feeling from the long time in the stirrups.

"Hold them!" Rand's voice floated across the slow-moving herd.

Opal looked down to see Ghost smiling up at her, as if to say, no worry, we'll take care of this.

When things settled down, Rand and Ghost took off again, leaving Opal a bit disgruntled that he wasn't letting her have some of the action. She felt pretty sure the other kids were feeling the same way.

"But you know this is equally important." She'd caught herself talking out loud just to hear a human voice instead of only bawling cattle. Up ahead she saw another small herd heading back to the campsite. Joel turned and waved to her. At least the rain had tamed the dust. Lowering clouds hinted at more to come.

By dusk all the drovers had their cattle in camp, and after a drink from one of the deeper holes of a mostly dried up creek, the herd settled down.

"Come and get it," Chandler hollered loud enough to be heard over the cattle and the wind.

All but Joe, who'd been assigned first

watch, loosed their horses into the remuda and stumbled back to camp. It took a while for the ground to quit coming up to meet their boot soles after being in the saddle all day.

"I'm hungry enough to eat that whole pot." Joel got in line behind Beans.

"Chandler made plenty. Sure some different to ride herd all day rather than cook." Beans bent his knees, which creaked a complaint. "Must be gettin' old." He took a tin plate off the stack and waited for Jacob to load on the beans, biscuits, and baked venison. "Looks mighty good, young feller."

"I learned from a good teacher." Jacob smiled at the older man. "Just don't ask me to bake a cake on that thing." He nodded toward the rack over the ripe coals. "You can thank Mrs. Harrison for the dessert tonight."

"What did she send?"

"A big pan of gingerbread."

Within minutes everyone had a plateful and found seats either on wood chunks or the wagon tongue. Opal grinned when Ada Mae squatted with her spurs on and nearly dumped her plate getting upright. Most people made that mistake only once. Halfway through the meal the rain started up again, blowing in sheer curtains across the land.

"At least there's no thunder and lightning." Rand leaned against a wagon wheel, scraping the remains off his plate with a final biscuit.

"That would spook the cattle?" Joel left off poking a stick into the coals.

"Been known to. You young'uns did a mighty fine job today." Rand nodded and smiled at each of them. "Glad to have you along."

Thank-yous echoed from around the fire. Raindrops sizzled.

Opal fought to keep her eyes open, and she could see Ada Mae leaning against her sister. The thought of leaning against a shoulder brought her right awake. The shoulder she'd thought of belonged to Mr. Chandler.

"Linc, you go relieve Joe so he can eat. There is plenty left for him, isn't there?"

"Yes, sir. I set some back." Chandler turned from washing off the plates they'd all dropped into the dishwater.

Opal twitched her mouth from side to side. Should she offer to help clean up? Why? None of the others did. Her eyes drifted closed.

"You kids spread your bedrolls under the

wagon. I reckon that'll keep you some dry. Chaps, you take second watch, and I'll do third. Beans, you can help Chandler with breakfast so we can hit the trail right early. You might all pray that we get no lightning and thunder tonight."

Opal laid the canvas down first, then folded her quilt in half and folded the other half of the canvas over it so she had a snug cocoon that she hoped would stay dry. *Never thought I'd be so tired I could sleep standing up.* On one hand, she was grateful for the rain they needed so badly. On the other, she hated being wet, or at least sleeping wet, about as much as Cat used to. Under the covers she shucked off her wet britches and tucked both boots and britches, along with her sheepskin jacket, under her quilt to make a crazy sort of pillow. She sighed. That was about as much as she could do to keep them from getting wetter. Whatever happened to singing around the campfire and swapping tall tales like the men said they often did on a long trail ride? Rain, that's what. Knowing the answer didn't help alleviate her feeling cheated.

In spite of the dirt clod digging into her hip, she fell asleep before she could even ask how the others were doing. Sometime during the night something woke her. She lay listening so hard she held her breath. When it came again, shivers ran up and down her spine, all the way to tingling her toes. Wolves. Their plaintive howls echoed across the prairie. Songs without words. Or was it Indians? She'd heard that attacking Indians imitated animal noises. *Go to sleep. There've been no Indian attacks around here.* But her orders to herself failed. The eerie howls came again. Restless bellers came from the bedded-down herd. A horse whinnied and another answered.

She started to peel back the covers from her warm nest when another sound settled her down again.

"Jesus walked dis lonesome valley. . . ." Linc's deep voice raised in the old songs of his people floated peace across the camp. "He had to walk it by hisself. Nobody else could walk it for him; he had to walk it by hisself."

Another voice joined in. Rand's.

Did she believe that Jesus was indeed walking — riding — right beside them? She'd always said she did, and now in the wee hours of the morning, she clung to that faith. *I will never leave thee nor forsake thee.* One of the verses she'd memorized at Ruby's insistence echoed in her mind. *Lo, I am with you always.* Sheltered under His mighty wings, held in the palm of His hand. The verses flowed like a spring that never ran dry, bubbling up comfort and peace that let her sleep again.

~*~

"All right, cowboys, up and at 'em."

Opal blinked in the darkness. Had the wolf songs been a dream? She could hear the others muttering as they dressed under the covers. Out to the west a star hung low on the horizon. Light lined the distant horizon on the east, a thin band that struggled to overcome the dark dome.

Getting her legs into pants still damp took a grunt or two, but before she stood to button them, she shoved her feet into her boots. At least it had quit raining.

"Breakfast is about ready," Mr. Chandler announced.

"Come and get it before we throw it in the fire," Beans added.

"He wouldn't." Ada Mae sat up, forgetting to duck. "Ouch."

"You got to remember that when you sleep under a wagon." Joel rolled his quilt, then folded the canvas and rolled it around the quilt and stuffed it in the wagon along with the others. He clapped his hat on his head. "Were those wolves howling last night?"

"Sure were. They do a mighty pretty song." Beans handed him a plate of mush with sausage and sprinkled brown sugar on top. "You want one biscuit or two?"

"Two."

Firelight flickered, thanks to the wood that had been kept dry under the wagon. Opal took her plate and sat on one of the logs close to the fire. How could she be so hungry so soon? Her whole body felt as if it had been a very short night. The eastern sky had lightened by the time everyone had caught their horse for the day and mounted up. Rand gave the instructions, and they headed out. Opal looked up. A dark V of honking geese was winging south, another reminder that winter lurked over the next hill.

By the time they'd driven the herd, doubled in size since morning, to the ford, deepening dusk hovered over the land, lightened by what light remained reflecting off the water.

"It looks higher than when we came over. You want to wait until morning?" Beans looked from the river to Rand.

"No. We can do it." Rand checked the

river again. "They've been through a lot worse than this."

Opal stared across the river. A lamp set a window to glowing. Now she knew what a comfort that sight could be. Almost as if to say, "Welcome. You are almost home."

"Beans, you lead them out. Chaps, you take the upriver side. Joe, downriver. Let's do this nice and slow so we have no problems."

Beans nudged his mount over the lip of the butte and down the well-used trail, a couple of the older cows following him as if they did this every day. The herd flowed after them, bawling, the calves floundering after their mothers. Joe and Chaps eased down the sides to keep the stock headed straight for the river, not allowing any to panic and run up and down the riverbank.

Rand left the young wranglers to keep order while he returned to the rear to give Jacob his orders. Joel and Virginia brought up the rear with the band of horses, many of which had stopped to graze what little grass they could find.

Opal sneezed at the dust raised by hooves cutting through the damp top layer. The rain had run off the soil more than soaking in, as they so desperately needed.

If only they could see better. Bawling

cows, splashing calves frantic to find their mothers. The men's voices floated back, encouraging the stock and one another.

With the stock over the edge, Opal headed on down to be ahead of the wagon. Bay sat back on her haunches when she started to slide, so Opal kept a tight rein to help her horse keep her feet. Joel caught up with her at the bottom.

"They all across?"

"I think so. They've quieted down."

The river rushed by, as if in a hurry to get rid of the extra water and return to its summer somnolence.

"Opal!"

She looked up the butte at Rand's call. "What do you need?"

"Help with the wagon. Come on back."

"Sure." She shrugged at Joel and nudged Bay back up the angled incline.

"Put a noose over that pole and keep it taut going down. We'll be the brakes to keep the wagon from running over the team."

She watched as Rand settled his rope over one pole and, giving ten feet or so of slack, cinched the end around his saddle horn. Then she did likewise.

"Slow and easy is the ticket here. Just like with the cows."

"Yes, sir." While she'd seen this done before, she'd never been the brake rider. "Easy, girl, just keep that rope tight." The wagon eased down the trail, the two horses pulling against it, the team in front mincing down the hill, tails twitching and ears laid back. When they reached the bottom, she let out a breath she didn't realize she'd been holding. One more obstacle was behind them.

"Good job." Rand left his noose snug on the wagon. "Take it straight across, Jacob. It might start to float, so keep a firm hand on the reins. I'll be upriver to help keep the rear end from floating sideways." He turned to Opal. "I'll yell when we get across. Then they can bring the horses down." Rand followed the wagon into the river, doing just what he'd explained. The wagon made it across without a problem. Rand yelled back, "All right, bring them down."

Opal repeated the order, but when she heard no response, she rode partway up the hill. "Bring them down, nice and easy."

"We're comin'."

She could hear the horses coming, so she returned to the river edge. "Joel?"

"Here."

Virginia led the horses into the river.

With the last one in, the three young wranglers followed.

Opal's mount had just found its feet again when a scream from downriver made her turn in her saddle. A horse whinnied in fear, thrashing and churning the water.

"Help! We're stuck. Help!"

Chapter Thirty-Four

"Rand, it's Ada Mae!"

"Ada Mae, stay on your horse! Everyone else, out of the river." Rand spurred his mount into the river. "Opal, shake out a loop and help me get her out."

Ada Mae's horse whinnied, primal fear turning it to a shriek.

"Hang on, Ada Mae, we're coming." Opal shook out her rope in spite of shaking hands. Quicksand. With the river up like this, they could drown before being pulled loose.

The horse screamed. Ada Mae screamed.

"See if you can get a loop on Ada Mae," Rand said. "I'll try for the horse's head."

"Keep talking to me, Ada Mae." Opal could barely see them out on the river. If

492

only they had waited until morning or crossed earlier.

"Help me."

"Calm down now. Talk to me."

"The water's too deep."

"I'm throwing a loop. Try to catch it." Opal felt the rope plop in the water. *God, please!* Nudging Bay back out belly deep so she could see better, she hauled the rope in and threw it again.

"I got it."

Opal heard the tears in the girl's voice. "Thank you, God. Ada Mae, listen. Put the rope over your head and settle it around your waist. Kick free of the stirrups, and I'll pull you in."

The horse whinnied again, frantic in its terror.

"Hold still, you . . ." Rand tried his rope again. "Get Ada Mae out of the way so she doesn't get hurt. Then I'll get the horse." He drove his horse farther into the river, all the while talking gently to the frightened pair.

"Back, Bay. Back up." Once again Opal felt a surge of gratitude that she'd voice-trained Bay, much against the laughing opinions of the cowhands. "Back."

Bay did as told, backing toward the riverbank so that Opal could use both hands to pull in the weeping girl.

When she could stand, Ada Mae slogged her way to the shore, clinging to Opal's stirrup.

"All right, come on up . . ."

Virginia jumped from her horse and grabbed her little sister, both of them crying as they clung together. "I should have been watching for you," Virginia choked out. "You coulda died."

"I-I was so scared." Ada Mae hiccupped, her sobs abating.

"Come on. You can ride behind me on the way home."

It was me who should have been watching out for the younger ones. Opal swallowed the rest of her tears. "No, Virginia, she'll freeze in those wet clothes. Let's get her up to the house. Give her a boost up behind me." Opal leaned over and extended her hand.

"I-I can't m-make it." Ada Mae's teeth were chattering, her hands icy cold.

Opal whipped off her jacket and threw it to Ada Mae. "Take yours off and put that on."

Beans' horse skidded to a stop. "Lord above, I'm sorry. I was tryin' to get those fool cattle settled." While he spoke he leaped to the ground and hoisted Ada Mae

494

up behind Opal. "Get her on up to the house. I'll go help Rand."

"Hang on." Opal kicked Bay into a gallop and, trailed by Virginia, headed for the house. Ada Mae clung to her, still coughing and sobbing.

"What happened?" Ruby met them at the door. "I heard you gallop up."

"Quicksand. Ada Mae's horse got in it."

Ruby disappeared and Opal swung her right leg over the saddle horn so she could help Ada Mae down. Between her and Virginia, they got Ada Mae up the steps and inside, where Ruby met them with a quilt.

"Go over by the fire, honey, and get your clothes off."

"I-I c-can't."

Virginia threw her gloves on the floor and unbuttoned her sister's shirt, all the while murmuring comfort and love. Opal held the quilt to shield Ada Mae from drafts. Already the heat felt like hands caressing her face. As soon as the little girl was naked, they bundled the quilt around her and rubbed her arms and legs through the quilt.

Ruby dragged the tub in from off the back porch and set it beside them. "We'll put her in this as soon as we can get warm water ready." At Little Squirrel's instructions, Joel dumped in a potful from the reservoir and returned for more. Within minutes they had additional water heating on the stove and Ada Mae folded into the tub of warm water set close enough to the fire to drive away the cold — and the fear. Opal and Virginia stood holding the quilt as a reflector.

"Here, let me do that," Ruby said. "You two go back and get your wet things off and set your boots back here to dry." She smiled down at Ada Mae. "Sounds like your teeth quit chattering."

"I know. I ain't never been so scared."

Rand and the men stopped outside the door. "Are men allowed in?"

"Of course. Get on in here and get warm."

Within minutes more boots lined the front of the fireplace and along the stove, and the men sank into the chairs around the table, hot coffee cups warming hands as the liquid warmed insides.

"That was a close one." Rand shook his head.

"What happened?" Jacob asked. "Sorry, but I never heard a thing with all the clattering in the wagon. I thought we were all across."

"And we were thinkin' on the cattle."

496

Chaps huffed a sigh. "Sorry, Boss."

"It was no one's fault. Just shows that you got to be on guard every minute. Seems we all got a mite complacent that close to home."

Opal handed Ada Mae a pair of pants she'd outgrown and a shirt. Why had she not waited until the last to cross the river? What was she thinking of? Not watching out for the younger ones, that was for sure. "You warm enough now?"

"I'm cookin'." Ada Mae grinned at her. "We better be gettin' on home. Ma will be worried."

"I'm thinking you might be staying here. Leastways that's what I heard Rand say. It will be safer to go on after the sun comes up."

"Ma knows we'll be there as soon as we can." Virginia handed her sister a cup of coffee well laced with sugar and cream. "Drink this."

Ada Mae took a sip and wrinkled her nose. "I don't understand why grown-ups think this is so good."

"Just be polite and drink it."

"Soup's ready." Ruby set a plate of sliced bread on the table. "Everyone come on over."

When silence fell, Rand cleared his

throat. "Lord God, we give you thanks for saving Ada Mae from the river, for giving us a good roundup, and for keeping us all safe. Thank you for the rain we needed so badly, thank you for the food we have to eat and the hands that prepared it. In your Son's precious name we pray. Amen."

"Eat, Pa." Per banged his spoon on the table, making everyone smile and Ada Mae and Joel laugh.

The next morning the men headed out on the east side of the river to bring in whatever other stock they found. After thanking Ruby for her hospitality one more time, the Robertson girls and Jacob rode on home, Ada Mae cheering that they wouldn't have to go to school that day.

"Rand said you did mighty well," Ruby said, one arm around Opal's shoulders, waving good-bye with her other.

Opal half snorted. "I almost let her get drowned. Some good." She stepped away from the comfort of Ruby's arm. "I better get on down there and make sure the cattle we brought in don't take off."

"Opal, they're in the pasture."

"Oh, I thought . . ." She closed her eyes against the morning brightness. "That was too close, Ruby, just too close. That old river, I think it's got it in for me."

"What do you mean?"

"Well, thanks to the river and me, Atticus near to got killed. And now Ada Mae nearly drowned. I used to love that river, but now, now I'm not so sure."

Per tugged at his mother's skirt. "Up, Ma."

Opal leaned down and swung him up on her shoulders. He dug his fingers into her hair and jerked his hands. "Ouch. Stop that."

Ruby reached up to untangle his hands. "Be gentle with Opal." She patted Opal's hair. "Be nice."

Per giggled and slapped his hands against her head. "Go, Opa, go."

"Rand said all of you did a fine job on the roundup."

"Yeah, we did. I was really proud of all of us."

"You trained them well."

Opal jiggled and swayed to keep Per content. She nibbled the side of her lower lip. "I think I'd rather train horses than people."

"Why?" Ruby reached up to Per. "Come here, you rough rider, you. Opal isn't your horse, and since you can't be gentle, you'll have to get down."

"I'll set him down." Opal took his hands and swung him to the floor with a "whee" and a gentle landing. "I better get to work."

"Just a minute."

Opal stopped and turned to look at Ruby. "What?"

"All is well that ends well."

"Is that another Bible verse?"

"No, just a well-used truism."

"Just another normal event in life in the badlands?"

"I guess you could say that."

"And I should be thankful in all things."

"I'd like to believe you are."

"Me too." As Opal headed to the barn for the chicken feed, she thought back to what Ruby had said. Rand was proud of her. He thought she'd done her best, and her best was good enough. No one died or was even hurt, really. Not even that stupid horse that got in a hurry and slipped into the quicksand. She stopped with one hand on the barn door. Thankful. Full of thanks. *How do I do that, God?* The rooster crowed. A cat wound its mewing way around her ankles. "Start with all this, eh? Why, it would take all morning to list everything I could be thankful for." She tipped her head back to see another V of geese honking their way southward.

"There's truly no place on earth I'd rather be than here on the Double H Ranch in the badlands of Dakotah Territory. Thank you, God, that I don't have to fly south every year. I can just stay put." The barn door creaked a greeting as she stepped into the dimness and inhaled the rich aroma of hay and grain and cows and chickens, along with dust and leather and harness oil — a fragrance far better than any perfume. Something else to be thankful for.

Chapter Thirty-Five

Ruby and Opal watched the men ride toward the river to take the cattle to the Triple Seven. *Go with God. Please, Lord, keep them safe, all the men, but you know I'm most concerned about my own. Selfish, I know.* Ruby turned back to the welcome warmth of the house. "How about stopping by the Robertsons' and telling Cora that I'll come visit her tomorrow?"

"Sure." Opal kept on going through the kitchen and out to the springhouse to get the milk bucket.

Ruby watched her in the dimness of the predawn day. Opal moved with grace, a pleasure to the eye. Even wearing britches, she could never be mistaken for a man. Tall, slender, her long hair fashioned in one braid, she was every inch a woman.

Her whistle chimed in with the sleepy songs of the chickadees and finches that roosted in the cottonwood behind the springhouse.

The rooster crowed down at the barn.

Ruby closed the door and returned to the stove. "You want another cup of coffee, Little Squirrel?"

"That be good."

Ruby poured two cups and set them on the table. "I'll have some of that corn bread. How about you?"

At the assent she poured molasses over the two cut pieces and set the bowls by the coffee cups. "Sit down. We can finish the dishes later." Ruby took a seat and propped her elbows on the table while she sipped her coffee.

"I dry more pumpkin today. Pick rest of beans."

"I'm glad we let the beans dry on the vines. We need more dried beans. The men at the line shacks always go through a lot of them."

"Easy to fix."

"Do you want to go to the line shack with Linc this winter?"

"If you want. Baby be born in winter."

"I'd rather you stay here where you'll be warm." *And I can watch out for you. No matter what you think, first babies and mothers can have problems.* Not that they had a doctor or anything yet in Medora, but there were enough women around to help one another out. Cora Robertson had been with her when Per was born.

Ruby rubbed her belly, thinking of the life growing inside her. Would that she would have a girl this time. *Not that I won't be joyful with another boy, Lord, you know that, but I think every woman wants a little girl too. What would we name her?*

She'd caught herself daydreaming about the baby more than once. That is, when Per let her have a moment's peace, like this precious time in the morning before he woke up. She reached for her Bible that she'd brought to the table. It was too cold out on the porch. How she would miss the time out there, especially watching the sunrise bring Chimney Butte to life. Since their home was snugged into the eastern wall of the valley, the sun had already been up some time by the time she could actually see it, but the reflections on the far wall and peaks came alive with the sun.

"Be hard winter." Little Squirrel took her cup to the dishpan.

"How do you know?"

"All the signs. Squirrels thick tail, coyote

pelt thick." She held her hands several inches apart. "Caterpillars too. Muskrats building extra big houses. Need more wood."

"We need to haul more up to the line shacks too, then." Ruby knew that the next big push was readying the place for winter — banking the house and chicken coop, cutting and splitting wood. After the first deep snow Rand would string ropes to the barn, to the springhouse, and to the smokehouse, as well as to the outhouse, in case blizzards made it impossible to see.

Like Rand had said, it was a good thing Chandler was there to do these things for the Robertsons. *What would I do if something happened to Rand?* The thought clogged her throat. *Would I be brave enough to remain on the ranch like Cora is doing? But, then, what would be my choices? I don't have enough money in the bank to live on forever. What would I do?*

She opened her Bible to the Psalms, where she always went when she needed comfort. At the same time she scolded herself over worrying about tomorrow. *Let the day's own troubles be sufficient for the day.* While not from the Psalms, that truth always made her stop and think. After all,

Jesus promised to care for even the sparrows, and she had no trouble believing she was of more value than the twittering little birds.

"Ma?" Per charged into the kitchen and threw himself against her knees. "Where Opa, Pa?"

"Opal is out milking."

"Me go." He darted toward the back door, stopped only by his mother's lightning grab for the back of his nightshirt.

"Breakfast first." She set him up in the seat Beans had built that sat on one of the regular chairs. "You sit there while I get you some oatmeal."

"Egg?"

"All right." She dished the remaining cereal out of the kettle and poured cream over it, along with a dollop of molasses, and set it in front of him. "Where's your bib?"

He stared around and shrugged as if he'd been searching for hours and could not find it. "Ma, eat."

"I know." She took the dish towel off the bar on the oven door and tied it around his neck. "We have to keep you clean somehow."

"Clean." He started to dig in with his fingers, but Ruby caught him and put the spoon in his hand.

"Use this." She took the toaster rack from the hook on the wall and, opening the stove lid, laid the rack in place, a slice of bread between the layers. The bread toasted nicely, as the coals were hot. She turned it over for the other side. Once browned, she set it aside and laid two chunks of wood in the firebox.

He was down to the milk in the bottom of the bowl when the back door opened.

"Opa."

"Good morning to you too." She set the jug of the oldest cream on the table. "Thought you might want to churn today. Or I can do it when I get home."

"Good." Ruby handed the butter-and-jam toast to her son. "Oh, I forgot, could you bring the salt pork in for the beans?"

"Sure."

"Opa!" Per tried pushing back from the table, but his mother stopped him.

"You finish eating. She'll be right back." Ruby drained the soaking water off the beans, saving some for the beans and the rest for the chickens, and started chopping onion. Her eyes watered immediately, and she sniffed back the tears. "I hate chopping onions."

"Down, Ma."

She caught him before he could

scramble down, wiped hands and face, and gave him a pat on the bottom to send him on his way.

"Ghos?"

"Gone on roundup with the men."

"Pa?"

"Gone on roundup. Get your toys."

Opal returned and set the hunk of salt pork on the table. "You need anything from town?"

"Not that I can think of, but if you would, please dress that young man there before you go."

"Come on, big boy." Opal swung him up on her shoulders and trotted them back to the bedroom, her boots clomping out the beat.

Ruby stirred in molasses, the chopped salt pork, and the onions, and then set the covered iron pot in the oven to bake all day. With corn bread she'd bake later, supper would be ready.

After Opal left and Per settled down with his blocks, Ruby took out her paper and ink. A letter to the Brandons was long overdue.

Dear Lydia and family,

I'm sorry to be so negligent in answering your letter, but as usual, things around here are in turmoil as we work to get as much as possible put by for winter, along with roundup and sending the steers that are ready to the abattoir. Rand reminds me how much easier things are now than they used to be, so I don't mind that I didn't live out here in the early days. My friend Cora Robertson and her husband were some of the earliest settlers, and her tales make my hair stand right up on end — tales of wolves taking down cattle and snatching pigs and young stock right out of the pens at the barn. I have heard them howling and seen their tracks, but I have yet to see one. Little Squirrel is promising a hard winter, though I have a hard time believing the signs that she listed. I guess we shall see. I have not felt the last few winters particularly easy but am grateful for all our blessings. Plenty of food and firewood being two things at the top of my list.

Opal refused to go to school this fall, and if the truth be told, I can hardly blame her. The teacher here is not really qualified to teach the older students, and you can guess what the thought of going away to Bismarck or Fargo for school does to her. So she and Pearl, who used to be the teacher here, have made an agreement to exchange instruction for household assistance, since Pearl and her husband have opened their home to boarders. There just is not enough housing here in Medora.

Rand and the men have left for the final phase of fall roundup. You would be so proud of Opal, the way she took the Robertson girls and Joel Chandler under her tutelage to instruct them in matters of riding horses, driving cattle, and roping, which is an art all in itself. I am always amazed and delighted at Opal's skill in all these things. As Rand says, she is a natural, especially in training horses, but I also know she has worked many long and hard hours to learn the skills.

While in my heart of hearts I wish she would go to finishing school and become the proper young woman I always dreamed of her becoming, I know that is my wish and not hers.

You would not recognize me, I have become so rounded. I don't remember showing so much change when I was carrying Per, but Cora Robertson, my dearest friend here on the frontier, says that each of her girls were different from the time she realized she was in the family way. She is holding up well after the loss of her husband. I don't know what I would do if I lost Rand, but I rest in the assurance that God would know and never fail us.

I do so treasure your letters. I take them out to read again and again. Opal said the children are looking forward to visiting next summer. What a wonderful treat that would be. Life on a ranch in Dakotah Territory is so different from life in New York, but then, if Mr. Roosevelt can find such joy in ranching, perhaps it behooves more easterners to come west. He says that the wide open skies and plains have made him look at all of life differently.

"Ma?"

"What, dear?"

"Potty."

"Oh my, yes." Ruby took him back to the bedroom to the chamber pot they kept under the bed and sat him down. At the rate he was learning, he would be out of diapers before the new baby was born. What a boon that would be.

She set him to rights and returned to her letter, bringing Lydia Brandon up to date on Per and his accomplishments.

I must go stir the beans; their good fragrance is already floating through the house. I pray that you all continue in health and prosperity, and that all is well with your souls. I love the verse in Third John that I have varied a little here. What have you been reading that would be good for me also? Please write back soon, dear friend, for your letters bring us such joy, especially now that the nights are getting longer again and the outside work is slowing down. Perhaps I'll get my mending caught up. I think of the sewing machine that burned in the fire and pray that one day I shall have one again.

Yours always,
Ruby

She read the letter again, addressed the envelope, and set it on the shelf that Rand had Carl build for her last Christmas. Opal could mail it on Friday when she returned to Pearl's for school.

Not needing to make dinner for all the men gave her a sense of freedom, heady enough to grab up Per and whirl him around the kitchen in a half-time waltz.

"More." He clapped when she stopped. "More, Ma."

"Let's go find Little Squirrel, or perhaps we can take the churn out on the back porch." She glanced out the window. Sure enough, the clouds had blown over and the sun was painting the yard and garden in that golden light that sparkled of fall. The number of choices of what to do next made her giddy, laughter bubbling up at the grin on Per's round little face.

She carried him with her out to the back porch. "Little Squirrel, let's go down to the river and have a picnic."

Little Squirrel looked up from where she fed more wood into the fire under the drying racks, hung with strips of pumpkin. "Go fishing? Could dry fish too."

"If you want. Remember you said you would teach me to weave willow baskets?"

Little Squirrel nodded, her dark eyes dancing. "Yes, need baskets. Cattail make good basket too. One day go dig cattail root. Good to eat."

"Oh, really? You get worms, and I'll fix our dinner."

"Fry fish."

"All right." *Oh, I wish Opal were home. She would love this.* Ruby returned to the house, gathered cookies and other supplies, including bacon grease and cornmeal and a frying pan, a blanket for Per to sleep on, and away they went.

~⟋

Opal found them later in the afternoon. "I was getting worried when you weren't around the house." She swung off her horse and dropped the reins. "Any fish left?"

"Not fried. Little Squirrel has a long line down there. She's going to dry them." Ruby laced one more willow branch in and out of the basket ribs.

"When did you learn to weave a basket?"

"Today."

"And you made all of that?" Opal hunkered down and admired the half-woven basket.

"Little Squirrel started it."

"Where's Per?"

"Fishing. He caught several."

"He landed them?"

"I'm sure he had help."

A burst of laughter from both baby and woman floated back from the point of the sandbar that had arisen during the dropping of the river.

"He's having fun."

"We've all been having fun." Ruby tipped the brim of her flat leather hat back. "We didn't have to cook dinner, so we ran away."

"Ran?" Opal glanced at Ruby's extending middle.

"You know what I mean."

Opal glanced up at the honking V of geese. "If they'd set down around here, I could bag us some of those tonight." She pointed to the saddle. "I have the gun."

"If you want to go, Little Squirrel could milk for you. Roast goose sounds wonderful."

"It's a shame I didn't bring Joel with me. He wants to learn to hunt."

"Opal, are you sure you — ?" Ruby flinched inside at the look in Opal's eyes.

"Not too many men will attack someone with a gun, even if she is female."

"True. Be careful."

"Ruby." Opal stood and shook her head the slightest amount but enough to convey her sentiments.

Ruby watched her mount and turn the horse away from the riverbank, then head upriver. *Please, Lord, take care of her. And thank you for this day to treasure.*

❧

She heard the horse lope into the yard when dusk had just given up to dark.

"Ruby."

She opened the door just as Opal called her name.

"Look what I got." Opal held up several geese, their feet knotted together with thongs. "And here." A deer lay across the horse's rump, antlers catching the light from the door.

"I'll take the geese. You going to hang the deer in the barn or the springhouse?"

"The tackle is in the springhouse. I'll ask Little Squirrel if she'll help me dress it out. It's a three point."

They finally turned in around midnight, what with dressing out four geese and a deer. Ruby laid her hand over Rand's side of the bed. "Keep him safe, dear Lord." Her back ached, and she'd just about dozed off when a cramp in her leg threw her out of bed. "Argh." She paused. What was that she heard? The chickens. Something was after the chickens.

"Opal, get the gun!" she called. And Rand had told her to take it easy.

Some time later Ruby crawled back in bed again. She could hear Opal muttering about missing her shot. The weasel got away, but without his prey. Would that all weasels could be apprehended.

Chapter Thirty-Six

I wish Atticus were here. Opal stared out across the dancers, patterns forming and changing as the whirling partners followed the singsong instructions of the caller. Since the roundup celebration was being held in the town square this time, ranchers and townspeople, farmers, even the army platoon and some of their families came out to the festivities. Rand and a crew had a fat steer turning slowly over the coals, the fragrance making her nose twitch.

"Are you all right?" Ruby stopped beside her in the shade of the cottonwood tree.

"Sure. Just catching my breath."

"I'm hoping to find mine again." Ruby patted the mound under her apron. "This one likes to push up against my lungs. Must be a girl. She loves to dance."

"How do you know?" Opal stared at her sister.

"I started dancing, and she started too. She's kicking up a storm."

Opal rolled her eyes. "Ruby."

"Just you wait until you have one."

"That'll be a l-o-n-g time." *Might not have been so long had Atticus stayed around.*

"Something's bothering you."

"How do you know?" *Tell her, silly.*

"Your eyes are wearing clouds."

"I-I wish Atticus were still here and things were back to the way they used to be."

"Oh, my dear Opal." Ruby put her arms around her sister. "So often we wish for things to change, but once it has happened, there is no going back."

"That's what Mrs. Brandon said too." Opal fought the tears that threatened to overflow. "H-he was my best friend. Why doesn't he write to me?"

"I wish I knew."

"Sometimes I think he may be dead, or he hates me." The dam burst and she sobbed against Ruby's shoulder. "It's not fair. He was such a good person. Everybody liked Atticus."

"It's true it's not fair." Ruby stroked Opal's hair and let her cry.

When the sobs turned to sniffles, Ruby handed Opal a handkerchief from her pocket. "Perhaps we should pray that he will write to you, to at least let you know where and how he is."

"Would you?"

"Of course." Ruby used her thumbs to smooth away the moisture under Opal's eyes. She cocked her head. "Ah, Rand is back to playing."

Opal sighed. "Think I'll go see how Per is doing."

"I'll do it. You go have fun." Ruby headed toward the area under another tree that had been blocked off for the smallest children. Some of the older children took turns playing with the babies, while others copied those dancing for a while, then ran yelling after someone who teased them.

Opal sniffed once more, swallowed the rest of the tears, and made her way back to the table where punch filled a tin tub and Pearl stood dispensing cups of the refreshment to those who stopped by.

"Hi, Opal. You want some?"

"Yes, please." She took the cup and sipped, watching the dancers over the rim. Linc and Little Squirrel waved as they sashayed by.

"You all right?"

"I guess." *Am I wearing a sign that says I'm sad?* "I'd rather be home working with the horses."

"I'm thinking the men here are just glad to be off their horses for a time."

"Most likely."

"Don't you like dancing? You looked to be having a good time."

"Miss Opal?"

She turned to see one of the hands from the Triple Seven waiting.

"Can I have this dance?"

"Sure." She set her cup down. "Thanks, Pearl."

As she whirled into the schottische, she saw Edith standing off to the side. The look on her face matched that of a lovesick cow.

Oh-oh. I bet Mr. Chandler hasn't been paying her enough attention. Opal glanced around to see Mr. Chandler dancing with a young woman and laughing at something as he twirled her under his arm. *He is one fine-looking man.* The thought caught her by such surprise she missed a beat and would have stumbled but for the firm hand of the man she danced with.

The deep blue of Mr. Chandler's shirt made his eyes seem bluer than ever, and the sun glinted on hair the color of prairie grass ready for haying. She turned away when she caught him glancing her way. When the dance ended, she headed back to the table for another drink. At a tap on her shoulder she turned, her elbow catching the midriff of the man behind her. The drink sloshed over the rim, splashed on her arm, and decorated Mr. Chandler's shirtfront.

"Oh, sorry." *Ground, swallow me up. How can I be so clumsy?*

With one hand he brushed off the droplets, all the while keeping his gaze on her. "Could I please have this dance?"

"I . . . ah . . ." She glanced down at the dark spots, traveled up over dark blue material stretched over a broad chest, past a square chin, faltered on lips that quirked a bit, leaped over a straight nose, and locked on eyes that crinkled at the outside edges, the blue of a hot summer sky, intense and yet hinting at gentleness.

"Miss Torvald?"

The sound of his voice broke her reverie. What was it he wanted?

"This dance. Would you dance with me? Please." The "please" tacked on at the end of the thought as if he'd just been reminded of his manners.

"Ah, sure." What in all that grew green

had happened to her? *You ninny. It's just Jacob Chandler. You've been trying to teach him to rope and ride. Why are you acting so silly?*

He stretched out his hand and took hers.

She allowed him to lead her out into the dancers, place one hand on her waist, and then hold her right hand in the air. The waltz plucked at her feet, and they never touched the ground until the music stopped.

"Thank you. Care to dance this next one?"

Opal nodded.

"All right, all you dancers, form your squares." Mr. Adams from the general store loved calling the square dances as much as the people loved dancing them. Rand on the guitar, Pearl on the piano, and one of the Triple Seven hands on the fiddle paused their playing as four couples moved to make up each square. "That's right, folks, there's room over here for one more pair." He nodded to the musicians, and the music started up again.

Opal curtsied, swung with her partner, and promenaded around the circle. Once around and she moved to a new partner. Chaps swung her around, and the pattern continued.

"You done caught that young man's attention," he told her as he swung her to his side before twirling her under an upraised hand.

Opal waited until they were close together again to ask, "Who? What?"

Chaps winked at her as he handed her off to the next partner.

Jacob crossed his arms and did a do-si-do around his partner, all the while wondering at the swell of emotion he'd felt when waltzing with Opal. He was right. The times he'd felt that before weren't counterfeit. Opal Torvald attracted him like no woman had since his days with Melody.

He passed his partner on to the next just in time to take Opal's hand again. Her smile set his heart to tapping to catch up with his feet.

Today she looked far different from the horse trainer in britches, long-sleeved shirt, and no-nonsense hat. Blue and white gingham suited her, as did a full skirt and puffed sleeves with white lace around the neckline.

He caught her on the spin and tucked her under his arm for a promenade back home. Tall as she was, she just fit. He smiled into her upturned face and released her into a grand right and left back home. Surely following the complicated patterns wasn't enough to set his heart to dancing this way.

At the end of the dance another man claimed her, and Jacob leaned back against a cottonwood trunk, the better to watch the dancers. He chuckled when he saw Joel, his face screwed up in concentration as he danced by with Ada Mae.

He wandered back over to the table and thanked the young woman pouring when she handed him a cup of punch.

"I don't think we've met."

"No. I'm Jacob Chandler. I work out at the Robertsons'."

"I'm Daisy Higgins and pleased to meet you. How do you like our badlands?" She handed a filled cup to someone else.

"Very much. Moving here has been a good thing, even though I'm still not much of a wrangler."

"My Charlie's not either. Not everyone was born to sit a horse." She handed a child a cup. "You're welcome," she replied to his thank-you.

Jacob lifted his cup. "Refill?"

"Sure enough." She dipped out more and filled his cup. "You come on by and visit us sometime. Anyone invited you to join us for church?"

"Ah, yes. My son and I will be coming next time." He almost explained that he had not come earlier due to that head injury, but instead he just nodded and turned away. Now he'd really committed himself. He followed his nose to the fire pit where half a beef was being turned on a spit. The fragrance made his mouth turn to liquid.

"You want to take a turn?" Joe from the Harrison ranch offered.

"Sure, why not?" Jacob took hold of the crank.

"Keep it nice and slow."

Jacob gave the crank a turn. The sizzle of dripping fat, the flare of the coals at the grease gave him a feeling of a different space, here away from the music and dance.

"Hi, Mr. Chandler, how are you?"

The voice from behind him caught him unaware, but he recognized it well.

"I'm fine, and you, Miss Robertson? I'd think you'd be over there dancing."

"I was hoping, ah . . ."

He gave the crank another slow turn.

"Can I get you anything? Something to drink? They've set cookies out."

"No thanks. I've got some." He indicated the cup he'd set on a nearby rock.

"I'm glad to see you are doing so well."

Guilt sizzled like the juices on the coals. "Thanks to the graciousness of you and your mother. No one has had better care. Thank you." Why couldn't he care for her? It would make things so easy.

But not if you care for another. The small voice could hardly be heard above the dying grease drops flaring in the yellow and white coals.

Surely someone would come to relieve him soon. He turned the crank again. The fire's flame heated his hands and face. Had he known he'd be doing this, he'd have brought his leather gloves along. *Why didn't I talk with Cora as I had planned?*

Time for brutal honesty. *Because I was uncomfortable. Lord, have I not learned my lesson? Apparently not. I do not want to hurt this lovely young woman, yet better a gentle hurt now than something terrible happening.*

What if Mrs. Robertson asks me to leave if I bring this up? There are other jobs, but none so perfect for both my son and me.

"Mr. Chandler?"

"Yes?" He kept his attention on turning

526

the crank. It had a tendency to whip around halfway through the turn, an easy way to crack a wrist.

"I . . . um . . . I could bring you another drink if you would like."

"Thank you, but I'm fine." As soon as he said that, a thirst the size of the badlands attacked his throat.

"Oh. Did I tell you about the new book I've been reading? It's *David Copperfield* by Charles Dickens. I'll be reading it to the family in the evenings now that it gets dark so early."

"Good for you."

"You could join us if you like. I'm sure Joel would enjoy the story too."

Not fair. The quicksand is sucking me down. If I stay in the bunkhouse and send Joel, I'm being surly. If I keep him with me, he'll miss out on a good thing. If I go, I encourage you.

"I . . . ah . . . I guess I will see you back at the dancing."

"Everyone seems to be having a good time." He glanced over to the musicians who were tuning up again, Rand one of them.

"Would you like me to ask one of the other men to take a turn there?"

Oh, please, yes. He wiped the running

527

sweat from his brow and temples. "Someone will surely come by."

"As you wish." Her tone wore a touch of starch.

He watched her march back to the gathering. *Now you've offended her.* He sighed. There was no winning this . . . this . . . what? It wasn't a battle, really, but an insidious attack.

After he endured a few more wrestling matches with the crank, Beans wandered over.

"Mite hot there, ain't it?"

"Yes."

"I better throw more wood on. The coals seem to be dyin' some."

Not that I can tell. He watched Beans stack the fire just so.

"There's an art to keeping the coals just right."

"Looks that way."

"You want me to take over for a bit?"

"If you'd like." Jacob stepped back from the heat. "If this tastes as good as it smells, there won't be one lick left over."

"Folks fight over the bones even. The sweetest meat is right down on the bones."

"You don't say." Jacob took out his handkerchief to wipe his brow and the back of his neck.

"You go on and get yerself a drink. If you want some cider, that's over to the store."

"Cider?"

"Got a bit of a kick to it, if you know what I mean."

"Oh." *I hope he means only apple cider and not the hard stuff. I'd hate to see someone get liquored up and create a scene.* He'd heard stories of the goings-on across the river, thanks to a few local and colorful characters.

"Thanks. You want me to spell you in a while?"

"Nah, you took your turn. Someone will amble on over. Should be slicing it for supper pretty soon."

Jacob nodded and headed for the punch table but veered off to the public pump. Something sweet wouldn't satisfy his thirst as well as plain water.

He pumped and drank, soaked his kerchief to mop his face and neck, drank some more, and pumped for a couple of little boys who then half-soaked themselves drinking from the spout. Within seconds he had a line of children waiting their turn, giggling and shouting to others.

Jacob resigned himself to his new duty, laughing and teasing them as they took turns. When he realized they were drinking then running to the end of the line to come up again, he let the pump handle slow to a stop.

"Sorry, that's all."

"Please, mister. One more time." The plaintive cry came from several hopeful faces.

"Nope. Your mas might come after me for letting you get all wet."

"But you washed our hands and faces too."

"So we're all clean for supper." Two held out hands for good measure.

"I've got a better idea. How would you like to hear a story?"

"You gots a book to read?"

"No, but some folks say I tell a good story. How about we go on over to that oak tree and sit in the shade?"

"And you'll tell us a story?" The children clustered around him, dancing and giggling their delight.

"What story you gonna tell?" One little girl took his hand, beaming up at him.

"I thought perhaps . . ." He rubbed his chin with one finger as if deep in thought.

" 'Three Billy Goats Gruff'?"

" 'Jack and the Beanstalk'?"

"How about 'David and Goliath'?" He

looked from upturned face to upturned face.

"Is it a good story?"

"Yes, it most certainly is." Jacob crossed his legs and sank to the ground, several children copying him, others just sprawling.

"Once a long time ago . . ."

"Before we was borned?" A little girl with freckles dancing across nose and cheeks asked the question.

"Long before any of us were born or even our mothers and fathers were born or our grandfathers. Way back in very early times a boy not much older than you was out in the countryside taking care of his father's sheep."

"My pa don't like sheep much. He says they are smelly and stupid and ruin the pasture."

Jacob nodded. "That's true. Sheep are all of those things, but they also provide us with wool for our clothes and blankets —"

"And stockings. My ma knits lots of socks."

"Very true. To help keep you warm in the winter, right?"

"My winter underwear itches. I don't like wool much."

"Let's get back to our story." While he

unfolded the story of David and Goliath to them, the children stared at him in rapt awe, giggling when he changed his voice to portray the parts, and falling silent as he waved an imaginary sling around his head to let the stones fly. When Goliath hit the ground, all the children applauded.

"And so we see that when God is on our side, we can slay even giants." He glanced up to see that Ada Mae and Joel had joined the group, along with other older children he didn't know.

"That's Joel's pa," Ada Mae announced to all the children. She pointed to the boy beside her.

The look Joel sent his father wore a touch of pride.

Jacob nodded, while inside his mind danced and his heart leaped. The feelings happened again when sometime later Joel joined him in the line waiting for a piece of the beef being served by four men who were slicing as fast as they were able.

~⋊

"That was some shindig," Mrs. Robertson commented on the ride home. "Times like this I miss my Ward so bad I can about taste it."

Jacob sighed. "I can't begin to understand how you feel, but I can say how sorry

I am you have to walk through this." Losing Melody when he'd planned to marry her had taught him something of grief. It hurt, clear to the bone and the innards. It colored the whole world in tones of gray and preyed on one like some vicious critter that slashed and ran, leaving you bleeding and reeling from the shock. Not just once, but over and over until you caught yourself watching the shadows and listening for the footfall, all the while knowing there was nothing there. The one you loved was gone, and there was nothing you could do about it but endure. Unless . . .

"I found comfort in His Word," Jacob offered.

"I'd be one of those demented ones picking at threads were it not for that. But no matter how much comfort I receive in the reading, I'm alone in my bed at night, and I'll never hear his voice again nor see his smile. My Ward had a smile that near to squeezed my heart to smithereens. That's what made me fall in love with him in the first place. He was never one to waste words, but with a smile like that, why, who needed words?"

"Mr. Robertson was a fine man. I could never thank him enough for taking on this easterner and my son."

"He was always like that. If someone needed something and he had it to give, he would." Mrs. Robertson dabbed at her eyes.

"Ma?"

She turned around to answer a question from Ada Mae. "Yes?"

"You seen my hat?"

"In the box there in the corner."

"Thank you."

Mrs. Robertson turned to Jacob. "You're an easy one to talk to."

"Thank you."

"I do hope you take on our little congregation. We need a pastor."

"How did . . ."

"I suspected you were far more than you were letting on."

"May I ask how?"

"Just a sense. But I knew you were playing close to your chest. When you gave the funeral for Ward, well, I can never thank you enough."

As they topped the rise to the homeplace, Jacob wished he'd driven more slowly. But then, one of the girls might have overheard. He had to talk about the situation with Miss Edith. But when? And how?

Back in the bunkhouse Jacob tucked the covers around his already sleeping son. Oh,

534

to have the resilience of youth, to play hard, work hard, and collapse into sleep without a care in the world. Or at least to be able to forget those cares in the comfort of sleep.

When will I be able to talk with Mrs. Robertson? Lord, it has to be soon, before that young woman gets hurt any worse than she already is going to be. Such an innocent. Why can't I love her? It would be so easy. Well, not easy but simple. But then I would be living another lie.

A lie I live because of another innocent, another one I wounded. I cannot, will not, do that again.

For some reason a picture of Mr. Dumfarthing came to his mind. Not the nearly dying man but the one later, the one so interested in discussing things of the spirit but with no patience for those around him in the present. An interesting dichotomy. *What has happened with you, my friend?*

You call him friend when you ran out on him too? Isn't it time you put your own life back in order?

"Yes, Lord, it is time." His whisper sounded loud in the silent soddy. He took out paper and ink, sharpened a wing feather he'd found in the chicken pen to use as a quill, and sat down to write.

Dear Mr. Dumfarthing,
   I am writing to beg your forgiveness for running out on you. I was a coward, pure and simple, and now I must tell you the story and let you judge whether you believe a correspondence could be possible, especially if it could be between friends. One of the lessons I have learned is the value of friendship. . . .

He wrote for three pages and signed his name, along with an address, before he sat back in his chair and rubbed his aching forehead. The headaches were still a recurrence since the accident, but they came less frequently now. As did the dizziness. He addressed an envelope and, now that the ink was dry, folded his closely written sheets, fitted them in the envelope, and dropped wax from the candle on the flap to seal it.

The letter he wrote to his family was far shorter, but at least they would know where he was living now and would have an address for him should they decide to write. If only he could write a letter to Mrs. Robertson and perhaps Miss Edith and be gone when they got them.

Ah, but that would be the coward's way out, and he'd resolved not to take that way anymore. He put away his things, blew out the lamp, hung his good clothes on the pegs along the wall, and just before crawling under the bedcovers, laid a hand on Joel's shoulder. "Lord, please, help me to show my son how much I love him. And if possible, let him believe that I am indeed his father. Now and for always. Thank you."

Morning was going to come mighty early, but he'd finally gotten some things off his chest. One, no, two, left to go.

Chapter Thirty-Seven

Opal threw back the sheet and went to kneel at the window, her arms crossed on the sill. She inhaled and nodded. Fall was indeed heading quickly for winter. Soon this window would be closed, the cracks stuffed until spring. Gone was the hot stillness of summer, of frogs croaking and crickets singing.

An owl hooted, a coyote yipped, and another joined in to make a chorus. From a distance a horse whinnied, another answered. What did they see or hear that made them restless? She listened closely now. Horses were better at guard duty than even a dog. Another whinny, and she pushed away from the window and flew out the door to call Rand. Something out of the ordinary was out there.

"Rand, there's —"

"I heard them too."

"I'll get dressed."

"No, you stay here. I'll take Ghost and get the men. Get the rifle down."

Opal wanted to argue, but someone needed to stay by the house, and she was as good a shot as any. Rumor had it that a small group of Indians had been stealing horses and cattle. So far their ranch had never had any trouble, but then, Rand treated the Indians like he did everyone — fairly and with respect.

Opal pulled on britches and shirt, knotting her hair back with a ribbon. Once she had her boots on, she headed for the front room and took her rifle from the gun rack. Levering a shell into the chamber, she eased out the front door and remained in the deep shadows. The moon peeped from behind a cloud, then hid again. Ghost whined at her feet. Rand must have told her to stay too.

"Come," she whispered as she slid back into the house and walked on through to the back door.

"I don't see anyone."

Gun ready, Opal spun toward the voice. "Oh, you startled me."

Ruby stood to the side of the window.

They exchanged brief glances, and Opal paused for a moment before easing back out the door and repeating her actions from the front of the log house. Two pairs of eyes were surely better than one.

The land had fallen silent, as if it too waited, holding its breath in order to see.

Opal's eyes ached from staring into every shadow, from studying each moving leaf and grass blade. Ghost sat quietly at her feet, further confirmation that nothing untoward moved.

She wagged her tail when Rand stepped onto the porch at the far end.

"Good thing she knew you, or you might have caught a bullet." Even though Opal trusted the dog, her heart still needed to settle back down.

The sound of horses galloping off in the distance sent them both to the front of the house.

"You see anything?" Rand called to the three approaching men.

"Two Indians. Took off when we showed up. Good thing we have a strong fence and the horses were in it." Chaps set the butt of his rifle on the porch floor. "They must be getting desperate."

"They don't eat horse. I'd give them a steer if they asked. But horse thieving . . ."

He shook his head. "And on a moonlit night too. Strange."

"You need anything else, Boss?"

Rand nodded. "Joe, you take guard the rest of the night. We'll keep an eye out for a while."

Though they stayed on guard for the next week, nothing else happened. A severe frost crept in one night, and they woke to a white-rimmed world. Opal's boot tracks to the barn to milk made a black trail in the sparkly grass.

"We'll dig up the rest of the potatoes," Rand announced after breakfast. "And bring up some river sand to cover the root crops. Opal, you take care of that. I don't want Ruby doing any heavy lifting."

Opal stared across the table at her sister. "You're all right?"

"I'm fine. Rand is being a mite protective, that's all."

"Chaps, you can go back to splitting wood. Beans says we're going to need to put in extra wood at the line shacks. Promises to be a hard winter. The rest of us can go pull in those trees we downed last year and any that the wind felled for us. Let's stay on this side of the river."

The men gave Beans a hard time about

his weather-predicting bones as they filed out of the kitchen.

Opal continued to study her sister. Were the circles under her eyes more pronounced? Had she seemed more tired lately? How come the cows could drop their calves off all by themselves and women needed help? She started to ask, thought the better of it, and pushed back her chair. Cleaning up the garden would most likely use up the day. That and studying, since tomorrow she went to Pearl's again. Rand had been making sure one of the men was always around the homeplace too. Was he being overprotective or just wise? She chose the latter and set her dishes in the steaming pan.

"It keeps cold like this, and we'll be butchering soon." Chaps forked up a mound of potatoes. He had finished splitting a pile of wood so had offered to help Opal dig up the potatoes.

Opal pointed to the dirt-crusted potatoes. "Per, you can help me put them in the sack." She did several to show him how. When he did as she said, she patted his bottom. "Good boy. You can help."

Together the three of them made their way down the row.

"Hey, Per, no." Chaps hid his laugh behind the back of a gloved hand as he swiped it across his face.

Opal turned. Per sat in the middle of the row, a ring of dirt circling his mouth as he tried to take another bite out of a potato about the size of his fist.

"Good grief." Opal surged to her feet and took the potato away. "We could at least wash it first."

Per reached for his treasure, eyes narrowing. "No, Opa."

"Well, that was sure clear." She turned to Chaps, who was now leaning on the fork handle. "Can it hurt him?"

"Only if he chokes on it."

"Opa!" One tear meandered down his fat cheek as he stood up.

"Oh, all right." She rubbed the dirt off on her pant leg, turning the potato to get it all. Washing would be better, but this was the way she always cleaned carrots before eating them. After all, what harm could a little dirt do?

She gave Per back his potato, and he plunked himself down again. Hard to do two things at a time at his age, like standing, biting, and chewing the crunchy white flesh.

"I'll wash you up later," she promised

and went back to putting potatoes into the gunnysack. From there they would dump them into the bin cleaned and ready in the root cellar. Turnips and rutabaga each had a bin, carrots another; onions were already dried, hanging by their braided tops. Anything that couldn't be stored or dried was already canned.

Ruby and Little Squirrel were justifiably proud of the shelves of food put up. Any game brought in and not needed immediately was either smoking or had been smoked and now hung in the springhouse.

By the time the triangle rang for dinner, Opal counted ten gunnysacks full of potatoes, tall and ready for hauling. She'd taken Per back into the house earlier when he'd gotten fussy but had stopped first for a quick washup at the pump to appease his mother.

As they continued to prepare for the coming winter, Opal finished off the two horses she'd been training and took them back to their owners so the Harrisons wouldn't have to feed them. Along with bringing the split wood to the line shacks, Rand hauled sacks of grain back from Medora for winter feed. They stocked the line shacks with a supply of canned food and dried food and lined the northern wall with firewood as an extra shelter. They made sure that the Robertsons' shack had the same preparations.

⁂

"It don't look good, Boss," Chaps said one evening after supper. He'd just returned from several days of checking on the grazing herds. "The grass is down to the ground already in too many places."

Rand slowly shook his head. "Sometimes fences don't sound like a bad idea. Would keep our own cattle closer to home and they wouldn't overgraze the land. Too many head have been brought in."

"Won't be a problem next year. Mark my words, many are going to die."

"We'll see how bad the snow gets, then cut down cottonwood trees if we must."

Opal sat at the table supposedly doing her lessons but instead listening to the men. The Indians had taught them to bring down the trees so the stock could feed on the tender branches. They'd not started feeding out the hay yet, but the stacks that looked so large in the summer now appeared pitifully small.

"Opal, how about stopping by the Robertsons' on your way to Pearl's in the morning? I'll have a sack ready for you."

"Sure." Opal knew the two women exchanged fabric pieces for quilts and clothing, along with yarn for knitting, especially the yarn that Little Squirrel had dyed during the summer. She'd used onion skins for a soft yellow, bark for a brown, and ground red rock for a shy red. While cattlemen hated sheep, they all appreciated the wool carded and spun to be knit into stockings, hats, scarves, and mittens or gloves. While knitting wasn't her favorite occupation, Opal could turn a heel with the best of them if she could sit still long enough.

~⚡

The sun just topped the eastern buttes as she rode Bay out of the cut, nudging her into an easy lope that ate up the mile to the Robertsons'.

"You just missed the girls," Mrs. Robertson said after greeting Opal and taking the sack from her. "Oh, good. More quilt pieces."

"Where's Edith?"

"She went to visit Mary. She really needs a couple of extra hands, what with her two little ones."

"Oh. I didn't know she was leaving."

"We thought it better this way." Cora nodded toward the stove. "You want a cup of coffee?"

"No, thanks. I need to be going."

"Thank Ruby for me."

"I will." Opal waved after mounting Bay. *Wonder what that was all about?* Loping in to Pearl's gave her plenty of time to ponder. No one had said anything about Edith's leaving. Was it because she was so sweet on Mr. Chandler? Virginia would tell her if they ever had time to talk again.

She dismounted and led Bay into the three-sided shelter behind Pearl's house. The framework of a barn rose right behind it so it would eventually become one building. Carl had nearly finished the addition to the house too.

As Rand often said, *"That man never lets any moss grow between his toes."*

Opal unsaddled her horse and tied her to a manger where Carl had left some dried cornstalks for the horse to eat. "I'll come out and water you later." Flipping her book-laden saddlebags over one shoulder, she headed into the house.

Music met her at the door. A piano. "I'm here," she called as she shut the kitchen door behind her.

"Come see what Carl brought home." Pearl's voice floated back from the front parlor.

"I can hear it." Opal hung up her outdoor things and followed the lovely notes, as pleasant to the ear as the fragrance of fresh bread was to the nose.

Pearl turned on the bench, her smile rivaling the sunshine coming in the windows. "Can you believe it? My father had this shipped out to us. In one of my letters I mentioned how I missed my music, and here it is, an early Christmas present." Her long fingers flew up and down the keyboard, bringing forth crashing waves, a tinkling brook, a lullaby, and a call to adventure.

"You want to try it?" Pearl let her hands fall in her lap.

"I've not played since Dove House."

"Perhaps we could do a duet for the Christmas program."

Opal sat down on the bench. "Where are the kids?"

"Over to Cimarron's. Carl dropped them off. You know how nice it is to have close neighbors like that?"

Opal settled her hands on the keys. Cool to the touch. She played a series of chords, then several scales. Her grin said it all.

"See, I told you you wouldn't forget."

Opal played a simple song, missing a couple of notes and slower than she'd have liked. "Need practice all right." She turned to look at Pearl beside her. "Sure makes me think of Belle. You ever wonder what happened to her?"

"Not really. She and I weren't much of friends."

"She was a terror at times, but she was good to me."

"Well, we better get busy. You have all your homework done?"

"Even the essay. I'm not much fond of the Greek tragedies. Not of Greek anything." Opal wrinkled her nose.

"You'd rather not study that?"

"Do I have a choice?"

"Latin is more important as a language, but the Greek philosophers and sages are well worth learning from."

Opal made a face.

"Besides, it's good discipline."

"Like calculus?"

"Yes. The more you develop your reasoning powers, the easier college will be for you."

Opal shook her head. "Pearl, I am not going to college or some finishing school for young ladies. That's not what I need to make a life here in the badlands."

Pearl studied her young charge. "But the more intelligent and educated you are, the more you will be an interesting woman to talk with and the more you will give your children and your husband. In spite of what men say and think, women have fine minds that need education just as the prairie needs sun and rain." She rose and moved to the bookshelves that lined the north wall. Pulling off a book, she brought it to Opal. "Here's Plato's *The Republic*. Look for what it says about the value of a good mind. Read Proverbs also, keeping in mind that when the Bible talks of man and men, it frequently means humankind, but then, you would know that if you were studying Greek more closely."

Opal nibbled on her bottom lip. "I'd rather read Mr. Roosevelt. He, at least, speaks my language."

"You mean English or Western?"

Opal cocked her head, a grin lighting both eyes and cheeks. "Yes."

Later, as she and Bay loped on home, Opal veered off the trail to check on a place where she often saw deer. It wasn't long before, with a gutted deer slung over the back of her saddle, she trotted up to the springhouse and dismounted. The kitchen windows glowed a lamplit welcome.

Ruby stepped out on the porch. "I was getting worried."

"I know, but when this spike stood right there and stared at me, I couldn't resist."

"Supper's nearly ready. We have company."

"Who?"

"Mr. Chandler."

"Ah. I'll be in soon as I hang this."

"Let the men do that. I think you should put on a real skirt."

"Aww, Ruby."

"Don't give me any trouble. It's about time you started dressing like a young lady when we have guests."

Chapter Thirty-Eight

"So what will life be like in a line shack?" Jacob pushed back his plate.

"Would you care for another piece of cake?" Ruby refilled his coffee cup.

"No, thank you. I won't be able to get back on that horse as it is." He patted his middle. "Delicious meal."

"You're planning on manning one of the line shacks?" Rand leaned back in his chair, studying the younger man.

"Yes, sir. Mrs. Robertson says it must be done, and the girls surely cannot do it."

"I heard of one woman who did. But she was mighty tough. It gets real lonely out there. What about your boy?"

"He will move into the house. I hate to leave them with no man on hand, but what else can we do?"

"Hire another hand."

"I don't think she has the finances for that. We haven't discussed her money situation, but I know that, though they trade butter and eggs at the store, the beeves sold this fall were her mainstay."

"We'll send one of our men out to spell you. Chaps, tell him about life in a line shack."

Chaps creaked his chair back on two legs. "That wind is what gets to you. That and the cold. Your job is to ride out each day halfway to the other shack and make sure you head any cattle you find back toward the river. Cattle drift before the wind, a dangerous thing. If they get out on the open prairie they won't have any protection. Most likely we'll never find them — at least not alive. Winter is a lot different here than where you came from."

Jacob glanced up, hoping to catch Opal's gaze. The firelight sent lights and shadows dancing across her face, highlighting her cheekbones, shrouding her eyes in mystery.

He brought his attention back to what one of the other men was saying. When he looked up again, she'd moved to a chair in the other room, where a lamp lighted the pages of her book.

Why could he talk with her so freely out

553

on the range, but here she withdrew like she'd never helped him, broken and bleeding, up on a horse and gotten him back to the house with utmost caution?

"I don't think I ever thanked you, Miss Torvald, for taking such good care of me that day I hit the ground." He raised his voice slightly so she would hear. He was still careful about jerking his head or standing up too quickly.

"You're welcome." She marked her place with one finger. "At least out on the prairie you won't have to worry about tree branches."

One of the men choked on a snicker. Another buried his grin behind a coffee cup.

"It happens to the best of us, Jacob." Rand raised his cup in salute. "In fact, every man here has hit the ground more than once, usually in rather undignified circumstances. Welcome to ranch life."

"Thank you. Miss Torvald tried her best to train me, er, all of us, in ranching skills."

"Have you been practicing?" Opal asked.

"Every chance I get." *Not that there are many.* "What is that you are reading?"

"Plato's *Republic*."

"In Latin?"

"No, English. My Latin isn't that proficient."

"I used to have a copy of Plato's works in Latin."

"Pearl — Mrs. Hegland — has one if you would like to borrow it."

For Jacob the rest of the room seemed to disappear, and all the focus turned toward the pool of light around her, the chair, and the braided rug at her feet where a fluffy orange-and-white cat lay curled with tail covering its nose.

He sighed and pushed back the chair he sat in. "I need to be heading back. Joel will have his homework done by now. Ada Mae will make certain of that. Thank you for the coffee and cake, Mrs. Harrison. And the advice, Rand. I'll see you all in church some Sunday?"

"That you will, and I'm certain you can take over our pulpit any time you feel ready."

"Thank you. I'm praying about that." He smiled at Opal. "Since you coached me in riding and roping, perhaps I could return the favor if you'd like help with Latin and Greek."

Opal shrugged. "Perhaps. I don't much care for them."

Talk about a straightforward gaze. Jacob quelled the urge to sit back down. Now he knew more than ever what he wanted to talk with Rand about, only by himself, in the proper way.

"Hear you tell a good story," Opal added. "Perhaps you'd all come over for a get-together on Saturday. Beans tells good stories too." She glanced over at Ruby. "All right?"

"Of course. We'll pull taffy and roast pumpkin seeds." Ruby smiled at her husband. "That sounds like fun, doesn't it?"

"Indeed. You want to write Mrs. Robertson a note?"

"Of course." Ruby started to stand, but Opal beat her to it.

"Here's paper and pencil." She crossed the room, supplies in hand.

Jacob felt his heart kick up a pace when she drew near. His arms remembered the dance, holding her so properly. Perhaps they could dance again on Saturday. "Could I talk with you a moment, Rand?"

"Sure." Rand studied him for a moment. "Soon as that invite is done, I'll walk you to your horse."

The good-nights were said, and Rand followed him out the door.

"I was going to wait for a better place and time."

"No time like the present." The two men faced each other in the dimness lit by the square of light from the window.

Lord, help me. Why is this so difficult? "I . . . I . . ." *Oh, just say it.* "I want your permission to call on Opal, er, Miss Torvald."

"Call on, as in court?"

"Yes, sir."

"Good grief, man, she's far too young for that." Rand took a step forward.

"Really?" Jacob could hear Rand sucking in his breath, exploding his answer.

"She's only fourteen."

"Oh! Sorry. I mean, I assumed she was at least seventeen or eighteen. I mean, she is so capable and . . ." *Good grief is right. She's still a child.*

"That she is, but nevertheless, she's too young to be thinking of marriage. Besides, you have a son who is half her age."

Jacob sucked in a deep and calming breath. "She is worth waiting for."

Rand was silent for a moment and then spoke firmly, as though forcing his voice to be reasonable. "You cannot mention this to her until her sixteenth birthday, if you are so inclined then. I believe you are a man of honor, and —"

"And yes, I will obey your instructions. When is her birthday?"

"May sixteenth."

"Pretty much a year and a half."

"Pretty much."

Had Rand stepped back, or was it his imagination? "You have my word, Rand." Jacob extended his right hand.

Without hesitation Rand took his hand, and they sealed the pact.

But what if someone else comes along and . . .

"Good night." Rand nodded.

"Good night." The ride home gave Jacob plenty of time to think. Good thing he'd talked with Mrs. Robertson when he did, no matter how difficult that had been. He thought back to their conversation. He'd found her on the back porch sorting through the dried beans. Edith and Emily had taken the wagon into town for supplies.

"Can I speak with you?" he'd asked.

"Of course. How can I help you?" She drizzled dried beans from one flat box to another, letting the wind do its work blowing out the chaff.

"It . . . it's about Miss Edith, and um . . ." He sighed. "This is really difficult. Your daughter is a lovely young woman and will make some man a fine wife one day, but —"

"But not you."

"Right. I mean, if I . . ."

"That's quite all right, Mr. Chandler. I'll have a talk with her."

"I feel like a heel. Sometimes I wish I did care for her, but she seems just like one of my younger sisters."

"Thank you for being honest with me. I know she thinks very highly of you and dreams young woman dreams. I would have been very pleased had you chosen her for your wife."

"I'm sorry."

"Me too."

And he still was. He was sorry for hurting her feelings. The house had not been the same since she went to her sister's. Not that he'd wanted to change his mind, but everyone missed Edith.

His horse picked up the pace as they neared home.

And now the woman, or rather the girl, who had caught him so completely was off limits for a year and a half. *Lord, if this is all part of your plan, I'm feeling a mite like that Jacob of long ago. At least I only have to wait two years, not seven.*

Chapter Thirty-Nine

In November winter arrived in a fluttery white dress, dancing on the breezes, hiding the browns and tans of fall, and capping roofs and fence posts in glittering blankets and tall hats.

While the men were out stringing ropes from house to outhouse, to springhouse, to smokehouse, and to the barn in preparation for probable blizzards, Opal got out the toboggan and took Per for a ride behind the horse. His shrieking glee made everyone laugh, and when Rand set him in front and slid down the hill, the child hooted even louder.

"See, Ma." He waved and tried to stand but for his father keeping a firm hand around his waist. "Opa!"

Ruby stood on the porch, waving back

and laughing too. "I want a ride," she announced when Opal stopped by the porch.

"Do you, I mean, should you . . . ?"

"No, I won't, but I can want one, can't I?"

"Whew." Opal did a swipe of her brow. "I thought for a moment I was going to have to tie you to that post."

"As if Rand would let me on that toboggan like this." Ruby motioned to her rounding middle.

"As if you could get on the toboggan like that."

"I'll have you know, young lady . . ." Ruby's shaking her finger made Opal laugh again. "Someday you'll be in this shape, and you won't find it so funny."

"If I have to give up horses and cattle to have children, I think I'd just as soon not. Besides —" she rested her crossed arms on the saddle horn and leaned forward, lowering her voice — "what man will put up with his wife wearing britches?"

"A man who loves you enough to ignore them or . . ." She paused.

"Or?"

"Or one you love enough to give them up."

Opal shook her head, eyes slitting just enough to make her point. "Never." The picture of a certain man with wheat-colored hair and eyes like bits of Dakotah skies strode through her mind. Funny how he'd been acting like a friend but now managed to disappear whenever she came around. He'd begged off a day of roping too, saying he had too much to do right then. She, along with the Robertson girls and Joel, had had a merry time.

Over the next days, after the first snow melted, Opal surprised herself by discovering she actually missed all the kids she was used to seeing every day in school. Riding back and forth had always been fun, and there had been some pleasure in setting up Mr. Finch, like putting grasshoppers in his lunch box. When he'd opened the box, they jumped out and he jumped up, dumping his dinner on the floor and enduring the laughter of the children, several of whom also had grasshoppers in their dinner buckets and thought it a huge joke. Somehow Mr. Finch was not able to take a joke well.

Opal glanced up at the gray, low-slung sky. Looked like snow for sure, and Beans would be right again. The men needed to get back in off the range if it started coming down heavy.

She raised the collar on her sheepskin coat to keep the north wind from blowing down her neck. Maybe going riding wasn't such a good idea after all.

But if she went back up to the house, she'd have to help with the sausage making. They'd ground up most of a deer and the remainder of the pork, and now Ruby and Little Squirrel were stuffing sausages to hang in the smokehouse along with the venison haunches. Pretty soon they'd let the fresh meat freeze instead of smoking or curing it all. Opal saddled Bay and rode back up to the house for the rifle. She'd seen two deer up the draw. Bringing in another one wouldn't hurt.

Snowflakes were drifting down when she turned back for home, a four-point slung behind the saddle.

Perhaps she should take this deer over to the Robertsons'. Was Mr. Chandler a good enough shot to bring in game for the table? She knew that none of the girls had the stomach for it nor were they proficient enough with the gun. Given time and training, Ada Mae would be able to hunt. She'd dogged Opal's every step and copied everything she did, even to the extent of wearing britches.

"We can dress it tonight and take it over

tomorrow." The sound of her words made Bay's ears twitch. She drew up to the springhouse to see Chaps unloading a deer too.

"Hey, you. Two more hides for tanning, huh?" He hung his deer on the hook and turned to take hers.

"If I'd known you got one, I could have stayed inside by the fire."

"Sure, as if you ever wanted to stay in the house." He untied one latigo holding the deer behind the saddle while she undid the other. "Where'd you get this one?"

"About a mile south, right along the game trail to the river. And you?"

" 'Bout a mile north on the other side. Couple of them were still bedded down. Joe brought in grouse." He glanced up at the sky. "We could be in for it."

While the first snow had been such a delight, it had all melted away, but now with December arriving, this could be the beginning of real winter.

"I thought I'd take the deer I shot over to Robertsons' in the morning on my way to Pearl's," Opal announced when she entered the house.

"Sounds good. Give that gravy another stir, will you?" Ruby set Per in his high seat.

"Where's Rand?"

"He and Beans aren't back yet."

"But it's almost dark."

"Thank you, Opal. Surely I can tell dark from light too."

Opal blinked at the snap in Ruby's tone. *What's the matter with you?* But she stirred the gravy without comment. "Where's Little Squirrel?"

"I sent her off to rest. She's just not doing well."

Opal waited a moment for more information to be forthcoming. When Ruby shut the oven door with more force than normal, she was sure something was wrong. But what?

"Ma? Opa?" Per lifted his arms in supplication. He hated being tied in his chair almost as much as he hated waiting for anything. "Down."

Opal shook her head. "Sorry."

"Down, pease?" He tugged at the towel tying him in.

"Can he have the heel?" Opal asked.

"Hmm? What? Oh yes." Ruby stood still, listening. "That wind has picked up."

"Is Ghost with them?"

"I guess. She's not around here."

"She'll lead them home." But Ruby's worry was contagious, and fear for the missing men lurked in the corners and leaped aboard their shoulders when they passed by.

"Is Linc with Little Squirrel?"

Ruby nodded. "We better go ahead and eat while it's hot. You go ring the triangle."

Wind-driven snow blasted her face when she stepped outside to clang the triangle. Ignoring the snow, she slammed the bar around the three sides, keeping it ringing as a beacon for those trying to find home.

"Perhaps he stopped somewhere." Opal hoped to sound casual and convincing. If the wind was driving this hard here in the valley, it would be really fierce up on the buttes. "Which side of the river are they on?"

"West."

No wonder Ruby was snappy. Fording the river in the dark and snow could be dangerous, especially if they missed the ford and slipped into a quicksand hole like Ada Mae had.

The four of them sat down at the table, bowing their heads for grace in the normal way, waiting for Rand to pronounce the blessing, only he was still out in the snow.

The silence stretched.

You can say grace, you know, Opal's inner voice chided.

She opened her eyes enough to see Ruby

take in a deep breath, but before she could speak, Chaps cleared his throat and began.

"Dear Lord, thou who hast control over the wind and the waves, please abate this storm long enough for Rand and Beans to get home. Give them a guiding star and safe passage across the river."

Opal swallowed tears and heard Ruby sniff.

"We thank thee for this food prepared with hands of love and for this house that shelters us from the storms. Thank you for listening and hearing our prayers. Amen."

"Men." Per clapped once and grinned at those around the table.

"Thank you." Ruby picked up the platter of sliced venison haunch and passed it to Joe on her left. Rand's chair at the other end of the table stood as a grim reminder of those missing.

Conversation consisted of "pass the butter," "thank you," and "please pass." Ruby started to get up for the coffeepot, but Opal shook her head at her.

"I'll get it." Watching Ruby push herself to her feet and waddle around the table was getting to be too much. Without Little Squirrel to help, Opal figured she should step into the gap.

"Thank you." Ruby held her refilled cup

between both hands after adding cream and sugar, something she never did.

Opal fixed a plate of cookies and passed them around, giving Per the first one, which earned her a smile that made them all grin.

"He's some boy." Chaps reached over and tickled the little guy's tummy.

"He sure is." Opal picked up the slack when Ruby didn't answer.

"Don't you worry none, Miss Ruby. They'll make it home," Joe assured her.

Ruby nodded, forcing a smile to answer.

"I'll go clang the triangle." Chaps pushed back his chair. "I remember the time a clanging triangle brought me home. Leastways here, once in the valley, you know you're goin' wrong when you're climbing a hill. Works kinda like a funnel, you know."

They all paused to listen when he opened the door. Had the wind died some?

The clanging triangle started up and continued on and on. Opal felt that her ears might keep on ringing. While the beat slowed, the metal rang on.

Opal started to clear the table, and Ruby rose to help her.

"I'll do it."

"No, the busier my hands, the easier my

mind." Ruby took a cloth and wiped Per's hands and face. She untied his belt and let him scramble down. Lifting him had become more difficult as her stomach protruded.

The silence before Chaps returned to the kitchen made them pause and then pick up conversation when he came back in, dusting snow from shirt and shoulders.

"The wind dropped some. We're not in a full blizzard."

"That's some comfort."

"Ruby, why don't you go sit in that chair and read to us?" Opal stuck more wood in the fire. "I'll do the dishes. Oh, should we take food down to Linc and Little Squirrel?"

"No, he took bread and meat." Ruby took Per by the hand and led him to the rocking chair, where they settled into the circle of lamplight.

"Where Pa?"

"Looking for cattle."

"Dark."

"Yes. He'll be home soon."

Per snuggled against her side with his head on her shoulder. "Read, Ma."

Opal glanced over her shoulder. Funny how Per, who was always so busy, loved to be read to as much as any of them. She dipped another plate in the rinse water and set it in the wooden rack to drain.

Chaps opened the door, and the wind dusted snow inside, blowing a chill across the floor. The clanging started again. How could a triangle sound cheerful in the daylight and mournful in a snowstorm? Opal ignored the thought and paid attention to the story.

Mr. Chandler tells a really good story. Ruby's voice and even the three-tone clanging faded. Memories of waltzing with him, of his fighting with the lariat, of the terrible ride back to the Robertsons' with him so wounded invaded her mind. He was a far better dancer than he was a rancher. That thought jerked her back to the room where the story fell from Ruby's lips in a pleasing cadence. Per lay against her shoulder, his long lashes brushing his rosy cheeks and his thumb and forefinger securely in his mouth.

Opal moved the coffeepot to the hotter part of the stove.

"Surely they've bedded down somewhere by now." Joe poured himself another cup of coffee, now blacker than a moonless night.

Chaps joined him. They turned back to listen to the reading, blowing on the surface before sipping from steaming cups.

Opal dumped the dishwater in the slop pail, wiped out the enameled pan, and hung it on a nail behind the stove. She laid the wrung-out cloth over it and moved the pan of rinse water to the top of the reservoir.

"You want me to make cornmeal mush and set it for frying in the morning?"

"Yes, thank you." Ruby stuck a piece of paper in place for a bookmark. She half covered her mouth to hide a yawn but gave up as it stretched her face.

"Why don't you go on to bed?"

"Because I'm waiting for Rand."

"And will your worrying and waiting bring him home any sooner?"

"Now you sound like Bestemor."

"No, I sound like Ruby, who needs her sleep." Opal set a pot of water to boiling and brought the cornmeal out of the pantry, along with a pan of cracklings. "I'll take Per."

"Thank you, Opal. What would I do without you?"

Opal took the sleeping child from Ruby's arms and carried him down the hall to his room. She changed his diaper, pulled up clean soakers, and tucked him in bed. " 'Night, little guy." She kissed his cheek and headed back for the kitchen, stopping at Ruby's room on the way. "He never even woke up."

"If only I could do that. I mean, sleep like that." Standing behind a screen in the corner, Ruby laid her layers of clothing over the top of the screen. Her flowered flannel nightdress settled down her arms, and she waddled toward the bed, tying the neck ribbon as she went.

"You want a warm stone for your feet?"

Ruby sank down on the edge of the bed. "No, I want Rand."

Her big sister looked like a little girl pleading for a puppy.

"Let me brush your hair." Anything to take the fear from her sister's eyes. "I'll be right back." Opal headed for the kitchen for the stones they kept under the stove.

"It's clearin'." Chaps came in from the back porch.

"Thank God." Opal moved the pan of boiling water to a cooler part of the stove, retrieved a stone, and returned to Ruby's room. "Chaps said it's clearing."

Ruby closed her eyes and chewed her bottom lip. "Thank you, Father. Oh, thank you, thank you."

Opal slipped the stone in the bed, removed the pins from her sister's hair, and took up the hairbrush. With long gentle strokes she worked the few tangles loose and brushed love all through the glorious blond hair.

Ruby let her head fall forward and propped her hands on the bed beside her. "If I don't go to bed soon, I'm going to collapse right here, and with all the extra weight I'm carrying, you'll never get me into bed." Her murmur hardly moved her lips.

"Then I'll quit now. I wouldn't want to have to rig a rope and tackle to heave you into bed." Opal tied the hair mass off with a ribbon and lifted the covers for Ruby to crawl under. She kissed her sister's cheek. "Now, don't forget to say your prayers," she admonished, the very thing Ruby used to say to her.

"Thank you, Mother Opal." Ruby smiled and turned on her side. "I haven't quit praying since darkness fell."

Opal returned to the kitchen. Would she ever learn to pray like Ruby did? Was it something that came with age?

"I put more wood in."

"Thanks, Chaps." She pulled the pot to the hotter stove front and poured the golden meal into a smaller bowl of cold water, stirring as she poured. No one liked lumpy cornmeal. Once she had that smooth and liquid, she poured it slowly into the boiling water, stirring all the while. Oatmeal was far easier to make.

The men headed for the bunkhouse after ringing the triangle one more time. Opal read until the cornmeal mush was cooked, then poured it into bread pans to set. Leaving one lamp burning in a window just in case, she headed down the hall to her room. "Lord," she whispered, "please bring them home safe." After sliding her hot stone under the covers of her bed, she pushed back the curtains to stare up at the sky, now a round bowl of black velvet, pinned in place by stars of all sizes and twinkle power. "Lord, please bring Rand and Beans home safe and sound. I don't ask for a whole lot because I don't want to bother you, but now I'm really asking. If there is something you want me to do, let me know, and I'll do my best."

White covered the ground and drew curved corners on the windowpanes. She thought back to supper. The snowfall had escalated to blizzard proportions and yet, these few hours later, the world was still, as only it can be when buried in new snow. Chaps had prayed for the blizzard to cease.

He had reminded God that He had power over wind and weather. Was this an answer? How could it not be?

She let the curtain fall and sat down to take off her boots. Shirt unbuttoned and one boot off, she froze, not even daring to breathe. Was that a dog bark?

She listened so hard her ears ached.

The bark came again, closer this time.

She slammed her foot back in her boot and buttoned her shirt as she ran on her tiptoes to the front door.

Ghost leaped and yipped when Opal flung open the door. Rand's "Halloo" floated through the darkness.

"Down, girl. You are soaking wet."

"Take her in by the fire." Rand rode up and dismounted. "Sure hope you have something hot you can fix for two near-to-frozen cowboys."

Opal threw herself into his waiting arms. "I was so afraid. . . ." *We could have been left like Mrs. Robertson.*

"Hey. We holed up till the snow quit, then came on in." He hugged her close. "How's Ruby?"

"Sleeping."

"Not now." Ruby met her husband at the door and hugged him as close as her front would allow.

"I'll put the horses away." Beans took the reins.

"Thanks. Then come and eat."

Later, when the men had been fed and all was well again, Opal stood at her window again. "Lord, when you decide to answer prayers, you sure don't let any grass grow under your feet. Thank you. I think I need to believe in you more."

While her stone had decidedly cooled off, her heart felt bigger and warmer than it ever had. Rand and Beans were home safe. She'd rubbed Ghost near dry with a towel, and now she lay sleeping behind the stove.

"God, I have one more question. You could still the wind and the snow, and you did. You could have made Atticus well and whole again, but as far as I know, you . . . Is *why* an all right question to ask?"

Chapter Forty

"That has to be the prettiest Christmas tree ever."

"Ah, my Ruby, you always say that."

"Only because it is." She inhaled the pine fragrance and let her head fall back against Rand's shoulder. "I think tonight I heard the angels singing."

"That was the boys. They're practicing for tomorrow." He rested his chin on the top of her head, his arms around her, hands covering hers on the readymade shelf of baby.

Their hands bounced upward as Ruby uttered, "Oof."

"That one sure can kick."

"You ought to feel it from my point of view." She puffed out a breath. "He or she, as the case may be, is far more active than Per was, and look at him go."

"Not now, thank you, he just went to sleep."

"I wish we could have gone to church."

"I know, but with the snow falling like it is, I just didn't want to chance it."

"Rand, can you believe how blessed we are?"

"Sometimes no."

They chuckled when their hands bounced again.

"I think this baby could come soon."

"Is there something you are not telling me?"

"Just a feeling. Twinges, backache, you know."

"Now, how would I know?" He stepped slightly back and kneaded her shoulders with firm hands. "Tip your head to the right."

"Wish I could lay on my stomach and let you work on my lower back. Ah." Her "ah" turned into more of a groan.

"What? Am I hurting you?"

"No, not you. This child of yours. He's doing somersaults."

"Let's go to bed. Morning will come far too soon." Rand blew out the lamp near them and banked the fire in the fireplace and then the one in the kitchen stove. The cat and Ghost lay curled together behind the stove, both of them looking up but neither moving.

"I wouldn't move either." Rand set the lid back in place. The cat yawned, showing pink tongue and white teeth. Ghost's tail brushed the floor. "Merry Christmas, animals." He picked up the last two heated stones and followed his yawning wife to the bedroom.

Sometime later Ruby woke with a grunt. She shifted her hips, trying to relieve the cramp. In a moment she relaxed and snuggled herself closer to her husband, sleeping spoon fashion behind her.

The third time she woke, she gave up. This was no muscle cramp. She pulled herself to the side of the bed, leaving the warmth of her quilted cocoon.

"What is it?" Rand's voice came softly through the dark.

"Looks like this baby is getting anxious."

"You mean now?"

"Well, not right now but soon." Ruby sat up on the edge of the bed. "If it's a girl, we name her Mary, and if a boy we call him Joseph."

"We could call him Harold."

"Harold? Hmm." She squirmed against another surge.

"Sure, as in 'Hark, the Herald Angels Sing.'"

Ruby groaned, this time at his joke, if one could call it that. "You better go put wood on the fire. Think I'll be doing some walking for a while."

Rand walked with her, entertaining her with stories of the calves he'd helped into the world and a tale of puppies he hand-fed as a boy.

"You want me to go get Little Squirrel?"

"No. She needs her rest. It'll be a long time yet." She clung to Rand's arm, fingers digging into his wrist until the contraction rolled on. She stood panting in the aftermath.

"You need to put that sheet of canvas under the sheet of our bed and fold another sheet over it."

Rand did as she instructed, and together they tucked the bed back together. "You sure you should be doing this?"

"Of course. I have a box of supplies all made up. It's there under the bench by the wall. You'll need lots of hot water so start the boiler. There's plenty of water in the barrel on the porch."

"If it isn't frozen solid."

"It wasn't earlier." This time the contraction brought on a groan. "Wish I had sent Per and Opal to the Robertsons'."

"Too much snow. I could take them to Little Squirrel."

"No."

"Then I'll go get Little Squirrel."

"No. Ohhh." She straightened, kneading her back with her fists.

"Ruby, you need a woman with you."

"Why? You've helped calves be born. This is no different."

"I can't do this!" He dropped the round lid back on the reservoir, the clatter making Ruby grimace again. Either that or the pain rolling through her did.

"Of . . . course . . . you . . . can." A pant separated each word. She placed the scissors, string, and some cloth pads in the water about to boil.

"Oh." The gush of water down her legs told her they'd reached the next stage.

"Please, let me go get Little Squirrel."

"Only if we have an emergency." She clung to the back of a chair and panted her way through the contraction.

An hour later, with his wife sound asleep, his new daughter, Mary, in the crook of her arm, and the bloody sheets in a bundle in the corner ready to be soaked in tepid water, Rand watched the first

581

streaks of Christmas Day light the eastern sky. While his hands had quit shaking, he still quivered inside. No wonder this was women's work. Strong man as he was, he'd barely survived, or at least that was the way it felt.

He dashed away another tear as he thought again to the glory of holding that squalling baby in his hands. He'd laid her on her mother's chest and dripped his tears on Ruby's sweaty face. His brave wife had neither screamed nor fainted, while he'd nearly keeled over. Only the knowledge that she needed him kept him on his feet and inside the house. No wonder most men were banished from the birthing room.

"Rand?"

He turned back to the bed at the soft call. "I'm here." *I'm here all right, and I'll always be here.*

"Merry Christmas." Ruby smiled at him and kissed the downy head of their daughter. "You did just fine."

"You are the one who did just fine. Ruby, darling, I love you more than I ever thought possible. Thank you for giving me the privilege of staying with you and being the first one to meet our new daughter."

"I know it wasn't proper."

"And since when did we give a frog's leap about propriety?" He turned her hand and kissed her palm, then closed her fingers over the kiss to keep it warm. "That was one of the big reasons why I came west, to escape from proper, and 'this is the way it should be done.'" He mimicked a woman's voice, making Ruby smile.

She could still feel the imprint in her hand. *Ah, my Lord, thank you for bringing us through the birthing. I know my time was easy compared to others I've helped, but one forgets how hard it is. Thank you that we ignored conventions. Having Rand with me . . . I-I cannot begin to thank you enough. Our little Mary.* Ruby laid her weary head back on the pillows. Granted, she'd slept awhile but hardly enough to make a dent in her weariness.

"Ruby?" Opal's voice came softly, along with a knock on the door.

"Come in."

Opal stuck her head in. "Are you all right?"

"More than all right. Come meet your new niece."

Opal glanced at Rand. "Niece?"

Rand smiled from Ruby to Opal.

"You already had the baby?" Opal tiptoed in, a grin nearly splitting her face.

"Your sister is one tough lady." Rand stood by the bed. "And she made me into one tough man. I'll never make fun of cows having calves again nor of women being the weaker sex." He took Ruby's hand. "Wait till Per hears about this."

"How could you? I mean, I never heard a thing." Opal stared down at the little head in the crook of Ruby's arm. "It's a girl?"

"We're calling her Mary, since she was born on Christmas Day."

Opal knelt beside the bed and touched the baby's downy head with one finger. "She's all right and you're all right?" She looked up at Ruby, concern wrinkling her forehead.

"Far as we know. It was an easy birthing and —"

"And she's lying through her teeth." Rand shook his head. "I can't begin to tell you —"

"Don't listen to him."

"But what about Little Squirrel? I thought she was coming."

"Ruby wouldn't let me call her."

"She's not been feeling well. She needed the rest."

Opal stared from one to the other. "I

think I'll go make breakfast. You both look like you need a long nap." She pushed herself to her feet. "What a Christmas present."

As she left the room, Ruby motioned Rand closer. "The presents. They're in the bottom of the chifforobe and behind the box in the pantry. We didn't put them under the tree last night."

"That's because we were going to do so this morning, but we were slightly busy." He dropped a kiss on her forehead. "I'm off to do your bidding."

A yawn caught her before she could cover her mouth. "Thank you."

"And you sleep. Don't worry about a thing." He shut the door gently behind himself.

Ruby settle into the pillow and let her eyes drift closed. She never got further than "Thank you, Father" before she dropped into exhausted sleep.

"Merry Christmas, Linc." Rand smiled over the top of his coffee cup when Linc burst through the door. "What's wrong?"

"Boss, Little Squirrel is some sick. Can Miss Ruby come see to her?" Linc had never talked so fast in all the time Rand had known him.

"No, she had the baby last night." Rand set his coffee cup down and stood. "You want Mrs. Robertson? Is Little Squirrel having the baby?"

"No. Yes. I don't know, Boss. She's sick, not de baby. Don't know what to do."

"All right. I'll send Joe over for Mrs. Robertson."

"No, I need de preacher man worse." At Rand's questioning look, he added, "Shoulda married dat woman long ago, but going to do so now."

"I thought you *were* married." Rand's eyes widened.

"Was by Indian way, but I want a proper Christian way before . . ." Linc's voice trailed off. He stopped to blow his nose.

"If you say so. Joe can go on out to relieve him early. Soon as he eats. Since you can't leave to take Chap's place, he'll have to stay put." Rand turned to Opal. "How long until it's ready?"

"Soon as the biscuits are done."

"Good. I'll get the men and harness the team. Linc, you want to take some breakfast out to Little Squirrel?"

"She can't eat. Heavin' up all night." Linc buttoned his sheepskin coat again. "Thanks, Boss." He turned to the door and let in a blast of cold air as he slipped through the opening.

Rand shrugged into his coat, all the while giving instructions to Opal. "If Ruby wakes, tell her what is going on, but we'll let her sleep as long as possible. I hear Per. You go on and get him."

Opal pushed the pan of scrambled eggs to the back of the stove and hurried down the hall, tiptoeing so her boot heels would be silent. She swooped Per up, grabbed his clean clothes, and hustled him out to the kitchen in time to give the eggs another stir.

"Merry Christmas, Opal, Per." The men came in, scraping snow off their boots and shrugging out of their coats.

"Merry Christmas. Give me a minute while I change this little guy, and I'll have the breakfast on the table."

"You go ahead. I'll take care of the food." Beans moved toward the stove.

"Biscuits are in the oven. Ham in one skillet, eggs in the other. Oatmeal cooking in the big pot."

"Where Ma?"

"Sleeping." She stripped him and, taking a rag and warm water, wiped him down and dried him before pinning another diaper into place. She pulled up his soakers and slipped a clean shift over his head, then stuffed his flapping arms into a cardigan sweater. "You hungry?"

"Ya, hungy. Bread."

"Biscuit."

"Bread."

"You are one stubborn fella." She set him in his seat on a chair and tied the towel around his middle.

"Hey there, Per." Joe sat beside him. "You need some help?"

"Where Pa?"

"Out in the barn. He'll be back."

Opal set a bowl of oatmeal and a biscuit with jam in front of Per. He promptly licked all the jam off the biscuit and held it out. "More?"

The hands sat down at the table.

"Good thing that snowstorm quit during the night. We can get out to the line shacks."

"You riding or taking the sledge?"

"Sledge." Joe shoveled eggs and biscuit into his mouth.

"More."

Opal handed Per another biscuit with jam. "Should just give you the jar and a spoon."

"He'd like that right fine." Joe pushed back his chair. "I'll go help Rand harness up the team."

"I'll fix a box of cookies and things for you. Sorry you'll miss Christmas dinner." She stopped a moment. "Maybe I should send one of the geese with you."

"No decent oven to bake it. We'll make do." Joe tickled Per under the chin. "There's a box out on the porch. For under the . . ." He nodded toward the tree.

"Thanks. This sure isn't the way we planned Christmas Day."

"From what I hear, babies don't go along on anyone's plans but their own."

"Seems that way." Opal set two plates on the counter and piled cookies and dough-nuts on top of the remaining biscuits. She tied a dishcloth around them and set them in a box, along with dried apples, thick slices of ham, and raw potatoes. "You better cook these before they freeze."

"I know. The nearer I can get with the horses, the better."

Rand came in the door. "You have a good day for traveling. Be careful."

"I will. Merry Christmas, all." Joe headed out the door.

Rand followed. "Remember to tell Chandler to come on over here."

"I will."

"When you see Chaps, tell him what happened with Linc and apologize that he didn't get the break. Let him know I'll make it up to him."

"Will do."

Opal and Rand watched Joe drive off, harness bells jingling and the wagon bed swooshing along on the sledge runners. Hay half filled the wagon bed, providing feed for the horses while they waited for the return of the men in the line shack. Weather permitting, Rand rotated the men every week or two, not like many of the ranchers who left men in the line shacks most of the winter without a break.

"Guess I'll clean up and start stuffing those geese."

"You know how?"

"Ra-nd."

"All right. Just checking. I'm thinking we should bring Little Squirrel up here where it's warmer."

"What if she is contagious?"

Rand clapped a hand on Opal's shoulder. "Young lady, you have a mighty good head on your shoulders. Why don't you go check on Ruby while I take care of this boy of mine."

Per looked up from smearing jam all over the table as far as he could reach.

"Pa, see."

"I see. Looks like you need a bath."

Opal grinned at them both. "As you said, I'll go check on Ruby. Then I'm going to eat breakfast. How about you?" *Merry Christmas, everyone, and please, God, take care of Little Squirrel.*

Chapter Forty-One

"Hiyup!" Jacob swung his rope, trying to convince the cattle heading east that they'd rather return west. It was Christmas Day, and except for the cattle and the horse he rode, he felt mighty alone on this vast prairie. Off in the distance he could see the thread of smoke rising from the other line shack, letting him know he was not totally alone in this sea of white.

Being out on the horse was much better than being tied up in the cabin by the snowstorm. He'd already figured that out. Thank God for a kerosene lamp, plenty of wood and food, and his Bible. He'd studied the accounts of Christ's birth and the various visitors to that crude manger, filling him with wonder all over again at the intricate plan God laid out for His people. A newborn baby sent to earth from heaven to bring His people back to himself.

"Because He loves us." Jacob leaned forward to clap a gloved hand on his horse's shoulder. He and Ned were getting to be fairly close companions, or perhaps it was that he was finally learning how to talk horse. They drove the cattle back to the breaks and watched them make their way down into the valley. Looking over his shoulder, he could still see the smoke rising from his shack. He turned and headed north to see if any animals had strayed through that section.

It was slow going through the new snowfall of the last several days, at times up to the horse's knees. Where the wind had swept it off the frozen layers beneath, Ned picked up his feet and even tossed his head once in a while, a slight show of spirit that made Jacob smile.

"You'll get an extra helping of grain when we get back to the shack. Most likely that's the best Christmas present you could ask for — other than a warm stall in a real barn."

Ned pricked his ears, looking off to the south, then whinnied, the sound shattering the silence, which suited Jacob more than the constant whining and shrieking of the wind. No wonder people went stir crazy out here.

"Someone coming?"

Ned whinnied again, this time receiving an answer that even Jacob could hear.

"Company." He wouldn't be spending the day alone with his books and the growing stack of letters, some of which would most likely never be read by the young woman to whom they were written. As he and Ned made their way back to the line shack Jacob thought of the pages he had written to Opal. Perhaps they were for his own enlightenment, as he had started with his life on the farm, the second son of six children. He had written of the good times, like fishing in the creek and chasing his little sister with a garter snake, and he'd written of the sad time when she had died of the croup. He would never forget the sound of her coughing and choking. The family had gathered around her bed, praying for God to make her well again. He had, but she lived with Him, not them.

By the time he reached the shack, he could see the team pulling the sledge with one man aboard. Guess he was to leave Ned at the shack.

"Sorry, old boy, I thought you were to

get a break too. You still get the extra oats I promised." He unsaddled the horse, threw him some hay, and poured two measures of grain into the feedbox.

"Merry Christmas," he called as the jingling team stopped, steam blowing from their flared nostrils.

"Merry Christmas to you too." Joe climbed out of the bed of the sledge. "Get your stuff. You're needed at our spread."

"What's up?"

"Linc's squaw is some sick. He came in saying he wanted to marry her, like right now. So I came for you a day early."

"What about Chaps?"

"He'll stay out since Linc can't come. I'll tell him when I see him."

"Come on in while I get my stuff together."

"Nah. I'll pitch some of this hay into your shed and feed the horses. How's the kerosene level?"

"Adequate, but we can refill the can if you brought some."

"I'll do that."

"I got rabbit stewing. Snared one yesterday."

"Miss Opal is roasting goose. Oh, Ruby had her baby last night. A little girl." While the men talked, they forked the hay into the shed.

"All is well?" Jacob asked over his shoulder as he swung open the door, letting stew fragrance freeze on the air. He gathered his writing and reading supplies, his few clothes, and stuffed them all into a satchel, since he would be using the sledge and needn't use only saddlebags. While he left blank paper, he was careful to gather up all the written sheets, laying his Bible on top. *Lord God, don't take Little Squirrel away from Linc, please. Lay your hand of healing on her, and let this marriage last for many years.* He stood with his eyes closed a moment longer, then sighed. Here he'd been thinking on his own plight, and Linc might be losing the one he loved.

He glanced around the single room to see that all was in order and checked to see if the coffee was still warm. Though the stew bubbled gently, the coffee had gone cold. Not surprising, since he'd been gone several hours. He fed the woodstove maw, moved the coffee to the heating front, and took two cups down from their hooks on the wall. No cupboards, only shelves, pegs, and hooks lined the wall.

"You ready?" A blast of freezing air announced Joe's entrance.

"Coffee will be ready in a minute."

"That's all right. You drink it, then you better be on your way. Merry Christmas."

The team headed for home at a good clip, harness bells singing a song of winter. Jacob kept up a litany of prayers for Linc and Little Squirrel as the loose snow swooshed around them. He drove the team into the barn and tied them to a hitching post.

"Thank you for comin'." Linc met him at the door of their home and helped him out of his coat. "You really be a preacher man?"

"Yes. I served a parish in Pennsylvania before coming here." Jacob dug in his satchel for the Bible. "How's Little Squirrel?"

"She's awake."

A knock on the door caught their attention. "Linc, it's Opal."

"And Rand."

Linc opened the door and stepped back. "Gettin' right crowded in here."

"How's Little Squirrel?" Opal carried a basket over her arm. "I brought you some things. Ruby sends her love. She'd be here if she'd not had the baby."

"Ah knows that. Let's get on wid it."

"Good. Miss Torvald, you can be the

witness for Little Squirrel." Jacob jerked his attention back from the rosy-cheeked young woman and moved to the side of the bed where Little Squirrel lay beneath a stack of quilts topped by a buffalo hide. "Little Squirrel, do you want this marriage?"

She nodded, her eyes huge in her shrunken face. "Linc say good for us." The words fought past the phlegm in her throat.

"Have you eaten anything?" Opal asked softly, kneeling beside the pole-and-post bed frame.

"She finally keep down warm water." Linc stood beside Opal.

"I brought some broth. Ruby said we have to get some nourishment into her."

"Preacher, say yer words."

Jacob nodded. "You sit beside her on the bed and take her hands." While Linc did as told Jacob found his place and cleared his throat. "Dearly beloved, we are gathered here in the sight of God and this company to witness the marriage of Linc and Little Squirrel. God says that where two are joined together, let not man put asunder. Marriage is a holy institution, blessed by God, and given to us as a gift. Do you, Linc, take this woman for your wedded wife?"

"Ah do."

"Do you promise to love her and protect her as long as you both shall live?"

"Ah do."

"Little Squirrel, do you take Linc for your wedded husband?"

Her "I do" came like a breath.

"Do you promise to love him, honor, and serve him as long as you both shall live?" *Oh, Lord God, let this marriage continue.*

"I do." Stronger this time, she clenched his hands.

"Then in the sight of God and this company, I pronounce you husband and wife. You may kiss the bride."

Linc bent down and kissed his wife with such love and tenderness in his eyes that Jacob blinked several times. He looked up to see tears streaming down Opal's cheeks and heard Rand clearing his throat.

"Let us pray. Father God, creator of all things, especially of the love between a man and a woman, thank you for this union, for this couple here. We plead for your hand to intervene and bring healing to Little Squirrel. Bring comfort and peace; let her swallow the broth and keep it down so she can grow strong again and care for her husband and the child she carries. We thank you in advance. Give these two long years together and the joy of living as your children. Amen."

"Amen." The others echoed his words.

"I take care of my wife. Ya'll get on back to the house." He clasped Jacob's hand. "Thank you for comin'. That were a right nice ceremony."

"I'll fill out a paper to say this is real and legal. I'll bring it by some other day."

"Dat be good."

"You have enough food in case the weather shifts?"

"We do. I laid some by, just in case."

"Keep spooning her the broth, whether she likes it or not." Opal pushed her arms into her coat sleeves. "I'll make more with the goose carcasses."

"You're a good man, Linc. We'll keep praying for Little Squirrel." Rand shook Linc's hand.

"Thank you. God bless."

When they arrived back at the house, stamping the snow off boots and legs, Beans shut the door behind them. "Things all right out there?"

"Yes. Well, they are married. Now I hope she makes it through." Rand shucked off his gloves and coat.

"She's tougher'n she looks."

"You seen her since yesterday?"

Beans nodded. "Stopped by this mornin'. Made sure they had enough wood and food."

Rand clapped his foreman and former cook on the shoulder. "You're a good man, Beans. Remind me to give you a bonus."

Beans snorted. "Ain't likely. I peeled the potatoes. The rolls is ready to go in the oven when those geese get some more done. Opal, you did a fine bit of work here this mornin'."

"Thanks. Think I'll go check on Ruby."

"She and the little'uns are sleepin' real peaceful-like."

"Thanks, Beans. When she wakes up, we can have Christmas dinner."

Her smile caught Jacob right in the heart.

"I better be getting on home. All right if I borrow a horse?" Jacob looked to Rand.

"I'll go saddle one up." Beans reached for his jacket.

"I can do it. You stay here. Just tell me which one."

"You're welcome to stay, but I know you want to spend Christmas with your boy. It'll be a good surprise for him." Rand shrugged into his coat. "Come on with me."

"Merry Christmas, Mr. Chandler." Opal held the door open for them.

"A blessed Christmas to you too." Jacob followed Rand out the door, wishing he could stay yet grateful he could see Joel today after all.

"Why, Mr. Chandler, what a wonderful surprise." Cora Robertson met him at the door.

"They needed me over at the Harrisons', so I came back early. I need to go out and get some things from the soddy and put the horse away."

"We were just sitting down to dinner. We'll wait."

"Pa, you came back." Joel peered out the door at him. His smile was all the Christmas present Jacob needed.

"I'll be back up as soon as I can." Jacob touched the brim of his hat, his gaze meeting Mrs. Robertson's. Her nod let him know she understood. He turned back to the horse, knowing his cheeks ached from smiling already. *He called me Pa.*

"Oh, Mr. Chandler, there is a letter here for you." Mrs. Robertson handed it out to him before closing the door.

"Thank you." Jacob glanced at the return address. Mr. Dumfarthing. *Ah, good news? I hope so.* He put the horse away, slogged to the soddy, and started a fire in the stove so the room would be warm later. While waiting for the wood to catch, he stood by the window to read his letter. The spidery writing told him the old man had written this himself. He had to be better, then.

Dear Reverend Chandler,

You cannot begin to imagine my delight at hearing from you. While many lamented your perfidy in leaving so abruptly, I knew there had to be something terrible that happened to drive you away. I thank you for entrusting your story to me. You can be assured that it will go no further.

Someone told me that forgiveness is an attribute of our God that never changes, as is mercy, and that our heavenly Father wishes we would be as merciful to each other and ourselves as He is. Today I extend that mercy to you in the hope that you will do so for yourself. We all do things in our lives that we are ashamed of, and often others suffer because of our actions. As I read the Word of God, I understand the consequences of sin far better than I ever did, but I also believe in His bounteous grace and forgiveness. I have you, my friend, to thank for that. Without your persistence, I might have died a mean and bitter old man before my time, for bitterness was eating away at my heart and soul.

While I am not robust, I am able to attend church when the weather is good — the cold air is just too hard on my chest. The new pastor is an older man, and we are grateful for him. He has not the *joie de vivre* of our young Pastor Chandler, but his sermons are sound, and he calls on me every week, since I requested that. We both enjoy a game of chess and discussing the political situation.

I have news for you also. I wish it were better. Two days after you left, they found the body of the young woman far downriver. They laid her to rest here in our cemetery. I wish there were a different, more pleasing end to that story here, but tell your boy to look no more. His mother is enjoying her new life in the heavenly kingdom, where she is now able to breathe without coughing.

I would be honored if you would continue in a correspondence with me, and if you like, I will extend your greeting to others who have asked after you. May our Lord richly bless you as you bless others in your new homeland. I have included a bank draft that could be used for the benefit of your new congregation when you decide to pick up the mantle again. I know God will be hounding you if you don't.

Yours with joy in the service
of our King,
Evan Dumfarthing

Jacob set the damper so the wood would burn longer and retrieved a tow sack of presents. *He wrote to me. Father God, what a wonderful gift. And look where he is.* This promised to be both a joyful and a sad afternoon. *Perhaps I should wait to tell Joel until later tonight.* He shut the door tightly behind him. *Oh, I forgot to tell them about the new baby. What a day for news. Good news.*

That night, after an afternoon of feasting, exchanging presents, games, and laughter, followed by chores and more good food, Jacob and Joel returned to the soddy, both of them wearing the broad-brimmed western hats the Robertsons had purchased for them.

Joel fingered the brim, as he'd been doing since he first put it on, then hung it on a peg on the wall.

"Pretty fine, aren't they?" Jacob said, doing the same.

"Thank you for the chaps."

"You are most welcome." Jacob had used his time in the line cabin to turn a tanned steer hide into chaps for his son. "Guess I better learn how to tan hides too. And make boots. You're growing faster than a . . ." He started to say *weed* but changed it to *corn*.

"Ada Mae gave me her boots. She outgrew them, but I got paper stuffed in the toes." He sat down on his bunk and held out his boot, pushing his finger in at the end of his big toe.

"Pretty big, all right." Jacob put more wood in the fire. "Joel, I got some news in that letter today." He sat down by his son, who froze in place like a rabbit hiding in the brush.

"So?"

"Mr. Dumfarthing, a man from my Pennsylvania church, wrote and said that they found . . ." Jacob paused and sighed out his sorrow. "They found your mother's body somewhere downriver. They buried her there by the church."

Joel nodded. "I figured she was dead, or she woulda sent me a letter." He let out a long breath, and his shoulders rounded. He dashed his fists across his eyes and sniffed.

Jacob laid a hand on his son's shoulder. "I am so sorry to tell you that."

Joel leaned into his father's hand, and Jacob gathered him close. "You and I, we're a family now."

Joel sniffed again. "The girls don't got a pa, and I don't got a ma." He didn't say any more, though Jacob waited. After the boy snuggled down under the covers, Jacob patted his shoulder.

"Good night, son."

" 'Night, Pa." Joel cleared his throat. "Ah, my name is Joel Chandler now for real, isn't it? I mean, not O'Shaunasy anymore?"

"If you like, son."

"I do."

Jacob thought of writing a letter back to Mr. Dumfarthing, but instead he banked the fire and blew out the lamp. So many changes in a year, in less than a year. He had so much to be thankful for. What would the new year bring? 1887. What joy it would be to tell the congregation they had a gift of five hundred dollars for the new church. And his son had called him Pa.

Chapter Forty-Two

"Company's coming."

At Rand's announcement Opal flew to the front door. That was one of the things she liked most about Christmas, friends coming by in sleighs with harness bells jingling. This year their family would stay home because of the baby, but others would come to the Harrison ranch. As long as the weather held.

"Hey, Charlie!" She waved from the porch, recognizing his team before she could see his face. Who was that on the seat beside him? A man, not Daisy. That was for certain.

As the sleigh drew closer, her heart picked up the beat. Could it be? "Atticus! Rand, it's Atticus!" She leaped from the porch as the horses trotted up to the hitching post. "Atticus. God does answer prayer."

He stepped from the sleigh and caught her as she threw herself in his arms.

"Atticus. Welcome home, boy." Rand waited on the porch, his silvered breath dancing on the frigid air. "Get back in here, girl, before you freeze to death."

"Look what I found along the road, just passing our house." Charlie stepped from the sleigh. "Merry Christmas, everyone."

Opal sniffed and stepped back to look up into Atticus's eyes. "You're all right now?"

"Pretty much."

"Good." She thumped him a good one on the chest.

"What's that for?" His jaw dropped.

"For not writing, that's what. We never knew if you lived or died or were crippled or what. What kind of friend are you?"

"A cold one if you all don't get on in here." Rand glanced back at the door where Opal could hear small fists banging.

"Pa! Opa! Out!"

Opal locked her arm through Atticus's. "Come on in. Hurry, Charlie, we have news!" She matched her steps to Atticus's, as he slightly favored one leg on the steps. *He's here! He's actually here. Thank you, God. This is the best Christmas present*

609

ever. You brought him home. Thank you, thank you.

"I just hope the coffee is hot." Charlie threw a heavy blanket across each horse. "Can't stay long, but what is the news?" He clapped his hands together to warm them and came through the door, stamping his feet.

"We have a baby."

"A baby? Ruby had her baby? Well, Merry Christmas."

"Yes." Opal looked into the eyes of the young man who, while so familiar, seemed a stranger. "Merry Christmas, Atticus." She reached for his coat to hang it on the coat tree by the door.

"Come over by the fire and get the chill out of your bones," Rand invited. "Opal, you better move that coffeepot to the front."

"Sure smells good in here." Charlie sniffed the air like a hound dog. "Daisy will be tickled to hear the news. Mother and baby are . . . ?"

"Sound asleep, although I don't know how, after all this ruckus." Rand threw an arm around Atticus standing beside him, both with their backsides to the blaze in the fireplace.

Beans brought cups of coffee to the visitors. "You take cream or sugar?"

Both men shook their heads and accepted the cups.

"So, Atticus, what a surprise," Opal said.

"I thought to get here yesterday, but the train was held up east of Fargo by the snow." He sipped from his cup. "I wanted to surprise you."

"You did that all right." Opal fought back all the questions she wanted to ask. Surely Atticus would tell his story. He never had liked her prompting him. He had a scar on his right temple, a limp. What else did he still carry from that terrible beating?

"So where did your folks settle?" Rand took the initiative.

"Back in Ohio where we were from. Pa's workin' for my uncle. He still has the wanderlust, but this out here took the starch right outta him."

"How's the rest of the family?"

Atticus half shrugged. "The kids are in school. Ma . . . I think Ma is most grateful to be away from the . . . the mean . . ." He shrugged again and shook his head.

"Cruel is the word, son. Your family was never treated decent here, and I'm sorry for that."

"Not bad by any of you. There are good

people here in Medora too."

"So that means you are staying?" Opal picked up Per and held him on her lap.

"Ah, no. I'm heading west."

Opal stared at him, shock dropping her jaw. "But . . . but why?"

"I'm scouting a new place for my family. Out in Oregon Territory, where land is good for homesteaders, for farmers, not just for ranchers."

"Oh."

Charlie drained his cup and set it on the table. "Well, thanks for the coffee, but I better be gettin' on home or Daisy will come after me. I promised her a sleigh ride before dark. She'll want to make a beeline for here to see Ruby and the baby, but maybe we better wait until tomorrow." He started for his coat. "Oh. I better know that baby's name, or I'm in ice water up to my neck."

Rand chuckled. "Her name is Mary, since she was born on Christmas Day." He turned to Atticus. "But you'll stay for supper, right? And the night? That train west won't be by until tomorrow. Unless you'll stay a few more days."

"Until tomorrow. And thank you for asking."

Rand walked Charlie to the door. Opal

played with Per, all the while keeping an eye on Atticus. What was different about him? He still looked a mite peaked. As if he spent too much time inside. And yet there was an air about him.

"One day isn't much of a visit," she said to him.

"I almost didn't get off the train."

"Oh, Atticus, you wouldn't. I mean, you couldn't just pass us by." *I mean, pass me by. You're still my best friend.* "I-I've missed you a lot, a whole lot. I didn't know if you were dead or alive. I kept praying God would make you all right again."

"He did." Atticus sat down on the stool beside her chair. He poked at Per with one finger, making the little one giggle. "Mostly. Anything ever happen to those two?" He looked up from entertaining Per, his eyes dark with — with what?

"One's dead. The other is in jail in Dickinson. A bullet ricocheted and killed Mr. Robertson."

"Oh no. Not Mr. Robertson too." He tipped his head back and closed his eyes. "That poor family."

"Atticus, I am so sorry. Will you forgive me?" Opal swallowed the tears that threatened to gush.

"For what?" His eyes clear again, he stared at her.

"For all that. Everyone else has been paying for my stupid mistake." Surely there was a better word than *mistake* for all the tragedy that had happened.

"Sure I forgive you, if that's what you want. But, Opal, I don't hold no grudge against you."

"I thought when you never wrote . . ."

"You know I can't write." He studied his hands. "Well, not much anyway."

"You could have asked Robert to write for you."

Atticus sighed. "Yeah, I coulda. But it was like I couldn't think clear for so long, and when I could, I didn't want to think on it anymore."

Nor on me either? But she didn't ask that.

"I wanted to put it all as far from me as I could."

"If we don't eat pretty soon, everything's gonna be burnt to a crisp," Beans said after banging a couple of pans around.

Per slid to the floor and headed for the kitchen. Opal watched him go.

"I should be in there helping." She stared at her twining fingers. She'd never been this uncomfortable with him before.

He stood and pulled her to her feet. "We can talk more later."

Rand returned from checking on Ruby. "They're back to sleep again. I'll take her a plate later."

When they gathered around the table for a long overdue dinner, Rand bowed his head. "Lord, we have so much to be thankful for — new life, safety, a snug home around us, Atticus's return, that you are making Little Squirrel better and protecting her baby, that Linc and she are married, that we have food to eat, and that we have a chance to rejoice in the time you sent your Son as a baby here to us. Today I appreciate in a new way what that meant. Thank you for this bounty we have and for keeping Ruby safe through the birthing." His voice choked. "I cannot say thank you enough. In your Son's precious name, amen."

Opal sniffed and joined Beans in bringing the long-delayed food to the table. Roast goose, stuffing, mashed potatoes, leather beans with bacon and onion, gravy, applesauce, pickles, rolls, butter.

"Is that everything?"

"Where Ma?"

"Sleeping." Opal gave him a roll to hold him until she could dish up his plate.

"Sick?"

"No. Resting." Rand tousled his son's hair. "You eat now."

They finished dinner and the men headed outside to take care of the chores and get Atticus situated in the bunkhouse. Opal was washing dishes when Ruby wandered into the kitchen.

"Merry Christmas. I never dreamed I'd sleep this long."

"Merry Christmas. Are you supposed to be out of bed?"

Per saw her and came running to throw his arms around her legs. "Ma!" He pointed at the tree and jabbered a bunch of his own words.

"I'm feeling pretty good, actually." Ruby leaned down and kissed the top of her son's head.

"Up."

"I'm afraid not. Where's Rand?"

"He's out making sure there is bedding in the bunkhouse for Atticus."

"Atticus is here?" Ruby gingerly sat down on a chair and stood up again with a groan. "Well, that part's not working so well. When did he come?"

"Sometime between Mr. Chandler's performing the wedding for Linc and Little Squirrel and our finally eating Christmas dinner." She set the last plate in the rinse water. "Beans is out doing the chores."

"I see, I guess."

"Ma, up." Per tugged at her robe.

Opal dried her hands and scooped him up. "Can I fix you something to eat?"

"Whatever is left over. I'm starved. How is Atticus?"

"Looks good. Wait until you see." Opal sighed. "But —" She cut off what she was going to say when she heard boots clumping on the porch and men's voices. "He's not a boy any longer, that's for sure. And he's on his way west."

Ruby put her hands to her tousled hair. "I'm not presentable for company. Bring my plate back to me, will you, please?"

"Sure." Opal watched her sister leave the room, moving pretty swiftly for a brand-new mother.

"Ma?" Per put his head on Opal's shoulder and stuck his two fingers in his mouth. His tiny sniff told her he felt abandoned. "Sorry, little guy, but one of these days you'll think your baby sister is pretty special." Opal held him on her hip while she put slices of goose, a scoop of stuffing, potatoes, and gravy on a plate and slid it in the oven to warm.

"You're hungry already?" Rand teased as he and Atticus came in the doorway.

"No. That's for Ruby." Opal set Per down and he aimed for his father's legs, looking up at him and jabbering a whole string of sounds.

"I know you have lots to say, but I sure don't know a thing you said." Rand picked up his son and headed for a chair by the fire. "Come sit down, Atticus. Looks to me like we have some presents to open pretty soon."

Opal took the warmed plate in to Ruby, who had crawled back in bed. "Can you sit up?"

"Sort of, if you will help prop the pillows behind me."

Opal did and, after settling her sister, stopped at the cradle at the bottom of the bed to watch the baby sleep. "How come animal babies are cuter than human babies?"

"Opal!" Ruby spoke around a mouthful of potatoes.

"Well, calves and colts would be running around, chicks would be feeding themselves, and baby pigs would be lined up nursing. She's just laying here, waiting to be cared for."

"Lying."

"What?" Opal stared at her sister, then chuckled. "Oh, all right. She's lying here."

"You go on out, and when she wakes up, I'll bring her out to introduce her to her brother."

"You sure?"

"If I need help, I'll call."

~🙶

Later that evening, after the gifts were opened and the pumpkin pie devoured, along with most of the leftovers, and after Opal put Per to bed, she checked on Ruby, who had never made it out to show off her beautiful baby.

"How are they?" Rand asked when she returned.

"Sleeping. All of them." She looked over to see Atticus smiling at her. For the first time, he looked like he used to. Mostly.

She tried to remember. Had he ever sat in their house before? Other than for a meal? "Can I get anything for you gentlemen?"

Rand yawned. "Not for me, thanks."

"I'd best be finding my way out the bunkhouse." Atticus stood and held out his hand. "Thank you, Mr. Harrison."

"I think you can call me Rand by now." Rand stood too. "Good night." He wandered down the hall.

Atticus lifted his jacket off the hook. "Good night, Opal." He touched a finger to her cheek and headed out the door.

"Good night." *Is this all? He stops here on his way west and this is it? I know it's not proper to sit here and talk by ourselves, but . . .* She thought of yanking the door open and yelling at him to come back. She thought of donning her jacket and boots and tramping after him.

But those were the actions of the early summer Opal. She leaned her forehead against the door. *I know I've learned something through all this, but right now . . .* Her sigh made her sniff again. She banked the fire and blew out the lamp. For a change she couldn't hear the wind howling or whining at the edges of the windows. All was silent. She tiptoed down the hall and, after making sure Per was snugly tucked in, went on to her own room.

With her pillows banked behind her, she wrapped her arms around her knees so she could sit up and think. If she lay down, she'd most likely be asleep before taking three breaths. Atticus had come to visit. He seemed well and pretty much restored. "God, you did hear my prayers, and I thank you for that. I truly do. In fact, I can't thank you enough. For that. But what about the rest of it? Two men died and two were wounded. There's no way to fix that."

She rested her cheek on her quilt-covered knees. The beginnings of her coyote blanket covered the end of her bed. Four skins did not a full cover make, but Ruby had sewn them carefully together as a beginning. "Your Word says you turn things into good for those who love you. Do I not love you enough?"

She stroked the fur, feeling the richness, the depth of the pelt. She thought about the verse again. Romans 8:28. "I know, it says that in everything you work for good. So are you still working? In all this, I mean." She snuggled back down and pulled the coyote pelts up over her.

"Are you changing me into something different, as Ruby and Rand did with these pelts?" She waited. No sound, no answer. But inside, she knew there was an answer, for God had already changed her.

The next day Opal rode with Atticus and Rand to the train station. Her heart felt heavy as she stood on the platform waiting to say good-bye. Would she ever see him again?

"I'll be back." Atticus looked into her eyes so deeply it made her shiver.

Relief flooded her. She nodded. "I'll be here."

"All aboard!" The call stretched out like the steam pouring from behind the train wheels. "Come on, young fella, if you're going west."

Atticus squeezed her hand and strode off to mount the train stairs. He waved one more time and disappeared into the car.

Opal sighed.

The engine chugged. The train wheels squealed. Atticus appeared at a window and waved.

Opal looked at Rand. "I offered to marry him." *If he'd stay.* She turned and waved at Atticus again.

"And?"

"He said I was too young."

"You are."

"I know. But I think God has something more for me than being a good horse trainer."

"Oh, I'm sure he does."

"Let's go home." She waved at the train until it was so far down the track that only the smoke showed where it had been. Funny, but this didn't feel as much like an ending as a beginning.